GRAPHITE

MEN LIKE GRAPHITE ARE STABLE IN STANDARD CONDITIONS

GRAPHITE

UNDER HIGH PRESSURE, THEY CAN CONVERT TO DIAMONDS

Book 1

A S J WELLS

Copyright © 2024 A S J Wells

The moral right of the author has been asserted.

Apart from any fair dealing for the purposes of research or private study, or criticism or review, as permitted under the Copyright, Designs and Patents Act 1988, this publication may only be reproduced, stored or transmitted, in any form or by any means, with the prior permission in writing of the publishers, or in the case of reprographic reproduction in accordance with the terms of licences issued by the Copyright Licensing Agency. Enquiries concerning reproduction outside those terms should be sent to the publishers.

This is a work of fiction. Names, characters, businesses, places, events and incidents are either the products of the author's imagination or used in a fictitious manner. Any resemblance to actual persons, living or dead, or actual events is purely coincidental.

Troubador Publishing Ltd
Unit E2 Airfield Business Park,
Harrison Road, Market Harborough,
Leicestershire LE16 7UL
Tel: 0116 279 2299
Email: books@troubador.co.uk
Web: www.troubador.co.uk

ISBN 978 1 805145 48 6

British Library Cataloguing in Publication Data.
A catalogue record for this book is available from the British Library.

Printed and bound by CPI Group (UK) Ltd, Croydon, CR0 4YY
Typeset in 11pt Minion Pro by Troubador Publishing Ltd, Leicester, UK

To my wife of 63 years & our brilliant daughters, Juliet & Sally

CHAPTER 1

No one can make you feel inferior without your consent
Eleanor Roosevelt

Working and sleeping and eating and shitting…

Maurice mused, part in anger and part in despair, then put his fingers to his lips as he glanced around the town square nervously in case someone had heard his thoughts. *My long-departed mother would have severely reprimanded me for such language, though my father would simply have frowned and, with a faint smile, shaken his head almost imperceptibly. He was not only my hero but a real-life one.* He smiled at the memory, and his pale, lean face lit up momentarily.

I remember how frustrated I was at Dad's pacifist attitude. He avoided any form of argument or confrontation, and it reached a pitch one day when my friends were bragging about their fathers being so macho and they suggested mine was more mouse than man. I was almost in tears when I got home and told Mum. It was then she made me promise never to tell anyone what she was going to show me. She unlocked a drawer and produced a box containing medals for bravery that Dad had received during the Falklands War. Apparently, he had been so embarrassed by all the celebrations in his honour he insisted it would never happen again.

It explained everything to me! He was large and very strong and never made a fuss. When he realised I knew his secret, he opened up to me. Away from the horrors of war, he decided there was no need for violence; physical or psychological. It broke our hearts when he was killed in a train crash... although, I know it's wrong, but it did put me in a better light at school when the other kids' parents told them about the local press headlines: 'Death of a Hero'. Remembering his creed, I did try to keep a low profile. Anyway, the shock flattened Mum and she died a few years later, when I was at college, he reflected sadly, before continuing to review his current situation. It was one of those grim grey days, and Maurice Jenkins was in one of those matching moods.

Depressing moods, contemplating his life, were occurring more frequently that autumn. It was always a bad time of year for him. Shops were full of Christmas goods and the media spoke of little else. The public was becoming ever more involved in preparations for the season's festivities, which always eluded him. *I've no relatives or friends in the area except for my French neighbours and their two kids I play with sometimes. Perhaps I fit in with them because of my French name. It was given me by Mum in an attempt to be different and because they both enjoyed a trip to France. Didn't stop the English master from calling me Morris Minor!* The neighbours had gone back to France for a period, making him feel more lonely! However, after even his darkest moments, he was still able to dream; not of fame or fortune but of escape!

His life lacked any brightness – indeed, it was completely without any sort of levity or inspiration; it needed a spark! Somehow, he realised this and could glimpse, at the end of his current chapter of unfulfilled existence, not a light but at least a twinkle. Contemplating this future, he foresaw the twinkle as being in someone's eye. So certain was he that it became an obsession that dominated his life, both waking and sleeping. Sometimes, after noticing an attractive woman, he considered the possibility of the twinkle of love. Watching a TV comedy, he could recognise the twinkle of laughter. *Then there are all the other possibilities; fun, pride, fear, and even rage or hatred. No! To aspire to a brighter future for me, the twinkle must be a favourable one – but not at this moment.*

The blast from a car's horn interrupted his line of thought. *Stupid man! It may be foul weather, but it's better to be cold and alive than dead! Good job that driver was paying attention and saw the man dash out from behind the bus. The pedestrian would've been – quick and dead. Oh, I like that! The quick and the dead. What a thing to break my mood.* He paused to look round the raggedly evolved historic square. The weather, the season and all other circumstances had led him to a point of – *suicide?*

No! He still enjoyed some moments of his solitary life. Anyway, he didn't have the courage. His mind turned to his *raison d'être* or perhaps, more aptly, his excuse for living.

Some have lives like… like graphite: theirs can be an existence of a sombre hue, but as with the mineral they can leave their mark. This can readily be erased, yet where is the harm? Many have headstones or plaques or even monuments erected in their memory. Some leave great works of art, literature, music or science, and many honour them after death. Does this improve their passing lot? Perhaps. If there is some form of conscious afterlife.

Hardly a sight for sore eyes! The wind blew an old woman's skirt up while she was struggling to hold her shopping. *God! Am I that desperate that I should notice such a thing? No!*

Everyone noticed. The reason was the movement of the skirt; and more unusual is the mere fact she is wearing a skirt. It took his mind off death.

Is there any evidence of post-mortal satisfaction for the greats or the unknowns? Therefore, a nobody, a veritable non-entity, could achieve satisfaction during life and not be discouraged by thoughts of not leaving a 'mark'. The obvious dangers in this philosophy are denial of an afterlife and the possibility of irresponsibility in one's actions.

Pausing to reflect on his earlier thoughts, he gazed at the roadway, unseeingly at first, then noted the yellow lines. *Graphite! There is graphite in my life! It's the graphite line I've drawn around my comfort zone.* The thoughts troubled Maurice, a lonely bachelor of twenty-nine, stuck in a mundane '9-to-5' office job with a large insurance company. Clever enough to become an actuary, he was too complacent to try. His hobbies were long solitary walks in the surrounding countryside, and playing the stock market with theoretical money. Although his stocks and shares 'game' brought him theoretical riches, he lacked the confidence to invest real money. The arrival of digital cameras brought him a new activity, and he would print the best shots he took of plants on walks.

He'd had little chance of promotion or even office romance, and was far too restrained to try and make the break. Tall, and lean, from his reluctance to spend money on food, he could have been a natural at sport, yet he never tried once his schooldays were over. He didn't realise that some women considered him to be quite handsome; one even thought he looked like Robert Redford, except his hair was more straw colour than blond. His whole appearance, from well-combed hair to neat apparel, was successfully designed to avoid attention. He was too cautious to make even a tentative approach to any woman. The office grapevine classified him as a strange and secretive loner.

Once, a couple of the more mature females had tried to defend him from male colleagues' ridicule, but he hated this sympathy and retreated further into his shell. His only memorable occurrences in the previous year were tripping when entering a bus, and the resulting bruise, and the time, which he tried hard to forget, when he allowed himself to be taken to a colleague's farewell function in a pub. He had dared to drink a whole pint of bitter in an attempt to blend in. He managed to sneak away early and with a devil-may-care attitude had traversed the road away from any crossing, resulting in a cyclist's curses.

Today, he delayed at work to complete a task that had been annoying him all week, and missed his usual bus. Thus, he was sitting with resignation, alone with his dark thoughts, in the dirty bus shelter. Jigging his legs up and down, and pulling the collar of his black raincoat tighter round his neck, he tried to keep warm in the cold, damp air.

"Bus late as usual." The monotone remark partly aroused him from his contemplation.

Maurice was about to grunt an acknowledgement when he saw the speaker, in a yellow safety jacket, was emptying a litter bin and looking directly at him. He felt strangely compelled to reply, then the man in yellow continued.

"I'm sorry if I'm mistaken, and I'm certainly no psychiatrist, but I couldn't help noticing that you looked miles away and seemed very depressed. I like to cheer people up when I can, and I thought you needed cheering."

Maurice stared at his newfound mentor, whose pallor was not enhanced by the streetlights. He realised the man was sincere, and how correct his reasoning was. Then he gave the stranger a grateful smile, nodded, and spoke slowly.

"You're most observant, and you've 'bin' quite right in your diagnosis. Sorry! Couldn't resist the pun."

"I've heard worse," the man interjected with a half-smile.

"Anyway, I don't mind admitting I was feeling very sorry for myself, and you snapped me out of it." He got to his feet and held his hand out to the binman as he continued. "Bit late yourself, aren't you? Wouldn't fancy your job, particularly in these conditions. Though I do realise it's an essential job."

"S'pose so," the binman grunted as he put a fresh bag into the bin. Looking round, directly at Maurice once more, he removed his glove before shaking his hand. He paused and spoke more clearly.

"Any job is better than none, but the way some people treat me as a non-person can be – irritating. It's rare for anyone to recognise how important it is to keep the town clean. In the years I've been doing this, you're the first stranger to speak to me about it. Usually, the only people who acknowledge me are a couple of small shopkeepers and the local police."

"I can't believe that. Surely you must do the same route and see some of the same people?"

"I do."

Maurice noted that the binman had to be his own age or slightly younger, and wondered just how he came to be in such an undesirable job. *Perhaps I'm wrong, but from the way he has been doing his work, and at the end of an unpleasant day, I reckon he takes his responsibility seriously. In fact, with his blond hair and two-tone blue eyes, he could be a model or an actor.* Glancing around to see if the situation was set up for TV or film, he continued his questions.

"Don't you speak to some people as you just did to me?"

"Yes. All most ever do is give me a nod or grunt a minimal reply. Why are you looking around? Are you worried someone might see you talking to me?"

"Good heavens, no! It's just that... well," Maurice paused with embarrassment, "don't get me wrong, but you look – out of place. I wondered if this was a set-up." He looked around the Square once more.

"A set-up? Out of place? What on earth do you mean?" The binman stepped closer and frowned at Maurice.

"To be honest, I think you look too young and handsome to be in such a job!"

"Aha. When it comes down to the basics, you're just as biased as everyone else." He stepped back to his cart and prepared to move away.

Maurice rose from his seat once more and caught him by the elbow. "I'm sorry. I didn't mean it to sound like that."

"Are you gay or something?" The binman eyed Maurice's hand on his arm. Whipping his hand away, Maurice stepped back and spread both hands out.

"No! It's just that – I was feeling very depressed and you broke it for me, and I didn't want my mood to upset someone else. You must admit you're not Mr Average Binman."

"I suppose not." He let go of his cart and turned to Maurice, who continued with his theme.

"Any job may be better than none, but there must be other council work. Why choose this one?"

"There is, but this has two advantages. One is that I'm outdoors, and the other is that I'm not under constant surveillance."

The abject picture they presented initially brightened as they chatted. Although they had not been thrown together by some crisis, a bond of mutual empathy grew between them as they compared their lives.

"Why don't you try for some other career?" Maurice enquired, voicing his own, earlier, thoughts.

"I keep meaning to, but keep putting it off!" He visibly relaxed as he warmed to the conversation with Maurice. "I have a beautiful wife and two great kids. We live in a small house in the country with a large garden." He relaxed more as he talked, prompted by Maurice's question. "Unfortunately, to make ends meet, Helen has to work as well. With that and trying to give time to the kids, we grow some veg and stuff but don't get the best out of the garden." His analysis of his life really took hold, as if he was bearing his soul to a psychiatrist.

"Neither of us went to college and often wish we could find some way to go now. I like to think that I do exercise my mind while doing this work routine." He nodded his head as if to reassure himself.

"How **can** you do that?" Maurice asked, his curiosity roused by this enigma.

"I cast my mind over more profound matters and it helps time pass."

"Such as?"

"Well, I like to analyse everyday things such as the way people walk and the differences in their feet. I notice minute things and once decided that even a fly can cast a long shadow in a dying sun. A better example is now…"

"Now?"

"Yes. I hope I have helped you by talking to you. After all, it is a privilege – a privilege for anyone to be able to help others. Anyway, I suppose I should make the effort to change."

Maurice was so taken up by his newfound friend's oratory he didn't detect his slight West Country accent. Roused from his melancholy, Maurice spoke with an authority, displaying some alter ego.

"Go for it! Don't wait for New Year's resolutions and all that rubbish. Oops! Sorry about that, but in view of your current work, it is probably apt. **Act now**. If you don't try to break out of a rut, you'll never know what might've been."

"You're right, of course. I'll think about it when I get home." He nodded thoughtfully.

"That's the danger! Get home, get comfortable, put it off until tomorrow – the day that never comes." Maurice enunciated, as if rehearsing lines for a play, with his eyes unfocused.

The binman peered at Maurice, frowned slightly and enquired in a soft tone, "Are you talking to me or to yourself? I don't know what work you do, but I reckon you could be considering the same thing you're telling me to do."

Startled, Maurice stared into the other man's eyes and paused before replying. "You're right. **You are right!**" he almost shouted, looking around to see if any passers-by had noticed. He looked at his feet, which he had been stamping to offset the cold, pursed his lips in contemplation and then looked back at his new companion.

"Tell you what. It's almost six weeks to Christmas. I'll meet you right here at 5pm on Christmas Eve, and we can show each other that we have made our moves. That way, we have a mutual deadline, compelling us to take some action, even if we are strangers. In fact, being strangers could help." He looked for a sign of approbation.

"I'm Maurice Jenkins. I work for Oslava Insurance in offices just off the Square." He held out his hand to the binman, who approached him slowly. They shook hands firmly.

"I'm Arnold Phillips. You know who I work for. Very pleased to meet you. It's a deal. See you here Christmas Eve."

With a wave of his hand, he grasped his cart and pressed on with his duties.

Maurice watched Arnold go and reflected on his somewhat hasty agreement. *I've not even stopped to consider if I'll be available. Why shouldn't I be? On reflection, the encounter seems like a fairy tale, except that my fairy godmother is a binman! Is it the plot for a comedy or a thriller? Is Arnold 'MAGIC BINMAN' or 'SUPER BINMAN'? Perhaps this is where my future lies – scriptwriter? No matter, our discussion has broken my mood and motivated me. Twinkle! No twinkle! Still...*

As he slumped back on the seat and peered around the mist-dampened square, normally full of tourists, now with a few late shoppers trudging home, his spirits started to flag again, and he drew his knees tighter together to keep out the cold. His attention was caught by a nearby couple in a passionate embrace. Embarrassed that he might be seen watching, he looked around the Square.

It was the heart of old Houghbury. On two sides there were rows of medieval houses with lots of black timbers showing, and the higher floors projecting over each lower one. They had all been converted into shops or offices. A few were now part of national chains, and the rest were the type of selective quality enterprises one expected in such a notable market town, beloved of the affluent and tourists. The third side had some Georgian and Victorian buildings, which were occupied by banks, a department store, a large drugstore, a supermarket, and some pubs and eating establishments. Two impressive edifices dominated the fourth side. An enormous church, parts of which dated back to the fourteenth century, and the incongruous civic building. What started its existence as the town hall had grown more outlandish with each addition. It now included a market hall, a library and the police station. The centre of the Square had a few flowerbeds around a pathetic fountain, near an equally pitiful town clock. The most magnificent structure was the war memorial constructed through the donations of the entire population of Houghbury.

That always made Maurice laugh. *Just how many of the townsfolk had the means to contribute after the war?* One area of the Square was full of market stalls twice a week, and was used as a car park for the rest of the time. Then there was the row of shelters beside a lay-by allocated for the buses. As his gaze moved around the various features, noting how the lights in the buildings compensated for the poor street lighting, he saw his own reflection in the glass side of the bus shelter. His dour visage enhanced his dismal mood.

A nobody, nowhere, doing nothing; **now** *is my time to change. I'll walk home! It's only a mile or so. If I stay here, I'll go mad – or madder than I already am.* Forcing himself to walk briskly, he left the Square. Was he walking briskly to appear more athletic or to get warm? More likely to get to the sanctuary of his studio flat.

He was striding down the main street, with its intermittent traffic, when a toddler on a scooter dashed round a corner in front of him, pushing furiously. The little boy's face, twinkling with enthusiasm, partially roused Maurice from his lethargy. Instinctively stepping aside, he watched in horror as the scooter's front wheel struck a crack in the pavement, toppling the child into the roadway. Time stood still as Maurice reacted with a speed unknown in his earlier existence. He leapt to the kerb, bent down and plucked the boy from the gutter as a car sped by, narrowly missing Maurice's head as he straightened. Then time and sound caught up as he regained his balance and gasped for air once more. The boy was yelling in terror and struggling!

The entire incident had taken seconds. The mother, a young woman with long blonde hair, came round the corner. Her frowning face distorted into a mask of fear and extreme anger when she beheld her precious son screaming in the arms of a total stranger. Dropping her bags, she snatched her boy and yelled for the police. A crowd from nowhere gathered around them, and some men held Maurice with more vigour than necessary.

"He fell off his scooter! I picked him up from the road!" pleaded Maurice, trying to be heard above the multitude of voices. The onlookers had been roused to a vigilante pitch by the mother's cries.

"That's what they all say! If I hadn't arrived when I did, this man could've run off with my little Charlie!" The stressed mother sobbed distraughtly to the gathering, which became more aggravated, rapidly descending into mob madness.

"'Angin' is too good for 'is sort."

"'E looks the sort."

"Probably got a record."

"Bet he's a known paedophile!"

"Yeah! 'Spect 'e's on the pervert list already."

The muttering from the crowd grew louder and angrier as yet more people arrived and pressed forward to see what was happening. Maurice became terrified and unable to make himself heard. His heart was pounding, his mouth dried and he broke into a cold sweat. Amidst all the jostling, someone punched Maurice in his solar plexus. Unable to bend, with his arms held wide and tightly, he retched dryly, and tears misted his grey-blue eyes.

"'E looks guilty as 'ell!" someone muttered.

"Kick him in the crotch! That'll pacify his obscene desires," an educated voice proposed spitefully from the rear of the ever-growing crowd. There was a murmur of assent from many, while others turned to seek the speaker. The men holding his arms stepped apart roughly and stretched Maurice painfully. Then a pugnacious man stepped up to fulfil the suggestion. He swung his booted foot at the target area.

Maurice, acting with unaccustomed speed again due to his raised level of adrenaline, pulled with the man on his left arm. This caused the man on his right arm to become the target and receive an excruciating kick on his left thigh. With a cry of anguish, he released his hold and crumpled to the pavement. Two or three other members of the mob surged forward and grabbed Maurice. Blaming him for the fallen man's injury, they had just started to punch and slap him when the police car arrived. It had an immediate calming effect, and when the grip on his arms was relaxed, Maurice was able to bend slightly.

"I saw it all!" cried out an onlooker, desperate for attention.

"I've got it on film!" declared a corpulent bystander.

Others started vying for attention, while some faded away, not wishing to be involved further.

"What's going on here? Who phoned for the police?" demanded the elderly constable.

"It's that man!" exclaimed the mother.

"What? He rang the police?" enquired PC Baxter, indicating the man on the ground with a half-quizzical and half-humorous expression on his face.

"No!" The mother almost shrieked in frustration. "It's my Charlie."

"Oh! He rang for us?"

"**No! No!** That man tried to steal my Charlie!"

"Why is he lying on the ground?" Baxter became serious.

"**Not him**," several voices shouted. "**Him**!" This was no Garden of Gethsemane moment, as five or six accusing arms pointed at Maurice.

"Is this true?" asked Baxter.

"**Yes**," shouted several members of the shrinking throng.

"No!" spluttered Maurice, his feeble protestation lost amidst the other voices.

Baxter sensed the mood of the remaining crowd and moved alongside Maurice. He grasped his arm. Looking around, he noted the number of people leaving, among whom was a guilty-looking man from the very front of the mob, who moved away faster at Baxter's next question.

"And why is this other person on the ground?" The injured man's moans could be heard clearly, as the rest became silent.

"It was his fault!" whined the man who had held Maurice's left arm.

"How was it his fault?"

"The kick was aimed for him and he dodged."

The ludicrous statement caused Baxter to tighten his lips, suppressing his inner laughter. The second constable, a woman, began taking names of possible witnesses, while her colleague handcuffed Maurice. In an attempt to placate his obviously aggrieved prisoner, the PC spoke softly to him as he placed him carefully in the back of the car.

"It's for your own safety, sir. They're an angry mob. We'll get it all sorted later."

Meanwhile, the WPC had collected six witness names and addresses. She also collected the camera from the fat man, giving him a receipt for it. The worsening weather and failing light encouraged the rest to depart. An ambulance arrived and took a bewildered Charlie and his stressed mother to hospital for a check-up. It also collected the ever-moaning injured man on a stretcher.

Maurice sat in the back of the car gathering his thoughts and feeling almost as if he had been rescued from one of his own nightmares. *In the tempest I'm enduring, there was one moment of... bravery. Yes, real bravery, like the shining light in any storm. The mother's face as she entered the ambulance changed to a most loving beauty.* As the car moved away, one of his erstwhile captors glared directly through the window, pointed decisively at Maurice and slowly drew his finger across his throat in a meaningful gesture. It cut abruptly into his thoughts and he stared unseeingly through the front windscreen.

At the police station, he was taken to an interview room and the handcuffs were removed. His heart was still beating faster than normal, but he felt calmer as he thanked Baxter for his help.

"If you'll sit there, sir, I'll be back in a moment."

"Can't I go now?"

"I'm sorry, sir, but this is a serious charge, and you'll have to be interviewed formally."

"Surely you don't believe..." Maurice's voice died as Baxter left the room. Outside the room, Inspector George Banbury intercepted Baxter.

"What have you got there, Baxter?" To everyone else at the station, he was Joe – good old Joe. Only Banbury refused to address him as such. The inspector's peers realised it was the way the weak Banbury protected his misplaced status.

"Man accused of attempted child abduction... sir." Joe added the 'sir' reluctantly.

"Right! Give me the facts, then get the charge sheets and I'll help you question him." Joe went as directed, with a deep frown. *Jumped-up little twat! He doesn't mean question, he means interrogate, and he'll do it. Any opportunity to have power over another person.*

Maurice was amazed when Joe returned with Banbury, whose hostility, adding to his earlier experience, left him confused and fumbling for answers. Once, Joe tried to intervene, to his own detriment, to remind Banbury that Maurice was entitled to a phone call. So aggressive was Banbury that Maurice began to doubt his own innocence. The outcome was that he was 'remanded in custody, pending further enquiries'. He did not know anyone to phone and was appointed a solicitor. His first dazed thought in the cell where he had been placed was relief at finding a kind of sanctuary.

Reflecting on the events that had put him there, his mood changed from acceptance to anger. *My unselfish action in helping another person has resulted in my current predicament. Earlier, I was dwelling on my failure to find a place in society. My conversation with Arnold helped lower my imagined barriers. Now – after an attempt to be a part of it – I have become a branded outcast! The whole scenario is a nightmare. From fairy tale to horror story – I must wake up soon.*

The kindly Baxter brought a mug of tea, and explained police and court procedures to him. Faced with a sign of humanity, however small, his wrath dissipated.

This whole affair will be cleared up in the morning. That nice policeman realises how ridiculous the accusation is. The others will soon see that I saved the boy and did not try to abduct him. He accepted the food offered him later but had difficulty in swallowing, so most was left and removed.

Lying down on the bed, he stretched out several times, opening and closing his eyes. *Somehow, it must be possible to return to my nice, safe and boring life. I know – I'll make the most of the situation. I'm on one of those gimmicky holidays where you get back to – what?* Then the lights went out. A sharp reminder he was not in control and could not leave this restricted space. *Sleep. That's the answer! I must go to sleep. It will deaden my fears and pass time quicker.* He could not relax enough for sleep, as his worries intensified the harder he tried. It must have taken hold of him at some stage because he awoke with a numb arm where he had been lying on it. It was still dark and the rest of the building was quiet.

The police interviewed their six witnesses and the mother. The latter stated that when she arrived on the scene, the accused already had her son in his arms. She hastily added that her son was screaming! This was underlined by the other witnesses only becoming aware of the scene after the mother screamed. Police also checked the street security cameras and found none covered the scene of the alleged crime. On examining the video taken by one of the witnesses, they discovered it too only recorded the melee after Maurice had been grabbed.

"Sorry, sir," stated Sergeant Pollock at the reception desk, as he returned the camera. "We require footage of the accused actually perpetrating the alleged crime. Though," he breathed in a mock conspiratorial tone, "in the unlikely event that the accused should be found not guilty, he could use it to sue his aggressors. Apart from that, I'm afraid it's worthless!"

"**Worthless!**" the somewhat obese witness squeaked. "We'll see about that! I'm sure the media will want it!"

"Don't waste your time, sir," the sergeant advised very seriously. "The media won't dare to use it unless the accused is found guilty, or they could be sued."

"I'll bloody well hang on to it and hope he's found guilty then!" the obese man grumbled as he waddled out of the room.

The other witnesses proved more reliable, yet not even the mother had seen Maurice actually pick up the boy. Background checks on Maurice showed that he was a loner with no previous convictions, and no known interests for a man of his age. His flat was searched and three pieces of evidence were found which would help the Crown's case. One was a few soft porn magazines, another was some children's comics, but the most damning evidence was a series of photos of naked children in suggestive positions. The Crown Prosecution Service decided to proceed with the case on the grounds that the circumstantial evidence was overpowering.

"Why does a grown man buy kiddies' comics? Jenkins is a mature, seemingly intelligent man. They **must** be for enticing kids," growled one of the investigators.

"Forget comics," instructed Inspector Banbury. "These photos will convict the evil bastard!"

"You were lucky to find them, guv!" exclaimed one officer, looking intently at the inspector.

"There's no such thing as luck! It's hard graft and planning that screws these animals." He said it with a relish his colleagues had grown accustomed to. Such was his hard-line reputation that staff would give concealed Nazi salutes to indicate his impending presence.

Someone had once had a glimpse inside George Banbury's locked cupboard and felt compelled to tell a few colleagues that it contained numerous books only a fascist would want to keep. Adding to his reputation was his appearance; his dark brown hair was severely combed with an exact parting on one side; his face was bony and colourless with a thin moustache and mean mouth; and he did not walk, he marched! The rumour was that he had gained promotion by blackmail.

When his defence lawyer, Terence Schott, asked him about the items, Maurice explained.

"I may be single, but I do have normal sexual desires and I would like a girlfriend. As to the comics, I used to buy them to read to a French neighbour's children, helping them with their English. They've returned to France and I don't know when they'll be back. I just never got round to throwing them out. Perhaps they remind me of happier times. Anyway, is there some law against me having them?"

"No," replied his lawyer, studying Maurice closely, "but what about these photos of naked kids?"

"**Naked kids**? You're joking!" Maurice protested.

"It's **no** joke! The police found them in your room!" Schott's grave look frightened Maurice, who looked with horror at the copies shown him.

"**No! No! No!**" he exclaimed. "**Never**. I've never had or seen such disgusting things."

"Calm down, Maurice!" Schott had never seen his client so animated. "The point is the police say they found them in your room."

"They're lying! Unless someone else has had access to my room since I was last there, the police must've planted them!" His accusation was very positive, and inwardly Schott agreed with him.

"It's their word against yours, but it does not look good in view of the charges against you."

The case was heard in less than a month, because of a vacancy and because it was considered an open-and-shut one. The police did a brief check of his story as a matter of routine. They had checked that CCTV cameras did not cover the site of his alleged crime. There were no defence witnesses to corroborate his statement that he had plucked little Charlie from in front of a car. That fact added to his guilt, as there were quite a few people about at the time and it was considered highly unlikely for none of them to see his claimed action. No car driver reported the incident. Mob rule and unfounded prejudice weighed heavily against him.

Schott was keen and ambitious, and tried to show that the prosecution's case was based purely on circumstantial evidence plus a strong play on bias, but it was always an uphill struggle. Despite Maurice denying all knowledge of the offending photos, the police were believed, and he was found guilty and sentenced to three years in prison. His nightmare was now complete.

I made a momentous decision to change my life, but not like this. After all the determination I experienced after talking to… a binman – Arnold! Now I will never keep our Christmas Eve appointment, although he may read the case in the local press. The journey to the prison gave him time for thought.

The induction from arrival to placement in his allocated cell was a mind-bruising whirl. Lying on his new bed, he closed his eyes to shut out the surroundings. *Why on earth did I change my routine? Who the hell would want to become a member of a society where they so readily believe the worst of someone? Human nature? Such mob responses are highlighted by numerous examples throughout history. Witch hunts; religious persecution; Ku Klux Klan – my god! Even such an educated and philosophical society as twentieth-century Germans elected such a man as Hitler! I was right to keep to myself. It may not have been an inspiring life but it was safe – and comfortable.*

His intense gloom was not helped by the arrival of his cellmate, who was an aggressive example of low life. He turned his back on his new companion and tried to sleep. *How will the press report my conviction? Who will read it? Who cares?*

CHAPTER 2

'CONVICTED CHILD-NAPPER BLAMES PHANTOM CAR' was the headline in the **Houghbury Herald**. Many locals, including the 'obese man' and a woman who had been crossing the road 25 metres from the incident, noted the heading. The latter rang the police as soon as she was able.

"Can I speak to the person in charge of the Jenkins case, please?"

Unfortunately, she was talking to an officer who had had a really bad day and was five minutes from going home. The last thing he needed was some complicated conversation with a woman who sounded desperate. He took a deep breath and tried to be polite, yet, above all, to quickly transfer her.

"That case is closed, madam. The officers handling it are not available at present."

Dismayed by the cold reception to her wish to be helpful, she begged nervously. "Isn't there **anyone** I can talk to about it?"

Feeling a bit sorry for the caller, but not enough to undertake the task himself, he looked around and considered the alternatives. Taking a statement could be protracted and make him late for dinner. Doing nothing would add to the shadow he was currently under for losing his temper with a suspect.

"Let me have your details, and I'll pass them to the relevant officers tomorrow." He tried to sound encouraging.

"My name is Diana Gumbrill. Mrs Diana Gumbrill. My phone number is," there was a pause before she gave the number, as if reading it, "Tilstead, 4 8 9 1 5 4."

"That's the Houghbury code, isn't it?" the officer said as he wrote it down.

"I suppose so," she mumbled.

"Where are you ringing from?" he asked suspiciously.

"From my home."

"Which is where?"

"Where I live!"

"**What** is your address?" He was losing patience and wondered if she was making fun of him.

"Number 2, Ash Cottages, Tilstead," she replied promptly, and added, "are you sure there's no one I could talk to now?"

"You could try his lawyer." It just occurred to him that this was the answer to his problem. He could get rid of a potentially hysterical caller and upset one of those pain-in-the-neck lawyers at the same time.

"Who is his lawyer?"

"Just a moment, please." With a glance at the clock and his hand on the mouthpiece, he turned to a passing colleague. "Jim – the Maurice Jenkins case. Which lawyer was appointed for the defence?"

"As I remember, it was young Schott. Why?"

"Woman on the phone is asking." Then, clearing his throat, he spoke into the phone. "It was a Mr Schott. That's S-C-H-O-T-T. I think his office is in Houghbury Square. Was there anything else, madam?" His tired tone sent a different message to his words.

"No, thank you, Officer."

He had felt compelled to obtain and pass on her information. However, she had always had difficulty in talking to strangers, particularly on the phone, and she was only too pleased to terminate the strained phone call.

"I expect the officers on the case will want to contact you when they can," the officer added hastily as he replaced the phone, and he almost smiled with relief.

She found Schott's number and rang it quickly, aware that his office could be closed at 5pm. However, Schott was a late starter and finisher, so he agreed to listen to her. He was delighted to hear her version of events, as it vindicated the sympathy he felt for his client.

"Why didn't you come forward sooner?"

"I only saw him save the child, in the headlights of the car. I was dashing across the road before the car, as I was anxious to catch my bus, you know, the number 8." She paused for some acknowledgement of the bus, but Schott was silent, so she reasoned that he needed more information.

"It goes out to our village, a bit round the houses – it's a pretty run but not at this time of year and in the dark. Have you ever been on that route, Mr Schott?" She was rambling and losing the thread of events, as her nerves took command once more.

"No." Schott paused to cover his growing impatience. "What happened after Jenkins picked up the boy?"

"Oh… er yes! I never saw what happened next, 'cos I was down the side street where the number 8 stops." Again, she paused for some reaction. "**You know**, next to the burger place. They say their burgers are very good – not that I've tried them myself, you understand. Have you ever had one, Mr Schott?"

"**No**! Please can you tell me anything else you saw that night?" He was beginning to wonder if this was a genuine caller or just someone winding him up.

"Oh yes – er, the man who saved the little boy." She spoke as if she had completely forgotten the reason for her call. "I presumed that man would be receiving the thanks of the child's parents. As soon as I saw the details of the case in the **Herald**, I was horrified. How could such a thing happen to someone who should be getting a medal, not a prison sentence?"

"Could you come to my office tomorrow morning, to make a statement?" Schott enunciated every word meticulously.

"Not until after 1pm, I'm afraid. I go to work in the morning. I work for a firm selling stuff through the web."

"That'll be fine. I'll have an early lunch." He spoke his last thought aloud, attempting to encourage what could be a vital witness.

His obvious willingness to help Maurice Jenkins did encourage her, and she made a note of the appointment in her diary. Her husband had given it to her because her wandering thoughts constantly annoyed him. They each failed to see that their own behaviour was a reaction to that of their partner. The trouble began soon after they were wed. His fastidious nature made her nervous and she became more careless, which made him aggressive, and that made her even more woolly- minded.

At the meeting in his office, Schott had prepared his desk with some photos and the town map. Mrs Gumbrill had an image of lawyers that made her tense, and it was only her strong sense of the injustice committed, plus the feeling that she had suddenly become important, that obliged her to attend. Schott was not what she had envisaged. He was very tall, lean and young – well, he could only have been in his early thirties. With his dark hair and 'grandee' beard, he made her think of Don Juan. It was his casual dress, with dark blue trousers and a polo-neck shirt, plus the warmth of his greeting that made her relax. After the preliminaries, he led her to the desk and pointed to the map.

"Where did Jenkins seize the boy?" he asked softly.

"Round the waist," she blurted nervously.

"No." Schott spoke patiently. "Where on this map? Which spot on which street did he get hold of the boy around the waist?"

"That's where he grabbed the boy from in front of the car," she said, pointing with an available pencil.

"Can you show me where you were at the time of the incident?"

"There. I was crossing the road; from there to there. That is where I caught my bus, and there is the burger café," she continued.

Bugger the burgers, he thought.

"Why didn't you wait for the car to pass you?"

"Well, I was already partway across when I heard it coming. So I looked to see if it was safe to continue. That's when I saw the man grab the child from the path of the car. As I said before, I had no reason to believe my presence would be required, so I just carried on to catch my bus – outside the burger café," she added for good measure.

"Can you describe the car?" requested Schott, making notes, although he had already explained that he would be recording the interview for his secretary to type up.

"Not really. All I can say is it was probably a largish one from the size of the headlights," she guessed, gazing abstractly at the furthest wall.

"Was it travelling very fast?"

"No! Had it been, I would **not** have crossed in front of it."

"Do you know the town well?"

"Yes. Been in the area most of my life."

"In view of Jenkins having been convicted, I have to tell you that there should be a retrial, at which you will be cross-examined intensively."

"Okay."

"One question they are bound to ask is, do you know Jenkins at all?"

"No."

"Can you tell me which of these men is the one you saw grab the little boy – round the waist?" he added for good measure, though she failed to recognise the sarcasm. He pointed to a series of photos.

"That one," she indicated. "It was only a fleeting glance, but I saw him clearly in the headlights as he stooped down."

"Think carefully before answering this one. Will you or anyone you know benefit from your testimony?"

"**Definitely not**! In fact, this is costing me time and money to come here." She looked at Schott meaningfully.

"I'm sorry about that. I can't recompense you in any way, or it could be misconstrued that you have been bribed. Have you been asked to do this by anyone or any organisation, such as the media?"

"**No! No**! I've never met or even heard of Jenkins before. And, to the best of my knowledge," she inserted the phrase she had heard in TV police dramas, "I don't know **anyone** who does!" She was getting angry, thinking to herself – *I try to help and am treated like a criminal. And it's costing me.*

"Does your job bring you into contact with anyone who knows Jenkins?" He tried to cover every possibility.

"I shouldn't think so. There's only the owner and two warehousemen."

"What exactly do you do, Mrs Gumbrill?"

"Well, the boss gets the orders and payments from the web. He gives me the orders. I note them down, prepare the invoice and delivery notes, plus mailing labels, and pass them to the warehouse. When the goods have gone, I receive confirmation, clear the record and file it," she recited, as if instructing a new clerk. "What else can I tell you?" Her angry mood overcame her normal nervous disposition.

Schott noted her ill humour and, with a sympathetic smile, said, "Forgive me for pushing you, but that is what can happen in court, and I want you to be prepared."

"Surprising, isn't it?" she remarked casually as she calmed down. "The story in the paper shows Jenkins as a dangerous loner. Yet from his actions, he's a hero, and from his photo, he's quite handsome. I wouldn't mind meeting him in the burger bar. They say they're very good burgers. Have you ever tried them, Mr Schott?"

He began to wonder what event had snared her into such an obsession with the café. She was gazing tenderly at Maurice's photo on the desk. He ignored her question and stood looking at her carefully for several moments. She was lost in her own world. He placed the recording of their interview in his secretary's tray and glanced at her quizzically, again.

"Are you quite sure you don't know him, Mrs Gumbrill?"

"What? Oh yes. I mean no." She was embarrassed for a moment, being caught off guard. "Must say, though, I wouldn't mind getting to know him!"

"Mrs Gumbrill! You're a happily married woman! What would your husband say if he could hear you now?" he said jocularly, trying to imagine this very ordinary housewife, with her tightly permed dark hair and prim dress, getting involved in extra-marital affairs.

"Well, I am married, I suppose. But I don't think my husband could give a toss what I get up to. Apart from this diary, he has never given me anything but trouble!"

Schott regarded her closely. *I wonder if my enthusiasm for her evidence is misplaced. She could be doing this to get close to Jenkins, although, to the best of my memory, there's not been a picture of him in the paper. On the other hand, she could be a bored housewife seeking attention.*

He looked at her more carefully.

She must be mid-forties, and has a pleasing if old-fashioned appearance. You can't tell a book by its cover in her case. Her dithering is not in keeping with the picture she presents. Thinking back, I recall how attractive she looked when she became irate. Anger activates appearance, he reasoned, as if reciting some advert. Shaking himself mentally, he returned to the task at hand.

"Thank you for helping. I'll try to get the case reopened, but nothing is certain. We really need the car driver to come forward. Without a more accurate description of the car, we have little hope of tracing him. Should you remember anything at all, however small, about the car, please let me know immediately." He shook her soft, warm hand rather firmly, and escorted her to the street. "Thank you again. I'll be in touch."

Even in the cold autumn light, he is not bad-looking, she thought as she smiled back at him. He watched her walk away across the Square. He was turning to re-enter his office when he had a revelation. CCTV! He looked intently all round the Square. Yes, there were at least four cameras covering the area. They could record traffic moving through the Square and vehicles in the car park. *As the mystery car had been coming from the direction of the Square, it could have been recorded on one of the cameras. Ah!* he thought, *I hope it was not market day, or there will be less chance of finding the car when the Square was full of stalls.*

It occurs to me that I could be wasting my time with all the effort required re-opening the case on the grounds of such a shaky witness, particularly coming forward so late. From my contact with the police, I guess they would not want to re-open it, and would use minimum time on the matter. They would prefer to undermine Mrs Gumbrill, although, the case having brought me some publicity, contesting the verdict could be even better. To have some chance of success, I really need the car driver. Nobody has admitted being the driver so far, despite media publicity. Schott studied the facts intensely. *I am forced to the conclusion that if there had been a car, either the driver is frightened to come forward or he does not live in the region.*

Where to begin looking? Checking all the relevant CCTV tapes will not only be time- consuming but pointless, without some better description of the vehicle. Perhaps Jenkins has some ideas. I will have to visit him soon.

CHAPTER 3

The media can act very quickly when they get a scoop, and that happened in this instance. The 'obese man' sold his video immediately the verdict was announced. The local TV station moved hastily, because scoops were a rare commodity in their part of rural England. They knew national TV and press would be very interested, even though it was only a three-minute recording by an amateur. Thus, an edited version was broadcast, with the announcement of the case and its outcome, the next day in the local news slot.

It got a mixed reception from those members of the public who appeared in it. Some were proud to be seen on TV whatever they were doing, and would have enjoyed making fools of themselves in the less pleasant game shows. Others chose to ignore it as far as they could and would not discuss it with acquaintances that mentioned it, except to excuse their behaviour.

The 'member' of the mob most horrified to see how bestial his behaviour had been was the one who shouted, "Kick him in the crotch." As a Roman Catholic priest, Sean Anderson was not only ashamed of his behaviour, he was frightened that anyone, particularly from his congregation, would recognise him. As a young man in a position of responsibility, he compensated for his average stature and youthful appearance by always holding himself very erect, to the point of actual stiffness. *Why did I speak so aggressively?* he asked himself again and again. He prayed for guidance and forgiveness, yet still felt scarred by the episode.

Yes! He had been recognised! The bishop rang him to demand an explanation. A 'devout' member of Sean's church had reported him. The bishop would not say who, and instructed Sean to meet him at once. Throughout his drive to the meeting, Sean desperately contemplated his fall from grace. He tried listening to a topical programme on his car radio, but his thoughts returned, time and time again, to his troubles.

Why did I do it? What will the bishop say? How can I excuse myself? His mind racing in circles, he swerved to avoid a cyclist. The return to reality caused him to hear a few words from the radio. One word marked itself very precisely into his deliberations: REACTION.

The solution to my dilemma has been hovering over me all the time like some evil spirit I wish to ignore. What I shouted in that unguarded moment, caught up in the outrage – or was it the hysteria? – of the mob, was a reaction. A spoken-aloud reaction to the long-suppressed thoughts I've harboured about the unsavoury activities of some of my fellow clergy. In normal circumstances, I would have called them brother clergy. Yet, despite my avowed Christian beliefs, which instruct me to love all men as brothers, I cannot apply it to anyone, particularly priests, who abuse children. He silently prayed for forgiveness, as he should have forgiven those who had caused him offence.

Surely the Lord will forgive my momentary transgression and understand why I succumbed to temptation. After all, to err is human, even if one is a priest. Less troubled by his impending meeting, he almost enjoyed the rest of his journey. *The bishop has always been a model Christian and will accept my behaviour as momentary human weakness. Until that dreadful moment,* he reflected, *my service to the Church had been exemplary.*

The atmosphere when he entered the bishop's office was decidedly cool. Sean was not disheartened, as he knew he would ultimately be forgiven after some form of admonishing.

"Well, Anderson, thank you for coming so promptly. The sooner we can sort out this sorry affair, the better for all of us. I'm sure you agree?" The bishop, who spoke pedantically, was wearing a sombre suit, with a face to match. His expression belied the fact he was exceptionally young to hold such a status. Apart from the deeper frown shadowing his small hazel eyes, the only item out of place, Sean noted, was his hair. It was slightly tousled, as if he had recently been scratching his head.

"Yes, Your Grace," Sean acknowledged with an attempted smile.

"Please sit," the bishop instructed while looking at some notes on his desk. "I've managed to see the offending TV clip since I spoke on the phone, and I'm appalled. **What is** your explanation?"

"I was at a loss to comprehend my own behaviour, Your Grace. I've searched for an explanation, and with the Lord's help, I think I've found it." He swallowed briefly before continuing.

"It was a belated reaction to a long-held and subliminal abhorrence for members of our church who have proved to be paedophiles. I'm sorry to say I was overcome by the heat of the moment and voiced my thoughts aloud. I hope you understand and can forgive me." He adopted a humble tone, which was foreign to his nature.

The bishop stared at him for several elongated seconds, creating a fraught atmosphere. Then he peered down at his notes before clearing his throat.

"We all have angry thoughts which our calling requires us to reason through, not to voice aloud, and certainly not in a public place. In fact, you did more than voice them. You shouted! If you've harboured such intense feelings about our brothers who have fallen by the wayside, or other matters concerning our church, you should discuss them with us." He paused and Sean felt obliged to speak.

"I do understand that. It's just that I feel the Church is not dealing strongly enough with these cases." He paused and added bluntly, "Though I have issues with some of the Church's current policies, it's not my place to voice them." The lower lid of the bishop's left eye moved very slightly. It had the effect of making his brown eyes even darker. Slowly, as if to control some inner turmoil, he ran his index finger up and down his forehead. He looked from Sean to his notes and back again. Then, after taking a deep breath, he spoke as if choosing each word in turn.

"Our church is – governed – by the word of God, as set down in the Holy Bible…"

"By man," Sean muttered, becoming impatient with the protracted lesson he had to listen to. The bishop turned his head slightly as if to hear better, and his eyes narrowed.

"Anderson!" The vehemence in his voice made Sean stiffen. "Are you doubting the word of the Lord?"

"No. It's just that the Bible was written by man, and man is fallible. So it is possible that the Lord's words may not have been set down verbatim." Sean had attended this meeting as a guilty man about to be sentenced. However, the stress of the last few hours and the unnecessarily pompous attitude of his superior had burst the dam on mental disagreements he had with the rules of the Church.

The bishop was plainly offended and gripped his hands together as he struggled to retain his composure. Slowly, like some sports action replay on TV, he examined his notes, before looking up once more.

"This is not the only complaint I have received from members of your congregation. The first was a few months ago, and I chose to disregard it at the time as being malicious gossip. It stated that you said in a sermon that Christ was not God on Earth!" He paused for a reaction.

"Oh yes!" Anderson smiled as he recollected the occasion, causing the lines of anxiety on his face to disappear. "I encourage my flock to ask questions on any part of the Bible or our church, which they feel needs clarification. One member asked how Jesus could feel pain and die for us if he was God's son. In my next sermon, I tried to explain that he was not a part of God while on Earth, but a flesh-and-blood human. He assumed his rightful place and powers when he ascended to Heaven. There was great doubt in the mind of the person who posed the question, and I felt it was my duty to dispel it. I also considered the possibility that others may have had the same doubt."

"I see. An interesting hypothesis to relieve doubt. Whether it would be acceptable to a higher authority, I don't care to debate at this time. However, of much more serious nature are the complaints about one of your more recent sermons. There were several in a similar vein, so I do not believe they are malicious or mistaken in their understanding of what you said. They state, in different degrees, that you described Christ as," he paused, as if the words he was to utter were an anathema, "a homosexual." His voice dropped almost to a whisper. The bishop toyed with a pen while he spoke, and Sean was temporarily distracted. He realised, with constriction in his throat, that the matter was not going to be resolved today.

The bishop had not reached his present position by bending the rules, and he would be reporting the interview and outcome to a higher authority. *The Church is like an army*, reasoned Sean to himself. *The army of Christ. Like any army, it has very strict rules, which can change only very slowly. Am I to be used as the sacrificial offering to appease the bad press the Church has received in recent years?* The chilling silence in the room brought him back from his desperate thoughts.

"Well?" the Bishop, staring at him intently, asked abruptly.

"They said **what**?" Sean asked, swallowing hard, trying to sound as if he was in disbelief. Swallowing again, he added, "Your Grace."

"They said you told them that Christ was a homosexual!"

"Oh dear! Obviously, I conveyed the wrong message!"

"Well, what **did** you say? What message did you fail to deliver?"

Sean took a deep breath. "Again, my sermon was based on a member's question. If Jesus was truly human, did he have human emotions and desires? My answer was that he probably did, but as the Son of God he would have had the strength to suppress them. I thought I had satisfied their curiosity, but during the following week I was left a consequential written query. As all of Jesus's disciples were men, could he have been suppressing homosexual desires? The following Sunday, I had a different sermon prepared, but I felt compelled to give the enquirer a brief answer. The gist of it was that whatever salacious thoughts or desires Jesus had were definitely suppressed, whether they were heterosexual or homosexual." Sean spoke bluntly, thinking it obvious to anyone of intelligence that he had not maligned Christ. His superior bent over his notes, writing as if to catch up with his thoughts.

"Do you believe Christ had homosexual thoughts?"

"He was a man, so he could've."

"Do you have homosexual thoughts?"

This meeting is turning into an interrogation, thought Sean. *Is this high-flyer trying to trap me for his advantage? I cannot sense any empathy for my position. However, while I am not prepared to lie or grovel for my benefit, I am damned if I am going to help him!*

"Don't we all?"

"I **beg** your pardon."

"Don't tell me that, with your Christian love for your fellow man, you have never wondered about its more earthly manifestation?" Sean pressed on, trying to gain some advantage. Unfortunately, his adversary was better versed in the art of political debate and redressed the balance quickly. He put down his pen and sat back on his chair. He clasped his hands and forced a smile to his lips, but not his eyes, as he carefully replied.

"As Christians and priests, it is our duty to enquire and wonder about all the ways of humankind. It does not behove us to have thoughts beyond the boundaries set down by our church. As Christ suppressed such thoughts, so must we. Do you have such thoughts?"

Sean knew he was on dangerous ground; he knew the person he faced would always try to give a textbook reply, but he had to make one more attempt.

"Naturally. It's all part of natural animal instincts." *Oops*, he thought, *I should have said human, not animal.* "But, like you, I'm sure, they are not acted on but are suppressed," he retorted, hoping the blunt implication would cover his earlier mistake. It almost worked. The bishop leant forward angrily and the tension showed in his raised shoulders.

"Like me! You're nothing like me, or you wouldn't be in the mess you're in now! You would do well to remember where you are and why you are here. It is your failure to suppress your thoughts that has caused this situation!"

Sean became annoyed. *Recently, I have been having more frequent doubts about my vocation. I feel I am in it more by chance than choice. Perhaps I was too ready to fall in with my family's wishes. At the outset, I enjoyed a sense of helping people, which has become questionable as time has passed. The complaints by my congregation illustrated my concerns for the true value of my profession in modern times.* He returned to the attack.

"Yes. I've been weak. As a mere human, I find it difficult to be pure of mind, even if I am of body." *Oops! I hope that sounds more positive than offensive.* "I must confess I've had strong animal attractions for some of the women in my church, and I contained them." Sean paused as he realised what he had just stated. He continued with a nervous laugh. "I meant I contained my animal attractions, not the women. I hope they have been hidden. The animal attractions, I mean!" His nerves were taking over.

Shaking his head at Sean's attempt at humour, the bishop's expression was cold, and he tapped his pen on his notes in vexation.

"That's the second time you mentioned animal instincts! How far do **you** believe Darwin's theory of evolution?"

"I'm sorry, I've never read any Darwin, but some of the points that I've heard about evolution seem to make sense – as accepted by the Church," he hastily added.

"Many things may appear to make sense, but there can always be a counterargument. Our faith can be our ultimate defence against the wilder hypotheses. I suggest you renew your knowledge of the Bible to understand the sense **it** makes, and to strengthen your own faith."

"Darwinian or not, there are instincts which are a part of being a human. I don't see these as sins, only as the weakness of being human. I think it gives one added strength to recognise one's fallibility. Don't you agree?" He tried to gain some ground by asking questions once more.

"We recognise the fallibility in lay persons, but we have to be above such things." His pomposity really annoyed Sean, and caused him to interrupt.

"I thought only Christ was perfect?"

"And **still is**!" was the swift retort.

"I said 'was' and I meant 'was'. We are talking about human fallibility! Christ was a human while he was alive on Earth. Now he has joined his Father in Heaven, he is no longer a human." Plainly irritated by Sean's attempt to debate with him, the bishop rose to his feet.

"You are **not** here for a theological discussion. You **are** here to explain your actions and why they have led to complaints from your congregation! Your reasoning thus far makes me question whether your beliefs are suitable for a Catholic priest. This is a more serious problem than I envisaged." He paused.

Ah! thought Sean, feeling irritated by what he conceived as his superior's inequitable approach. *So the great man does have mere human emotions!*

The bishop closed the file on his desk with deliberate composure and continued. "I will have to give the matter a great deal of thought, and I suggest you do the same. You will take a month's sabbatical, away from the area. I **have** a suitable candidate to cover your absence. When you return, we will meet again to discuss your future in the Church. Thank you for coming. Make full use of your time away." He held out his hand and Sean touched it reluctantly.

He was striding from the room without a word, when the bishop, who had returned to his notes, called to him.

"One more thing. I believe you are a keen amateur artist, and I've heard you have had great success in selling some of your paintings for church funds?"

"Heard? Heard from who? Perhaps another malevolent alleged Christian in my congregation." Sean was so disturbed by his unworthy punishment he voiced his thoughts aloud.

"Anderson! This is the unsuitable behaviour that brought you here today. Perhaps you will do me the courtesy of answering my question?"

"Yes. Most are sold for church funds," he stated bluntly, as he half turned to face his 'inquisitor'.

"You sell others then?"

"Yes. It helps to cover the cost of my materials!"

"Oh! Well, that's all right then. I commend you for your work on behalf of the Church. I was concerned that you might be making a second living out of it."

Sean gritted his teeth and, with a nod of his head to the bishop, he left. He was controlling his anger and dismay with difficulty, and knew that if he spoke again he would only worsen his situation.

The whole way home, he gripped the steering wheel so hard his knuckles were white. As he entered his house, he spotted one of his flock and gave a friendly wave. The woman gave him an icy look and walked away. *Perhaps the Bishop is right. An absence will give me an opportunity to think clearly about my beliefs and my future, and it will give a chance for the dust to settle.*

The next day, he was feeling much calmer. As it was winter, he went online to find a holiday in warmer climes. A cruise around South America to the Galapagos and the Panama Canal! No, that was too expensive and too far. Most of the available places were too expensive. *The Galapagos? Ah yes – Darwin. What were the bishop's points about Darwin? Perhaps I should enlighten myself on the subject.*

Eventually, he found an offer for a room in a hotel in Malaga for a whole month. He rang the bishop and gave him the plans and agreed a handover date with his relief priest. "It will be a good time to study the Bible again," he explained to the bishop. He also decided to take Shakespeare's *King Lear*, as a challenge, as well as his artist materials.

CHAPTER 4

Crossing from the Square, a few days after her interview with Schott, Diana Gumbrill noticed the headlights of an approaching car were similar to those she had seen at the Jenkins incident. Stepping to one side, she peered past the rear lights of the disappearing vehicle and tried to see the name. Having enjoyed her small moment of importance, she decided *to visit that nice Mr Schott again, particularly as his office is close by. And – he is very attractive to an unsatisfied woman in her – er – thirties.* Schott was working late as usual and admitted her, despite the interruption to his train of thought. She looked so enthusiastic that his hopes were raised for some vital information.

"I've **just** seen the car again," she boasted.

"How do you know it was the same car? You said before that you only saw the headlights!" he asked with gentle firmness.

"That's just it! It wasn't until a couple of minutes ago, when I saw it again, that I remembered it had distinctive lights. It's just hard for me to describe, as I know a car by its colour, not its make. I've just never really noticed cars' lights being much different from each other. When I noticed Jenkins grab the boy from the front of that car, I just thought they were ordinary lights. Anyway, I just saw lights tonight like the ones I saw that evening. I don't know how, but they did stand out." She was obviously enjoying his attention again and was drawing out the reason for her visit.

"Yes! Yes! But what was the car?" he asked impatiently. *Just! Just! Just! She'll just drive me crazy.* He often received attention from women who saw him as a good catch because of his looks and his status. However, he was very wary of this obviously-very-frustrated married woman, particularly as he was alone in his offices. He beckoned for her to sit in the chair on the other side of his desk.

"Ah, well. I knew you would want more details." She spoke in an artificially husky voice, causing Terry to cough in order to suppress a laugh at her. "So I stood at the side of the road and checked it out, as well as I could. You have to remember it was dark. All I had to see by were streetlights. My eyes were still adjusting from looking at the headlights. Then there was the rear lights – and it was driving away quite fast."

"What **did** you see?" Schott had difficulty keeping his exasperation out of his voice. Returning to her normal voice, she continued.

"Well, it had a yellow number plate, and," she paused as she had seen the announcers do in TV game shows, "the number began with a two. Or was it Z? And then, I think it was B three." She smiled flirtatiously at him.

This woman, thought Schott, *looks like a spaniel waiting for praise. She would try the patience of... of Nelson Mandela.* "We can't be certain it was the actual car, can we?" He tried to make her face reality.

"I suppose not." She shrugged her shoulders and fingered the neck of her coat.

"Can you remember the rest of the number?" He almost pleaded.

"No. It was very dirty and I'm not a fast reader."

Now she is acting like the same spaniel begging for scraps. I wonder how credible she will appear in court. The word bumpkin occurs to me, but I shall ignore it. After all, she has come forward as a good citizen. "We'll need more information if we're to trace the actual car and its driver."

"I couldn't see the name, but it was a... sort of... grey colour," she announced proudly.

"**A sort of grey colour**." He gripped the edge of the desk to prevent more overt displays of losing his patience. *It has been a very trying day, and this meeting caps the lot.* "Do you recall anything else about it – the shape or size or the insignia?" *I know I am clutching at straws, but she* is *my only favourable witness, and I do not want to lose her.*

"What's insignia mean?" She gazed at him blankly.

"Insignia means the trademark or symbol or sign used by manufacturers to identify their products." Inwardly, he was about to count to ten to calm himself, yet dare not lest she start on her life history. *I must treat this interview as good training for cross-examination in court.*

"Well." She paused once more to keep his attention.

*It's **not** well,* he thought. *It'll soon be ill if the silly woman cannot provide something more substantial than 'a sort of grey colour'.*

"There was some sort of sign on the back of the car."

Again, she paused. Schott could bear it no longer. He stood abruptly and, aware of the personal risk, walked around the desk and handed her a pencil and piece of paper.

"Draw it, please," he commanded in as kindly a voice as he could muster.

"It was just the usual car shape!" she exclaimed, taken aback by his sudden move.

He turned away; walked across the room; opened and

closed the drawer of a filing cabinet, with no purpose other than to control himself, and turned back to her with a very forced smile on his lips. His eyes were cold and far from smiling as he stared closely into hers, took a deep breath and spoke as softly as he could.

"I'm sorry if you misunderstood me. What I'd like you to draw is the insignia; the sign on the back of the car."

She looked from him to the piece of paper and back. "I'm not very good at drawing," she apologised weakly. Her moment of glory was fading fast.

"It doesn't matter. All I need is some idea, however vague, and I'll do the rest." His laugh was genuine. As if transported to become an observer of the scene, he understood the comedy he was participating in. *Concentrate,* he told himself. *The sooner I get this done, the better for both of us.*

"I know it wasn't this, but this is what it reminded me of." She drew five interlocking rings across the middle of the paper and handed it to Schott. He looked at it, back to her, and back to the drawing, without any sound or expression. Her initial enthusiasm had deserted her and she began to wish she had not bothered at all. She rose from her chair and was preparing to leave, when Schott waved the drawing at her. He walked round his desk, produced another piece of paper and drew on it carefully. He held up his work for her to see.

"Could this be what you saw on the car?" His excitement was palpable. She stepped closer.

"Yes! That's it! How can you tell?"

"My dear Mrs Gumbrill. What you have drawn is the Olympic Games symbol, with five rings. What I have drawn is four rings – the insignia of Audi cars." He paused and looked at her. "Do you think the car you saw tonight was the actual one you saw Jenkins save the boy from?"

"I don't know. Are there many cars like it?" She was bemused by his changed attitude.

"Unfortunately, yes. There are thousands. However, there could only have been a dozen or so passing through Houghbury that night. That narrows the field down considerably. Thank you for coming forward again. If you remember anything else, do let me know. Otherwise, I'll contact you."

He stroked his chin and thought, *That will happen when I want – what? Torture or a laugh?* He escorted her to the outer door and very deliberately locked it behind her.

As soon as he was able to, Schott contacted Inspector Banbury, who had been in charge of the Jenkins case, and asked for it to be re-opened.

"Re-opened, Mr Schott!" Banbury's eyes narrowed as he peered over the top of his reading glasses at Terry. "I know you're fairly new in town and are anxious to make a name for yourself, but this is not the case to do it with. Jenkins is a filthy pervert and he's where he ought to be: in prison. It was an open-and-shut case. The evidence was overwhelming."

He was so vehement in his antipathy for Maurice that Terry wondered if he had some vested interest in ensuring Maurice stayed in prison. He stared at the inspector for several moments until Banbury became agitated and removed his glasses. He placed them carefully in their case and then sat back in his chair. "Why do you want it re-opened? Do you have new evidence?" He inclined his head, raised his eyebrows and gave his impression of a smile of confidence.

"Yes, Inspector. I certainly do have fresh evidence, in the shape of an eyewitness." He showed the inspector Mrs Gumbrill's statement with the addition of the make of car.

"Where did you find this…" Banbury gave a meaningful pause "…eye witness?"

"The lady came to your police station and was directed to me. She—"

"Why didn't she come forward at the trial?" Banbury interrupted.

"Because she didn't know there was a trial until she saw the report in the local paper." Despite Banbury's attempt to pretend to perform his duty as an impartial public servant, his prejudice shone through. An ordinary member of that public would have been intimidated by Banbury's hostile questioning; not Terry, who was accustomed to such tactics in court. In fact, the sight of the pompous policeman, with his prematurely bald head, small eyes, and fat nose and lips made him want to laugh.

"**So** she had no previous knowledge of Jenkins's arrest, yet she says here **she saw** him save the boy. How come she didn't see the hullabaloo that followed the mother's arrival?" Again, an insinuating pause, and he finished with a note of triumph.

Terry continued to stare intently into Banbury's eyes and very calmly suggested, "If you read on, you will see that Mrs Gumbrill was rushing for a bus and didn't see what ensued. When you, and your colleagues, have read the statement, I want the CCTV cameras in the Square checked for any Audis passing through at that time."

"**Want? You want!** It's not up to **you** to decide how we proceed!" Conscious that he was fighting a losing battle, Banbury lost his temper.

Terry's eyes narrowed slightly as he took a deep breath and stated firmly, "Sorry! Not want, I **insist** on them being checked. I will put in a formal request to the chief constable, and I think it will look better if I can mention your cooperation."

"I didn't say I wouldn't do it," Banbury replied, shuffling papers on his desk. "We do have an officer who could do it when he's in next. Now, if that's all, I've an urgent phone call to make." He tried to close their meeting and dismiss Terry at the same time. Terry stood motionless for a few seconds and then stepped briskly forward and held out his hand. Banbury started to back away and then realised it was for a handshake.

Terry returned to his office in the knowledge that Banbury would have to be watched carefully in case he tried to sabotage the review. Then he advised the prosecution service that he would be entering an appeal.

A visit to Jenkins in prison was next on his agenda, where his news was most warmly welcomed. Jenkins not only suffered from captivity but also from hostility from the other prisoners, and Schott was disconcerted by the change in his client. His colour could have been described as prison pallor, except he had not been inside long enough. The change was so marked that the lawyer made a point of checking Jenkins's health with the prison doctor later. Coupled with his previous depression, he was at an all-time low, which the authorities recognised, keeping him under close surveillance. The mere fact that somebody could corroborate the truth lifted his spirits. Not wishing to make him overconfident, Schott explained how they still had to find the actual car. Maurice admitted he had no idea of the make of the car but agreed, for what it was worth, that it had been a 'sort of grey colour'.

"I know it's a bit of a cheek, after all you're doing for me, but I wondered if you could do me a favour?" Maurice requested tentatively.

"Depends what it is," Schott replied.

"Remember how I told you about the events leading up to me grabbing the boy?"

"Yes." Schott nodded cautiously.

"My discussion and subsequent agreement with Arnold Phillips was intended to kick-start both our lives. I'd like to think he had more success than me, and might believe in my innocence. We made an arrangement to meet at that bus shelter, in the Square, at 5pm on Christmas Eve. I'd love to know if he keeps our date. So, if you happened to be in the area at the time, could you check for me, please?" Even as he asked, he realised how ridiculous he sounded.

"I can't promise, though there is a chance I could be there. If Banbury does his job, I may have good news for you before then."

After he left, Maurice returned to his cellblock, and the temporary elevation of his spirits flattened somewhat as the doors clanged. *I'm getting out soon*, he repeated to himself every few minutes. His request about Arnold had been a shot in the dark, and he just hoped his momentary acquaintance had prospered from their meeting.

The slings and arrows of outrageous fortune

The next day, Inspector Banbury visited him, opened a folder and studied it very deliberately. Too deliberately, Maurice decided. He knew from his previous dealings with Banbury that the inspector loved to make a drama out of any situation. The visit must have been prompted by Schott's new information and Banbury must be viewed as hostile, so Maurice kept his guard up.

"Do you know a William Gumbrill?" Banbury quizzed, in his best TV cop manner.

Maurice put his hand to his mouth, as if to cover a cough, but really to hide his amusement at Banbury's behaviour. Then he paused and made great play of considering the question.

"Er uh! No! I don't think so. Should I?" He inclined his head on one side and gazed at Banbury with what he hoped was a mixture of awe and innocence. This annoyed the inspector greatly.

"Don't play the innocent with me, Jenkins." Maurice had to hide his laughter, and thought of Shakespeare – *All the world's a stage and all the people are players*. Somehow, Banbury sensed his mirth and continued.

"He works with you, or did before your arrest!" He was at once angry and triumphant.

The smile faded behind Maurice's hand and he frowned. Casting his mind back over his workplace, he envisaged everyone there. *No, definitely no Gumbrill. I would not forget a name like that.* "Sorry. You must have the wrong office. I don't know of any Gumbrill." He eased back on his seat once more and waited for the next act. This was the best entertainment he had had in prison.

"Let's try again, Jenkins. Can you picture anyone at your former office who was overweight and—"

"Lots!" Maurice interrupted with a laugh.

"**And**," Banbury continued without a change in his stony face, "wears brown-rimmed round glasses, has a thick grey moustache, and is bald?" He almost smiled as he finished.

"Oh! **Bill**!" The revelation made him sit very upright. "**Why**? What's old Bill been up to?"

"So you do know William Gumbrill?" Banbury continued, ignoring Maurice's innuendo.

"If that's his name, I…" Suddenly he understood the reason for the interrogation. "Gumbrill. Is he related to Diana Gumbrill, my new witness?"

"He's her husband. When did you last see him?" The inspector had the bit between his teeth now.

"Funny you should ask. He visited the prison, soon after I was sent here, to collect my office keys. You can check with the guards." Maurice was puzzled by the questions.

"What did you discuss?"

"Work. Which key was which. You know, the usual things."

"Did you talk about your case?"

"No!"

"You expect me to believe a colleague visits you in prison and doesn't ask you about your crime?" Banbury forced an artificial laugh.

"He asked, but all I said was that he wouldn't believe me if I said I was innocent. He would just have to wait, as I was doing, for the evidence to be found."

"So you told him you needed evidence?"

"Yes. It's true. I did need a witness who saw what really happened!"

"So you arranged with William Gumbrill to provide one. And he made the mistake of using his own wife. How were you going to repay him?" Banbury was triumphant and openly gloated.

"I arranged nothing. I hardly know the man. His visit here is the only time I've said more than a couple of words to him. In fact, I only speak to him when it is absolutely necessary, as he's a cold fish, always creeping around management. Even so, surely you can't believe he would be so stupid as to use his own wife, even if I had asked him, which I most certainly did not!"

"Which do you think the court will believe? That it's a pure one-in-a-million chance that your new witness is married to the very man who earlier visited you in prison, or that it was a set-up that backfired?"

Banbury left, without disguising a victorious smirk. Maurice's few hours of hope had been shattered. He returned to his cell, oblivious to the crude remarks and hard jolts from passing inmates. Wrapped in his personal hell, he became more tortured when he was alone at visiting time. One more observant guard noticed his acute depression and advised the prison psychiatrist, who arranged an interview with Maurice. He seemed to be more interested in his own appearance than the problems of the prisoner before him. His attitude reflected his many years of doing the same tedious work, listening to the fanciful stories of so many lowlifes. He dished out the same advice, whatever the case, like some old-fashioned doctor giving aspirin for every illness.

Maurice recognised the boredom of someone supposedly sent to help him, and it brought out the devil in him. He played along with the psychiatrist and began to enjoy himself. This time, there was no Banbury trying to outflank him, so he acted out the first type of character he could imagine. He picked suicidal ignoramus and had some difficulty in hiding his enjoyment. When he was alone again, he reconsidered the session, realised how much it had lifted his spirits and wondered if the 'shrink' had been cleverer than he thought. The result had been good, whatever the truth.

Writing scripts was something I thought of, after my meeting with Arnold. Perhaps I could try comedies. There's nothing else to keep my mind off my predicament, so should I start now? It could be a laugh. He frowned thoughtfully and suddenly realised what he had just thought. "I hope it will be!" He spoke out loud with a big grin, causing nearby inmates to stare at him.

He managed to get a notebook and pencils and then stared at the blank paper. *How to actually begin? The TV series* Porridge *was one of my favourite comedies. Will the real thing, which I am now experiencing, be as good, or possibly even better? Thinking back to other TV comedies, I remember one called* The Office, *which I found far less amusing than my own experiences in a real office. The best test would be to note every potentially funny event, starting with the early part of the meeting I just had with the frightening Banbury.*

Mentally shaking himself, he tried looking to the future for a favourable result in his appeal, and good news about Arnold.

CHAPTER 5

The TV item was seen by Arnold Phillips as he sat with his wife having an after-dinner coffee. True to his resolve, he had sought openings for a new career.

"I know—" He stopped abruptly, realising that his wife would not understand why he was about to disrupt their steady and safe, though unexciting, lifestyle after a brief conversation with a convicted paedophile.

"You know what, dear?" she enquired lethargically.

He had been compelled to marry her before their daughter was born. With no parents able to support them, they had foregone further education in order to set up a home together. Despite their poverty and lack of years, they had a maturity grown through necessity. They also had a strong marital bond developed from that maturity and from their mutual love and loyalty, underpinned by considerable jealousy.

Helen matched Arnold for appearances; with her long raven hair and fine features, she would be known as beautiful in any language. The locals gossiped that such a young couple with such extraordinary good looks would soon stray and separate. The partnership survived and grew ever stronger because of their deprived childhood, forced marriage, jealousy and mutual respect. Each attracted would-be suitors but remained loyal. Things might have been different had they lived in a big city, but their environment was most conducive to a stable relationship (no horses involved).

Rudton, where they lived in a small semi-detached house, was a village of approximately 200 persons, about 3 miles from Houghbury. The house was blessed with a much larger garden than modern ones could possess, and must have been built originally for a farm worker. Arnold and Helen improved their family's health and finances by growing vegetables and fruit in the rear garden. The front was left rough, with grass, remains of a rockery, a tired hedge and a few flowers.

Their daughter, Nicola, now eight, and son, Roger, six, were doing very well at school, and provided the real spark in their marriage. Helen sometimes felt a sense of injustice that one careless moment had apparently changed their lives forever. Then she would look at Arnold and understand how fortunate she was to be in such a wonderful relationship.

To help pay the bills, she took any job she could find in the area. She worked on a farm for a little while, but it left her too tired to perform her domestic duties, even with Arnold helping. Sometimes, she had helped in the village shop, but they cut back because of ever-increasing competition from hypermarkets and the internet. Finally, through a friend, she started cleaning for the owners of a large country house. They were pleased with her work and sense of responsibility, and helped her get cleaning jobs at other large houses. She left one because the owner made improper advances, and the rumours about her departure served to protect her elsewhere.

Although she was shocked by Arnold's sudden decision to seek a better career, she supported him. She also decided to undertake a course to improve her lot and to be better able to help Arnold and their children.

"Er, uh, I know that street. I could've been working nearby when that happened," Arnold mumbled anxiously, covering his potential embarrassment.

"Good job you weren't. Knowing your fondness for lost causes, you'd probably have tried to rescue him from that mob. Then you could've been arrested for aiding and abetting. He got what he deserved. Imagine if it had been one of our kids."

"You're right as usual, dear. Though I must say he didn't look… er…" He paused and held his hands out, palms up, as he sought the best words to use.

"Didn't look what? Guilty? The type?" She questioned him impatiently, wanting to concentrate on the next local news item.

"Well. Yes. It may not be possible to categorise people into perverts and non-perverts, but he didn't look guilty." He was anxious to finish the topic but knew Helen would be curious if he failed to conclude the subject properly.

"How can you say whether he looked guilty or not? He just looked terrified!"

"I suppose so. It's just that I hate to see mob rule. Anyway, the police must've checked the facts for the court to find him guilty."

"Of course. Oh, look. There's the Houghbury Christmas market!" Helen drew his attention to the TV and closed their exchange.

Arnold looked at the TV without seeing it, as his thoughts raced on about Maurice. *He seemed such an honest and friendly man. Even though our meeting was brief, I can't identify him as the perpetrator of such a crime. Yet when we parted, Maurice was waiting for a bus. How could he have been caught snatching a little boy a few streets away, only minutes later? Was he waiting for his prey at the bus stop?* Unwittingly, he scratched his head. *Did I upset his plans? Perhaps he'd been forced to move because I'd recognise him in future.* He looked around the room, searching in his mind for an answer. *No! There were too many other people about – or wasn't he really waiting for a bus, but for everyone else to leave?*

The more he concentrated on his encounter with the convicted man, the more doubts he had. *Maurice could've merely passed the time of day with me. He'd no reason to create any sort of image with a stranger he might never meet again. If he really did have evil intentions, he'd have kept as low a profile as possible, and not engage in a protracted discussion.* Carefully, he reconstructed the meeting. *He even rose from his seat and touched me to stop me from taking offence. Perhaps he did it to establish an alibi. No! That could not be the reason if he intended committing a crime within walking distance and only minutes later.*

He paused in his recollections to admire Helen. *How could Maurice have benefitted from our meeting? Come to that, I've benefitted! That meeting kick-started my life. Should I feel grateful, or relieved? Grateful for the new impetus, or relieved that we've not met again? Something still feels wrong, and it nags me. It wasn't Maurice's attitude or appearance, but there's definitely something that doesn't gel with his subsequent actions.*

Then he found the answer and it caused him to take a sharp breath and to sit upright.

"Now what's the matter?" Helen demanded angrily as his sudden movement disturbed her. Arnold shook himself mentally and stretched his left leg.

"Sorry. Just a touch of cramp. I must've been sitting awkwardly." He relaxed again, his mind returning to his dilemma. *The problem is his **name**! Maurice gave me his real name! He did not seem to be a simpleton; far from it. If he was planning to snatch a child, would he have given his real name to a stranger minutes before?* He closed his eyes as he re-envisaged the meeting.

Despite the outcome of the case, and Helen's independent summary of the situation, I still have a shadow of a doubt lingering in my mind. Although I can see no point in pursuing the matter, inwardly, I feel disappointed. Then Helen interrupted his analysis.

"I'd better check the kids've finished their homework, so they can watch one of their programmes before bed. Can you get the washing-up done?"

"Okay."

"Incidentally, you haven't told me how you got on with your application for assistance from the council for your degree course." She started to put away her mending of the kids' clothes. Arnold cleared his throat as he rose to go to the kitchen.

"I was going to discuss it with you when the kids were in bed. Basically, they've agreed to give me some financial help, but, due to current staffing problems, they can't let me have time off. What they suggest is I make up for time lost on courses during the week by working the hours at the weekend." He turned to look at her. "It throws extra pressure on you, looking after the kids on Saturdays. We can chat about it later." He continued into the kitchen before Helen could reply.

They worked out a schedule later, covering their courses, their jobs, the children and the use of their old car. The latter was vital for getting to and from work, the schools, and now to their courses. Fortunately, Helen's course was mostly via the post, and she only had to meet her tutor or fellow students once or twice a month. There would be extra strain in the household, but their joint enthusiasm swept them along.

The children? Well, Nicola and Roger thought it was great that their parents were to become students. Nicola was really keen because she felt she would be able to talk more openly about them. She had made the mistake when she first started school of declaring her father's occupation as 'binman'. At playgroups, she had learnt that kids can be physically cruel. Then she found their mental cruelty was much more painful. Roger, having been warned by his sister, said his father 'worked for the council'. Now they would be able to brag that their parents were students on advanced courses. At that early stage, they did not understand the sacrifices in 'quality' time that would affect them.

Eager to get started on their respective courses, they did some intensive domestic planning as well as pre-course reading. Realising some tasks would be neglected once studying began in earnest, they undertook all the repairs, decorations and changes to their little home that they had been putting off for years.

"I'll finish the ceiling tomorrow, dear. I want to watch the football now," Arnold sighed one day as he prepared to clean his paint roller.

"Oh no, you don't," Helen retorted swiftly. "You're just going to have to get used to making some sacrifices when our courses start, and TV is one of them. Also, you will save time by not having to clean up before the job is fully done."

"I suppose you're right. It's just that I get so bored with painting."

"Tell me about it! How do you think I feel with all this cleaning I have to do?"

"At least you have different houses to look after. That's some variety, isn't it?"

"I could say the same about your bins!" Helen's frustration showed in her raised voice. Arnold was about to reply that she was talking a load of rubbish, which hopefully she would have found funny, when the door opened and Nicola came in.

"I can't sleep! You're making too much noise," she said wearily.

"Saved by the bell," Arnold whispered to Helen. They looked at each other and smiled.

Helen put an arm around Nicola and as she led her from the room, she turned to Arnold, nodded her head and spoke with a laugh. "Another lesson learnt!"

One lesson he could not learn was certainty in Maurice Jenkins's guilt. He rethought, time and again, about their meeting, particularly when passing the bus shelter in Houghbury Square. *It would help to know all the facts of the case, and not just the newspaper's version. If I enquire too closely, I might become a suspect or be cast in the same mould.* A visit to the library, one lunchtime, gave him more facts but failed to clear his doubts. To visit Maurice was the obvious answer, but he lacked the conviction, or was it the courage, to attempt it.

Christmas Eve provided him with an early finish, so he was able to do last-minute shopping. As Helen had the car, he had to catch a bus from the Square. It was nearly 4pm, so he only had ten minutes before his bus left. Clutching his bags, he looked around the area and was reminded once more of that fateful meeting. As the queue moved to board his bus, something caused him to pause.

"You getting this bus or what?" the man behind him growled, giving him a nudge. That decided him. He hated the mob violence Maurice Jenkins had endured, and he also disliked being pushed around by strangers.

"No. Thank you!" he declared sarcastically, and stepped aside with a slight bow of his head. *Is that the real reason for delaying or is there a subliminal curiosity making me keep my appointment with Jenkins?*

As the bus left, he realised how impetuous he'd been, as the next one was a whole hour later. To kill time, and keep warm, he walked around the Square. It was nearly 5pm when he happened to pass the bus shelter where he had met Maurice. He stopped and looked. There were just two women and three kids waiting. He was about to move back to his own bus stop, when a tall man tapped his arm.

"Excuse me. Are you Arnold Phillips?" the man enquired in a formal manner.

Is this a coincidence? Did this man hear my conversation with Maurice? Does he have bad news about my family? Just who is he?

"Who are you?" he retorted.

"My name is Schott. I'm Maurice Jenkins's lawyer."

Arnold paused and looked intently at the man, before answering cautiously, "I'm Arnold Phillips. Why do you ask?"

"Maurice asked me to come here. He hoped you would keep your appointment despite what you may have read about him."

"I'm here more by chance than by arrangement. I can't stop. My bus is due to leave shortly."

"Don't worry about your bus. I'll give you a lift home and then we can talk about Jenkins's case. I can see you're suspicious, so have one of my business cards." Terry handed one to him. "If you have read about the case, you will have seen that I defended Jenkins, though unsuccessfully, I'm afraid."

Arnold took the card almost grudgingly and read it. "Okay. But I live some distance away."

"I know where you live. When Jenkins told me about you, I did some checking. My car is parked nearby and we can talk while I get you home."

With his shopping safely stowed in the boot, Arnold began to relax and enjoy the unexpected luxury of Schott's car. *How can I explain this to Helen?* he worried.

"Why do you want to talk to me? I only met Maurice Jenkins briefly on that one occasion. The case is closed, isn't it?" Despite his caution, his need to find an answer to his earlier puzzlement over Maurice's crime took hold.

"He claims he is innocent: that he had just snatched the boy from the path of a car. Until now, there have been no witnesses to prove it. I now have a witness, whose reliability is suspect. She has provided details of the car involved, and we are checking for it. When I visited Jenkins in prison to tell him of these developments, he mentioned your date and asked me to keep it for him. Idiot!" Schott shouted out as he was forced to swerve around a cyclist coming out of a side road.

"Do you **really** believe he is innocent?" Arnold doubted that he would get a true answer from the person being paid to defend Maurice.

"Strange as it may seem, I'm inclined to believe him. Our hopes of a successful appeal rest on finding the driver of the car. If he exists, why hasn't he come forward? He could have something to hide, or he may not live in this area. Which is why I decided to meet you tonight."

"I don't see how I can help. The first I knew of the case was when I saw it on the TV."

"Jenkins claims he had a long discussion with you moments earlier?" queried Schott.

"Yes, but I don't think anything was said that could help you."

"How come you had a chat when you are strangers?"

"I think I made some comment about the bus as I was passing him, and much to my surprise, he answered." The warmth and motion of the car made him drowsy, and he shook himself. "It's extremely rare for anyone to notice me at my work. It's even rarer for one to engage me in fruitful conversation. People normally ignore me completely. Our conversation grew from that."

"How did he seem to you?"

"Seemed like a pleasant young man. Nothing abnormal really."

"What sort of mood was he in?"

"Ah! Now there you have something. Although I thought he was very gracious in talking to me, I think he was very depressed. In fact, when he started giving me advice about changing my job, I suggested he was putting his own life as a parallel. He seemed to cheer up as we chatted."

"Were you surprised when you heard about his alleged crime?"

"To be honest, I was. I've chewed it over in my mind. I don't think he is that sort. I realise it's not always possible to tell. But then it struck me. If he had any intention of committing such a crime, why did he talk at length with me moments earlier, and why did he give me his real name?"

"The prosecution would claim that it was a spur-of-the-moment crime. Do you think he could have done it?"

"**No**." Arnold paused. He shook his head. "If I come off the fence, I must admit I think he is innocent. You could say I'm biased because I've every reason to be grateful to him. He kick-started my life and my wife's. Because of him, we are both about to undertake courses to better our lot. Plus, it's proved a bonus for our kids, as they have a new pride in us." Arnold's smile, as he considered the recent changes in his life, froze as the car shook violently.

"Wow! Where did that wind come from? The weather forecast did warn about the chance of gales, but that gust was more like a mini tornado!" Schott slowed the car for safety.

"You don't know this road too well, do you? This stretch is notorious for being a wind tunnel when the wind is in a certain direction. Even so, that was exceptional. What exactly did you hope to learn from me tonight, about Maurice?"

"You've told me what I wanted, and that is Jenkins's apparent frame of mind just prior to the incident. Apart from adding grist to the mill, you have strengthened my belief in his innocence, and shown that I'm not wasting my time."

He turned the car down the lane towards the village and had to brake abruptly as the headlights revealed a tree across it.

"Shit! Oh, pardon my French. Which way do I go now, to get you home?"

"It's all right. I can walk from here. It's not far. The alternative car route is miles away." Arnold undid his seat belt and prepared to get out.

"It's foul out there; wind and rain. I don't mind diverting."

"No. It's all right. We – country folk – are hardened to such conditions. It'll only take a few minutes. Quicker than dragging you all across the countryside. Could you open the boot so I can get my shopping, please?"

"One last thing, do you remember any particular cars leaving the Square at that time? It's the one piece of evidence that is absolutely vital," Schott asked as he reluctantly got out.

"Sorry, I don't." After shaking Schott's hand and retrieving his bags, he set off around the fallen tree. The lawyer dived back into the car, turned it and left. He did not see Arnold trip over a branch in the sudden darkness left by the car's lights. Resembling gnarled fists of some monster, other branches struck him and spun him off the roadway. As he sprawled into the side ditch, a bramble cut his cheek, before his whole face was immersed in the muddy waters.

Spluttering furiously, he gasped for air and spat as much filthy water into the void of the night as he could manage, though some had already been swallowed. He climbed back shakily to the bank on his knees. With his eyes trying desperately to adjust to the total darkness, he felt about for his bags. Then he had to search for the missing contents. As he scrambled around, he thought, *If only I had the car keys as they've a mini torch attached. But, of course, if I had the car keys, I'd have the car and wouldn't be in this position. If I'd one of those modern phones, I could use that as a light.* His suppositions were not helping him feel any better, so he concentrated on the task at hand.

The hedges were protecting him from the worst of the wind, but not from the rain, which had become torrential. Cold, icy water was running down his neck. His trousers were soaked and muddy, and his hands were becoming numb as he shivered and groped his way along the roadside.

My shopping and the presents! His dedication to his family overcame his gross discomfort as he retrieved as many items as he could remember. Battered and bruised, with an intense pain in his left leg, he squatted on a branch and did his best to check by touch that he had everything. Standing up, he cracked his head on another branch, bringing tears to his eyes. Had there been anyone else there, and had they been able to see him, they would not have noticed the tears, as his face was a sheet of water from the rain.

With considerable pain, he started home, soaked from head to toe and limping badly due to a strange pain in his left leg. The dark of the terrible night disappeared as he blacked out and collapsed in a heap on the lane's rough tarmac surface.

CHAPTER 6

A little light reading was my intention, thought Sean Anderson, relaxing on the promenade in Malaga. *I came here for gentle exercise interspersed with good dining and light reading, to abandon all thoughts of Church and parish. Yet here I am catching up with some classical literature and scientific works, though I suppose they do require more concentration, which should keep my mind off my problems. Then again, some lines in Shakespeare's* King Lear *I find relevant to today's affairs. Some of the wisest are spoken by the fool, and one in particular I think is pertinent to my current position.*

In Chapter 3, Scene 2, the fool states in his speech, …When priests are more in word than matter… It is my objection to some priests not practising what they preach that got me into trouble.

With his thoughts meandering around his predicament, he became aware of his surroundings. An attractive woman smiled at him as she passed, and he instinctively smiled back. Then he remembered he did not have the protection of a priest's garb; he appeared to be a normal tourist. *If there is such a thing.* A visit to Marks and Spencer before he left England had provided him with what he conceived as suitable holiday wear. It certainly deprived him of his usual formal look and made him appear, well, classier than the average vacationer. A feeling of guilt froze his face and he looked along the promenade, wondering if anyone had noticed. *Of course! Nobody knows who or what I am, so I can escape my priestly restrictions – to some extent.*

Just then, an elegant young man stopped at the other end of the bench Sean was seated on.

"Is it all right if I sit 'ere? You're not saving it for anyone, are you?" His accented voice was as charming as his apparel.

"Perfectly all right." Sean tried to make his reply equally gracious.

"Sorry if I 'ave interrupted your Shakespeare. I'm a great admirer of 'is works, but I know it takes considerable concentration to get ze best out of zem." He pulled at the creases on his trousers as he sat carefully on the bench.

"I was doing some catching up. I've not had the opportunity to read any for several years. You didn't interrupt me, as I was just reflecting on how apt many of his sayings are, even today." Sean closed the book and placed it on his lap. Turning to his new companion, he studied him more closely. *He's probably a few years my senior and keeps himself in very good shape. With dark hair and eyes, he must be a local. Am I looking at a true ladies' man; one of those Don Juans who frequent the better resorts? Look out, ladies, there's a wolf about. Uh-oh! Thoughts like that brought me here in the first place. I must try harder to cleanse my mind, I think the bishop would say. Oh dear, immersed in my thoughts, I didn't notice that I'm staring at this lothario.*

The stranger returned his gaze and smiled amicably.

"Are you 'ere on 'oliday?" he enquired politely.

"Sort of. I've had a tough time at work, and they granted me a whole month's overdue leave to recuperate. That's why I'm doing lots of reading." He gave a slight cough and added, "Reading the books I've missed and which could broaden my horizons; classic literature and modern science. You know, the type of reading that requires more concentration than one can give during a normal working week." Suddenly Sean was chattering away, and to a stranger, after several days' communicative semi-isolation.

"I gave up science ven I left college, but I too like to catch up vit Shakespeare and Cervantes, of course, ven I'm on vacation. I must admit to being lazy, zough, as I read ze Spanish versions. You'll never guess vich one I read last?" With a sinister laugh, he bent and twisted his body.

"*The Hunchback of Notre-Dame!*" Sean chuckled and continued. "No! Only joking. You mean *Richard the Third*, don't you? Though you could have been stirring things on the blasted heath in *Macbeth*."

"Very good. I did mean Richard. Vat do you sink of ze aut'or's treatment of 'im?" The Spaniard straightened himself and enquired with a wry expression.

"Well, I don't blame Shakespeare. He only reflected the attitude of the times, which was to think ill of anyone who was disabled or unusual, and to pander to the views of the current hierarchy. After all, history is not written by the participants but by those who follow, who may have prejudiced views. However, his harsh treatment of Richard has since been cast in stone."

Sean's views met with the other man's approval and led to a lengthy discussion on the tragedy in comparison with prevailing attitudes. The Spaniard glanced at his watch during a lull in their sometimes-differing reflections on Shakespeare.

"I vould like to get a light lunch now. Perraps you vill join me?"

"That would be nice. I get tired of eating alone. I'm Sean, by the way." He held out his hand.

"My name is Miguel," he replied, taking Sean's hand in a firm, gentle grip, and holding it for what seemed an age.

Sean was impressed by Miguel's friendliness but was not accustomed to shaking hands quite so intimately. *I wonder what Miguel does for a living, and how he can take such a long time away from it. Or is he also on holiday?*

Miguel led Sean down a street away from the sea to a small Indian restaurant. From the manner in which he was treated by the owner, Sean realised it was a regular haunt of his.

"I know England 'as tousands of Indian-type eating places, and I 'ope you vill enjoy the dishes 'ere. Ze owners are good friends of mine, and zey always give me ze very best service."

"Delighted! I enjoy Asian food but rarely get to eat it. I notice you can speak their language."

"One of my great aptitudes is for languages," he replied with a too-warm smile, placing his hand on Sean's elbow and guiding him to a seat.

Oh dear, thought Sean. *He's gay. I will have to find some way to break it to him that I am not, though I do enjoy his company.*

"Are you on holiday at the moment, Miguel?" Sean peered unseeingly at the menu, to appear as casual as possible, hoping the answer would give him a clue as to how to deal with the situation.

"No. I am working. I 'ave an 'airdressing salon for ladies and *cavalieros*. So ven everyzing is running smoothly, I leave my manageress in charge and take a stroll along ze promenade."

The waiter came and took their order. Sean agreed to Miguel's suggestion.

"Vat line of work are you in, Sean, zat makes you need a period of relaxation?"

This was the moment Sean had been avoiding, though he did not know why. *After my bluntness with the bishop, why should I be so reticent with a stranger? Do I miss the protection of my priest's clothing, or am I attracted to this man in more than a friendly way?*

"Guess. I think you will not even get close." He gave a sickly smile as he spoke.

Miguel smiled back and studied Sean from head to toe, then stared into space.

"I just 'ope you won't find my diagnosis 'urtful. You 'ave soft 'ands and a slight build, so I rule out any form of manual labour. You said you vere catching up vit literature and scientific vorks, so zat eliminates zose fields. You do not 'ave ze bearing of a military person. You probably 'ave some form of office job. Vit your obvious intelligence, it von't be mundane. From your apparel, you do not 'ave a top income, so zat rules out ze financial world. I am tempted to say you are a public servant, but zen I am lost. Enlighten me, please."

"A very good analysis. In some respects, you could classify me as a public servant. I'm actually a Roman Catholic priest in western England." Sean paused and tried hard not to laugh at Miguel's astonishment. The latter rose from his chair with all his former confidence visibly drained from his visage. Before he could utter any words of embarrassment or apology, Sean caught his arm. "Don't leave, Miguel. I do appreciate that you may be gay and I don't reciprocate your leanings. The Catholic Church is against homosexuals in some forms, but I am not. I welcome your friendship, as you are a kindred spirit in other respects. I have some issues with the Church hierarchy which I have been given this enforced absence to resolve. So can you treat me as just a normal, straight tourist, please?"

Miguel hesitated, looked analytically at Sean, then smiled and returned to his chair.

"You're right. I am gay, and not ashamed to admit it. I 'ave enjoyed your company, and if you as a priest, knowing vat I am, can still be so pleasant vit me, zen so can I."

Their conversation during the meal was more constrained, and it was only when they were finishing their coffee that the obstacle to their friendship was broached.

"Vere is your church?" Miguel's curiosity about this strange alleged priest took hold.

"It's St Michael's in Houghbury. Do you know England very well?"

"Vell enough to know 'oughbury. A lovely old market town set in pretty countryside, as I remember." He moved his hands in a wide circle, as if to enhance his description.

"I presume you are a Catholic, Miguel?" Sean momentarily lapsed into his priestly tones.

"I'm sorry to admit I am not, zough I was raised as one. I may not read science books now, but studying evolution at college, zat enlightened me. Now I am vat you call a atist."

"The word is atheist. If you don't believe in God, what do you believe in?" Sean had always wanted to have a debate, or at least a discussion, with a non-believer. In this situation, he could use his freethinking to reason for the Church, unlike his meeting with the bishop.

"Ah! Zis is a 'ole different can of worms. I 'ave to get back to my salon now, but I vould like to discuss zis furter vit you. Per'aps ve could meet 'ere for lunch tomorrow, say, noon?"

"That would be good. Let me pay for today's meal. You can pay tomorrow. Incidentally, you mixed two expressions, though I am most impressed with your English. One is a different kettle of fish, and the other is to open a can of worms.

The main thing is you conveyed the right meaning, which is surely what language is all about." Sean finished paying the bill and they separated at the door.

Sean set off for his constitutional walk, reflecting on his encounter with – a Spanish atheistic homosexual hairdresser. He reconsidered his part in the meeting. I *wonder if I have been true to my faith or to myself. Do I just like to take an adverse position in any debate? In fact, do I tend to turn any discussion into a debate? Were my controversial sermons a symptom of my contrariness or my liberal mind or an underlying need to shock people?*

He strolled further and further off his usual route until he became lost. Darkness seemed to come so quickly.

Oh God, he prayed silently, *where am I?* Accustomed as he was to asking the Lord for guidance in his life, he was now asking simply for the road to his hotel. He approached the only person in the street to ask for directions. As he showed his hotel address to the short swarthy man, he heard a sound behind him. Too late! A blow to the back of his head knocked him to the ground. Dazed, he lay there, struggling to get up, but someone was holding his arms. He shouted for help in vain as one of his assailants went through his pockets and stole everything, even the crucifix around his neck. A distant shout made the robbers run off.

Head throbbing and feeling unstable, as a couple helped him to his feet, while several others appeared on the scene. With only a few phrases in Spanish, he had difficulty in communicating with the group around him. He found this hard to believe as nearly everyone he had previously met in Malaga knew some English.

At last, one of them comprehended that he was staying at the Hotel Regina. One of the group phoned for the police and waited with him while most others drifted away. He sat on a low wall while he waited and was visibly shivering when the police arrived. They took details quickly from the remaining bystanders then took him to hospital.

Checks revealed he was suffering from concussion and would have to be kept in for further observation. Did he know anyone at his hotel that could bring him a change of clothing? As he had not mixed at all with the other guests, the only person he could think of was Miguel.

"The only person I know here is a man I met today. His name is Miguel and he runs a hairdressing salon. He might help me," he explained to an elderly doctor and his attractive nurse. Yes, the nurse knew of Miguel, and she explained something in Spanish to the doctor, who frowned at her and then at Sean. They knew where to find him, so Sean could relax. Relax he did. So much so that, despite the throbbing head, his shivering finally stopped and he went to sleep.

He had no idea how long he was asleep, because when he awoke, the ward was as quiet as the grave. An unfortunate thought, he decided, in these circumstances. A movement on the other side of his bed made him roll onto his back to look.

"Some people are just plain lazy, lying about in bed before it's even midnight!" It was Miguel, trying to be cheerful. He leant forward, looked closely at Sean, and shook his head. "You're not safe to be out on your own ven it gets dark. 'Ow on earth did you vind up in such a dodgy neighbour'ood? Ze nurse told me all about it."

"Well, I could blame you!"

"ME? I get blamed for everyting. Zis time, I definitely 'ave a alibi." He laughed, and Sean tried to, but it hurt his head.

"You started me thinking about science and religion and life in general. I was so wrapped up with my thoughts that I didn't notice how far I had walked. I stopped to ask the only person in the vicinity how to get to my hotel. It must have been his accomplice who hit me."

"Did zey take much?" Miguel asked, very seriously.

"Everything! Even my crucifix and my hotel keycard. I was lucky some people heard my struggled shout, or I might not be here now. The robbers know I can identify one of them."

"Aha! Trust a priest to look on ze bright side. Vich reminds me, does anyone in the 'ospital or the police know you're a Roman Cat'olic priest?" Miguel had a wry expression as he asked.

"I don't think so, why?" Sean was puzzled by the question. He thought Miguel understood he was here as an ordinary tourist.

"You vould certainly get preferential treatment if zey knew, zough it's not my place to tell zem."

"I'd rather they didn't know. Here, I'm just another visitor from Britain and want to be treated as such!"

"Okay, **Such**. You see, I do know ze English sense of 'umour."

"Very good." Sean tried to laugh again and continued in a more serious vein. "Anyway, I'm against people being given preferential treatment. To me, it's like jumping the queue."

"Vat is jumping ze queue?" his new friend queried.

"It is when somebody does not wait for their turn in a line of people, and uses either their status or wealth to get to the front of the line. I see a lot of it in the Church. Some members do things in excess of what the normal member would do, in the hope of buying a place in Heaven. In other words, their actions go beyond mere Christianity." He paused from his tirade, and Miguel recognised that the subject was one of the priest's favourites.

"I must thank you very much for coming to see me. It's most **Christian** of you!" Sean continued, placing great emphasis on Christian.

"Zat's all right, but it's not Christian, it just ze 'uman thing to do!"

"Human or humane, they are looked on as Christian values, which you must have been taught as a child." Flat on his back and having difficulty in concentrating his eyes or his mind, Sean still felt compelled to defend his position as a representative of the Church. Miguel could see he was struggling to make his point, so with a mock bow, he started to leave.

"Ve can continue zis debate ven you are fit again. Meanwhile, I 'ave brought your night clothes and some clothes for ze morning. Don't worry about a ting. I 'ave explained your predicament to ze 'otel. Zey 'ave altered ze code on your room, and vill await your return. I'll check vit ze staff 'ere tomorrow to see 'ow you're getting on and vill visit ven I can. Is zere anyone in England I need to tell?"

"Nobody." He realised how tragic that sounded. "I hope I won't be in here long. Thank you once more. You are a good friend."

Miguel grasped Sean's hand briefly and left.

Nobody! Nobody? The only true friend I've had in recent years has been Jesus Christ. Even he had friends when he was on Earth. My fellow clergy and my parishioners are what? Not really friends, more associates or work colleagues. He spread his hands wide.

Perhaps this is why I find myself welcoming the friendship of a man of the type I would never have considered before. Am I clutching at straws? Is Miguel a case of better than nothing? Heavens above! Now I'm starting to have most unchristian thoughts – again! Whatever else Miguel is, he's been a very good friend on such short acquaintance, and he has a fine mind. Sean reviewed the events of the day, vaguely aware of the gentle touch of his nurse like some beautiful administering angel as he lay immersed in his thoughts, eventually surrendering to the soft arms of slumber.

CHAPTER 7

Harold Brown and his wife, Rachel, were returning home late on Christmas Eve after delivering presents for their grandchildren to receive in the morning. As they were turning into the lane to Rudton, they were forced to stop by a large car leaving. The driver wound down his window and waved for them to do the same.

"The road into Rudton is blocked by a fallen tree. I've notified the highways authority. Merry Christmas to you." He quickly wound up his window and drove away before they could reply.

"Who was that?" questioned Harold.

"I don't know, but he's right about the tree. I could just see it in our lights."

"Bloody hell! Four miles instead of 40 yards!" he muttered angrily, as he drove on past the end of the lane.

"Mind your language, Harry," Rachel instructed him. "We could've left the car and walked."

"No way!" he replied. "Firstly, we would've abandoned the car in a dangerous place, as the council will be moving that tree first thing—"

"First, first, first! We could've left it further back," she remonstrated, interrupting him.

"AND... and secondly it may be only 40 yards, but I'm not prepared to walk it in these conditions. And at **my** time of life!" he continued doggedly.

"**Your** time of life? Huh! A good walk in the rain might make you wake up to life."

They drove on in silence; he concentrating on the winding lanes and upset by her criticism; she angry at his attitude. They were a small plump couple and had retired to Rudton several years ago. They had selected the village because it was near to their daughter and her three children, and because it was very peaceful. They avoided any stress or excitement as far as possible, and a few hours with their grandchildren was all they could endure. They had been invited to stay with their daughter after delivering the presents, to save having to drive back again on Christmas Day.

"We'd love to, dear, but we have to go to Rudton Church in the morning," apologised Mrs Brown, trying to look disappointed, while her husband nodded his head in agreement.

"What do you mean, Mum, you rarely go to church. You don't **have** to!"

"We may not be regular Christians, but we like to go on Christmas Day and at Easter."

"I don't feel very nice letting you drive home on a night like this. If you must go, make sure you ring me when you're home."

"Honestly, she treats us as if we were her kids! You remember how we used to wait up to see that she got home all right? Now the boot's on the other foot," moaned Harold.

The drive to Rudton was slow due to the wind and rain, and the pensioners spent the time reminiscing about 'how things used to be'. The sudden turn of events caused by the fallen tree had not only given them uncalled-for excitement and stress but also erased their saga of happy days.

"What's that?" Harold asked as he turned the car in towards their drive.

"What's what?" retorted Rachel.

"I definitely saw something lying in the road between here and that bloody tree." He stopped the car, got out and, pulling his raincoat hood over his bald head, walked briskly to the object. When he reached the bundle, he bent over it and gave a desperate shout.

"Call the ambulance! It's a man and he's unconscious." Rachel was halfway to him, and could just understand him above the noise of the wind and rain. She reached into her pocket and switched on their cell phone, which she always carried in case of emergencies. When she got through, she was able to give the ambulancemen details of their discovery and how to avoid the fallen tree.

While they awaited the arrival of help, the old couple, who decided they should not move the man, covered him with an old eiderdown and then a large plastic sheet, which they retrieved from their garage.

"We may not be able to move him, but at least we are keeping him warm," Harold stated as he stepped back to join Rachel, who was holding a torch.

"Do we know who he is? He could be a local, 'cos there's his shopping bags," she surmised.

"Bring the torch round the other side and we'll see his face."

As the light shone on the scratched, muddy features, they both gave a gasp of horror.

"My god, it's young Arnold!" Harold spoke first as Rachel stood transfixed with her mouth open.

"Go and tell Helen, and I'll stay here with him. You'll need the torch to see your path safely." He did not like sending her alone, yet realised they had no option.

Left alone with the injured Arnold, Harold bent as best he could and tried to tuck the plastic sheet closer to the crumpled body. He knew the blood running over Arnold's face was not as bad as it seemed at first glance. It was being spread by the rain, which was gradually washing off the mud. Harold started to shiver and looked around fearfully into the total darkness. It was his worst nightmare come to life.

If only we had stayed with our daughter, we would not be in this predicament. I'm ashamed for having such an unchristian thought. As he stamped his feet and shoved his hands deep inside his pockets, he had a brighter thought – *we may have saved a man's life! I really hope we have. Arnold and Helen have always been such a nice couple, and several times Arnold has helped us when something went wrong in our bungalow.*

In the Phillipses' house, the normal excited anticipation of the next day had abated with the ever-increasing lateness of Arnold. Helen's futile phone calls to his workplace, which was shut for the holiday, and to the bus station to check the proper departure of local buses, revealed her anxiety to the children. All the shops would be closed, so even his last-minute shopping could not make him this late. In desperation, she was phoning Houghbury Hospital when there was a gentle knock at the door, answered by Nicola.

"Mummy, it's Mrs Brown at the door." Nicola ran into the lounge and interrupted her mother's phone call.

Putting her hand on the mouthpiece, Helen glared at Nicola and spoke hard and low.

"Invite her in, and ask her to wait as I'm making an urgent phone call."

Then Rachel burst into the room, and before Helen could protest, she exclaimed breathlessly, "Helen! It's Arnold! He's hurt! We've called the ambulance!"

"**How? Where is he?**" she cried as she replaced the phone and gave Rachel her full attention.

"We don't know what the matter with him is, but he's unconscious and lying on the road in Nether Lane on the edge of the village." Rachel sat down heavily and handed her torch to Helen.

"You take this. My 'arry's there. I'll look after the kids and get my breath back."

"Thanks. Nicola, get Mrs Brown a drink and be good while I'm out," she rattled nervously as she grabbed her coat and left.

The cold rain hit her like a mallet and slowed her slightly, then she broke into as fast a run as possible. It could not have been more than about 500 yards; yet, in her panic, it seemed infinitely longer. *He's been hit by a car! Perhaps it was the Browns who did it. What was he doing in Nether Lane? It's nowhere near the bus stop.* The torch illuminated the figure of Harold bending over a shape in the road. She did not stop to think as she knelt down beside Arnold and blurted out thoughtlessly,

"What have you done to him?"

"I've covered him to keep him warm." Fortunately, Harold did not understand the real meaning of her question, and he continued, "We didn't like to move him. He was in this position when we found him. He must have been walking down here because of the fallen tree further up the lane. We don't know what's wrong with him. We only spotted him in our car's lights as we turned into our drive. Rachel called the ambulance and told them how to avoid that damn tree. He is breathing, but he's not moved once, and there seems to be a lot of blood in the rain puddles. There were some shopping bags scattered around, so I gathered them up while waiting and put them over there." Harold rambled on nervously, embarrassed by her silence and her tears.

Helen crouched over Arnold, stroking his cheek with a trembling hand. She looked up at him, her face awash with rain and tears, and swallowed, unable to speak, and simply placed her hand over her heart and then showed it to him, palm upwards. For a couple of minutes, they remained motionless; statues in the all-prevailing gloom of that ferocious night. Then the tragic picture disintegrated in a plethora of sounds and lights as the ambulance arrived, closely followed by a police car. After a detailed examination and some first aid, Arnold, still unconscious, was stretchered into the ambulance.

"What's wrong with him? Will he live?" the tearful Helen sobbed.

"He's lost a lot of blood from a nasty cut on his left leg. Fortunately, it just missed his artery, and he appears to have been hit on the head. We've patched him up, and we'll put him on a drip while we get him to hospital, but we can't delay. It was lucky he was found when he was. Any longer and he might have died," the senior medic explained. "Do you want to come with us?"

"Yes, but I have to see to my kids." She felt desperate as she searched for a quick answer to her dilemma. Then she felt a gentle hand on her arm and saw it was one of the policemen.

"As it's urgent, I suggest you see to your kids and we'll take you to the hospital immediately afterwards," suggested the older one, PC Baxter. "We won't be far behind the ambulance."

"All right." Helen realised the sense in what he said, despite her reluctance to leave Arnold even for a few minutes. At that, the ambulance doors were shut and it sped away with lights flashing. Helen and Harold returned to her house in the police car. Harold briefly explained to the police how he had diverted because of the fallen tree and then how he had noticed the body in the road. When he mentioned the other car, Baxter said they would have to come back sometime soon and get full details. Then they reached the Phillipses' house and Helen and Harry went in.

Knowing that the Browns had children and grandchildren and had always been such trustworthy neighbours, Helen accepted their offer to look after her kids. She explained where everything was and their routines, as best as she could due to the pounding in her chest and constriction in her throat. She nervously pushed her wet hair back and left with the police. The younger policeman asked her how Arnold came to be in the lane at that time of night.

"I don't know. He should have been home much earlier. I was very worried and was trying to ring you to see if he had been in an accident. I tried everywhere else." She started to cry again, and Baxter spoke kindly.

"No need to explain now. We can work out what happened later. Let's get you to the hospital first." In the silence that followed, Helen's thoughts raced from Arnold's condition to the circumstances and back. Then she forced herself to calm down, knowing that he was in safe hands and there was really nothing she could do to help at the moment. She looked closely at Baxter and spoke to break her embarrassment at the awkward silence.

"You look familiar. I've seen you somewhere recently." Then to answer her question, she said, "You were the policeman I saw on TV arresting that dreadful pervert!"

"Yes," he replied reluctantly. "That was me. Though I would not describe Jenkins as a dreadful pervert. Apart from making the original arrest, I had nothing to do with the case. In fact, between you, me and the gatepost, I believed his story, despite the lack of evidence in his favour."

"You sound like my Arnold. He said Jenkins didn't look the type, but I told him he was just being swayed because he hates to see mob violence." She sighed and stopped her tears.

"I hate to trouble you at this time as we are at the hospital. Could you just answer one small thing? Do you know anyone who might have given Mr Phillips a lift home?"

"No. Why do you ask?" she queried as she unfastened her seat belt.

"Well, Mr Brown stated that a car was leaving Nether Lane and the driver warned them about the fallen tree. As there was no bus at that time, it is possible the car driver had given your husband a lift," the policeman explained as he opened the car door and helped her out.

"We hope Mr Phillips will make a full recovery. Here's my card, in case you need to contact us. Reception is through these doors and to the left. They'll know where Mr Phillips is now." With a quick goodbye and thanks, Helen dashed into the entrance.

Arnold was already being treated in Emergency. His great loss of blood and apparent concussion made him a priority. His leg wound was cleansed and sealed; his head cleaned up and the scratches seen to. Checking his faculties would have to wait for him to regain consciousness. However, the doctor in charge was satisfied that Arnold would make a full physical recovery. He was moved to one of the medical wards for the night and Helen sat with him for an hour. It was explained to her that he probably would not wake for several hours, so she did not need to stay. Reluctant as she was to desert him, concern for her children temporarily overcame that for Arnold, and she decided to return to them.

She informed the staff how she had to get back to her kids and would return in the morning, unless there were further developments. Asking where she could get the bus to Rudton, her luck changed. One of the staff was going off her shift in ten minutes, and could take her home as it was only just off her own route home.

Nicola and Roger were still up when she arrived home. Their usual excitement on Christmas Eve had been supplanted by concern for their father. The Browns had done their best to placate them, and were very pleased to see Helen.

"How is Arnold?" Rachel was the first to speak, as she helped Helen out of her coat.

"He's still unconscious, but they've patched him up and say he should make a full recovery," Helen replied, trying to put on a brave face for Nicola and Roger. "Everyone has been so kind. One of the policemen asked about the car you saw. He thinks the driver might have given Arnold a lift home. If it's true, then Arnold must know the man. He had no reason to get a lift as there's a bus every hour. What sort of man was he? Would you recognise him again? Did he seem a decent sort? Why would he have left Arnold at the top of the lane? Why didn't he bring him right to our door? Did he not want to be seen with Arnold? Why—" Her rambling was cut short by Harold, who took hold of her arm and made her sit down.

"I'll get you a cuppa. Just relax. Nicola and Roger can go back to bed now," Rachel insisted as she ushered the children out of the room. She explained their mother needed to rest for a while, and would probably come and see them later in their beds.

"This is very kind of you both," Helen sobbed.

"It's the least we can do after all the many kindnesses you and Arnold have shown us over the years. As to the man we saw in that car, he seemed very nice. After all, it's a foul night, and he didn't have to stop and tell us about the tree. It was a very posh car, and I'm sure we will know him if we meet him again." Harold did his best to comfort her, then Rachel returned with the tea and pulled him to one side.

"We should go now," she whispered. "As a mother, she will have plenty to take her mind off Arnold – even partially." Then she spoke a bit louder as she lectured him. "Women need to be busy to overcome stress, you know." Harold was about to say what about men, and decided the time was not ripe for one of their arguments on sexual superiority. He tightened his lips and nodded while Rachel spoke calmingly to Helen.

"If there's nothing else we can do for you at present, we'll be going home. Ring us if we can help in any way, however small. Good night, and don't worry. Arnold is in the best of hands." Harold followed Rachel's suggestion and, having shaken her hand, they left.

Helen tried in vain to busy herself and was grateful when she heard Nicola crying. She left her jobs and went to bed, where both children soon joined her, and snuggling together they eventually dozed off.

CHAPTER 8

Schott went to the police station to see a new client, and was surprised when Inspector Banbury invited him into his office. Closing the door, he asked Schott to be seated.

"I need to discuss the Jenkins case with you. I realise you've only been practising in Houghbury for a year or so, which could mean you are unfamiliar with many local facts. So—"

Schott's patience was tested by Banbury's over-pedantic manner of speaking, and he was very busy.

"What local facts?" he interrupted abruptly. Undeterred, Banbury plodded on.

"So I think… it only fair for me to tell you… that… your new witness… is… not credible. I checked up on her and have found she is married to a work colleague of Jenkins, who visited him in prison earlier. You really must double-check your facts before wasting our time." Banbury failed to disguise his smugness.

"Thank you for your advice. I hope for Jenkins's sake that I haven't been wasting your time. One fact you may **not** have is that Mrs Gumbrill does **not** have a happy marriage. Therefore, I doubt she would go to all this effort for her husband's sake. She is not the brightest of people, but **I** believe her." Schott paused for some reaction. When none was forthcoming, he continued. "Have you had any joy with the car?" Banbury sat forward in his chair and sorted papers on his desk. Pulling one clear, he peered at it.

"Fortunately for you, I had my staff examine the CCTV tapes for the Square for the appropriate time. This was done before I found the Gumbrill woman's evidence to be suspect. There were a couple of Audis fitting the description she gave, clearly seen because they each had to stop at the roadworks in the north-west corner of the Square. They were both checked with the Vehicle Licence Authority. One belongs to a local man, and the other to one in London. Phone calls established that they had seen nothing. I'm afraid you seem to have no grounds for an appeal!"

Undeterred, Schott kept a stony face to hide his disappointment at the news and his irritation at the obnoxious person gloating at him. He requested as calmly as possible, "Could you send me the relevant parts of the CCTV tapes, please? Oh, and of course the names and addresses of the owners. I don't doubt that your staff checked, but while there is the slightest chance of proving my client's innocence, I must double-check. I hope you understand, Inspector?" Schott spoke with all the deference he could muster. Banbury agreed while shaking his head at what he considered the fruitlessness of carrying on. Schott departed to see his new client in the station cells.

The next day, Schott received the tapes and the car owners' details. As soon as he was able, he sat with his assistant, Derek Lee, and peered closely at the tapes. The pictures of the cars were unusually clear as they waited at the temporary traffic lights. The streetlights were reflected in the windscreens so the drivers' faces were not visible; only their hands on their steering wheels could be seen. It was disappointing, but Schott refused to give up. As Derek fancied himself as a bit of a sleuth, Schott asked him to interview the drivers. Even if they had not seen Jenkins, they should be asked to describe what they had seen.

"I don't fancy going to London at this time, Terry, with my wife expecting, so will it be all right if I ask an old friend of mine in the Met to do it for me?" Derek requested hopefully.

"Of course you can. I trust he's reliable. I forgot about Sally's condition."

"Actually, my friend is a she, and yes, she's very reliable. She's my stepsister!" Derek corrected with a large grin.

"I didn't know you had a stepsister!"

"After my parents arrived here from Hong Kong, my mother, who was never very strong, died soon after I was born. My father later married a Kentish maid; they had a girl and later a boy. Birdie, who looks much like her mother, went to university and got a degree in Physics. Then, out of the blue, or should it be **in** the blue, she joined the police. She must be on the... er... fast track, because she is a sergeant already!" Derek explained proudly.

Terry moved his head back as if to have a clearer look and study his assistant in light of this revelation.

"Congratulations! You're obviously a talented family. I hope she can help without damaging her career. She's certainly in the right position for us. I'm back in court now, so let me know tomorrow how you get on."

Derek contacted his sister and explained the situation. She reacted immediately, explaining she knew the person he wanted checking. Thus, it was possible he had seen something but would not admit to it for fear of becoming involved. It was a delicate subject, but she would see what she could do.

Sergeant Birdie Lee could not tell her stepbrother any more about Ali Masood, the Audi owner. He had long been suspected of involvement in dubious activities, but nothing had been proven. In fact, it was Masood who was suspected of having his main adversary, and the station's legendary top investigator, Doug Evans, mysteriously assigned to Norwich. To question Masood about being in Houghbury might endanger any current investigation by the CID. She decided to wait until an opportunity presented itself for her to discuss it with them.

Meanwhile, Derek visited the owner of the other Audi, a Major Stubbs. He received a frosty reception, even more so when he explained the reason for his visit.

"Why is it necessary for you to ask questions on behalf of some lawyer chappy, when I've already told the police all I know! Explain yourself, young man."

"I'm dreadfully sorry to invade your privacy like this, but—"

"I should **damn** well think so!" the major interrupted loudly.

"The police may have asked you a few basic questions to cover the event, but we are hoping there may be some small item they overlooked."

"Why on earth would they overlook anything? I've every faith in our police force, and I resent someone like *you* suggesting otherwise!" The implication of his remark did not go unnoticed by Derek, who tightened his grip on his notebook and tried to ignore it.

"Mr Schott has new evidence on a case which he wants to appeal. His client was found guilty, and Mr Schott is convinced of his innocence."

"Which case is it?" The major almost issued an order.

"Before I say, I'd like to ask my questions so that your answers won't be swayed one way or another, even subconsciously."

Stubbs glared at Derek with a visage that had always terrified his subordinates in the army. "Right! Carry on, if you must, but be brief."

Derek noticed the look and to avoid any retaliatory expression, he looked at his notebook. "Firstly, on the night in question, did you see any incident on the roadway, in the vicinity of Houghbury Square? Such as anyone running across or falling in front of your car?" Derek was finding it hard to phrase his questions politely in the face of the major's overbearing hostility. He recognised a strong element of racism in Stubbs's attitude, which surprised him. He would have expected a former officer in the British Army to be accustomed to dealing with men from all parts of the world.

"Nothing! The only people to cross in front of my car were at those blasted roadworks. They're the reason I remember anything about that night."

"Was there anything or anybody who drew your attention or who you remember?"

Stubbs paused, looked around the room, deep in thought, then his eyes stopped, unseeing, on an object. He paused as if to say something then returned his gaze back to Derek and cleared his throat. Derek sensed that the major **had** remembered something.

"**Was** there anything else, sir?" Derek looked down at his notebook again, hoping the suggestion of humility, by lowering his eyes, could extract a favourable answer.

"Nothing, dammit! Apart from those roadworks and the foul weather. Now if you're quite finished, I've got to feed my dogs."

The solid oak door was slammed shut behind Derek to underline the fact he was not a welcome visitor and to discourage him from calling again. He walked as slowly as he could to reach his car, perhaps in a show of bravado. The sudden loud baying of many dogs caused him to lengthen his stride a trifle. As he drove down the major's driveway, Derek knew he had just encountered a living fossil; an example of the bigotry expected in a bygone era. He had met military officers before and they had always been helpful and polite.

Why was this one different? I can think of nothing untoward in my approach. It's because of my handling of people that Terry entrusts me with these interviews. However I try, I can't overcome a feeling of failure. There was definitely some fact being withheld by the major.

Back at the office, he handled his other work with as much concentration as possible. *Should I have been more firm in my questioning? No! That would have gleaned even less information. Did I miss a question? Try as I might, I can't think of one. If Stubbs is withholding something, what can it be? Did he fail to see anything relevant because he was ogling some woman? Or was he ogling a man or boy?* Dozens of questions flashed through his mind, but no answers. He jotted down a list of trigger words to help him review the meeting another time. He had only met Jenkins briefly on a couple of occasions, but shared Terry's belief in the man's innocence.

"How did you get on with Stubbs?" Terry's question broke Derek's thoughts.

"Badly! He's a caricature of an English officer a hundred years ago. How he came to be in the modern army is a mystery. He was very hostile. All he would admit to seeing was the roadworks. However, he appeared to remember something else but clammed up and dismissed me."

"I'm sorry. I should've gone myself. I'll try to see him next week."

"Don't! It was not just me he didn't like; it was the whole idea of being asked questions that he had already answered for the police. Unless Birdie draws a blank, I suggest we avoid Stubbs for the present." Derek knew his proposal was counter to Terry's enthusiasm, but he had to warn him.

Schott reluctantly accepted Derek's recommendation. When the opportunity presented itself, he checked on Stubbs's background. He was not surprised to find the man came from a long line of landed gentry, and it was almost certain that he had not got his commission on merit.

In London, Birdie Lee had made enquiries among her colleagues and was given clearance to ask Masood about Houghbury. To keep it low key, she met him at his home, in plain clothes. She was shown into his dining room and tried hard not to peruse the contents.

"Well, well! This makes a nice change. Are you the replacement for that creep Evans, who's been harassing me for years in some personal vendetta?" Masood grinned salaciously.

She managed to divert her gaze from his pale face to avoid any hint of an interrogation. *Not a person to meet on a dark night,* she thought, *with his black hair and beard, and evil eyes.*

"No, Sergeant Evans has a temporary assignment elsewhere." *I don't know Evans, but if this scum worries about him, my emphasising his absence as temporary might reinforce the worry.* "I'm here merely to ask about your visit to Houghbury," Birdie explained mildly.

"One of your lot's already asked me about me driving through Houghbury. What's it to do with you?" His aggressive attitude warned her to tread carefully.

"As they no doubt explained to you, there was an incident in the town that evening, and your car was one of several caught on CCTV. We are hoping one of the drivers may have seen something, anything, which might throw some light on the case," Birdie said gently.

"What sort of thing? I was just passing through, minding my own business." His abruptness tempted Birdie to adopt the more usual cross-examination style, and ask what that business was.

"Did you see anybody cross the road in front of your car?" She controlled her impulse and returned to her initial relaxed manner.

"I must've. Probably at traffic lights. I can't remember anything in particular."

"Did you notice any little children or anything unusual at all?"

"Not really. I just drove through what to me was just another small town, with no need to stop for anything."

"Well, thank you for your time. Houghbury will have to look elsewhere for a witness," she added, hoping to arouse his curiosity. She closed her notebook, prepared to leave, and asked indifferently, "Was your business in Houghbury itself?"

"No. As I said earlier, I was just passing through," he snapped. She turned to look at him.

"Sorry, so you did. It's just that I thought you would've avoided the town centre in the rush hour." There was the very slightest change in his demeanour, which Birdie's experience detected.

"Oh, I don't know. I'd heard it was an interesting town centre, and diverted to see for myself. Never thought it was going to cause me all **this** trouble." He returned to the offensive. She offered him her hand, which he ignored.

"Thank you for your time. If you should remember anything, however small, please let me know." She left as gracefully as she could, but there was something troubling her and she could not place it.

The next day, when she had time, she rang Derek to give him details of her interview with Masood. "No luck, I'm afraid, Derek. He's a tricky customer. Despite being assured that the case had nothing to do with him, he kept his answers to a minimum. I even asked why he was going through Houghbury centre when his business was not even in the town." She spoke apologetically.

"What did he say to that?"

"That he had heard it had an interesting centre which he was curious to see."

"He must have got his fill of the view while he was stuck at the roadworks in the Square," Derek laughed.

"Roadworks?" Birdie was puzzled.

"Yes. There were some serious ones in the corner of the Square, which caused long traffic queues. That's how the CCTV got such a clear view of the number plates. Why do you ask?"

"He never mentioned them. If the CCTV had a clear view, could you see the driver?"

"No. The streetlights reflected in the windscreen, and all we can make out is his hands on the steering wheel. We take it your Masood is black?"

"He is an Arab, but his skin is no darker than yours. Perhaps he was wearing gloves."

"No. The hands on the steering wheel were very dark; definitely not wearing gloves!"

"Very, very interesting! Whatever you do, Derek, don't tell a soul about this!"

"I'll have to tell Mr Schott."

"Okay, if you must, but impress on him the need for absolute secrecy at this stage. If my suspicions are correct, not only will you get the evidence you require but *so* will we." She sounded triumphant.

"Can you tell me why you're so pleased?"

"You would soon work it out for yourself. I think Masood was not the driver that evening. So why is he covering for the real driver? And, the real driver is probably the one you need. I assume you had no success with the other driver you mentioned?"

"Nothing! And he's a bigot from a bygone era. Although I did feel he remembered something he wouldn't divulge." Derek could scarcely disguise his irritation at the memory of the interview.

"It's Sod's law that both potential witnesses are being cagey. If I think of something to prick your driver with, I'll let you know. Speak to you soon, I hope. Love you, Derek." Before she had time to hear his reply, her inspector, Phil Tyler, entered the room and heard her last words.

"What's this, Sergeant? Having a secret affair, and in official time?" He winked as he spoke.

"Sorry to disappoint you, guv. That was my stepbrother. He works for a lawyer in Houghbury and he asked me to interview Masood about the night he drove through their town. It's to do with some appeal they're involved in. I cleared it with CID before going. I got nothing out of the wily basket, but this chat with my stepbrother has certainly thrown a brick in the pond. Better close the door."

"If you have really got something on him, we'll discuss it with CID." He shut the door.

"Right. Fact one is that Masood is the owner of an Audi caught on CCTV in Houghbury Square. Fact two is that Masood claims he was the driver. Fact three, there were serious traffic delays in the Square on the night in question, due to roadworks. Masood never mentioned them. Fact four is that the CCTV did not picture the driver but did see his hands, which did not look like Masood's. Conclusion is that Masood was not the driver, so who was and why the cover-up? If we can find the real driver, we may find the evidence against Masood which has eluded us for years. Also, the real driver may be the witness the Houghbury lawyer is seeking."

"Excellent! So it's not a lover but a chink in Masood's armour!" Tyler joked.

"Very funny! Good job I know you better or I'd be forced to report you to Race Relations!" She grinned at him as he rose from his chair.

"I'll arrange a meeting with CID for this afternoon. Can't wait to see their faces when you tell them your news. I think they'll have to do a lot of research before confronting Masood. Is there anything else Houghbury can help us with?" he pondered as he grasped the door handle.

"There may be. There was another potential witness who was hostile to my stepbrother, and he seemed to be withholding something. Apparently, the local police inspector is reluctant, to say the least, to help with the local appeal, so I don't know what to suggest."

"Is the inspector's name Banbury, by any chance?"

"Yes. How did you know?"

"It's a long story, but I know what an awkward sod he can be. Leave it with me. I'll get our CID to liaise with Houghbury CID and your Derek."

"I never said my stepbrother is called Derek!" Birdie queried instantly.

"Well, if he's not Derek, who is the one you gave your love to when I entered?"

"Touché!"

Fortunately, the CID had a meeting planned for that very afternoon, and their inspector, John Langley, agreed to Phil Tyler and Birdie Lee presenting their item. When they were introduced, most of the six officers present put on bored faces and yawns. Birdie ignored the reception and gave them the facts, except for the bit about the colour of the driver's hands, which she wanted to verify for herself. Slowly, the audience began to pay attention. One detective stood up and asked to speak.

"I think Sergeant Lee is right!" the speaker announced very firmly. "Masood keeps almost as close an eye on us as we do him, and he always covers his tracks. If he is expanding into the West Country, he may not have had the time or the connections to safeguard his activities. This development of a completely unconnected case could be the weakness we've been looking for. It's the proverbial unguarded back door."

"Ooh! Hark at the proverbial Kowalski," some excuse for an officer barracked quietly, while a couple at the back of the room nudged each other, and one whispered behind his hand, "There goes lover boy again. He'll try anything to get a bit of skirt, won't he?"

"Met his match this time! He's no chance with the ice maiden," his companion replied.

"I agree with Ivor Kowalski. We must thank Sergeant Lee for bringing this to our attention. When this meeting is finished, I would like to meet with Kowalski, Lee, and you, Phil, in my office, if that's all right. I'll try not to keep you too late. Meanwhile, the rest of you can put your thinking caps on and come up with some ideas," Langley instructed. When Birdie and Phil left, the meeting carried on with its remaining business.

Nearly an hour later, Ivor, Birdie and Phil joined Langley in his office. Birdie explained the involvement of her stepbrother and the hostility of the other driver. Phil told Langley about the negative attitude of Banbury. As Langley had met Chief Inspector Basil Watson of Houghbury CID, he would contact him. He would arrange for Kowalski to be sent to Houghbury in case Masood already had contacts there, and to facilitate better liaison. He asked Birdie to explain only the barest of details to Derek, and to expect a visit from Ivor.

As Derek still had the CCTV pictures, it might be less suspicious if he showed them to Ivor, thus avoiding any awkward questions from Banbury. Birdie had a long weekend coming up and said she would visit Derek and his pregnant wife. Her suggestion that she introduce Ivor to Derek was welcomed.

She was noted for her helpfulness and intelligence, and with her slim figure, she was not unattractive at a distance. Close to was a different matter. Her plain face suddenly became alive with unusual, hypnotic eyes; they were Chinese in shape but were a striking deep azure.

On this occasion, she had an ulterior motive. She wanted CID experience for a fresh challenge and to enhance her career prospects. Career, career, career! This was her tunnel vision. It irritated others in the force, yet the pleasant diplomatic manner she presented carried her through. She had no time for romance, though she had had offers. There had been a growing sense of guilt about her neglect of Derek and his wife, particularly now they were 'expecting'. Now she had been presented with a golden opportunity on both fronts.

It took a few days to make the arrangements for Ivor, and he would not arrive in Houghbury until the following Monday. So it was decided that Birdie would travel to Derek's on the

Friday, and return to work on the following Wednesday. Much as she loved her stepbrother, the thought of spending so many days with him and his dull wife was painful. Internet to the rescue! She researched the Houghbury area and made a list of the sights 'she simply **had** to see!' Despite more feelings of guilt, her naturally anti-social personality decided that tramping around ancient monuments and other buildings in midwinter was preferable to family visiting!

Of course, trekking around Houghbury could give her an insight into what Masood was up to before that Kowalski know-all arrived. At least he supported her at the CID meeting, and she argued with herself that she would have to appear cooperative to grease her path into the CID. But there was no harm in a little groundwork, which she could make to seem accidental knowledge. Being devious or, as some would say, two-faced was a defence she had started building at junior school, and which she honed the rest of her life.

If she had a weakness, it was her 'big brother', Derek. He had always looked after her, and she looked up to him. They were chalk and cheese; him open, her secretive. Even when she laughed at colleagues' jokes, it was planned, never spontaneous. Just once in the early part of her career she had lost control when a villain tried to get fresh with her. Then it had taken two other officers to get her off the man. As with any subject she undertook, she had to be best, and that included unarmed combat. Although the incident had led to a minor reprimand, it served to prevent any colleagues from making the same mistake.

She did not mind the various names the others called her, including cold fish, because she reasoned it was a sign of their innate jealousy of her. Those at the top saw her as an example of the perfect officer, and all reports on her reflected that. One barrier, which grew with her career, was that of not only being a female but of being very young too. Rarely did she 'let her hair down', and then it was in the form of a trip to the theatre, a concert or the opera. Perhaps the latter was her Achilles heel.

CHAPTER 9

"Santos," Miguel announced as he sat down beside Sean's hospital bed.

"Pardon?" replied Sean.

"You were about to ask my surname, weren't you?" Miguel's laugh was a few notes higher than his physique foretold.

I'm pleased to note that my new friend has dressed more sedately than the last time we met. I don't want hospital staff to know I'm a priest, but neither do I want them to think I'm gay, in case they do discover my profession.

"Yes, as a matter of fact, I was. When I was robbed, I felt very foolish asking for somebody called Miguel who has a hairdressing salon. It was lucky someone knew you. For all I know, there could be several Miguel hairdressers in town. Anyway, I hope you didn't mind me asking for you. I haven't mixed much since I've been here, and after a whole week, you're the only person I've talked with. Gosh! That must sound bad coming from one in my profession. The thing is, I came here as much to find myself as to recuperate. That's one of the reasons I was keen to talk to you, Miguel… Santos." He added the surname as if to reassure himself that he did know it now.

"There are other reasons?" Miguel raised his eyebrows in a quizzical manner.

"Well, there's Shakespeare," he replied laconically.

"And?" Miguel pressed him for more.

"Then there's your views on religion. I really would like to discuss them at length." Sean's statement was meant to be the final reason, and he wanted to change the subject.

"And?" Miguel continued to press him. This was entering territory that Sean had no wish to explore. If only the doctor or the nurse would interrupt.

"And nothing!" he answered abruptly.

Miguel put on a long face and tried to look deeply hurt. "You mean I am a... *recurso* for you?" He sought the proper word in English.

"What is *recurso*?" Sean's reply was cautious.

"You know! A thing you use."

"A thing I use!" Sean did not like the implications of this word in Spanish. His alarm showed openly on his face.

"You know. 'Ow can I put it? You use me to learn the things you want." He spread his hands in a gesture of innocence.

"Oh! You mean like a teacher or perhaps a resource." Sean's relief was obvious.

"**Si**! That is the word – resource. We say *recurso*. But is that all I mean to you? I thought we were friends or *simpatia*?"

"Yes, of course we are friends! I just took that as read."

"RED! What's coloured red?"

"No. No. Read as in read a book. I just accepted we are friends and did not think it necessary to say so. I'm sorry."

"Good. I must go back to work now. The doctor says you should be able to return to your 'otel this evening, so I will come after five to collect you."

After his departure, Sean was left alone with his thoughts. *I have many men friends, so why should friendship with Miguel disturb me? I even know that some of those friends are gay, and it has never bothered me. Is it because I feel vulnerable without the protection of my priest's garb? Of course that's it! There was the overfriendly smile I got from that woman on the promenade. My lady parishioners smiled at me, but not in the manner that woman did. After hiding behind my uniform and calling, I am suddenly exposed to the everyday temptations of the human race.*

Miguel is a good friend. If I am to be true to my beliefs, I must adopt a Christian attitude towards other people. The basis for some of my sermons seems particularly pertinent now. Only God could have known the innermost thoughts of Jesus and his disciples. Therefore, as Israel frowned upon homosexuality at that time, it was possible some of them had latent feelings, which exceeded that of spiritual love for their fellow disciples. He recalled his debate with the bishop.

If Christ could help those who were looked on as sinners, then I cannot reject those whose lifestyle I disapprove of. It will be interesting to hear what Miguel does believe in. I hope my profession will not colour his reasoning.

"Excuse me, Doctor, as I have some time to wait for the results of your tests and until I leave here, has anyone got a book I could read? In English, if possible," Sean asked his examining member of staff.

"We probably do have some in reception. I'll get an orderly to bring you up a few," he answered, without pausing in his examination of Sean. Soon after the doctor left, an orderly arrived with a book and explained in broken English that it had been left by an English tourist, because it had not been what he had expected: *RIVER OUT OF EDEN*.

This is either very fortuitous and a coincidence, or Miguel has told them I'm a priest. Ah well, if this is all they have got, it will have to do. Sean sat up in the bed and turned his reading light on.

Oh*! It is **not** at all what I expected either,* he thought as he read the rest of the title in smaller print, underneath:

RIVER OUT OF EDEN: A DARWINIAN VIEW OF LIFE

Very interesting, Sean thought, *just what the doctor ordered. Well, so he did! I will ask to borrow it when I leave. I intended checking up on Darwin. This book could be the answer.*

He started reading immediately. Patients in the vicinity were amused to see him nodding and shaking his head without realising he was being observed. They became curious to know just what the strange Englishman was reading so intensely. One of them even made enquiries and explained to the others. Then one bold individual, a devout Catholic and English speaker, spoke up when he understood the subject matter of the book.

"Excuse me, sir, but what would your priest say if he knew you were reading such a book?" He translated his question into Spanish for the others present. Sean looked up and smiled.

"I know he would say that we must keep open minds and try to understand other people's beliefs in order to reinforce our own."

He tried hard not to burst out laughing, and hid his grin behind the book. The enquirer proceeded to translate the reply. This led to much discussion, revealing the degree of openness of each person's mind. Sean concentrated on the words before him and was grateful that the heated arguments were too fast for him to attempt to translate.

Yes, he could return to his hotel, provided he did not participate in any excessive physical activity, and he must return if he experienced any serious headaches. He was advised to avoid overindulgence in food and alcohol, and must return for a check-up in seven days. The book was his to keep, although it was their last one in English. Sean promised to bring some replacements for the benefit of future English-speaking patients.

Miguel's offer to take him for a meal on the way to the hotel was politely refused, as Sean only wanted a snack that he would have in his room.

"The hospital gave me a book to read, the only one in English they had, and I am anxious to finish it. Hopefully, it will give me an insight into Darwin's theories so that I will be in a better position to discuss your beliefs with you," Sean explained, as diplomatically as possible. "I do appreciate your kindness, but I need an early night—"

"Falstaff won't do then!" Miguel interrupted with a laugh.

"Eh?" Sean looked baffled.

"You know! Falstaff was never an early knight." Miguel laughed again.

"Oh yes. I see what you mean. I'm afraid my mind isn't very alert at present."

"That does not sound good for studying Darwin. If you like, I will take you to lunch tomorrow. Business is slow at this time of year, so I am closing my salon for the afternoon. I will be able to test your new knowledge of evolution." He tried to wink and it appeared more like a grimace.

"I look forward to it. But what about all your other friends? Aren't you neglecting them?" Sean enquired, to hide his mirth at Miguel's facial contortion and discover more about his new friend.

"No. It's all right. This is a quiet time for us all, so most of them are on 'oliday. My own is booked for nine days' time."

"Where – ooh!" Sean's question was cut short as Miguel braked suddenly to avoid a woman's hat, blown into the road. The squeal of tyres caught the attention of other pedestrians who had been bent into the gusting wind.

"Sorry about zat, but vere zere's a 'at, zere's usually someone chasing it. 'Ope I didn't shake you too much. At least I made everyone look at us."

"I'm fine," Sean lied as his headache returned.

Once back at his hotel, he retired to his room and settled down with a cappuccino. He preferred tea, but not the way the hotel made it. He found it hard to concentrate on the book as his mind wandered over the events of the last few days. Putting the book aside, he tried to sleep, yet his thoughts still troubled him. He started to analyse them one by one.

Is the problem being friends with a homosexual? Is it the memory of the robbery? Is it not being open about my profession? Is it reading a book that could question some basis for my faith? No, he decided. *Each can be reasoned through without the need for a confessor or a psychiatrist.*

The episode of Miguel braking had not only jolted his body but his mind. His thoughts were cast back to the very incident that had propelled him here.

Where is the similarity? There was no sudden braking by a car then. No bag or wind! It was the bystanders! In both cases, nobody was paying any attention to the roadway until, in one case, the squeal of tyres, in the other, the cry of a woman! The man with the child in his arms could have been telling the truth. The reason nobody saw him snatch the child from in front of a car was because they were not looking!

Sean was horrified! *I joined in persecuting someone with a mindless mob, just as Christ had been persecuted. And I closed my mind to the possibility of the man's innocence. I will phone my replacement in the morning and find out, indirectly, what has happened to that man.*

Phoning from Spain to England would be expensive as it could take a long time just to reach the man filling in for him. Then he remembered that his housekeeper had a cell phone she was always using. Furthermore, often to his annoyance, she knew everything that was happening in the area; she was an important link in the Houghbury grapevine. Luckily, he had her number on his own cell phone in case of emergencies, so he could send her a text, which could be shorter and less cluttered with diversions.

Dear Mrs Cley, apart from being mugged, I am enjoying my rest here. Ask Father Donahue if there is anything I can help him with. Let me know if anyone in our church wants to speak to me. Any important news about Houghbury? What happened to the man who tried to steal the little boy near the bus station? Give my regards to all. Father Anderson

Regards! I would normally have said blessing. Have I discarded the terminology with the vestments? Too late to change as it's been sent. A few weeks ago, I was addressing my congregation from the pulpit. Now I keep contact by a short text message sent from my hotel in Spain!

I'll switch off my cell phone when I meet Miguel for lunch. Why should I? It's only a text reply that I am expecting, and even if Cley speaks to me, I have nothing to hide.

A couple of hours later, as he sat on the promenade reading his book, he felt his phone vibrate in his pocket. Text message received: *Dr Fr A, Sorry Uv Bin Mggd. Givn Ur No To Fr. D. He'll Send U Qs. Note In Chrch Re Qs For U. Nu*

Gas Main =Bad Traff In H. Kidnap=Jenkins Jld. Lwyr=Schott Applin. C

What would Shakespeare's works look like written in text format? Trust Mrs Cley to try to keep up with the younger generation. It's not a skill I have any intention of learning. I am sure it is efficient, but I am not sure I understand it. I will have to ask Miguel at lunch.

"It vill 'ave to be a joint effort, Sean. I'm familiar viz texting, but in Spanish," Miguel explained as they finished their meal. "You start and I vill give suggestions for any you don't know."

"*DR FR A,* – That is easy. It means – Dear Father Anderson. Then she is – sorry something?" Sean shrugged his shoulders and looked at Miguel.

"Vat did you tell 'er in your text, Sean?"

"Well, I did tell her I'd been mugged."

"Zat's it then! She must mean – sorry you 'ave been mugged. She's left out most of the – 'ow do you say – vocal." He pointed at the a and the u.

"Yes. You're right. She has abbreviated by leaving out most of the vowels. So the next bit reads – given your number to Father Donahue. He will send you Qs. What can that be?"

"Vat did you vant ze woman to tell Fat'er Dona'ue?"

"To see if there was anything I could help him with. Ah yes! It's questions! So the next bit means that they have put a notice in the church for anyone else who may have questions for me. I'm getting the hang of this now—"

"Vat is ze 'ang?" Miguel interrupted.

"To get the hang of means to understand something. The next piece is not really new news, as it means there are bad traffic hold-ups due to the new gas pipes being laid in Houghbury, the town where I live. I asked her what happened to the man who tried to snatch a little boy in the town. I saw him arrested. She has told me his name is Jenkins and that he's been JLD? JLD? Oh yes! She means jailed."

"I didn't know you 'ad ze death sentence in England?" Miguel blurted out.

"We don't. What makes you think that? Jailed means sent to prison."

"No, not that. It's ze next bit about being schott," Miguel explained.

"No! No! Schott is somebody's name. So what is LWYR? LWYR = Schott. He is somebody who has something to do with Jenkins."

"A policeman? A prison guard? A relative? A representative?" Miguel tried all the English names he could think of.

"Thanks, Miguel. You've put your finger on it. It—"

"I never touched you!" Miguel protested.

Sean laughed heartily. "I meant you have given me the answer. LWYR equals lawyer. It's Jenkins's lawyer, and he is going to appeal against the prison sentence."

"Who is zis Jenkins? Do you know 'im?" Miguel was baffled by Sean's obvious interest in the case, so the latter explained it at some length. He omitted his part in the mob reaction.

"It seems ze man got vat 'e deserved. 'Ow can zere be grounds for an appeal?"

"As I happened to be there when he was arrested, I have an interest in the matter. I thought he was most definitely guilty until you gave me room for doubt, yesterday."

"Me? Vat did I say?"

"It was when you braked hard to avoid that hat. I realised none of the people around had really noticed your car until you braked." Sean explained as simply as he could, while gazing into space, lost in his own thoughts.

"So 'ow could zat make you tink of dis... er... Jenkins?" he said, putting his hand gently on Sean's arm to bring him back to the present.

"Sorry. I was picturing the scene in England. The similarity is that nobody saw Jenkins actually pick up the boy. Like everyone else in the area, I only noticed him already holding the boy when the mother came on the scene and cried out. Jenkins claimed he had snatched the child from the path of a passing car. In the pressure of the moment, I'm sorry to say, like all the others, I thought the worst. Nobody believed Jenkins's story." Sean became aware of Miguel's hand on his arm and found it more natural than threatening, so he ignored it.

"Perhaps they have found a witness or the car driver who can corroborate Jenkins's story."

"Vat is coborate?"

"Corroborate means to agree with something. A witness or the car driver could have seen Jenkins pick up the boy, proving he was innocent."

"Do you sink 'e is innocent now?" Miguel shook Sean's arm to get a firm answer. Sean paused, as if to gather his thoughts while he covered up the shock of this unaccustomed contact with a fellow human. Deciding he was worrying unduly, he continued to ignore it.

"I can't say that. However, I am no longer certain of his guilt. His story could turn out to be true."

He rose from his seat to pay the bill, and Miguel withdrew his hand, sensing there was something about the incident in England that Sean was not telling him.

They had a minor disagreement over who was paying, and Miguel won on the understanding Sean would pay next time. As it was very warm, even for Malaga in winter, they sat outside a seafront café and discussed the reason for Miguel's rejection of religion. He was keen to have some wine but concurred with Sean's wish to avoid alcohol until he had seen the doctor again. Fortunately, the café proprietor made very pleasant lemon tea, which they both enjoyed.

Sean learnt that his new friend had been raised a devout Catholic and lost his faith due to an enthusiasm for science, a dislike for the Church's authority, and some 'eye-opening' philosophical lectures he attended at college. The final straw had been the realisation that he was gay, which the Catholic Church rejected. Sean appreciated many of the reasons had an element of logic, yet he was unwavering in his own belief in God. Later, Miguel took them for a walk around Malaga, pointing out interesting features normally overlooked by tourists. They parted at dusk so Sean could get an early night and return to his Darwin book.

CHAPTER 10

Derek was pleased to receive a visit from his 'kid sister'. He could show her what a happy family looked like, as he knew she was totally dedicated to her career. Then there was the other reason for her visit, the Jenkins case, which should benefit his own prospects. He managed to persuade her to meet Terence Schott, although it was Saturday.

Impressing on them the need for utmost secrecy, she gave them an outline of the case from the view of her CID. Then she also heard their thoughts on the Jenkins case. Derek had got to run some errands for his wife and said Birdie should use the time to explore Houghbury.

"If you'd care to join me for lunch, I can show you the interesting parts of our town, and point out those relevant to our Jenkins case," Terry suggested, thinking it would be a pleasure to be in the company of a highly educated, reasonably attractive young female. There was also the possibility he might find out more about the **real** reason for her visit at this time.

"That's kind of you, Mr Schott, but I don't like to take up your time." She tried to be polite, while thinking *Such an arrangement could be most useful for me.*

"It's no trouble at all, and please call me Terry. It'll be a pleasure to have company for lunch, and all I'd planned for this afternoon, due to the inclement weather, was possibly to have a physical workout... indoors." The statement caused Derek, as he was about to leave the room, to turn round abruptly and frown at his employer. Terry ignored his blatant surprise and spoke quickly to distract Birdie's attention.

"I'll reserve a table at one of my regular haunts while you put your coat on." Unseen by Birdie, Derek shrugged his shoulders and prepared to leave once more when Birdie asked for directions to their toilet and left the room. Left alone with Terry, Derek's curiosity took over.

"Why did you tell her you'd be going for a workout, Terry? The only exercise you get is doing one of your walks or cycle rides."

"I'm sorry. I couldn't think what else to say on the spur of the moment. Your sister's obviously very clever and... er... dynamic. What sort of impression would I make as your employer if I said I was going to watch a DVD? Apart from being your kith and kin, she'll be of great use in the Jenkins case. From my personal point of view, it'd be a treat to dine with somebody like her."

Going from apologetic to explanatory, his statements grew more positive. Birdie re-entered the room before Derek could reply, and with a wave of his hand, he left. She sensed that they had been talking about her, and decided questions about that and the reason for Derek's surprise at Terry going for a workout could wait until she saw Derek in the evening. Ever alert, even in allegedly relaxed company, she had seen Derek's reaction reflected in the glass doors of a bookcase.

Lunch started with a strained atmosphere, with both sparring for more feedback than they were giving. Birdie spotted some paintings for sale on the walls of the restaurant and felt obliged to comment on them.

"Why on earth do artists feel obliged to pander to popular taste, or, in this case, I presume it's the tourists? The one to the left of the old fireplace appears to have talent and is misusing it!"

"I'm so glad you said that. I've been saying much the same thing to George, the proprietor, but he won't listen. I told him the paintings were an insult to the craftsmanship of the fireplace."

At last, they had found common ground, which nurtured a mutual respect, possibly a friendship. On leaving the restaurant, Birdie immediately reconstructed the barriers she had spent years creating. Terry gave her a formal tour of the sites involved in the Jenkins case and explained the grounds for the appeal.

"I can see your witness is on shaky ground due to her husband's involvement. Why aren't there more witnesses to Jenkins's version of events? After all, Jenkins was quickly surrounded by an angry mob!" Birdie argued officiously.

"Well…" Terry was taken by surprise by her cold bluntness. "That's a good question," he lamely replied. *My god! Derek said she was dedicated but I never expected that! Just when I almost liked her. And teaching me to suck eggs!*

His reaction to her thoughts made her stiffen mentally. He then gave her a rather formal tour of a few highlights of the town and returned her to Derek's house to perform her familial duties. During the short drive, she managed to refrain from criticising his driving. *Perhaps I've already been a bit hard on this poor excuse for a lawyer – but he is Derek's boss. I'll try to be friendlier for Derek's sake…* and *he's no threat to me.*

She had seen where the traffic delays caused by the work on the gas main were on the evening of the Jenkins episode.

Terry had explained how locals had tried to avoid the site, yet the traffic chaos had been unforgettable for anyone caught up in it.

Sunday was spent pleasantly, as an ordinary person would have said, with Derek's family for breakfast and a delightful Sunday roast lunch. Birdie now understood one of the reasons Derek had married Sonia was her cooking. In the afternoon, it was cold but sunny, and Derek took her on a tour of the surrounding countryside, pointing out all the historical monuments, which she had expressed a desire to see. After that excellent if over-large lunch, and with her big brother 'lecturing' her, she was transported to her childhood and happy memories. She felt more relaxed than she had for many years. At one site, they walked up to some ancient defensive earth rings, and Birdie remembered the events in Schott's office.

"Why were you so surprised when Terry said he was going for a workout yesterday?"

"Was I?" Derek was caught out by the unexpected question.

"Yes. I saw your reaction reflected in his bookcase."

"To be honest…"

"You mean to tell me you've not been honest before?" Birdie laughed.

"I'll come quietly, Sergeant. You're right. He doesn't work out. His usual exercise is going for walks. I think he probably had something mundane planned, such as watching one of his many DVDs, but didn't want to appear wimpy in front of my clever sister."

He patted her on the back as he spoke. Anyone else attempting such a move would have found themselves on their back in seconds. Instead, she turned and gave him an affectionate smile.

"Is he a womaniser?"

"Definitely not."

"Oh. He's gay!"

"No. Wrong again. I think he had his fill of chasing girls for their looks when he was young. Now he's very selective. There's no shortage of women who see him as a great catch, but few of them ever attract him. I think he wished to be hospitable because you're my sister and can be of great use in our case."

"So he didn't find me attractive. He just had ulterior motives." She tried hard to keep from grinning at his embarrassment. He coughed as if winded by the walk.

"No, not at all. I'm sure he finds you very attractive. It's… well… you know… he wouldn't want to… well… you know…"

"I don't know, Derek. That's why I'm asking you." She was enjoying his discomfort and was not going to set him at ease quickly. Suddenly Derek stopped and turned to face her, catching sight of the twinkle in her eye before she could disguise it.

"Aha! So that's it! My boss tries to be sociable, and you act the detective trying to infer things are not what they seem. He's a very good boss, and it's not my place to pry into his private life. For all I know, he could be addicted to sex and planned to have his wicked way with you. Now I understand you fancy him and hoped he **would** have his way with you!" He grinned at her.

"Don't be silly. He's certainly not my type. I'm here to see you and Sonia, and do some background checks on my case. You know damn well I don't have time for all that romancing rubbish." She saw the grin fade from Derek's face and tried a different wind-up.

"Though I must say he **is** handsome and **marvellous** company, so – perhaps I should show an interest in him. What do you think?"

"That you're being ridiculous! Apart from me, you have nothing in common."

"We do! There's this case, and then there's art."

"Art who?" Derek demanded. He was fed up with playing her silly games.

"Art as in paintings. We discovered we've a mutual interest in art during our lunch, **together**." She laid extra stress on the last word to wind him up once more. This went too far for Derek, who was puffing as they neared the top of the earthworks.

"Good luck to you both then! Now turn around and you'll see why I dragged you up here."

"Good lord. It's the next best thing to being in a plane. What a view! The whole town and a large part of the surrounding countryside are laid out like a model. Pity I'll never get to appreciate this view with – Terry." She could not resist one last dig at her brother, who was still out of breath. She patted him affectionately on the back.

"So you're not going to get your hooks into him?" he puffed as he looked straight into her hypnotic eyes.

"No!" she laughed. "You've nothing to fear. If I did have any romantic ideas, they'd not include your precious Terry. I admit he's very pleasant, but he's most definitely **not** my type." Clouds covered the low sun and a chilling wind blew across the ramparts of the monument, adding to the historical, almost frightening atmosphere. Birdie shivered and he put his arm round her.

"No need to be frightened, little sister," he reassured her.

"This place certainly is eerie in this light, but it'd take a lot more to scare me, big brother. No, it's the cold. I didn't come prepared for climbing hills."

Derek kept his arm round her and she nestled against him for warmth. They started back down to the car park like that, and she became the kid sister once more. So completely relaxed, she forgot all about cases and careers. The only sound, apart from his heavy breathing, was the wind in some scrubby trees and bushes. The gloom intensified and they had to concentrate on their footfalls because of the many ruts in the already uneven surface.

Drunken swearing from the direction of the car park alerted them and they quickened their pace. Three young… men, for want of a better word, had arrived in a battered old car, and were trying to break into Derek's.

"Oi! That's my car!" Derek shouted as he rushed towards them. They started to run to their own car when they noticed their adversaries were a slight Chinese man and a young woman.

"Fuck me! It's only some courtin' couple. Come on, lads. Let's show them!" A repulsive crop-haired youth stopped and made the other two return with him. By this time, Birdie, who'd been unusually slow due to being cold, had reached Derek at his car.

"Get behind me, Birdie. I don't want you involved in this." Derek stepped in front of her.

"Ooh. Birdie, is it? 'ere, Birdie; 'ere, Birdie, pretty Birdie. We like to stroke birds, don't we, lads?" The burly loudmouth slapped the oldest man on the shoulder, egging him forward. The leader was tall, heavily built, and with a tattooed face that would intimidate anyone. Derek, who was pressing Birdie behind him against the car, held out an arm to fend off the thug.

"Don't you dare touch her, or you'll be sorry," Derek warned him.

"And who's going to stop 'im, chinky chap?" The loudmouth grabbed Derek's arm and pulled him aside, where the third follower helped hold of him.

"We've got him, Sid," called out the young blond lad, clutching one of Derek's arms as if his very life depended on it.

"Yeah, we got 'im good. Nah, you show the bitch what a real man's made of!" The loudmouth was almost drooling in anticipation and twisted Derek's arm with pleasure.

"You shouldn't hurt her too much, Sid," the blond lad proposed.

"Shut up, you! 'e can do whatever 'e likes, can't you, Sid?" urged the other.

The leader looked from one to the other and back at Birdie. There was just a slight hesitation in his step.

"Are you a man or a stupid mouse?" shouted the loudmouth. Sid took a deep breath and drew himself up to his full height, as if playing a part in some horror movie. The thug then advanced in his most terrifying manner to Birdie and held out his hand to caress her.

"Don't touch me! This is your final warning!" she instructed him very precisely.

"Are you put off, Sid? Show 'er you're a **proper** man," prompted the nasty one.

"**Ooh**! I'm real scared." Sid laughed and held his arms wide as if in surrender.

"No, Sid. Leave her alone. She could be your sister," the lad with untidy blond hair pleaded.

"She ain't his fuckin' sister, but she's going to get fucked." Loudmouth glared at the lad who was struggling to hold Derek, and then looked at the leader for approbation.

"Give it to 'er real good, Sid! She's beggin' for it! **Do it, man!**" the evil lad seemed to order his huge companion. Sid turned back to Birdie and lunged at her.

Derek, who hated violence in any form, knew what would happen and would normally have closed his eyes. In the current situation, some primeval urge made him watch with relish.

With an overconfidence from years of his aggressive behaviour and size frightening his victims, Sid grabbed for her shoulder. He had a massive advantage of both height and weight. His hand never reached her. In that instant, he was slightly off balance and moving towards her. With minimum use of her full ability, Birdie seized his arm and spun round, pulling him completely over and past her to the ground.

She put her foot on his neck and kept his arm locked in hers. Try as he might, Sid could not move. The lads holding Derek both let go at the same time to go to Sid's assistance. Derek tripped one and ran at the blond lad, who fled. Then the one on the ground scrambled to his feet and ran after him.

"Help! I can't breathe," Sid whimpered.

"Oh yes you can. But try to get up or escape and I'll shift my foot like so." She only held her foot on his windpipe for a few seconds, but it was enough to put genuine fear into his eyes.

"Derek, have you got any rope or suchlike in your car?" She smiled at him as if she had been shopping and made a clever purchase. He looked through the boot of the car and showed her a tow rope and some cable ties.

"Use the ties. Interlock one round each of his ankles. Then I'll do the same with his wrists." Once they had him secured, they loaded him into the back of the car and Birdie sat beside him, while Derek drove to Houghbury police station. There, they cut the ties around his ankles and marched him inside.

The duty officer did not welcome visitors when he had just come on duty, on a Sunday evening. He glanced reluctantly at the trio, and his look became concentrated when he saw the largest man had his hands tied.

"What's all this then?" He sat up straight.

"These buggers assaulted me!" Sid blurted out, before the others could speak.

"Let's hear what they have to say about it, shall we, Sidney Cracken?"

"You know this man, Officer?" Derek enquired.

"Yes, and I know you. You're Schott's clerk. Sid's been a visitor to these premises on more than one occasion. Usually for drunk and disorderly, though it usually takes more than one officer to bring him in. And who is this young lady?" The officer glowed with his knowledge. Birdie pulled Derek's arm so she could reply.

"I'm Mr Lee's kid sister, Sergeant." She tried to sound juvenile, mocking Derek's earlier comments.

"Kid sister! That's a laugh. She 'alf killed me! Totally unpro... unpro... without reason," Sid protested, and then as he looked down at the slim woman he realised how ridiculous it sounded. "Well, she bloody did! Don't know 'ow she fight like it," he continued.

"Why did you assault this poor... frail... young gentleman?" The sergeant looked directly at Birdie and struggled not to burst out laughing. She understood the humour in the question and replied in kind.

"I'm terribly sorry, Sergeant. I don't know what came over me. All this lad did was to try to carry out what his friends, well, one of them, told him to do. Putting it politely, he was to have sex with me. I didn't want him to, so when he grabbed at me, I forgot my manners and floored him. I hope I didn't do wrong. I tried not to hurt him too much as I could see he was, as you put it, rather frail." She glanced at her huge would-be assailant and felt he appeared to be no more than an overgrown frightened schoolboy. She instantly dismissed the thought.

Derek looked from Birdie to the sergeant and back, and then at Sid, in disbelief. In his legal world, such jesting was reserved for more private surroundings.

"Where'd you learn to fight like that?" The sergeant needed some facts to overcome his disbelief.

"In the Met. I'm Sergeant Lee and I'm meeting my colleague from our CID here tomorrow."

"Yes. I'd heard someone from the Met was coming. I'm Robert Pollock. The lads call me Bob." He shook her hand. "So you've officially arrested Sid?"

"No. I've an interest in the Met case, and of course that of my brother. However, I'm here on vacation for a family visit. I'm off duty, so I'd like you to treat this as a citizen's arrest by my brother."

The sergeant went through all the formalities of arresting Sid and taking statements.

Then, as they were leaving, he handed her a note he found on his desk.

"Nearly overlooked this. Apparently, there've been developments in the Met case and your man's only coming down for a couple of days, so he wants to meet you here at 10:30 tomorrow. Someone rang Mr Lee's home and left a message. You are staying there, aren't you?"

As Derek and Birdie drove home, Derek could not stop talking about the events of the afternoon. He'd had more excitement than he could have believed possible, and he swelled with pride at how Birdie had handled herself. Sonia had been worried because it had been dark for over an hour when they returned. She was even more worried when she heard what had happened to them.

Monday morning at the police station, Birdie and Ivor Kowalski had a meeting with Chief Inspector Basil Watson, in which Ivor explained the Ali Masood case and the very latest developments. Completely unexpectedly, Masood had rung the London office and asked for a message to be passed to Birdie. Phil Tyler had taken the message.

"Masood apologised for his bad memory, but there was one thing he should've mentioned about his journey through Houghbury, and that was the terrible traffic jams caused by some gasworks. It appears to clear up some of our suspicions, yet we still need to check on what exactly he was doing in this area," Ivor explained.

"There's an office you can use for a couple of days. Let me know how we can help. By the way, Sergeant Lee, congratulations on your arrest yesterday. I know you put it down as a citizen's arrest by your brother, but Bob told me the truth. Sid Cracken is a public nuisance, and was bound to get into more serious trouble one day. It's a good job it happened to someone who could fight back. We'll find the other two, and from what you've said in your statements, at least one of them's not destined for a life of crime. Cracken's greatest threat to society, until now, that is, has been the number of youngsters he leads astray. Just between us, you've rather upset Inspector Banbury, who was hoping his team would collar him."

Once they were alone, Ivor and Birdie quickly compared notes.

"How the hell did Masood find out about the roadworks? If it had been him in the car, he'd not have overlooked them when I interviewed him. Someone's been blabbing to him!" Birdie demanded irately.

"That's the reason I had to see you as soon as I could. Who've you told about Masood, and when?" Ivor tried to be as diplomatic as possible with his question. He didn't want to upset her as he rather fancied her. He had made enquiries about her and understood her dedication to her career excluded men friends. However, he enjoyed the challenge of adding another woman to his list of conquests. He had spent most of the weekend researching her on the pretext that she could have been the one through whom the information had leaked.

He found that she had only once turned down the chance of extra duty, and that was because she was going to some opera by Puccini. Thinking this could be the key to unlocking her heart, or more importantly her body, he did some intense studying of operas, Italian in particular.

"That's why I had to see you now. Don't take this the wrong way, but we have to explore all possible sources if there's been a leak. When did you explain our suspicions to your brother?" The question upset her sufficiently for her to fail to notice the excessively pleasant manner in which he posed it.

"If you must know, I actually explained it to my brother and his boss fully on Saturday morning. I did give my brother the outline reason for our interest on Friday afternoon and said he could tell his boss, but it had to be kept a secret between them. I'm absolutely sure they couldn't have known, or contacted Masood."

"Why're you so sure, Sergeant Lee?" He added name and rank to make the question sound more official and less personal. He had never seen her out of uniform before, and with the way her trim, desirable body grew more taut at his questions, he had difficulty in keeping his own thoughts official. Exercising extreme care in his handling of her, he knew his admiration of her physical attributes could reveal his lustful thoughts, so he gazed at his notebook.

"My brother and I've always been very close and trust each other completely. Furthermore, unless both Derek and I are bad judges of character, this lawyer, Schott, is young, keen, clever and ambitious." Although she was irritated, she did notice he was smiling. Pretending to glare at him, she appraised her companion and found him to be very handsome, with a most charming smile. She had not really noticed him before, although that was not surprising as she always saw anyone at work as merely a colleague, and never as a person. *Some woman has a real catch with him*, she thought. He continued to smile at her and she found it annoying. "Well! Are you satisfied?" she demanded.

"Very," he replied. "I was just thinking how beautiful you are when you're angry."

Wrong thing to say to Birdie! She hated flattery, even when it had a sincere ring about it. Her guard, which had slipped momentarily, was fully in force once more.

"Now, perhaps you'll tell me when and how Masood came up with the information." She addressed him as she would a suspect, with a cold, flat voice. Ivor knew at once that he had made a mistake. Informal chats with colleagues had warned him of her rejection of advances from any of them. He had been overconfident of his ability to charm any woman, and now he would have to tread extra carefully. He would delay using another approach and facts he had learnt about her until a more relaxed opportunity presented itself.

"That's the disturbing question. He rang the office early Saturday morning and said, in so many words, that he'd some information he'd like to be given to you. Then he explained about the roadworks delaying him in Houghbury. He said he forgot to tell you, because he was angry at your invasion of his privacy. What's wrong? What did I say to make you react so?" He noticed the slight widening of her eyes and her mouth opening.

"We've a mole in our office! Only someone there would've known about the omission of the roadworks being cause for suspicion, and—"

"Yes! Yes! We know that now we think we've cleared your contacts here."

"**And**," she continued, showing her annoyance at his interruption, "if he wanted information to be given to me, like you said, why didn't he actually ask for me?" She stared at Ivor, waiting for him to work it out for himself.

"Of course! You're right. As you'd interviewed him, he should've asked to speak to you. He didn't, because he knew you weren't in the office. If you didn't tell him, when you saw him, that you'd not be in on Saturday, how did he know for certain?" His glow of triumph nearly matched that for one of his romantic conquests.

"Precisely! It all boils down to the mole, who made a mistake in mentioning my absence. He must be the reason Masood has always been one step ahead of us. And the main suspect must be one of your CID mates at the meeting. If I can discount the inspectors and you, that leaves five officers."

CHAPTER 11

Christmas Day!

It dawned in a somewhat less favourable light than previous years for Helen. Nicola and Roger, boisterous with opening presents, were sheltered from most of her worries about Arnold. She left for the hospital with them and with *great* hopes. Disappointed at being uprooted from their new possessions, the youngsters read their new books in a reception room, waiting their turn to see their dad. They became frustrated at the lack of any action, either to see their father or to go home. A passing tea lady provided them with some soft drinks.

"We're sorry, Mrs Phillips, we'll have to keep your husband in for a few days longer. His wounds seem healthy enough, but he's having difficulty breathing, and he's very dizzy. We've run a few tests but can't find the cause. Has he had any health problems recently?" The doctor was ashamed to be admitting his ignorance of Arnold's illness.

"Nothing. With his outside physical job and then all our activities at home, he's not even had a cold."

Helen had arrived at the hospital prepared to take Arnold home with her. The news of his problems was like a simultaneous slap in the face and punch in the solar plexus. Noting the tremor in her voice and her crestfallen face, the doctor, Tim Smedley, held her arm and helped her sit on a chair. When he was certain she was calm enough, he perused Arnold's charts, to avoid looking directly at Helen.

"Does he have any allergies?"

"Not that we know of," she whispered shakily.

"Has he eaten anything unusual recently?" he persisted, hoping for some clue, however small.

"No." She paused for a moment, lost in reviewing their diet of the previous week. "Unless..." She paused again as she recollected the events of the fateful day.

"Unless what, Mrs Phillips?" he prompted her urgently.

"Unless he had something unusual in the afternoon. He should've eaten the cheese sandwiches I made for his lunch... he wasn't home at his expected time... he didn't catch the normal bus." Her statements came as if gasping for air. She took a deep breath and continued. "In fact, now I think of it, the Browns, who found him, thought he may've had a lift in the car they saw near the fallen tree."

"Do you know who could've given him a lift?" Smedley perked up. Perhaps the car driver could provide the answer he sought so desperately.

"No. We'll have to ask the Browns. How urgent is it?" She coughed to clear the lump in her throat.

"Very. The sooner I know the cause of your husband's sickness, the sooner he can go home. Could you phone them right now, please?" He handed her his mobile phone.

"I'll have to look up their number. I've never had reason to phone them as they only live a few yards away." Smedley had a volunteer fetch her a phone book.

"This lady will keep me advised of anything you discover. I must continue with my rounds now, but I won't be far away," he reassured her.

It took her some time to find the right number. Fortunately, the Browns were at home. They were sorry to hear the bad news about Arnold and gave Helen all the information they could about the strange car and the driver.

"He seemed quite young, was well spoken and could have had a beard." They again offered to help in any way they could despite the fact they would have to leave soon for church and then for Christmas with their grandchildren. Touched by their obvious support and offer, Helen sank still deeper into a pit of despair, and her beautiful face became haggard with worry. The orderly appreciated her state and quickly fetched the doctor, and then the all-curing cup of tea. She had made written notes of such facts as the Browns had supplied, and she gave them to Smedley at his request. She mentioned that PC Baxter had been extremely considerate and wondered if he or his colleagues could find the driver, as it was urgent. He agreed, and rang the police himself to underline how vital the information was.

The police on duty on Christmas Day did not usually welcome enquiries. However, although they were very relaxed, they were not yet full of Christmas spirit, and they had plenty of goodwill between them. Thus, they all put their heads together and considered the information. One pessimist pointed out they could be wasting their time as the car and driver might not be local.

"Who **is** the sick man?" one asked.

"It's Arnold the binman."

"Oh. What a shame, he's always seemed so pleasant. I've spoken to him on my rounds, often."

"**Arnold**!" one exclaimed. "I saw him chatting to Mr Schott at the bus stop in the Square yesterday! I thought it very strange at the time, which is why I remember it!"

"That's the answer! Schott fits the description, and so does his car!" The news was received with delight at the hospital, which was able to start contacting the lawyer immediately as the police had given them his ex-directory phone number. There was no answer, so they left a message explaining how urgent it was that he contact the hospital. Then they rang the police again.

"Leave it with us. We'll try and find him for you," Sergeant Pollock told them briskly.

He immediately rang Derek Lee. He would have to know where his boss was spending Christmas.

"He's spending the holiday with some cousin in London, so he can go to the opera on Boxing Day. I'm not sure of the address, but I can give you his mobile number," Derek informed Bob. The latter tried time and again to reach Schott, only to be informed that the number was not available. In desperation, with vital hours passing, he rang Derek again.

"We can't get hold of Schott, and it **is** a matter of life and death. We think he gave Arnold Phillips a lift home on Christmas Eve. Is it possible?" Bob said anxiously.

"Yes. It's quite possible. He went to meet him in the Square on behalf of Maurice Jenkins."

"We don't need to know what they talked about, just whether Schott could've given Phillips anything to eat?"

"Very unlikely! He only met Phillips for two reasons. One, because Jenkins had asked him, and two, because he felt Phillips could add something positive to the appeal we're building." Derek was getting a bit strained at these interruptions to his family's celebrations.

"Did he learn anything useful?"

"I don't know. I've not spoken to him since."

"Well, how can you be sure he never gave Phillips anything to eat?" Bob too was getting exasperated by the lack of any solid information.

"Simply because he never even carries a sweet in his car or on his person, and he certainly wouldn't treat anyone to a meal." Suddenly understanding the potential interpretation of his reply, he hastily added, "He's always very cautious about socialising with anyone as he considers it could infringe on his professional status."

Deciding he was heading up a blind alley, Bob rang off and told the hospital as much as he had managed to find out. This left Smedley none the wiser, and he advised Mrs Phillips to go home. She would be told as soon as they had any new information or there was any change in Arnold's condition. Helen could see that the most sensible thing would be to leave. She was not helping Arnold, and she knew the children would be fretting. Still, she waited, clutching his hand, until she felt calm enough to drive them home. She let them see Arnold briefly, explaining that he needed more rest and was sleeping, so they couldn't talk to him.

Christmas Day! Fighting against the wind and rain to reach their old car cleared her mind, and she tried to make a game of it for the kids. In her anxiety, she flooded the engine and had to wait several minutes for the excess fuel to clear. With the interminable noise from kids, wind, rain and squeaking wipers, she was in a private hell with no end in sight. Her head throbbed and there was an unaccustomed tightness in her chest.

At home, she became an automaton performing her household duties. Her nightmare, sometimes softened by a child's enthusiasm, lasted until they were asleep. Then she treated herself to a small glass of sherry from a bottle given to her for Christmas by one of her employers.

Thinking back on the events that had brought her to this situation, she reasoned that it was due to getting a lift instead of the bus. The sherry had given her a pleasant inner warmth, so she had a second glassful. *Arnold got the lift because Schott wanted to talk to him about that...* pervert, *Jenkins.* She filled her glass once more, spilling a few drops as her hand shook. *I remember Arnold's reaction to the TV item about Jenkins. How's my wonderful husband involved in the case?* **Had** *he been a witness and not told me?* In her distraught condition, aided by the consumption of alcohol to which she was unaccustomed, she reasoned that the source of her problems was the evil Jenkins. Unable to contain her hatred, she spoke aloud in slurred words of pure venom.

"Jenkins cun rot in pizzon for ever. God curz 'im 'n' make 'im zuffa fouzend times wot Arnol's got!" She reached the toilet in time to eject the day's excesses. She never remembered how she got to bed, where she awoke early on Boxing Day, fully clothed, with the entire world's rock bands playing in her head.

Struggling to retain her composure and perform her domestic duties, she decided she was not fit to drive to the hospital, at least for a while. She rang them to see how Arnold was progressing and was told to delay her visit anyway, as he was suffering a bad attack of diarrhoea and vomiting. Doctor Smedley was more convinced than ever that the sickness was caused by something Arnold had eaten. To uncover the source of the malady, it was essential for them to contact Terence Schott. The police were doing all they could, but Schott had obviously switched his mobile phone off for the holiday. Gleaning all possible information from Derek, they discovered his boss would be going to a particular opera in the evening. They contacted the theatre's manager, impressed upon him the urgency of the matter, and had him place suitable signs in the foyer.

In the afternoon, Helen attended the hospital with Nicola and Roger, who again brought books to read. She was horrified when she saw Arnold. His face was gaunt and lacked all colour, and his eyes were puffy and bloodshot. He was awake and showed that he recognised her. He tried to talk, but the effort brought on another bout of vomiting. She talked to him as normally as her fears would allow, trying to make light of her worries by describing a jolly Christmas from her imagination rather than the reality. She listed the kids' presents as if he did not already know what they were. Smedley refused to let her stay more than an hour or so because he could see it was not helping his patient but harming her and her children. She reluctantly left, once she had received an assurance that they would advise her immediately of any developments.

Somewhere inside her, she was pleased to leave. Not for lack of love for Arnold, or for cowardice, but because caring for Nicola and Roger tipped the balance of brain over heart. *I've every faith in the hospital staff and in God. Together, they'll ensure justice prevails and Arnold will soon recover. He's a good, good man. I count myself lucky to have such a man as my husband and as the father to my children.* Nicola and Roger were unusually quiet on the journey home and Helen knew they had begun to understand the seriousness of their father's illness.

Terry was most surprised to see his name advertised in the foyer. Being an out-of-towner, he had arrived early to allow for any mishaps. He went immediately to the manager's office, where the outline of the situation was explained to him, and he was left to contact Houghbury Hospital. He was astonished to find that Arnold Phillips had had an accident shortly after he left him, and that he was now seriously ill. He told the medical staff all that happened while he had been with

Arnold. They were satisfied Arnold could not have consumed anything in Schott's presence and asked him to repeat the facts to the Houghbury police. This he did at once, and he also explained to the police why he had met with Arnold on Christmas Eve. In case there were further developments, he agreed to make a statement at the police station on his return to Houghbury.

He just made it to his seat before the music began. It was some time before he could concentrate fully on the performance as he kept thinking of poor Arnold and wishing he had insisted on driving him all the way home. During the interval, he wished he had a companion, or better still, a soulmate with whom he could share his thoughts on Arnold as well as on the performance. He felt the tenor was struggling a bit and was definitely not up to his expected standard. *Perhaps the singer had overindulged the previous day?*

Next day at the hospital, Helen was pleased to see Arnold looking a little bit better. He was suffering considerably less from vomiting and diarrhoea, probably because he had little left to give. However, he was severely dehydrated and had been put on a drip. He managed to croak a few words of comfort to Helen and obviously derived some strength from her presence. She allowed Nicola and Roger to spend a few minutes with him, and he even managed a weak smile for them, though they were visibly amazed at his appearance. Encouraged by his improvement, Helen did not feel so guilty when it was time to leave.

On 28th December, she was due to return to work. The Browns had spread the word of her problems, and her employers, hearing the news on the country grapevine, insisted she should wait until Arnold was well. He did look a lot better when she visited him, and the doctors, who had had a discussion about potential causes, were hopeful it was down to him swallowing dirty ditchwater.

"I'm sorry for causing you all this trouble, darling," Arnold whispered to her.

"I should think so too," she tried to joke with him.

"How are Roger and Nicola with all this disruption to their holiday?"

"Don't worry about them. I think this episode has helped them mature more in these few days than in the previous several months." His interest gave her new hope and took away some of the ache in her chest she had been suffering since Christmas Eve.

"Shouldn't you be at work today, dear?"

"Yes. My bosses heard about you being in hospital and told me not to go in until you're well."

"They're very kind." He nodded his head slightly at the thought of people being so considerate. She nodded in return and smiled, though she was fighting back tears.

"Everyone's been so kind, particularly the Browns."

"What? The doddery old couple up the lane?" He frowned as he thought of the old-timers.

"*Yes*! The doddery old couple, as you put it, who **saved** your life!" She nearly raised her voice in anger at him, but remembered where they were.

"They did! How?" He could not believe he had understood her correctly.

"What was the last thing you remember before waking in hospital?"

"Intense pain in my leg and head, collecting the presents together, and then I must've passed out. Oh! And it was pouring with rain and there was a gale blowing." His eyes were screwed up as he relived the moments.

"It was the Browns who spotted you lying in the road. They covered you from the rain, called the ambulance and fetched me. They also looked after the kids while I came here. I actually got a lift in a police car!" He started to reply and apologise for being so thoughtless, when a coughing fit overcame him. Helen rang for the medical staff and they asked her to leave, as they feared Arnold was getting too excited, too soon.

The next day, they stuck to small talk and their plans for meeting the demands of the courses they were about to undertake. And how proud they were of their kids developing maturity. They were happy to be in each other's company, knowing they would soon be at home together.

"Have they cleared the old oak tree from the road yet?" Arnold enquired as she was leaving.

"Yes. They did it yesterday. Shame to see it go. It's been such a landmark for so many years. They said it was all the rain we've had over these past few months, which loosened its roots."

Once home, she busied herself to keep from thinking of Arnold's illness. She was unaware of the ripples her departing remark had made with the medical staff. Purely by chance, a nurse who heard about the tree was making polite conversation with a colleague in the canteen and was overheard by a doctor from another section, who knew of Arnold's mystery illness. He had once been keen on the study of fungi, and mention of the oak triggered a warning in his memory. He raced to find Smedley and explained his theory.

"Amanita phalloides is often found under oak trees! Your patient, I believe, fell into a ditch when he tripped over the roots of an oak tree?"

"Yes. I didn't know it was an oak tree. What difference does that make? And what is this amanita thingummy?"

"The common name for amanita phalloides is the mushroom known as death cap! Could your patient have swallowed some when he fell?"

"**Yes**! We **thought** he'd ingested something from the ditchwater, which had made him sick. He admitted getting a mouthful of dirty water and stuff, which he tried to spit out."

"How long has it been since then?"

"About five days. Why, what can we do now?"

"Virtually nothing! Check immediately. You may be in time, but I think you'll find his liver's been destroyed! Let's get started. I'm on my break, so I can help." He grabbed the arm of his colleague and they dashed back to Arnold. Full emergency procedures went into action, to little avail. Smedley called Helen and asked her to come immediately. She managed to get the Browns to look after the kids, even though it was very late, and then sped to the hospital. Such comfort as the staff offered her was meaningless as she sat there holding Arnold's hand, watching him die.

Her own life became meaningless! She could not even weigh her own children in the balance of her existence! *God,* she silently prayed, *bring my love back to me. Take this paralysing pain from my heart. Make this nightmare end.*

She never knew how long she remained there, frozen by his deathbed, like a heart-rending statue by one of the sculptors of old. Eventually, Smedley, with some assistance, managed to prise her almost-hysterical grip from Arnold's cold hand. They moved her to an empty room and gave her some tea, which was left to grow cold. She sat there, tense and unmoving; ignoring or just not hearing the words of consolation and counselling offered by experts and non-experts. She had no tears; her eyes were fixed on a corner of the ceiling as she converted pain and grief into anger and hatred.

The medical staff had experienced many reactions in bereavement cases, particularly in younger people when death was unexpected, but never this extreme. Smedley managed to contact the hospital psychiatrist and a specialised death counsellor. Their discussions were producing lots of theories and countertheories, when the nurse who had taken Helen home on that first night entered the fray.

"I've just heard the terrible news about Phillips, so I've come to offer my help." She interrupted nervously, realising these superiors wouldn't welcome her advice.

"**Who** do you think—" The psychiatrist was stopped by Smedley.

"Hang on! Tracey's met Mrs Phillips before. Let's hear her out. How can you help, Tracey?" He beckoned her into the room.

"I only gave her a lift home on Christmas Eve, so I don't really know her well. But, as a mother myself, I suggest I take her home right now, so she can be with her kids. Her natural maternal instincts will help her get through any sort of mental pain."

Immediately, the three 'superiors' nodded in agreement. Smedley took Tracey to collect Helen, leaving the other two explaining to each other how the result was what they had been working towards all the time. Smedley gave Helen a single sleeping pill to take, to help her through this first night. Giving her more would have been dangerous for someone whose medical history he did not know, and now the death could have unbalanced her.

Reluctant though she was to desert Arnold, even though life had deserted him, Helen allowed herself to be led like a child and placed in Tracey's car. They had nearly reached Rudton when Helen broke the awkward silence.

"How can I tell Nicola and Roger?" Her eyes began to moisten. Pleased to be able to talk at last, Tracey paused before replying.

"How old are they?"

"Nicola is eight and Roger is six."

"Do you go to church regularly?"

"No. Arnold is… was an atheist. I went to church and Sunday school when I was little, and I used to get the kids to say their prayers, until Arnold made me stop. It was the only big disagreement we ever had." The tears streamed down her face as the memories returned.

"I won't enter the argument, one way or the other, but it could be a whole lot easier for children at those ages if they think their father's gone to Heaven."

"You're right. Arnold'd call it the coward's way out, but I must soften the blow as best I can."

The car stopped outside her house. She carefully wiped her eyes and steeled herself, before thanking Tracey and getting out. Tracey waited until Helen was inside the house before leaving. The Browns recognised the tragedy showing in her face, and as the kids were in bed, they felt free to express their concern. Reassured by her self-control, they went home, insisting she call on them for any help or '**absolutely anything**' she needed. Walking the short distance to their own home, they held hands, which was unusual, and never spoke, which was *very* unusual!

Making sure Nicola and Roger were safely asleep, Helen took the sleeping pill with some water and went to bed. Tomorrow, she would have a lot to face up to.

CHAPTER 12

"'E didn't know that I didn't know that 'e knew 'im!" Mrs Gumbrill burst into Terry's office despite his secretary's best attempts to stop her.

"It's okay, Eileen, I'll deal with this. Derek…" Terry got up from his desk and handed some papers to his assistant sitting on the other side of it. "We'd nearly finished anyway. Can you complete the papers as far as we've got, and we'll cover the rest later." His staff left the room, with Mrs Gumbrill pacing around and waving her arms.

My witness! Terry thought. *I wouldn't even rely on her to do my shopping. Patience! Patience! Look upon this interlude as light entertainment. After all, it happens in the best of courtrooms as well.*

"Now, Mrs Gumbrill. **Who** doesn't know **who**?" He opened a notebook and pretended that he was about to take some details. Inwardly, he thought, *Some of her conversation could be worth recording for Maurice,* who had told him of his new project to write a comedy script.

"**My Bill**!" she announced, as if it was a fact of international importance. She was still pacing around the room, so he moved round his desk and gesticulated at a chair.

"Which one? Phone, electric, rates – which – one?" *Same old person. It's still a question of blood from a stone.*

"No, no, silly! My 'usband, Bill." She shook her head so

vigorously he almost wished it would fall off and prove she was not a real person.

"Oh. **Mr** Gumbrill. What's he been up to?" *What more damage could her spouse do to this case?*

"You know 'e went and saw Jenkins in prison?" She had calmed down enough to elaborate.

"Ye-es." *Now where is she heading?* Terry thought.

"You know that 'e works at the same office as Jenkins?" She seemed to fancy herself as a lecturer.

"Yes, I do." Terry did not know quite how he was expected to reply in this strange woman's melodrama.

"Well." She paused for effect. Had his desk been soft pine instead of hard oak, there would have been indentations on the edge as a record of her visits; such was the pressure he exerted from his frustration.

"Well..." she repeated. "**I** didn't know!" *And that's that,* he anticipated her adding.

His grip on the desk tightened, and his chair moved back slightly. He took a very deep breath, exhaled and said, "What... did... you... not... know, Mrs Gumbrill?"

"My name's Diana, by the way," she proclaimed, as if revealing herself as some great star.

"Do your friends call you Di?" he asked gently, for want of knowing how he was expected to reply. He wondered, *Will I one day get an award for patience or even gallantry for my behaviour in the face of such odds?*

"**No, they don't**. My friends all call me Mrs Gumbrill." She appeared most indignant at the very idea.

"Can we stick to the point, please? I'm very busy today." He tried to hasten her.

"Busy with **what**?" *Was there no end to this impossible woman's impertinence?*

"**My work**! Now what's the point that's so important that you interrupted my meeting?"

"The point? What point? I know nothing about any point. Is there something you're keeping from me, Mr Schott?" she demanded.

His nerves were frayed, his knuckles were gleaming white, and he was definitely seeing red.

"**You** burst into my office **without an appointment** and talk about people knowing and not knowing!" His outburst had a remarkable effect on her. Her face became anguished; she slumped in her chair and looked ready to cry. Then the reason for the visit came gushing forth.

"My Bill's always so quiet and unresponsive. Then, at Christmas, 'e 'ad an extra drink and got real stroppy with me. 'E said 'ow 'e knew about my visits 'ere, and they weren't going to do Jenkins any good, 'cos the inspector didn't believe me, 'cos 'e knew Bill worked with Jenkins and 'e knew I'm married to Bill, and Bill 'ad been to see Jenkins in prison, and they'd set me up to tell you what I saw. But I didn't know Bill knew Jenkins, or that 'e'd seen 'im in prison. I may not 'ave qualifications, but I do know what I saw." With that final flourish, she burst into tears.

Terry now felt not only embarrassed but guilty as well. He pressed his intercom and asked Eileen to bring in some tissues. The very arrival of his plump matronly secretary placated the troubled atmosphere in the office. Once Diana had calmed down, he explained that he knew she was trying to be helpful and that she had told the truth. He ushered her out of his room, and apologised for being so abrupt with her.

"That's all right, Mr Schott. You're not the one who should be apologising. It's the mother of the little toddler what Mr Jenkins saved who should be apologising to Jenkins."

After she left, Terry thought about what she had said.

Nobody's *spoken to the mother since the trial. Perhaps her little Charlie has said something. I'll have to interview her, but not until I've talked with Maurice Jenkins again.*

After Maurice was shown into the interview room where Terry was waiting, they shook hands and nothing of any importance was said until they were both seated.

"Have you heard about Arnold Phillips since I last saw you, Maurice?" He broached the subject cautiously.

"No. Did you manage to meet him on Christmas Eve?" Maurice was keen to hear if the rendezvous had been kept, and whether Arnold had made any progress on their pact.

"Yes, I did, but…" He hesitated, wondering how best to break the news.

"How is he? Has he started a course? Does **he** believe I'm guilty?" His enthusiastic search for answers trailed off as he noted the sombre expression on his lawyer's face.

"This is very difficult for me, Maurice. Before I answer all your questions, I must tell you Arnold died two days ago."

Maurice was horrified. *I only knew Arnold for less than thirty minutes, yet I felt there was a bond between us. Suddenly my wrongful incarceration seems so insignificant.* Unable to come to terms with the news, he waited for Terry to explain fully. As he listened to the events, as far as Terry knew them, he collated a series of questions.

"How was he when you met him?"

"Curious about who I was. In good health and looking forward to Christmas with his wife and two children. Not only was he booked on a degree course starting in the new year, but his wife, Helen, is going on a course too. Though I don't know if she'll be able to now she's lost Arnold."

"Did he realise I'm in prison?"

"Yes, but he thought you must be innocent, particularly as you gave him your real name."

"How come he was there when you went?"

"He said it was coincidence, but I think he felt obliged to be there," Terry reassured him.

"Gosh, I feel partly responsible. But for our pact he wouldn't have had the accident and finished up in hospital. What actually killed him?"

"You're no more responsible than I am. He was there of his own volition. He could just as easily have caught the bus and got off near the top of the lane. It was a chance in a million that he tripped and fell in the ditch, and that there was some death cap in the water he swallowed."

"What about his wife and kids? Who's looking after them? Have they got other family nearby?"

"His wife is **Helen**." He repeated her name, realising that Maurice had not been paying full attention earlier. "Then there's a girl, Nicola, who's eight, and a boy, Roger, who's six. They've no family in the area, and they are pretty poor. There's an old couple close by who help as much as they can."

"Is there anything I can do?" Maurice requested hopefully.

"At present, definitely not. I'm sorry to say Helen found out why he was late starting for home, and about your pact, and in her despair she blames you for her troubles. In fact, without knowing you, she thinks of you as a convicted pervert who caused her husband's death. When you do get out, I should avoid any contact with her, if I were you. I know her hatred for you is unreasonable, but I think it is one support helping her overcome her loss."

"That makes me feel dreadful! If you ever discover **any** way I can help, however small, do tell me."

"I will. Now we must consider your appeal. We've had no success with the car driver so far. The London police are still working on it. I'd like to try another angle. The boy you rescued, why did he cry out?" Terry opened his file in preparation.

"I don't think I hurt him much when I grabbed him. I've been thinking about it, and believe it was a combination of events. First, there was his fall from his scooter. That could've hurt him, and it was a shock. Then there was the noise of the car. Then, of course, there was the added shock of being snatched from the roadway, and the closeness of a complete stranger. I don't think the hysterical reaction of his mother helped either." Maurice shook his head at the painful memory.

"That's more or less what I reckoned." He marked some notes in the file.

"How can it help my case?" This new line of questioning puzzled Maurice.

"I'll get to that in a minute. Did the boy say anything at all?"

"No. All he did was scream and cry. He didn't utter a single word while I was there. How's that relevant?" Maurice pictured the incident, particularly the little boy.

"Because of his age, nobody interviewed the child. I'm wondering if he's ever said or shown signs of knowing anything about the incident. He may have blocked it out due to the terror of the moment, or due to his mother's reaction." Terry thought it appropriate to explain more fully his reasoning, partly to give Maurice more hope and partly to find any triggers for his memory.

"He may have been helped to forget for his own good. On the other hand, he could've been encouraged to relive events to prevent future nightmares and suchlike. If you were the parent and your child's memory of the event was not what you believed to be true, what would you do? Would you accept that you may have been wrong, or would you put it down to childish imagination and ignore it?" He spread his hands as if weighing objects, and stared intently into Maurice's eyes.

"I've only been friends with kids, and I appreciate that's not the same as being an actual parent. So I can't really answer your question. What do you intend doing about it?"

"Visiting the family. It can't do any more harm, and it may be useful."

After Terry left, Maurice returned to his cell block and reflected on the meeting. *The planned visit may be clutching at straws, but at least it's some action to keep my hopes alive.* There was an alphabetical notebook, which Terry had left for him. Maurice opened it nonchalantly and found a separate note inside from Terry. It told him to use it for recording observations and thoughts, which could be useful for future comedy sketches. It also told him about the recent episode with Diana, advising him to file it as he saw fit, but to make sure it was anonymous.

He was delighted and commenced putting entries into the book. He had tried to find characters among the prisoners and guards to match those of *Porridge*, with little success, and he decided to ignore them and seek his own characters. One lesson he quickly learnt was to make mental notes for recording later, as inmates were liable to get violent when they saw someone noting their actions. He concentrated on making notes, even making a start on a storyline. It helped to block out the reality of his situation.

When the lights went out, his suppressed thoughts surfaced once more. *A loner I have always been considered, but it was of my own volition. In prison, surrounded by hundreds of inmates and guards, my loneliness is enforced by others and is growing more unwelcome as time passes at a snail's pace. Snails! How wonderful it'd be to walk through long damp grass on the rolling hills around Houghbury and see snails of many types clinging to the leaves.*

Why did I bother to catch buses to and from work, when I could've enjoyed the air and the exercise of walking? Perhaps I could join some organisations when I get out. When! Even if I'm totally cleared, I know this incident will leave a scar on my reputation. Helping with children would be almost impossible, yet it used to be my greatest enjoyment.

To break the pattern of his thoughts, Maurice tried doing word association with objects around him. *Bed – rest – lying down – sleep – impossible! Door – rectangular – keeps out draughts – solid – metal – keeps in prisoners! Window – lets in light – view – world – small – bars – lock – no! Try another route. Bars – drinks – people – merry – drunk - ill – bed – hard – prison cell!* Cell – biology – *DNA – di – di – en – dead – 'nd – **Arnold**!*

The harder he tried to psychologically escape his predicament, the more it loomed over him. Therefore, he decided to face it directly.

One autumn day has changed so many lives due to one chance meeting! I tried to change my life for the better and I'm in prison. Arnold tried to change his life and that of his family. Now he's dead and his family are worse off, and I get the blame. Terry is distracted from his paying cases; others may be suffering too. Is there anyone *who could've gained from that encounter? Banbury! Of course! He seems to be having great pleasure at my expense. On the other hand, perhaps his gloating sense of satisfaction at my predicament has made him a more pleasant person at work, and his colleagues have benefitted –* "at my expense," he spoke aloud.

"What? What you on about, pervert?" His obnoxious cellmate stirred and grumbled aloud. Maurice considered him beneath contempt and refused to honour him with a reply, and continued with his private thoughts. *If it was not my own story, I'd be able to see some humour in it – 'good deed' puts man in jail. As time has passed, I no longer think of this experience as a nightmare from which I'll soon awake. There's nobody to blame except myself. I can even understand the mother and other people's reactions now that I'm distanced from the event.*

Then he had second thoughts, like some revelation induced by a ray of moonlight. *I was depressed and the meeting with Arnold shook me out of it. Prison has depressed me again and Arnold has lifted my spirits once more. Not by meeting him, but by news of his untimely death. It's shown my troubles to be really insignificant in comparison. Therefore, I am truly indebted to him.*

Trying for more placid thoughts, Maurice could not help thinking, *What on earth will tomorrow bring?*

CHAPTER 13

A warm January day in London caught everyone by surprise. The effect of a sudden shift in wind direction produced a welcome relief from seemingly endless weeks of dismal cloud cover and brought a relative heatwave. Birdie and Ivor decided they should keep their suspicions about a mole between themselves until they had more positive proof. To be seen discussing any developments would have made colleagues of all ranks suspicious, so they agreed, despite Birdie's initial reluctance, to simulate a romantic association. To this end, Ivor decided to play his trump card.

"I'm sorry if you don't like opera, but I've two tickets to *La Traviata* tomorrow, and if you're free I thought it'd strengthen the impression we're trying to create, if you'd accompany me?" Birdie's eyes widened and she nearly gave an enthusiastic yes, then her ingrained caution took hold.

"I suppose it would enhance the illusion of our association," she replied autocratically. "So, yes, I'll come. Don't start getting ideas, though." She hoped she had covered her enthusiasm, as she had wanted to see this performance, yet kept putting it off and then found there were no tickets left.

"No, of course. Though could I at least hold your hand from the taxi to the theatre in case anyone knows us?" he requested, trying to appear nonchalant.

"**No!** It's not necessary. Remember this is part of a subterfuge, not a real romantic relationship!"

It's only a crack in her defences and more will follow or all my experience will count for nothing, Ivor mused. *Now for step two.* "Absolutely. AND – *I* want *YOU* to remember ours is purely a working relationship. Not that I don't find you extremely attractive, and will be proud to be seen in your company." His tone matched his stony expression.

"Of course!" She was at once pleased he did find her attractive and insulted to be 'rejected'.

"Now, in case anyone should ask, the opera is by Peppy Verdi and is based on a play called *The Lady of the Cameos*. It's a tragedy." He didn't ask if she knew, because he needed to make it look as if he didn't know she was an opera fan.

"Very interesting. I'll try and remember." She managed to suppress her laughter and a strong desire to correct him. *He must be going to all this trouble for my sake. If he was really keen on the opera, he'd not get such basic facts wrong. 'Peppy'! The Italians would lynch him for that.* Guiseppe *Verdi is an Italian national hero.* **The Lady of the Cameos**: *that would upset the French. He means* **The Lady of the Camellias** *by Alexandre Dumas. For a person with a Russian-sounding name, he'd start an international incident with his ignorance. Though, in a way, it's a rather cute flaw in such a strong character.* Unwittingly, her rambling thoughts had brought the trace of a smile to her lips. Ivor noticed and was encouraged, unaware of the true reason, and continued with his plan.

"Getting the tickets was very hard and I only managed it as part of a package deal. The other part is for dinner for two at Le Bistro near the opera house. It's renowned for its French cuisine, so I hope you'll join me there beforehand." Birdie frowned and then remembered how she had not been out for a 'posh' meal for ages. *Anyway, in for a penny...* So she agreed.

Birdie decided to keep an open mind on the identity of the mole. *If a major criminal like Masood was avoiding arrest due to someone in the police force, then it could be anyone – even Ivor or my own inspector. Although the latter is most unlikely; I've known him for years as a happily married man of limited resources and with no direct involvement in the Masood case. I'll observe my colleagues – particularly those in CID – for behaviour and standard of living. Prime suspects on my list must be those who knew about my trip to Houghbury and the reason for it. This means those members of CID who were at the meeting... though there could be others if they had discussed it widely... I'm fairly certain Phil Tyler and myself were the only ones outside CID.* In exploring all possibilities, with some lateral thinking, she initially rejected and then reconsidered the possibility of the chief inspector, who'd authorised the trip.

Isolating herself from the others during her career did not mean she was unaware of the office gossip. She was well aware of her nickname as the 'ice maiden', and was only too pleased to honour it. Also, she knew Ivor's reputation with women and pretended to ignore the implications of her current association with him. Indeed, in some respects, she was flattered, as he was undoubtedly very attractive to women.

On their date at the opera, she fully prepared for any advances he might make. Ignoring to a large extent his ulterior motives, Birdie decided to respect the first date she had allowed herself to have in years. It would be honoured for the special occasion it was meant to be. She purchased a new outfit and took unusual care over her appearance. Ivor was amazed by the transformation and said so.

During their meal, he could scarcely keep his eyes off her, to the extent that she was both flattered and embarrassed. They had pinot grigio with the fish and shiraz with the meat. Birdie liked wine, having 'tested' the various grapes at college. However, as she had not imbibed for some time, it definitely took the edge off her faculties.

During the opera performance she observed him occasionally, mostly concentrating on the action on the stage. She noticed he enjoyed the more lively parts at the start, but his fidgeting during the father's solos annoyed her. It confirmed what she had suspected, that he was not a real fan of opera. Between Acts 2 and 3 they lightly discussed the performance. However, disappointed as she was that he was not really keen on opera, she was highly flattered that he had gone to the trouble of finding out it was a passion of hers. Then there was the fact he had actually managed to get tickets and was prepared to possibly suffer the show for her sake. In the last Act, she immersed herself completely in the performance and, aided by the wine she had drunk during the meal, was predictably overcome with tears at the end, although she did know it well.

Ivor was completely taken by surprise. The 'ice maiden' showing basic human emotions and weakness in public undermined his machismo and his plans, and he found himself comforting her.

The scenario released painful memories for him. The last time it had happened so genuinely was with his sweet mother at his father's funeral. That delicate moment brought a transformation for both of them. He erased all his plans for seduction with an overwhelming feeling of compassion for her. She had allowed her icy persona to melt a little, and had re-entered the human race. He had become more serious and responsible; she was less serious and might even bend towards being irresponsible. She had enjoyed being comforted, almost sheltered, in the arms of a strong, handsome male. For once, she was no longer a dedicated career person, just a very relaxed woman. It caused a stirring in her that more experienced women would have readily identified as lust!

He noted the change in her demeanour; how she kept close to him and held his arm as they left the theatre. Later, he was astonished when she insisted he came into her flat for a 'nightcap'. He felt obliged to comply, partly for the great honour of entering the inner sanctum, as it was nicknamed, and partly for the new tenderness he had for her. Their conversation was awkward and largely meaningless until she steeled herself and blushed slightly as she seized the initiative.

"Thank you for a wonderful evening. I know you're not an opera fan, and I am flattered you went to so much trouble in order to…" she swallowed to find an easier way to say it "…to make love to me."

She leant against him in a suggestive manner, surrendering herself to him. Here was the prize he had worked for. Now was the time for him to give the performance that had won many a fair maiden's heart – and body. Instead, he was stunned; almost disappointed that she had succumbed. Here was this highly desirable woman, sought after unsuccessfully by men for years, finally offering herself to a recognised Casanova. She was giving into lust and he could not respond! Never before had he failed to seize such an opportunity. It was his turn to feel awkward as he finally found the right words.

"You're right. I did want you **very** much. I know my reputation, of which I have been very proud, and I did want to add you to my list of conquests." He swallowed hard. "After this evening, I just can't!" His voice was shaky as the Alpha

Male crumpled. Birdie was flabbergasted and moved away from him.

"You don't find me attractive enough then. Or is your reputation a myth and built on mere hearsay?" Her voice had quickly returned to something like its normal positive tone.

"No! It's not that. It's just that something happened tonight that placed you in a different position in my mind. You could say you have gone from being the prize I desired to a woman I revere." He went on to explain how the moment at the end of the opera had reminded him of his mother. Birdie stared at him, open-mouthed and with a questioning frown. *Reminded him of **his mother**!*

"So you understand, I now see you as…" Birdie's frown deepened and her lips tightened as he sought to explain. "Er… as my younger sister." Birdie's face lit up with pleasure as she hugged him, holding his arms and looking into his eyes.

"Thank god! For one dreadful moment, I thought you were going to say as your mother!"

She laughed and bubbled. Now there were smiles all round as they both relaxed and were able to joke over coffee about their earlier relationship.

"Why have you never shown your sense of humour at work?" Ivor asked.

"You of all people know that as a… what do you call it… a career woman, I have to portray a cold exterior at all times if I want to be taken seriously." She raised her head and pretended to be looking down her nose at him.

"I suppose so. It's probably the only way you'll get through the 'glass ceiling' – as they call it." He added the last words in repetition to hers.

"How about you then? How come you've never shown compassion or other emotions at work?"

"You know my reputation with the fair sex. I play the role of the strong, dominant male, which is what many women like for… er… romance – no – for sex! What would happen if I suddenly altered character and played the type most women want for a lasting relationship?"

"Oh! And what do you think that is, Romeo?" she interrupted.

"Why, little boy lost. The type that brings out the mothering instinct in you ladies."

"With your physique, that would be hard to believe." Birdie laughed as she leant back to admire him. He raised both arms as if to show off his biceps, then hung his head and pretended to weep.

"Which do you prefer?" he asked her jauntily.

"Now we're siblings, I prefer you as you are. You weren't really my type anyway."

"A few minutes ago, I thought I **was** your type!" he quizzed her.

"I'm only human, Ivor. It's not easy being the Ice Maiden. I do have normal desires. What with good food, a liberal quantity of wine, the emotions stirred by the opera, and – and you **are** – an attractive member of your species, I guess, I nearly succumbed!" She placed her hand over her heart as she confessed.

They discussed their search for the mole, and as Ivor was in the CID, Birdie gave him her thoughts about his colleagues. He nodded with half-hearted agreement on most of them, then laughed aloud at one of her perceptions.

"You're wrong about Doug Evans. As a ladies' man, I should be jealous of his good looks and physique, but I'm not. He is a fitness fanatic and somewhat vain, and shows no interest in the opposite sex."

"You mean he's gay?" Birdie announced with surprise.

"There's no evidence he is. However, the reason I

laughed is because only you, little sister, come close to him for dedication to the job. I may be mistaken, but if anyone is going to collar Masood, the odds are on him." He paused to consider elaborating. "I believe Doug had a relation who was a victim of Masood and the case is a very personal one to him." He almost whispered to emphasise the confidentiality of what he was revealing. "Hierarchy have tried to use others on the case to prevent it becoming a personal vendetta."

"If he's off the case, what makes you think he'll be the one to catch Masood? Particularly now he's in Norwich."

"I'm the only one who knows this, so I'm trusting you not to tell anyone. He still works on the case in private for those personal reasons. We're good friends and he trusts me, and he sometimes needs my help. He's suspected for some time that Masood has an accomplice in our office, and will be delighted that we agree."

"Good friends, eh? He doesn't care for women, eh? You refused my advances! I'm beginning to wonder if your reputation with the ladies is a front to cover your true leanings!" Birdie goaded him. Ivor started to protest then noticed the strange look in her eyes. He changed his whole demeanour, trying to look crestfallen.

"Alas! Uncovered, and by a woman! You want me to admit that all the lovely ladies I've been with were transvestites?" He tried to keep an expression of guilt.

"Sorry to crush your confession, but I've actually met a couple of your former conquests, and they both spoke highly of your lovemaking. Doug's desires may be in doubt, never yours!" Birdie quipped.

"Hang on, Miss Ice Maiden! If you knew all about me, why did you come on this date?"

"I reckoned I could resist even your legendary charms. If I should weaken – well – I knew I couldn't keep my – virtue forever. And **who** better to lose it to than an expert? It would've been all part of life's education! So you see, Ivor, for me, this had to be a win-win situation," she explained at length, despite his attempts to interrupt.

"Damn me! I thought I was the one with the great plan to trap you, and it transpires you were just using me!" He held up his arms in mock surrender. She quickly poked him in the ribs and he crumpled.

"Is it better to transpire than perspire?" She tried to poke him again, but he grabbed her hands and looked closely into her eyes.

"Enough, Sergeant Sister! So you've found my ticklish spot. Let's get down to business again." He pushed her away, but she wriggled back towards him suggestively.

"What business is that then?" He stared at her and abruptly got to his feet and began taking his clothes off. She hesitated in surprise for a moment and then resumed her official bearing.

"We're discussing your friend, Doug Evans." Ivor sat down after readjusting his apparel.

"Can't we use him right now?" Birdie frowned.

"That's another reason to find the mole. Although the villains don't know the level of his current involvement, this Houghbury incident has worried them enough to organise Doug's temporary assignment to Norwich!"

"So, with the urgency to find the mole, it's down to you and me, big brother." She smiled at the thought of working closely with her new buddy. Ivor kissed her on the forehead.

"Sleep well, little sister."

She grinned and replied, "And you, big brother."

As agreed with Ivor, Birdie went to see the superintendent the next day. She told him about her suspicions but left Ivor out of it.

"I'm glad you've come to me, Sergeant Lee. We don't want Internal Affairs involved at this stage, as it'd upset the staff and might all be for nothing."

"But, sir—" Birdie tried to interject until he raised his hand.

"Hear me out, Sergeant. This could lead to a major internal investigation, or it could turn out to be a case of careless talk. You must explore all possibilities until we're sure one way or another. Nobody, including me, should be left out of your enquiries. You must look at it from every angle." He paused to study her closely. "Has any officer been living beyond his means? On the other hand, could this Mamood have been told of your absence and the roadworks unwittingly by an officer who overheard others talking?"

"I'll look into it, sir. By the way, sir, the suspect's name is Masood, not Mamood. How do you want me to report?"

"As I said, include everyone and everything in your investigation. Do it aside from your normal work and update me in a week's time. Of course," he added with a laugh, "if it's me you suspect, you'll have to take it to someone higher." Birdie laughed with him and left.

She did not really see anything to laugh at, only the unusual sound of Superintendent Thwaite laughing, and her nervousness in his imperious presence. Thwaite was quite young to hold his rank; he never needed to raise his voice as he was always in total command of everyone and every situation. She explained the superintendent's attitude to Ivor, and they decided to split the task. As Birdie had the authority from Thwaite, she would check the Personnel files, for which the cover was classification of staff according to a new grading. Ivor would check all papers on Masood to find a link with Houghbury.

Once more unto the breach...

Meanwhile, Terry Schott visited Major Stubbs.

"To apologise for any discourtesy by my assistant." Having done so, he casually asked, "I know it's a long shot, but I was hoping that a person of your distinction and sense of duty might have remembered something else about that day you were stuck at the roadworks in Houghbury?" He used his most cajoling voice, which he had developed in court with hostile witnesses.

"There was one thing that did strike me as strange that day, though it's probably nothing to concern you." He paused for effect.

"Yes? What was that?" Terry tried to look curious without showing too much enthusiasm. *I don't want Banbury being told, in case there's relevant evidence* he *might destroy.*

"I saw a newer and more expensive Audi being driven by some young wog!" His disgust was blatant, and Terry managed to keep a calm exterior.

"Do you mean an African or Asian?"

"Asian, I think, but very dark – as was the woman beside him. How the hell they could afford it, I don't know." He shook his head in disbelief.

"You're certain there were two of them?" Terry asked casually, as this new piece of information had made him stiffen.

"Yes."

"And both were dark Asians?"

"Yes! I saw a TV programme only last week about Malaya, and these two looked exactly like the natives there."

"Would you recognise the driver if you saw him again?" Terry was excited and tried not to let it turn his questioning into a full-blooded interrogation.

"Definitely! Impudent w... person actually grinned directly at me!"

"Thank you very much, Major Stubbs. I'm sorry to have troubled you again." He felt he should make the major feel important in case he had to approach him again, so he added, "Your information could put a top criminal behind bars." As they shook hands at the door, Stubbs had his last word.

"Hope that nasty b-b-blighter gets what he deserves!"

Terry relayed the information through Derek to Birdie. She informed Ivor, who then concentrated his search on dark Asians in any photos in the Masood file. Knowing how dangerous the latter was reported to be, they kept it to themselves about the car's passenger. There were a few men fitting the description in the Masood photos, and Ivor set about eliminating them. He arrived at a possible, Arun Ramas, currently in prison for possession of drugs. Birdie decided it would be best if she interviewed him. She also decided not to tell anyone of her interest in Ramas. Ivor agreed she should interview Ramas as soon as possible.

She had to clear her normal duties first to avoid any suspicions from the suspected mole in the CID, as Masood was really their case. Checking Ramas's details, Ivor found he did have a sister, who was a qualified nurse currently abroad on a skiing holiday. These facts were all kept secret between Ivor and Birdie.

On arrival at the prison, Birdie was given strange looks and escorted to the governor.

"What interest do you have in Ramas?" the governor demanded.

"We think he may be the witness to an incident for which a man's been imprisoned." She left out the Masood angle.

"Witness or not, he's no use to you now. He was found hanged in his cell."

"Why wasn't I told? It would've saved me a wasted journey!" Her annoyance shone through.

"It only happened yesterday and we're still investigating it. When you asked to visit him so soon after the event, we were naturally very curious. We're keeping it under wraps until we get some answers. Is there anything you know that can help?" He tapped his desk to remind her that she was on his territory now.

"I only found out that he could've been the witness we want yesterday! As the description of the possible witness is not only vague but came from a somewhat hostile source, this Ramas might not be the one we want. If we find that he was the one, we'll let you know the full implications from our side."

Before reporting to Thwaite on her progress so far, she had to tell Ivor.

"He was dead soon after we found out about him! Masood is one jump ahead of us all the time. Did he think we might find the real driver, or was he told by someone that we had? This young man must have been doing dirty work for Masood and deviated for his own reasons. If that is the case, then it's odds-on Masood didn't sanction Ramas taking his sister along. Whether it's forward planning or inside information, we must keep the sister's existence secret." Her voice was hushed, as if the very walls had ears.

"I agree. We must find the sister before anyone else realises she was there. She may even have some idea what her brother was involved in," he whispered back at her.

"I have to report in. If there is a spy at the station, I think I know a way of trapping him and getting at Masood that way. In my report, I'll let slip that I've got a lead that would incriminate Masood, and I'll keep it to myself until I've checked the facts."

The superintendent was keen to hear how far she had got, and made sure they could not be overheard or interrupted.

"I've got no further with finding any spy in the office, so it might be a case of careless talk. A possible witness in the Houghbury case is dead in mysterious circumstances, so that appears to be a blind alley."

"Is that why you visited Blackwall Prison?" Thwaite asked suddenly.

"Yes. How did you know about it?"

"It would've been better if you'd consulted me first. The governor rang me to check on your visit and I'd some awkward explaining to do! Make sure you keep me fully informed in future, Sergeant." His anger was tangible as his chiselled jaw tightened very slightly. His rugged features would have made him attractive but for his permanently cold expression.

"I'm sorry, sir. I thought I'd tell you when I did have something definite. I did pick up one potential lead when I visited the prison. It might incriminate Masood, but I won't know until I've made a few more checks." Birdie tried to seem offhand.

"What's this new lead?" Thwaite leant across his desk as if making sure nobody could hear her reply.

"Sorry, sir. I'm not telling anyone until I'm sure it's not a wild goose chase, not even Inspector Tyler or you. As I explained to the inspector, it occurred to me that, with Masood's wealth and influence, our offices could be bugged. By the time you get the building swept for any devices, it could be too late, sir. I'll have definite news for you, one way or another, by the end of the week." Thwaite's forehead furrowed almost imperceptibly as he nodded his agreement.

"Good job, Sergeant. In the circumstances, I agree with the need for secrecy and wish you good luck. I look forward to hearing better news in a few days then."

That evening, Birdie met with Ivor at her flat and told him how her report to her superior had gone. He thought she was pushing her luck in pretending to have a new lead and was visibly angry with her. She snapped back that he was taking his big-brother role too far, and he left early, saying he had more files to check. Birdie was alone and upset. She finally had a close friend in the force and she had rudely rejected his concern for her. How could she make amends? She was certainly not going to run after him to apologise.

Mulling over these thoughts, she was disturbed by a gentle knock on her door. Her spirits lifted immediately. *Ivor has come back to make peace.*

With a broad grin, she opened the door. It was open only a fraction when it was smashed into her, sending her reeling. Before she could regain her balance, two extremely large villains flattened her. They trussed her up and taped her mouth with such vehemence that she had trouble breathing. *It's against my nature,* she thought as she tried desperately to free her mouth, *but I wish I'd screamed immediately, as a normal woman would have done.* She continued to struggle with what little movement she was capable of. Then they carried her out to a waiting car and deposited her very roughly in the boot, driving off at speed.

CHAPTER 14

Terry had Derek check Judith Donnelly's details in preparation for an interview. He discovered her parents were part of the 'county set', and they had not been pleased when her time at college had been spent with 'radicals', one of whom she married. Though she did a science degree to ensure the backing of her parents, her real love was art, which she studied on the side. From her artistic leanings, she loved to dress and behave to some extent like a peasant, which was also a disappointment to her parents. Even they would not describe her as pretty, yet her tall slim figure, her dignified bearing, her natural blonde hair and her fine features made her a woman to be admired in any company. Charlie was her only child and she doted on him, often making her husband, Tom, jealous.

Perhaps it had been her ancestry that caused her highly strung reaction to finding Maurice holding her son. Perhaps it was the culmination of a stress-laden day. They had returned from a supposed holiday, which had turned into one of Tom's family reunions. At these gatherings, Tom showed an alter ego, in which he treated Judith as his lackey. Normally, he was reasonably attentive and helpful, and she suffered his extra lack of affection in the presence of his relatives. This holiday proved to be the last straw, and she had finally given vent to her wrath at breakfast when he gloated over photos he had taken during the vacation. Later, she had dented her car on a post in the Houghbury car park. The shops **never** seemed to have the items she wanted. Then, to cap it all, Charlie on his new scooter was a major worry.

The dam holding her emotions burst when she saw Maurice holding Charlie, and they were swept along by a reinforcing surge from the noisy crowd. She calmed down at the hospital and was more her normal self by the time she got home. Tom realised he had overstepped the mark and tried to fulfil his role as a father and husband. It was much easier than a simple apology, and he tried to overlook the damage to the car. The comfort of the moment helped Judith block out the guilt she felt for her behaviour with the 'pervert'. This block she carried forward, unquestioned, with Charlie. She blotted the event out for both of them, and could not even discuss it with Tom after that day.

She was greatly relieved when the case was closed and she no longer had to suffer any doubts about her performance. Doubts born out of her very-stiff-upper-lip childhood. It reminded her of the relief she felt when she finished her degree in Biology. Tom had been teaching Physics at the local comprehensive school, and she had taught Biology there until the arrival of her son.

Tom found a better job in Nottingham, which should partly compensate for her loss of income. He had found a small flat there to live in while he searched for a house. She had not been there yet as there was no space for her and their son, but she didn't mind as she was kept busy with Charlie, her domestic duties and the art club she had joined. She still thought her true ability was as an artist, but there were no suitable openings and they needed the money it could have taken.

Terry was delighted with the amount of background

information Derek had obtained on the Donnellys. However, it still left him with the problem of how to meet and talk to Judith.

"Does she have any extra-curricular activities?" Terry pondered aloud to Derek.

"There is her art, which she has returned to now she's given up teaching. I've been told she's very good at it," Derek responded, wondering why it had not been included in his notes.

"Very good at what? Art or teaching?"

"I meant art, but she was highly valued as a teacher."

"What sort of art?" Terry enquired distractedly.

"I believe she does mostly watercolour paintings of still life based on her scientific knowledge."

"Like what?" Terry showed minimal interest as he doodled on his scrap paper.

"Do you really want to know, or are you just interrogating me out of habit!" Derek wondered if Terry would even notice if he left the room.

"Sorry! I keep thinking about where I can find the key to unlock Judith Connelly's memory. What were we talking about?"

"You were asking about Judith's watercolours." Derek spoke the words very slowly and deliberately.

"Oh yes. Well?" Terry pushed his doodles away and sat back.

"The ones she currently has on show at an amateur exhibition are all of plants. You know. The usual boring subjects, though with some degree of technical accuracy, I've been told. Probably due to her qualification."

"I'm interested in art. Boring or not, what are her main subjects?" Terry made an effort to concentrate.

"I don't know. You can see them for yourself in St Mark's Hall." Much as he admired his boss, Derek had lost patience with his current musings.

Desperate to find a means of talking to a potential lead, Terry decided he would waste part of his break dragging himself to look at the amateur art exhibition. So, after an early lunch, he went to St Mark's Hall. He put on a show of genuine interest, even discussing some with the artists on hand. There were a few he looked on favourably, and he compared them openly with the sellers' list. Any subterfuge was unnecessary as he was very attracted by one of a fungus on the side of a tree. On checking the list, he found it was by J Talbot-Hunt. Checking with the 'desk person', he was informed that it was still for sale and that the artist sold her work under her maiden name.

"Very wise, I'm sure. Could save some problems if she were to get divorced." Terry nodded sagely.

"**What** makes you think she might get divorced?" the desk woman snapped at him.

"I'm sorry. I didn't mean anything by that remark. It's just a habit of mine to consider such things. I'm a lawyer, you see," he explained hurriedly.

"Oh? I expect you see lots of tragic cases, but Judith is unlikely to be one of them," she stated coldly.

"I take it that Judith, whatever her married name is, is happily married then?" Terry tried to appear nonchalant, disguising his interest in Judith.

"Very happy now, though she nearly had a tragedy in her family." She paused for effect, acting as if she was all-knowledgeable. As Terry just looked at her blankly, she continued. "If you're a local, you must have read or heard of the case a few months ago, where a man tried to snatch a child in the centre of town?"

"Yes, I know the case. Why?" He decided to make a partial admission in case someone recognised him.

"It was Judith's boy that was snatched!" She had an air of confidential triumph in her announcement. Terry wanted more background information without appearing to snoop, so he threw a brick in the proverbial pond.

"A Mrs Connelly – no! Donnelly, if I remember correctly. It was the Jenkins case," he stated as a matter of fact.

"That's right. We were all shocked in our little art group. We never thought anything like that could happen here." Terry would not have been surprised if she had tutted as she shook her head.

"Does she talk about it much?" Terry enquired casually.

"No. Since the bounder was sent to prison, she's never mentioned it, and we don't like to trouble her."

"I wonder how her son is now." He spoke dreamily, as if voicing his thoughts aloud.

"Well," she paused and glanced around the hall, "I don't like to talk behind a person's back, but I believe she's blocked that episode out of her and her son's lives." There seemed little more to be gleaned from this 'non-gossiper', so he returned to the task at hand.

"I love that picture of hers. Do you think she'd do a subject I want in this same style?" He pointed at the fungus painting, gazing at it in genuine appreciation. He had been prepared to put on a false show of enthusiasm, particularly as he was not usually attracted to plant pictures. In this case, he was very attracted to this one. Perhaps it was the three-dimensional effect, or the use of light, or the natural accuracy; most probably it was a combination.

"You should ask her yourself." The woman ran her finger down a chart on the desk. "She will be on duty here from two until three." She looked up at Terry and her expression melted almost to a smile.

"I'll try to call back then, thank you." Mentally forgiving her earlier frostiness, he indicated a couple of pictures he reckoned were hers. "The use of colour in those two is very good, though the style is not to my taste," he added as he left, thinking, *Would I ever need to kiss the Blarney Stone?*

Realising that Judith Donnelly would almost certainly recognise him, he debated whether to return himself or to send Derek. *It is something I have to face up to, and, hopefully so will Judith Donnelly,* he decided.

At half past two, Terry recognised her as soon as he entered the hall. Slowly, recognition dawned on Judith's face as he approached her. She turned away from him as if to avoid meeting him. The action only served to encourage him, as he interpreted it as a wish to evade painful memories. He knew the actual incident must have been traumatic, and her appearance in court even more so.

"Mrs Donnelly? I thought I recognised you. I was here earlier, admiring your paintings, and the lady at the desk said you might be prepared to undertake a commission from me." he suggested taking her lead.

"Oh, it was **you,** was it?" She cleared her throat and turned to face him. "Beryl told me someone was interested in my fungus painting."

"Yes." He looked around cautiously and continued. "I visit galleries when I can, but I never expected to find something I would seriously like at an amateur exhibition." He had lowered his voice, as if taking her into his confidence so he wouldn't upset the other artists.

"So what would you want me to do?" Then she added quickly, "**If I** were prepared to."

"It would form a pair with that fungus painting, which I would like to buy. Similar in many respects, but the fungus would be amanita phalloides." He pointed at her painting while taking note of her reaction.

"Death cap!" Her surprise was palpable.

"Ah! You know it. So do you think you could do such a painting for me?" He tried to put on a friendly face, aware that her memory of him must be as an antagonist in the court.

"Why on earth do you want amanita phalloides as the subject of a picture?" She shook her head in disbelief. He had anticipated the question and had partly prepared his answer.

"You obviously recognised me, so you will understand how the insularity and stresses of my work can make me immune to people's everyday problems. Often, I find myself cast in a leading role in a play – I mean case – in which I have little or no belief." She seemed as if she wanted him to expand his statement, so he continued very positively.

"Someone I know has just died from ingesting it. The hospital found out too late to do anything. He leaves a young wife and two children. Their finances were bad enough before he died, so they must be dreadful now. Friends and neighbours do what they can, but it is a real tragedy. I want a painting of the culprit in my office to ensure I never forget, however busy I am." Judith's shoulders relaxed as he talked, and for a moment she forgot about Charlie and Tom.

"Why did the hospital find out too late?" He had aroused her curiosity. He made a show of being reluctant to tell her more, then sighed in resignation.

"I didn't want to say more because my involvement is somewhat painful to me. Putting it briefly, I met him in town on behalf of a client. As it was a very bad night, I gave him a lift home. He insisted on walking the last stretch. He fell over a fallen tree; landed in a ditch and must've swallowed death cap with some ditchwater. He was taken to hospital suffering from concussion and some nasty cuts." He paused, deciding not to say more at present.

"Was the fallen tree an oak?" she enquired, knowing the answer.

"I believe it was. Why?"

"Because amanita phalloides usually grows on oaks."

"Will you do the painting for me, please?" he begged.

"Why me? I'm sure some of the others could do it." Was it false modesty or the need for reassurance of the quality of her work that made her ask?

"That's easy to answer. It's the excellent quality of your paintings and your obvious knowledge of plants and fungi." This was going far smoother than he ever imagined. Better to delay any mention of the Jenkins case, anxious though he was to conclude the case for an appeal. "Do you study them?" he enquired casually.

"Yes. It was part of my university course. And thanks for your kind words. How could I possibly refuse now?"

"That's great. If you could do some quick sketches to show me, of your vision for the painting, we could meet, say, for coffee, in a few days. If that's possible?" He tried not to sound too pushy.

"I usually come in to do shopping on Thursday mornings. That gives me three days to rough out something to show you." She pursed her lips as she had an afterthought. "Only one thing, though, I'll have to bring my little boy."

The gods are shining on me today, Terry decided as he suppressed a look of triumph and they finalised arrangements.

Thursday, 11:30am, they met in 'Grounds' coffee bar in the Square. After the normal pleasantries and getting coffees for themselves and a fruit juice for Charlie, they were able to examine her sketches. Meanwhile, the boy was content to colour the pictures provided by the waitress.

"These are very good. Having seen three different perspectives, I would like the view of the fungus in that one on the tree, but could you get more of the tree in, please?" He studied the drawings and kept what he hoped was a friendly eye on Charlie. Now the opportunity was at hand, he was having difficulty in knowing how to proceed with his real purpose.

"No trouble. In fact, I think you are right. The death cap will be less prominent, but the overall picture will be more pleasing." She pencilled in some alterations. Terry waited for the right moment. He never had this problem in a courtroom; a place where he felt at home and others did not.

"That sad story you told me that is the reason for this painting. Was it a man called Phillips from Rudton?" She looked up and inclined her head slightly.

"Yes, it was. How did you know?" Terry suppressed the feeling of elation that arose from her introduction of the subject.

"I told my husband about it, and he remembered seeing an item in the local paper. Being curious, and from an ingrained habit of researching matters, I checked with the newspaper's archives and found the details. The only question I have left to complete the scenario is who your client was, but I suppose that is confidential." She was too clever to actually flutter her eyelashes, though she did smile at him somewhat coquettishly. He took a deep breath, looked at Charlie, then back at Judith.

"It's not confidential, but I hoped not to mention it," he lied, trying to draw her into his scheme slowly, so she would not raise any psychological barriers. He placed his hands on the table symbolically.

"Arnold Phillips had agreed to meet at that time and place with Maurice Jenkins. Please don't say anything until I explain it fully." She was stunned, and would probably have left immediately but for the need to collect her son without alarming him. "I know you believe you have every reason to despise Jenkins, but I think you are mistaken. I believe his account of events is true. Before you reject any such thoughts, I ask – no – I beg you to keep an open mind. If he **is** telling the truth, he is not the villain you see him as, but a hero who saved your boy's life. I already have one witness who saw Jenkins pluck Charlie from the path of a car, and we hope to find that driver soon—"

"Then why hasn't there been an official appeal?" she interrupted bitterly.

"You're a clever woman and a devoted mother. How will you feel if Jenkins really did save your boy, and you refused to even consider the possibility?" He tapped the table with one finger, to underline his question. He then explained the circumstances leading up to the event and how it would have changed the Phillips family's life for the better.

"One fact I ask you to consider carefully is," he paused to ensure he had her full attention, "that Jenkins gave Arnold his real name. If Jenkins is such an evil person, would he have done that?"

"I'm not sure. But then, why didn't you produce the witness at the trial?" she countered assertively. He briefly tried to explain and was forced to admit that the relationship between the witness and a colleague of Jenkins had delayed an appeal until the car driver was found.

"Arnold Phillips believed Jenkins to be innocent. This is not just another case for me. I truly believe he is innocent. Have you ever had second thoughts about him? Even slight doubt about his guilt." He stared directly into her eyes and noted a reaction she hastily covered.

"Never!" she protested. Terry decided to strike at her weakness.

"What does Charlie think? Shall we ask him?" He turned towards the boy, who was still scribbling away.

"**Certainly not**! You leave him out of this," she demanded.

"Has he ever mentioned the incident?"

"**No**!"

"Have you ever asked him?" Terry almost demanded, yet guessing what the answer would be.

"**No**, and you're not going to now!"

"Don't you think there is a danger in trying to get him to block it out?"

"He doesn't."

"So he **has** talked about it?"

"He may have."

"When?"

"Well, he did ramble on somewhat when it first happened. It was sort of confused and nobody paid any attention to it. Since then, he's had some bad nights, yet he never mentions any details."

"I've no wish to upset your lovely little boy, but I'd like to show him Jenkins's photo, just to see his reaction. May I – please?" he entreated, looking from mother to son and back.

Judith returned his gaze then looked at Charlie. She was deeply immersed in thought, and Terry waited patiently for an answer. The only sound at the table was Charlie muttering as he coloured a picture. Someone dropping a tray broke the moment. The sudden noise startled the adults, while the child looked around very calmly.

"You've certainly brought him up well. Most children his age would've been really startled by that noise. Your Charlie accepted it for what it was. Here's the photo of Jenkins. Can you show it to him and ask if he remembers the man?" Terry kept his voice low and flat, so Charlie would continue to ignore them, and slid the photo under the table to Judith. Reluctantly, she placed it on her lap, looked from Terry to Charlie and then down at the photo. She bit her lower lip and gave Terry an almost hostile look.

"Very well. **But** if it upsets him, you can forget your paintings!" She gently got hold of her son's arm. "Charlie, dear, I want you to look at a photo and tell me if you know the person." The little boy peered at it and frowned as he tried to remember.

"Was he the man who picked me up when I fell off my scooter, Mummy?" He looked questioningly at Judith. She looked from the boy to the man in surprise.

"Yes, dear. That's the man. Finish your drink. We have to leave now." As she got up from the table, she handed the photo back to Terry. "I hope you're satisfied now! I'll do the paintings, but don't try to involve Charlie again!"

"Thank you for doing that. I realise it wasn't easy. It doesn't give me anything to use in the Jenkins appeal. It does show that your son was not so traumatised by the incident to make him have a lasting fear of Jenkins." He smiled at them, shook their hands and left Judith putting her son into his coat.

CHAPTER 15

Sometimes, when all was quiet and he closed his eyes, Maurice could almost believe he was free. He could be lost in a world of his own imagining. He could be anywhere he chose to be, and with anyone he wanted to be with. Though the latter could lead him back to reality, as he had very few acquaintances worthy of the honour. Arnold would enter his dream world, and reality would thrust itself upon him once more. Or a door would close with that unmistakable prison sound. Or, and this was the worst of all, his cellmate, Rymer, would nudge him into life. Cellmate? More of a cellfoe! Rymer would do everything within his limited capacity to annoy Maurice, short of actual physical violence.

There was nothing in Rymer's character to admire. Until Maurice met him, he thought such a person existed solely in poor-quality movies. He knew that only his own superior size and fitness prevented the cowardly Rymer from attacking him. He dreaded to think what would happen if he was to become ill. Rymer's taunts and regular minor obstructions had become part of his daily schedule, and he treated them with the contempt the perpetrator deserved, while staying safe behind his comfort line.

This was one of those blessed moments when Rymer was away on some basic duties and Maurice had the cell to himself. *Now I can let my mind soar to the clouds, or I can retrieve my notebook from its hiding place.* With little else to occupy his mind, he reflected on the last few months of existence. *Yes, that's the word, existence! Yet, if I'm really to live life to the full, I must start now. As Oscar Wilde said, "We are all in the gutter, but some of us are looking at the stars." I'm by no means in the gutter! I may be in prison but I do have a bed, a roof over my head and sufficient meals. Many are worse off than I am. Even though I'm treated with contempt by the guards and my fellow prisoners, I know my innocence will eventually be proved. I may be physically incarcerated but my mind is free. Free for me to use more positively in future.*

He listened to the sounds from outside his cell to make certain it was safe to do his notes.

I've made a start on collecting jokes from inmates like old Buster. Yesterday, or was it the previous day, he was bragging how tough his home neighbourhood was, and said, "It's so tough, even the lollipop woman is built like Arnold Schwarzenegger." Then there was the miserable couple chatting. One said, "I don't like the look of that guard!" The second muttered, "Then look at another one!" All jokes and anecdotes will have to be collated into some sort of sketch when I get out. He instinctively looked up at the small cell window.

When I get out! Even to be outside in this torrential rain would be paradise compared to being here. To feel the rain beating against my face would be the blessed acknowledgement of really being alive. How long before I can have such a pleasure? It's no good counting the days. I must plan for my future now. What do I really want to do? What am I qualified to do? The only difference between pre-prison and post-prison qualifications will be the experience of prison – unless I set myself to actually learn some new skills. I don't expect to be here long enough to complete any course. So, what I can do is observe and record everything for possible future use – with caution!

Caution! Caution or prudence! If only my neighbour, Pru Gravillons, hadn't left the country. She would've given me a good character reference. She'd have told everyone how I regularly cared for her little kids, Monique and Gaston. I think she trusted me completely with them. They're the reason I still had the books and comics that I helped them to read. At other times, I took them to the playground when their father was away on business. I suppose I was just filling in for him and he seemed to appreciate it. Oh dear! They asked me to look after their apartment and their plants. They'll think I'm not to be trusted after all, and couldn't be bothered.

My name is mud in all quarters now, and I can't put it right while I'm stuck in here. The hardest will be Arnold's wife. She's every reason to hate me, and I do feel responsible for his death even though there are many excuses I could put forward. I had an immediate empathy with Arnold, so the chances are that I could have liked his wife – whatever she's like.

He gazed unseeingly at the cell window. *Whatever else happens, I must do something for her and the kids. Living in a small village, they'll be well known, and I'll be most unwelcome. The locals would recognise me immediately as the cause of the family's misfortunes. It might be possible to give financial help through a third party, although with my current state of affairs it couldn't amount to much. No doubt my fellow inmates could suggest some get-rich-quick scheme, if I was that desperate. If only I was not known, I could give the Phillipses the things I do have – time, effort and compassion.*

Terry's been relentless in his efforts to free me. Hopefully, he might even discover some way for me to help Arnold's family. Perhaps they are well cared for already. That would make me feel better but wouldn't absolve my obligation to them. Absolve! The word reminds me what Terry said about the TV item on my arrest. He said the 'kick-him' member of the mob was a priest! I wonder if he's sought absolution from God for such an unchristian outburst? Terry might know. I must make a list of questions to ask him tomorrow.

Wasting time. It's funny how one line of thought can lead to another. In here, I've time to spare, which must be used if I'm really to live life to the full. If I start a course in here, it'll be unfinished if I get an early release. An outside course isn't possible. Or – if I start an Open University course, I could complete it wherever I am. What subject? Well, one that I must be capable of completing, and it must be marketable for a better-paid and more fulfilling job. Maths! I've already got university entrance qualifications in both Pure and Applied Maths. They are the basis for many choices of careers, like teaching and engineering. I'll see the instructional officer right away.

"More bad news, I'm afraid, Maurice!" Terry's words crushed Maurice's hopes for a fruitful meeting.

"Bugger it! Sorry about that. I feel I'm punching at jelly every time I try to find a light at the end of the tunnel. What's it this time, Terry?" Maurice thumped the table with his fist in an unusual display of aggression.

"There are two items and both must be kept absolutely secret." He leant towards Maurice and lowered his voice.

"Of course," replied Maurice. "Though there's nobody in here I want to talk to, let alone share secrets with."

"We thought we'd found the real driver of the car you saved the boy from, but he was found hanged in prison. And Derek, you know, my assistant, well, his sister's a police sergeant in London. She was doing some checking for us and she's been kidnapped!" Terry's whispered words pierced

Maurice's brain as if from a megaphone. Unable to speak in the face of such further tragedies emanating from his incident, he shakily pushed his list across the table. Terry picked it up and scanned it quickly.

"With all the other events, I forgot to tell you about Arnold Phillips's funeral. I felt obliged to attend due to my part in his final moments. Also, I knew you'd wish to participate, even if I were in *locum tenens*, so—"

"In local tenants?" Maurice was baffled, and finally managed to speak.

"In *LOCUM TENENS*." Terry spelt it out. "It means I was there in your place, as your representative. Anyway, I sent a wreath from Schott and Associates. It might've been too obvious if I'd said 'and friends'. As it was, I think his wife suspected."

"Were there many there?" Maurice cleared the lump in his throat.

"About a dozen. His wife and the two children, a representative from the hospital, the old couple who found him, a couple of her employers, someone from the council, a couple of police and a few friends. Not a lot to show for a good man's life."

"I only met him that one time, but I think you're right. He was a **good** man." Maurice nodded his approval.

"A good man, which is more than can be said for that priest. I hear he suddenly went on a month's vacation. No doubt prompted by his superiors. Whether he'll return to his former church is still a mystery." Terry paused, sat upright and attempted a smile.

"Some good news! The woman whose boy you saved has been reconciled with her wealthy parents. She's a skilful painter and I'm buying a pair of her pictures." Terry went on to explain at length how he had managed to meet with Judith and Charlie. He noted Maurice's other questions, particularly about studying with the Open University, and agreed to get whatever materials he required.

After he left, Maurice, though relieved that some benefit had been derived from his 'crime', grew very angry at the other news. *This bad dream – no! – this hell – just gets worse. The more I think about it, the angrier I get. I want to... to what? Have to hit something – or someone. I'd hit Rymer but he's not here when I want him. Bugger it! It may cross my graphite line but I will hit someone! Let them feel the pain I feel.*

On the way back to his cell, he met Sidney Cracken. The story of his capture by a slight woman was a legend, and Sid did everything possible to overturn it. Maurice stepped in his path. *Who better than this mindless gorilla?*

"You must feel safe in here, Sid, away from all those wild women." He taunted Sidney, looked down at him with disdain and tried to pass. Maurice hit him hard with his shoulder and that was too much for Sidney. In the brawl that ensued, he punched and kicked Maurice nearly senseless until stopped reluctantly by **three** prison officers, while other prisoners had been egging Sid on. Maurice was taken to the prison hospital and patched up.

When interviewed, he admitted that he had started the affray, and onlookers agreed. One added that Maurice had only slapped at Cracken, and reckoned he had wanted to get beaten up. The prison psychiatrist interviewed Maurice later when he was better. On discovering that Maurice had just left a meeting with his lawyer when he attacked Cracken, he checked the details with Terry. The psychiatrist decided Maurice had acted partly from frustration and partly guilt, using the opportunity for physical pain to relieve his mental anguish. Having perused Maurice's file, the psychiatrist realised that the outburst of anger was almost certainly a one-off incident.

However, he would still need to be watched for any future signs of such behaviour. It was decided to isolate Maurice and keep a close eye on him lest he try even more desperate measures.

It was Cracken who was given an internal course on anger management. During it, the specialist discovered Sid's problem was not his low intelligence; it was his antipathy for the whole world. He had been mistreated by his parents, his siblings and at school because he was considered stupid. He could not understand why Maurice had aroused him and was positively baffled by him accepting the blame. Whenever anything had gone wrong when he was there, even if not involved, he got the blame. He could never defend himself intellectually, only physically. Hence, every incident would end in a fight against someone or everyone. Now something different had happened to him and he had all the time his slow brain could need to think about it.

Alone in his new temporary cell, Maurice wondered if two broken ribs and multiple bruises had exonerated him or really relieved his mental problems in any small way. *Was I seeking mental absolution?* he thought. *That word again. I wonder if the priest has cleared his conscience?* He perused his new accommodation. **Bliss**! *Solitary confinement! This isn't what I'd planned but seems a golden reward for the physical pain I've endured from Sid.* He laughed aloud, causing a passing officer to check on him.

My thoughtless provocation of Sid could've seen me back in my own cell at the mercy of Rymer. Instead, I can think and write without his constant baiting. I hope they get Derek's sister back safely and soon. From what I've heard of her, I think I would like to meet her one day. What did Terry say about her? That she's a single-minded career woman, attractive and clever, and unfettered with husband or boyfriend. The more I think of it, the more I reckon Terry might have a romantic interest in her. Well, if she's my type, may the best man win! He laughed aloud at his sudden arrogance.

Returned to his old cell with Rymer, the latter unexpectedly made himself scarce when Sid Cracken entered. Fearing the worst, Maurice sat submissively on the edge of his bed and raised his hands.

"I give up, Sid. I told them it was all my fault, and I'm very sorry for getting you into trouble."

"Nah, don't get the wind up. I've come to thank you for taking the blame. Nobody's never done that for me, no 'ow." His voice was almost beseeching, and Maurice indicated for him to sit down.

"You're joking, Sid? It can't always be your fault for every problem?" He smiled softly.

"'Cos I ain't too bright. I'm no good for nuffink, they're all against me. All I can do is fight!"

"Well, there you are, you're good at fighting." Maurice tried to sound encouraging.

"No, I ain't! This little woman – turns out to be a cop – floors me with ease. That's why I'm in 'ere."

Maurice gazed at the erstwhile brute slumped beside him like some naughty child. Suddenly he felt a deep sense of compassion for this man who had landed him in hospital. *Further than that, I feel responsible for him. How can I help him?* he thought, finally erasing his graphite line. Perhaps Sid, the pugilist, had hidden talents. Maurice had read about autism and wondered if Sid had something like it. There could be no harm in trying to find out; after all, there was nothing else he could think of to talk about.

"Do you like music? Can you play an instrument?" Maurice persisted.

"Nah!" Sid sounded even more depressed.

"Do you read a lot?"

"Can 'ardly read."

"Are you good at maths?" Sid looked at him blankly. "You know – adding and subtracting."

"I can add 2 and 2 when I 'ave to." His gloomy visage took Maurice's mind off his own troubles and he desperately sought some topic for this poor man to be good at. He could never have imagined feeling sorry for this brute of a human being. He doodled on the cover of his notebook as he sought inspiration.

"Can you draw or paint?" Maurice asked despairingly.

"Funny you should ask that. I loved drawing, but my parents told me not to waste my time as there was no money in it," Sid reminisced fondly. Maurice almost burst out laughing at the thought of such an oversized lout doing any intricate pencil or pen work. He returned to the task at hand, which he perceived to be helping someone worse off than himself.

"Right! No better time than the present! Here's a page from my notebook and a pencil. I want you to draw..." he looked around his cell for something challenging "...to draw me." Sid looked at him in disbelief for a few moments, before regaining his speech.

"What... now?" he uttered in amazement.

"Yes! Right now, before my awkward cellmate returns." He sat opposite Sid and turned his face so it was partly in profile. Sid studied him for a minute and then started scribbling away. They had been sitting like that for less than ten minutes when Rymer entered, saw what Sid was doing and broke into a vindictive chuckle.

"Ho, ho, ho! The dummy is trying to draw. Whatever next?" Sid flushed, screwed up his drawing and prepared to leave. Maurice stopped him and turned on Rymer.

"**You**, Rymer, are the lowest of the low and have no right to speak ill of **any** man, let alone **my good friend** Sid Cracken." He faced up to the culprit in an unusual show of anger. Rymer swung at him, but his hand was caught in mid-air by Sid, who promptly twisted it and sent Rymer flying out of the cell. He landed at the feet of a passing officer, who helped him up. Marching him back into the cell, he demanded an explanation, and was obliged at some length by Maurice. After consulting the governor, it was decided to move Rymer out of Maurice's cell and move Sid in.

The officials had great difficulty in understanding what had transpired. Maurice had been seriously beaten up by a man he was now prepared to share with, when none of the other prisoners would.

When the move was completed, Sid looked at Maurice with virtual hero worship, and spoke first.

"You called me your good friend! Nobody's ever called me good or friend before. And you'll share your room with me. I don't know 'ow to thank you." Unused to such adulation, and from such a surprising source, Maurice hunted for a reply.

"You can start by letting me see your drawing." He held out his hand, prepared to compliment where none was deserved. Sid anxiously pulled out the ball of paper from his waistband and handed it to his friend. Flattening it carefully, he ignored the smudges caused by all the creases and glanced at it. Then he gazed in silence for what seemed like an hour to Sid, who could stand it no longer.

"I'm sorry I've wasted your time. I've let you down. I know you were trying to be 'elpful, but I'm just no good at anyfink." He hung his head in genuine shame. Finally, Maurice was able to speak, and with complete conviction (no easier for a convict!).

"Sid! It's brilliant. You're a natural. I'm no art expert, but I do know real talent when I see it."

Maurice managed to get some sketching pads of different sizes and a selection of drawing pencils right up to **9H**, the very hardest graphite pencil, for his new companion. He tried to get him tuition without success. Sid's reputation discouraged all possible tutors, as it did other prisoners from attacking Maurice physically or verbally. This unaccountable relationship blossomed for both. Sid began to see a purpose in his life, and he had a real friend and mentor. Maurice was no longer wrapped up in self-pity, as he had another and more testing project – he had a big child to look after – Sid.

After this experience, I really think that anything is possible. So, come on, life.

CHAPTER 16

The priest, Sean, had not really cleared his conscience. He had almost cleared his memory. With the delight of almost total relaxation, immersion in his reading, and the subsequent meetings and discussions with Miguel, his mind became totally absorbed with current events. There was still over a week of his holiday left when Miguel departed for his own vacation.

"Remember, Sean, you must broaden your mind viz lateral t'inking, and broaden your life viz new experiences. I'm sorry to be leaving you just ven our debates are reaching some form of consensus. I can agree zat faith can 'elp people even zough zer's no scientific basis for it. It's not for me, I'm afraid; I still see it as unproven superstition. You must email me ven you're back in England. I'm interested to know 'ow you'll resolve your dilemma. For me, you should leave ze Church and join me as my partner. I'll miss you very much."

Saying that, he placed a hand on each of Sean's cheeks and kissed him passionately on the mouth. Sean was too startled to resist! He simply froze like a statue and stared with complete surprise at Miguel, who smiled intimately at him. Since leaving his parents and college, the only things he had kissed were religious objects and children's foreheads. There was no feeling of the revulsion he would have expected had he been forewarned. Neither was there a sense of great pleasure.

"Don't look so startled, Sean. Your virginity's still intact." Miguel laughed loudly and waited for some response.

Now, Sean's facial expression changed to guilt. *Should I've reacted more negatively? The moment's passed, so I'll pretend it never happened.* "I'm truly sorry you're leaving. I'll miss your companionship and assistance, and, of course, our unfinished debate. I promise I'll send you an email when matters have been decided at home," he responded diplomatically, changing the subject.

"Don't take too long. I might even email you first," Miguel said as his parting shot.

Left alone, Sean's mind was racing with different emotions and he headed for his hotel. He delayed at a *bodega* for some wine to steady his nerves. He consumed a large Rioja while trying hard to read his book. Every time he lost the thread of the scientific theories, he took a large gulp of wine and restarted. He had always been so sure of his faith and his celibacy, and suddenly those principles were challenged. He had been firm as a rock and now he was on the quicksand of possibilities. Staring at the open page of his book, his thoughts fixed on earlier events, he nodded his head automatically every time someone stopped and asked him a question. It was the waiter refilling his glass and taking payment from the change Sean had carelessly left on the table.

When he rose to leave, he noticed the ship was rolling in heavy seas. *What ship? I'm on land*, he recalled. As he staggered against a table, a waiter dashed over to help him, and led him to the door. Then a feminine voice came from somewhere close by.

"*Está bien. Sé donde vive. Yo tendré cuidado de él. Su nombre es Anderson.*" A slim, dark-haired young woman, nearly his own height, grasped his elbow firmly and guided him along the pavement.

"Werez ye tooking mi?" Sean slurred, as he tried desperately to walk straight and look at his new companion at the same time.

"Do not worry, *señor* Anderson. I take you to your 'otel. My name ees Maria. I nurse you in 'ospital."

Funny name, Ospital! Don't remember him, thought Sean.

Fortunately, it was not too far to his hotel, and she managed to get him to his room. Once inside, he staggered to the bathroom and was very sick in the toilet. As he knelt there with his head hanging almost inside the bowl, a moment of lucidity made him aware of the white porcelain surrounding him. *If this is the virginal white of heaven, why does my stomach hurt, and who is trying to break out of my head?*

Maria used all her nursing skills to clean him up and prepare him for bed. Room service brought a large cafetière of strong coffee, and she forced Sean to drink as much as possible. He vomited in the toilet once more, then fell asleep on top of the bed.

Maria managed to get him under the covers. He was extremely pale; even his lips had lost their colour and were almost blue, so she decided to stay. Fortunately, she had her mobile phone with her, so she was able to inform her family what had happened. Checking on her patient regularly, his pulse and breathing, she settled herself on the sofa and fell asleep reading a magazine.

Sean got up once during the night to use the toilet and noticed something on the sofa. In the half-light, he thought it must be a new arrangement of cushions. He returned his shaking body and pounding head to the safety of his bed. He was disturbed about 7am by movement in his room and a shadow falling over him. He tried to lift his head, but the intense throbbing made him lie back again.

"Is that you, Miguel?" he mumbled, the effort hurting his abused head.

"No, *señor* Anderson. It's Maria Caballero from the 'ospital. You were very ill last night so I put you to bed and stay to see you okay." She had just refreshed herself in the bathroom and she spoke slowly. Sean had difficulty comprehending, so Maria went through all the events from the time she collected him outside the *bodega*. This forced him to have a hazy recollection and he stared at this attractive *señorita* in his room.

"How do you know me? How did you know where I live? Why did you stay here? Who——?" Maria interrupted him and raised both arms in the air.

"Slowly, slowly! One question at a time. First, I know you and ver you live because I nursed you in ze 'ospital. Secondly, I stayed 'ere because you ver very ill last night, and in view of your earlier experience, I t'ought it best to keep an eye on you." She paused to study his face for recognition. "'Onestly, *señor*, I don't take advantage of nurse and patient relationship. I admit I found you very attractive when you arrived in 'ospital, but then I realise you are – 'ow you say – gay." Sean looked at her intently and burst out laughing. Maria looked crestfallen, almost in tears.

"Vy you laugh at me? I'm sorry I say I like you, but it's true! I know I shouldn't—"

"No, no, no! It's not you; it's me that's sorry. I'm not gay. Miguel is just a friend who helped me. The truth is I'm…"

He pretended to clear his throat as he changed what he was about to say. As he paused, his head and primarily his eyes cleared and he observed his administering angel. *An angel! That's it! That's why she's familiar. She's the angel in the hospital who roused the primal man in me. Or to 'gird up now thy loins like a man'* as it says in the Bible in Job. *Fully alert now, I can study her more clearly.*

Typical Spanish woman is my first impression. She's quite tall for a woman, with a slim build, which disguises the strength required to handle me last night. Wavy short hair frames a most attractive face, with dark almond-shaped eyes, full lips, firm chin and olive skin. Her nose is what? Roman? No. She probably has Moorish blood in her. The more I analyse her, the more I can imagine her portrait hanging in a gallery of stars. How could such a vision be available to assist me, suffering from selfish overindulgence?

In truth, she was quite pretty, but certainly no outstanding 'vision'. Perhaps Sean's view of her was enhanced by some emotional chemistry.

"The truth is, I'm extremely flattered to receive the attention of such a beautiful *señorita*." *What am I saying? What's happening to me? Why can't I be honest and tell her I'm a priest? Am I ashamed? Is there some part of me that wants to know her better? Yesterday, my sexual composure was challenged by Miguel and now by this Maria. Did the bishop really detect some fundamental flaw in my character, which goes beyond mere reasoning? Am I losing my faith? No, I don't think so. In some ways, my discussions with Miguel have strengthened it. What's wrong? Is it me or is it my church? My head feels too heavy to think more deeply.* While he had these thoughts, Maria was talking excitably, largely in Spanish.

The occasional pieces that registered with Sean gave him a précis of her life. Her long-term boyfriend had deserted her for an affluent blonde tourist. In her tragic disillusionment, she threw herself into her career as a nurse, which became her sole love. She still lived with her parents. Men she resisted because "Zay air peegs." She became attracted to Sean because he was so different from any other man she had known.

"I'm very sorry I disappointed you. Perhaps now you understand I'm not gay, we **can** be good friends. You've been very kind to me. I owe you a lot for helping me. My friend Miguel has gone away on his holiday, just when I was getting used to having company. I'm here for four weeks to sort out my life, and having a friend to talk with has helped me. I'd very much value your companionship, whenever possible, for my last few days. I must be honest and tell you it could only be friendship," he beseeched her, knowing his request was selfish and unlikely to gain a positive response.

"Why only friends?" Her curiosity prevented any other answer.

"I'd rather not tell you at present as it'd colour our friendship." Sean struggled to contain the truth.

"Are you married?" she persisted.

"No." *Some would say I'm married to the Church*, he thought.

"You 'ave a girlfriend?"

"No." *Is this the Spanish Inquisition?*

"Are you…" she paused with slight embarrassment "…'ow you say, not able to have sex?" She blushed as she said it, even though it was easier in a language not her own. Still, she could not look directly at him as she said it.

"The word in English is impotent. The answer is not as far as I know. I work for an organisation that prefers me not to have sex or get married."

"*Sí, impotente*. Is same in Spanish," she muttered absent-mindedly, while she digested his information and tried to find a follow-up. He decided he should change the balance.

"Did you have sex with your long-term boyfriend?" Putting the blunt question, he hoped he didn't sound like a priest. She frowned as she looked at him, then lowered her eyes and almost whispered, "Yes."

He found her ensuing blush absolutely charming, and was strongly tempted to put an arm around her in comfort as he continued. "There's no need to be embarrassed. Such things are becoming accepted as part of this modern world."

He almost forgot he was not in a confessional, and nearly added, 'my child'. He quickly continued. "**How** could he leave a beautiful, clever woman like you? What could any woman have that is better than you?" She was almost in tears as she forced a shaky reply.

"Money! She was rich!"

Sean's remorse at pressing the point made him put an arm around her at last. She burst into tears as she pressed her face into his chest. *The situation would have been safer for me had I been wearing my priest's attire. This thought leads me to realise I have been hiding from life, behind religious trappings, for too long. Just as others hide behind their uniforms in rigidly carrying out their tasks, be it police or waiters or the Gestapo or nurses.*

With these considerations, he continued and asked her gently, "Have you sought comfort in the Church, my… er… Maria?" Lifting her wet face, she looked at him.

"*Sí*! I mean yes. It was useless. The replies were *automatico* or *autocratico*. If you understand, you choose which is right. There was no compassion or *acuerdo*. Trust in the Lord is what they would say. **Why should I trust 'im**?" She raised her voice to an unexpected level. "**What 'as 'e ever done for me?**" Her voice returned to normal. "It was then that I tried different religions. To me, dealing with life and death on a daily basis, they are all based on superstition and not scientific fact." She had pulled away from him as she gave vent to her wrath.

Should I tell her now? Sean considered. *No. I'm only here for another ten days. She can be a pleasant and useful companion for that short time. No need to spoil it with my true status.*

"Now that's very interesting!" Sean exclaimed with unforced enthusiasm. "That's exactly the topic I'd love to discuss with you. It's—"

"What is topic?" she interrupted. Sean got out his Spanish-English dictionary and went through the pages, with Maria looking over his arm. He pointed at the English word and she read the translation. "*Ah, sí. Etam.*"

He handed her the book and asked, "What is the word you used earlier? You said compassion and *akwerdo*. She thumbed through the pages, found the word and showed it to him.

"Understanding. Now I understand." He laughed and continued. "*Sí!* I want to talk to you about science and religion. It's what Miguel and I discussed."

"Miguel, Miguel. You always mention Miguel. You make me *celosa!*" She smiled coquettishly at him. Sean turned the pages in his dictionary and found the translation of *celoso/celosa*.

"Jealous! Ah, Maria, how I'd love to think you'd ever be *celosa* because of me." *What am I doing? Has this hangover made me mad? I'm actually flirting with the poor girl.*

"'Ow do you talk about religion and science, *señor* Anderson?" She altered the direction of their conversation, although his last remark and becoming friendly visibly pleased her as she relaxed.

"Maria!" he protested. "Please call me Sean. The thing we talk about is the need for faith in an age of great scientific knowledge."

"Sean. What sort of name is that?"

"It's spelled S-E-A-N. It's an Irish name. When it is spelled S-I-A-N, it's a Welsh girl's name, and it's pronounced 'Sharn'," he explained, encouraging her continued curiosity.

"Okay. I vill," Maria suddenly announced.

"Will what?" Sean was perplexed.

"'Ave meetings viz you sometimes for talking, now zat I feel I can trust you." She smiled and held out her hand for a shake of agreement.

Am I going mad? Have events in Spain so traumatised me that I seek such an assent? he reasoned. Then he exceeded his priestly boundaries as he grasped her hand and, with a flourish of gallantry, pressed it to his lips and bowed. Her face lit up with pleasure and she gave a mock curtsey. They discussed times and places to meet, though not at his hotel, and she left to go on duty.

For nine wonderful days they met and talked about the use and misuse of faith and its various guises. Other topics were touched upon as they relaxed ever more in each other's company. When she mentioned funny or strange occurrences at her work, he had great difficulty in reciprocating due to concealing his true position.

The more they learnt of each other's likes and dislikes, the stronger the bond between them. What had started as a mutual affinity had developed into an overpowering attraction. Within such a short space of time, their understanding of the other one reached a level that many couples usually attain only after years of association.

Yes, there were all the signs of early love! Regularly, they found themselves holding hands as they mulled over some earth-shattering yet meaningless topic. Maria never imagined she would ever feel such an attachment to a man again. It caused her a problem a few times at work, when she was caught daydreaming. She had to keep reminding herself to maintain her guard, because as much as she cared for Sean, she knew there was some dark secret he was withholding from her. What sort of organisation could constrain him so?

For his part, Sean became increasingly worried. *I have never had such a strong... strong what? Friendship? No! Much as I hate to admit it, it is more than that. It is affection! I greatly enjoy her company and want to... to care for her. Much as I enjoyed my time with Miguel, I never counted the minutes until our next meeting. Am I so changed that I have a situation in which I willingly deny my profession? I loved my way of life and now...? Now I am...? I have an infatuation for this vibrant woman. I could never hurt her, yet I must tell her the truth before I leave.*

Several times, over those few Elysian days, holding hands and gazing into each other's eyes became as natural in their relationship as ordinary friends meeting and greeting. For Maria, her pulse quickened and she struggled to regulate her breathing. For Sean, he was unaware of breathing at all, only of the knot in his stomach. Their discussions were really only camouflage. Neither could argue any point very strongly. Hence, their mutual understanding led to Maria accepting there is a place for faith, and Sean acknowledging its shortcomings. Their meetings were always in very public places, yet they were alone, cosseted in their own sphere of happiness. Her friends would pass by and greet her without her noticing.

Alone, in their own beds, each would reflect on the rash stupidity of the relationship; Maria on not exercising more caution because of her earlier disappointment; Sean on feelings he should not have. Yet both were impatient for their next rendezvous. Finally, on his last day, Sean invited her to his room for tea. He wanted to have total privacy when he revealed his profession.

"You're leaving and you've bad news for me. I know you 'ave some terrible secret you 'ave been keeping from me, Sean. You 'ave other woman, or is it man? Tell me quickly, please." She was trembling as she spoke. Sean took hold of her hands and made her sit facing him.

"You're right. I do have a secret. Please listen carefully and let me explain all." He tightened his hold on her hands and leant forward, taking a deep breath. "It's my profession! I'm a Catholic priest."

"*MIERDA*! I cannot believe it! Why didn't you tell me sooner!" She tried to pull back.

"Please listen. I'm here on extended holiday to reconsider my position in the Church, under orders from my bishop. I didn't want anyone to know. Miguel found out and kept the secret. If I had told you earlier, you would never have become my friend. We wouldn't have had such good meetings." He paused for her to comment, which she did after a long silence.

"It 'elps you. It 'urts me!" She tightened her lips in an effort to control her emotions.

"I know that's how it seems. Let me explain fully." She listened to his every word as he gave her a complete account from his outburst at the Jenkins incident up to parting with Miguel.

"He knew what I am and that we'd never be more than good friends. In some way, he did help me to find my true path. When we parted, he kissed me full on the lips and I was shocked, but not repulsed. I began to wonder about my natural human desires, which I've suppressed for so long. I tried to read a serious book and found I was unable to concentrate. That's when I obviously drank too much wine, while deep in thought. Then you came into my life like some guardian angel." He shook his head.

"No, as a veritable **goddess**! My emotions challenged my mind and training once more. After a mere ten days, *you* mean more to me than my calling as a priest of the Catholic Church. I'm not practised in dealing with such emotions. So," he paused and looked into the very depths of her almond eyes, "if you care for me, even half as much as I do for you, I ask you to do me a great favour." He paused again, tried to judge her reactions and took a metaphorical deep breath before continuing.

"I have to return to England to sort out my life there. Can you, please, wait for me to make a decision in one month? By then, I'll know if my feelings for you are lust, simple affection, or, as I currently feel, **real, deep, true and everlasting love**." Finishing with a burst of passion, he finally released her hands, unaware of the pressure he had been exerting on them. He sat back and waited hopefully.

Maria slumped back in her chair and rubbed her hands gently. Staring down at them, as if studying the marks left by Sean's intense grip, she thought long and hard about all he had said. After what seemed like an eternity to Sean, she leant forward and delicately grasped his knees. She looked up at him, nodded her head and smiled warmly.

"I'm very flattered viz vat you said. I agree you must return to England and consider your future carefully. I must not be ze reason for ruining your life as a priest, and I can see you are dedicated despite all zat 'as 'appened. You 'ave much to give to the world. I should not vant to destroy zat." She patted his knees to reinforce her statement, and hesitated. Sean's face was a picture of misery at vant he took to be an outright rejection. She noticed and patted his knees more firmly as she continued.

"*Sin embargo, si elige me estaré esperando un mes o dos, o todo el tiempo que tarda para usted sin duda.*" She said it in Spanish with great drama and fervour. He had difficulty in interpreting any of the words, as they had also been spoken very quickly. The colour drained from his face and he was close to tears as she laughed and translated.

"Vat I said was – 'owever, if you choose me, I vill be vaiting for one mont' or duo, as long as it takes for you to be sure." Sean's face was transformed and his shoulders dropped as the tension left them. Finally, he kissed her and held her tightly against him.

The scent of this divine creature and the warmth of her body were overpowering to Sean. With great difficulty, he separated them. "We must part now before we do something we regret later. I'll see you home. There must be no lengthy farewells, or you will break what little of my newfound heart you don't own already."

CHAPTER 17

While Birdie was getting into trouble, Ivor had been doing out-of-hours checking on all the staff, fortified by an excess of strong black coffee. Once, when his mind wandered, he suddenly saw the funny side. *My original plan was for Birdie to stimulate me sexually. Instead, she has provoked me mentally, into doing this extra work, for which my stimulation is simply caffeine.* He started with the junior grades and worked his way up. One or two had blemishes in their careers, but nothing to link them to Masood. He found that the chief inspector had met the suspected drug lord on several occasions, but there was no evidence of financial or other gain. The superintendent, Bernard Thwaite, had never met Masood. Nothing to implicate anyone locally, so he thought he would try to search further afield.

He stopped and tried a different line of approach. *What was it Birdie called it? Lateral thinking. If someone has benefitted from an association with Masood over several years, how is that master criminal benefitting? Is there some way in which he has gained wealth and power, and not just avoided capture?*

Examination of the complete history showed that virtually all of Masood's criminal rivals had been convicted, leaving him as the number one suspected criminal. Ivor then checked how each rival had been caught. They were all convicted as a result of one fast-rising officer's brilliant work or –? No! It was too much of a coincidence. It had to be from information from the person who benefitted most – Masood. That officer was Thwaite! The case against the superintendent was overwhelming when Ivor examined his career. Thwaite had dealt with all the major cases in their district and obtained convictions in most. The only case he had never touched, according to the record, was Masood's. No wonder he was so confident that he could suggest Birdie check on everyone including himself.

Staying on nearly all night, Ivor wrote a detailed report on his checks and listed the facts implicating Thwaite. He was extremely tired, having been working non-stop since leaving Birdie. Unable to decide how to proceed, he had fallen asleep at his desk when Phil Tyler, Birdie's inspector, woke him.

"Ivor! I thought you should be the first to know. Sergeant Lee's been kidnapped. It happened about nine last night. A neighbour heard some noise and looked out onto the street. She recognised Birdie, who appeared to be unconscious, and saw her placed in the boot of a car. She left us a message on the phone, which I just heard. I know you two are… well… close friends and working on something together." His anxiety was patent. Ivor just sat there, stunned.

"Did the neighbour get the car registration?"

"Yes. It's being checked right now. Have you any idea who'd want to snatch her?" Tyler sounded desperate.

"**Definitely**! It's Masood! We were following up on the Houghbury lead and happened to uncover that he has a spy in this office. Birdie was trying a long shot, by letting it be known that she'd definite information to convict Masood and would present it before the end of the week." Ivor was now wide awake and very angry.

"Who'd she tell?" Tyler prompted.

"Nobody apart from the superintendent, I think. However, I've found the spy **since** I left her just before nine last night."

"Who is it?" Tyler demanded.

"All the evidence is in this report." He produced it from his locked drawer. "There are also copies sent to Birdie's and my home computer." He looked around to ensure they were alone and then handed it to the inspector.

"**Wow**! No wonder you're being doubly careful. What are you going to do with it?"

"It is going to Internal, but first I'm going to see Thwaite with it, to try and save Birdie. I'd appreciate it if you came with me."

"Of course I'll come. I'll back you to the hilt." They started down the corridor to the superintendent's office.

"One thing puzzling me is your concern for Birdie. It's more than I'd expect for one of your conquests?"

"Sorry to disappoint you, but she's not a conquest as you put it. Strange as it may seem, and I know many won't believe it, ours is purely a type of... brother and sister relationship," Ivor whispered as they neared their goal. Tyler looked incredulous. They arrived at Thwaite's office, confirmed there was nobody with him and marched in despite protestations.

"How dare you burst in here! What do you think you're doing?" The superintendent leant forward and closed the file he had been reading. His formidable presence made them hesitate and they looked at each other. He may have cheated to attain his rank, but he had never lacked bearing and was always in full command of every situation; truly a man to be feared. Then they thought of Birdie and, encouraged by each other's support, they proceeded with their plan.

"Mr Thwaite, Officer Kowalski has something to say to you, and I'm here as a witness," the inspector declared firmly. The superintendent rose from his chair, glared at each of them in turn, and spoke with all his given authority.

"You will kindly address me as sir! Whatever you have to say can wait for a proper appointment." Under normal circumstances, his rank and natural air of authority would have stopped them once more in their tracks, but it was swept aside by their concern for Birdie.

"**It cannot wait**, **Thwaite**! Unless you wish to add accessory to murder to the list of your other crimes," Ivor blurted out anxiously.

"You **will** address me as sir! And you **will** leave immediately!" He reached for his phone, but Tyler held it down. He was almost terrified by this domineering man, and only the impetus of their charge into the superintendent's office kept him going.

"**You** have lost any right to be called sir. **You** will sit and listen to Officer Kowalski quickly or, as he said correctly, you will be charged with accessory to the murder of a policewoman." As Tyler spoke these last words, Chief Inspector Ron Bennett overheard them as he hurried into the room. Thwaite's secretary had summoned him.

"**Explain yourselves immediately**!" he almost shouted as he marched towards the two intruders.

"Sir," said Ivor, addressing Bennett and turning his back on Thwaite, "I'll put it simply. We knew someone in this building had been passing information to Masood, which is why we've never collared him. Thwaite knew of Sergeant Lee's suspicions, and to throw her off the scent he instructed her to check on everyone to find the mole. He thought his impeccable record would keep him in the clear. Over many years, Thwaite has helped Masood in return for information, which furthered his career and got rid of Masood's rivals. Thwaite has had a hand in virtually all the major cases in the area, but never Masood! I have written a full report to substantiate my accusations.

"Finally, Sergeant Lee informed me last night that she had told Thwaite that she could produce definite evidence, by the end of this week, which would convict Masood. Last night, soon after I left her apartment, Sergeant Lee's body was seen being placed in the boot of a car by two men. There is every reason to believe they are Masood's men." He took a deep breath. "The only person who could've given him the information to warrant such drastic action was Thwaite. Internal Affairs will undoubtedly act on my report and deal with Thwaite appropriately. However, if Sergeant Lee is alive still, she could be killed at any moment, and then the charges against this… traitor will be much more serious. If you agree, we must have him stop Masood now!"

Bennett looked from Ivor to Tyler. The latter was nodding his head vigorously. Then he turned to the superintendent and studied him thoughtfully.

"Absolute rubbish! I have **never** given any information to Masood! I demand you remove these two and put them on suspension pending further enquiries. I will take that report as evidence of their insubordination." Thwaite reached out his hand to grasp the papers, but Ivor pulled away.

Without any warning, the chief inspector grabbed the superintendent's arm, glared into his face and barked at him.

"You will do no such thing! I am backing Inspector Tyler and Officer Kowalski one hundred percent!"

"Don't be ridiculous! Let go of me at once." Thwaite's voice lost a little of its authority, and was there an underlying sense of doubt in it and his bearing?

"Now that we have Ivor's proof, many pieces of unusual information begin to make sense." Bennett spoke very precisely, as if the fog of ignorance was clearing. Tyler and Kowalski looked at each other in satisfied wonderment as Bennett continued; his eyes narrowed and with a deep frown on his forehead.

"I always thought it was your obsession with the job that made you insist on knowing everything that went on in the office; not just administration matters." He paused and nodded his head. "On reflection, I think perhaps you took more interest and made notes when items concerned Masood. Also, I used to wonder how you got the proof to put away so many of his rivals. Furthermore, I recollect being a trifle puzzled when you had Detective Sergeant Evans detached to Norwich because you thought he was taking the case too personally. **Now**, you will sit and do everything within your power and your relationship with Masood to save Sergeant Lee. **I mean now!**" he snapped at the startled Thwaite.

"Kowalski, stay here. Tyler, get every available officer ready to act. We'll need armed officers. Tell them all an officer's life is at risk due to the treachery of our Superintendent Thwaite. Then we'll get Internal Affairs to handle him." He turned back to the ruminating Thwaite and thrust his fist into his face. The others had never seen the chief inspector use his position so aggressively before.

"Well, Thwaite. Where is she being held or where might we find her?" He placed pen and paper in front of the speechless superintendent, who was clearly shaken by the turn of events and visibly paled. He paused, thought carefully, and then hastily scribbled down a few addresses.

"They're the only ones **I** know. Masood might have been my informant, but I **never** gave him information."

"You've lost any credibility. Save your excuses for Internal." Bennett warned him, taking the list and passing it to Ivor.

"Pass this to Tyler and Langley. They're to send officers to each address immediately. They have twenty minutes to get in position, quietly, and await instructions. At that time, I'll have Thwaite ring Masood, and for both of their sakes, I hope we're not too late." The chief inspector had always been admired by staff for his management skills, knowledge of the job and his intelligence, but this was much more action positive than they had seen before. Man of action was an understatement.

Once they knew of Birdie's kidnap, and of their superintendent's betrayal, every officer wanted to take part. It was difficult to leave even a skeleton team to cover the station's public duties. All officers were in position at the premises on the list and some other suspect places.

"I never told Masood, or anyone, about my discussion with Sergeant Lee. I would never endanger anyone's life. If I can do anything to help Sergeant Lee, I will," Thwaite protested.

"Be that as it may, you could ring Masood and, if he is responsible, warn him not to be too hasty." Bennett ignored his erstwhile boss's protestations.

"I really don't know him, but if you think it might help, I will. What's his phone number?" His voice became less masterful as he was forced to consider the accusations against him. Thwaite was given tea to steady his obvious nerves, and to make the call to Masood as natural as possible. He was told how much he could tell the criminal. Then he made the call with Bennett and the duty sergeant standing by to prevent any untoward messaging, and with the line set up, after eliminating some interference, for recording.

Having seen him appear decidedly shaky only moments before, they were impressed with the act he put on for Masood. After the event, they decided there must have been a hidden code word, which they had not allowed for, as Masood was totally non-committal. He thanked Thwaite for his news and said he would have his staff ask around for any information about the missing officer. Reviewing the recording, they could find nothing to incriminate Masood or Thwaite.

There was no unusual activity at any of the addresses being watched, and no sign of the kidnappers' car. It was not registered to Masood or any of his known accomplices. Ivor feared the worst and was at his wits' end. Then he remembered Doug Evans had the most knowledge of Masood. Ivor contacted Doug immediately and explained the problem. Doug recognised the descriptions of the kidnappers given by Birdie's neighbour, and believed them to be contract 'collectors' for illegal gambling joints and drug dealers, etc., who could be used by Masood. He did not have the positive proof required for conviction but had once trailed them to an abandoned house.

Ivor got Tyler's agreement to take a colleague and two armed officers to check. On arrival at the house, they left their car nearby and approached with caution. It was boarded up at the windows, and there were piles of rubbish in the small front 'garden'. There was a rough unsurfaced lane between the house and a sort of factory building, which overshadowed it. They could just make out a car parked down the lane. It **was** the one they sought! The team split up, with the two extra armed officers making for the rear of the decrepit house. Ivor was desperate! He could not wait for them to get in position and took it upon himself to burst in through the front door. Any tiredness or pain was overcome by his concern for Birdie and the effect of too much caffeine. There were sudden movements in a rear room and he charged straight in.

Birdie was tied to a chair and had obviously been beaten by the two lowlifes that turned to face him. As he leapt at the first one, the other fired at him and he crashed to the floor. His colleague was close behind and ducked rapidly back. The crook with the gun pointed it at Birdie's head and ordered the hiding officer to drop his gun. The officer threw down his gun and stepped forward. A shot from somewhere made him drop to the floor. As he looked up, he saw the threatening crook on the floor and the other with his hands in the air. The two officers assigned to the rear of the house had shot one thug and were advancing on the other. Through the remaining slit for vision left in Birdie's bruised and swollen eyes, she recognised Ivor on the floor.

The three standing officers retrieved the crook's gun and made sure neither could do any more damage. They called for backup and an ambulance and untied Birdie. However, they decided not to move her in case they aggravated her multiple injuries. Apart from the cuts and bruises that showed, her right arm was hanging at an unnatural angle. She tried to talk but could not open her mouth, so she grunted and looked from the closest officer down to Ivor's crumpled body. The officer made a twisting motion with his hand to indicate Ivor's condition was touch and go. She tried to rise and was held down gently by her colleague. Much as they envied her abilities and made fun of her as 'the Ice Maiden', they had great respect for her. Her condition made them all **very** angry. They handled the handcuffed crook roughly yet resisted the temptation to exact the revenge his treatment of Birdie deserved.

After five or six minutes, the ambulance and more police

arrived. It took all the medics to get Birdie onto a stretcher with minimal pain. Those officers allowed into the building all wanted to help carry her and Ivor to the ambulance. The wounded crook was a completely different story. It was not help but hindrance they offered, and the two inspectors had to restrain them. Tyler had the other crook placed in a car quickly to remove further temptation. The premises were sealed off for forensics and the 'collector's' gun removed. A search of the surrounding area included the kidnap car, which was then hauled away for examination.

All the way to the hospital, Birdie tried to turn her head to see Ivor. *He can't be dead or he wouldn't be in this ambulance,* she reassured herself.

At Emergency, they were separated. He was still unconscious and scarcely breathing. She suffered pain at every movement, but none as great as her emotional pain. The injured hitman arrived and was found to be in no immediate danger. The police marksman had accurately shattered the man's shoulder as he redirected his weapon from Birdie to Ivor's colleague. It was a potentially lifesaving shot, yet it drew much criticism from the hierarchy, who needed firm proof that **any** shot was necessary. Birdie's colleagues had a different opinion – they thought the criminal should have died!

The media soon found out about the shooting and arrived at the crime scene and later at the hospital. Police protection was provided for all three in the Emergency ward and later when they were transferred to the main hospital. Chief Inspector Bennett was kept very busy explaining why he had taken such drastic action, deploying so many staff and arresting Superintendent Thwaite. The evidence produced by Ivor, backed up by Bennett's report, was presented to Internal Affairs. Meanwhile, Inspector Tyler was landed with the task of sorting out the administrative problems caused by the speed of the unforeseen mission. Inspector Langley had readily participated because the outcome should provide the evidence against Masood that he had been seeking for years.

The uninjured crook, Jack Fellows, was interrogated formally. The calibre of his lawyer should have been beyond the means of such a minor criminal, and nobody was sure how the lawyer was contacted or appointed, though they had their suspicions. Watching the interaction between the lawyer and his client, Langley decided the crook was really afraid of his representative. Every question put to the thug made him look at the lawyer, as if unable to answer without approval. Despite every effort of the interrogators, they were unable to establish any link between the prisoner and Masood.

At the outset of the interrogation, he tried to make the police believe he and his partner had just found Sergeant Lee and were trying to release her. His partner shot at the man bursting into the room because they both thought he was one of her captors. When he was told that he and his 'partner' had been seen kidnapping the sergeant, he confessed, saying it was a contract job. He had no idea who had employed them as the instructions plus half the money came through the post. He did not know what they were meant to discover, only that they had to get her to talk about her current cases.

"What did she tell you?" Langley asked, almost casually.

"She kept saying Masood would get nothing out of 'er." The lawyer nodded at his client.

"So you know Masood?" Langley fired his question quickly. The crook looked around the room, but it was fairly plain he was looking for a sign from the lawyer.

"No, I don't."

"But you've heard of him?" Langley pressed on. Again, the prisoner gazed about, as if in a trance.

"Yeah! 'E's some big local businessman, ain't 'e?" The prisoner shrugged his shoulders and grinned.

"Is he?" Langley put the question to the prisoner but looked at the lawyer, who looked away at his client, as if avoiding Langley's piercing eyes. The crook was again perusing the entire room.

"So I've 'eard say in the pubs."

"What sort of business is he in?" Langley kept looking from the prisoner to the lawyer and back.

"Dunno. Is it transport or summink?" He appeared to be getting too relaxed and confident as he looked around the room once again. Langley realised he had to change tack.

"You're an interior decorator by trade, are you, Mr Fellows?" He smiled at the two men facing him across the table.

"A what?" The prisoner frowned at Langley.

"An interior decorator. You design and decorate people's houses and flats for a living, do you?"

"Blimey, no! What gave you that idea?"

"Well, I couldn't help noticing how you keep studying the walls in this room." Langley's fellow interrogator put his hand over his mouth to suppress his laughter. Langley turned a page in his notebook and continued in a more serious vein.

"I remind you that the very least you will be charged with is kidnapping, and with assaulting a police officer. If the officer your accomplice shot does not live, you will be charged with accessory to murder." The prisoner's face dropped like a stone as he looked at his lawyer for assistance, noting how his counsel shrugged his shoulders.

"I didn't know she's a copper," he retorted.

"But you've already said you were to find out what cases she's currently working on!"

The accused looked directly at his lawyer, and Langley addressed the recording apparatus.

"For the record, the prisoner has conferred visually with his counsel."

"Yeah, well, I didn't know she was with the police." The interrogation continued in circles for another half-hour, and then finished for the day.

Bennett realised their hoped-for breakthrough had not materialised. They had yet to question the wounded crook but knew they would get the same answers. Both villains were more in fear of Masood than a lengthy jail sentence. With Inspector Tyler, he visited Birdie and Ivor in hospital, where they were closely guarded. Ivor was still unconscious and his condition was described as critical. Birdie had multiple bruises, broken ribs and a broken arm. She recognised Bennett and Tyler through her puffy eyes even though she was very drowsy from painkillers.

"When can I see Ivor?" she murmured anxiously.

"Not for a while yet. We have to put you back in one piece first," Tyler replied, with a nod of assent from Bennett.

"Did we get Masood?" Duty above pain! This was the Sergeant Lee of old.

"We've been unable to prove a connection between your assailants and Masood yet. However, we do have the mole. It was Thwaite all the time. He's now under suspension thanks to you and Ivor. Ivor proved he had gained all his promotions through information given him by Masood. Information which saw most of Masood's rivals behind bars. Do you feel up to telling us the new evidence you were hoping for?" Tyler placed a hand gently on her good shoulder to prevent her from trying to rise as he spoke.

Birdie looked around as best she could, then motioned them closer and whispered, "Nobody else must know of this or we'd have another witness murdered! Do you both promise? It's good that Thwaite has been caught, but there could be another spy. Money opens many doors." She paused for them to agree and for the pain in her chest to subside.

Instinctively, her colleagues looked at each other and then around the room. They leant forward and spoke softly. "We promise." They waited patiently for her to continue.

"I wouldn't be surprised if Masood has the station bugged, and probably an agent in this very hospital. There's a witness in Houghbury who had a good view of the driver of Masood's car and the passenger. He's not keen on 'coloureds' and has a problem telling them apart." Again, she paused for her pain to subside.

A doctor entered to examine her and the two men sat back. "I think you'd better leave now. Your visit is obviously distressing my patient." He turned and instructed her colleagues. Behind his back, Birdie shook her head as best she could, and her eyes were wide in panic. Sergeant Lee panicking? It was unheard of!

"**No! You leave!**" snapped Bennett. "This is urgent police business." The startled doctor was ushered from the room by Tyler. As the door closed behind the man, Bennett suddenly turned to Tyler.

"Did you see his ID?"

"No! I'll check it now," Tyler replied as he dashed after their visitor, who was making his way down the corridor. "Hey! You, Doctor! Show me your ID." The request caught the man off guard and he sprinted round the corner with Tyler in pursuit. He failed to catch the suspect doctor, and on his return, he reprimanded the officer on guard.

"Nobody, and I mean nobody, whether they look like medical staff or even police or firemen, gets into this room without proper ID. Even then, they are to be accompanied at all times."

"Very good, sir. But what if they want to examine... the Ice Maiden? Shouldn't we have a WPC available?" The poor constable was suitably ashamed of his lack of foresight, and momentarily forgot Birdie's real name.

"You're right. I'll arrange for one immediately. Meanwhile, I never want to hear Sergeant Lee's nickname again! After what she's been through, I think she deserves better."

He re-entered Birdie's room, with the officer still mumbling his apologies. Ensuring they could not be overheard, Bennett and Tyler leant over Birdie once more.

"I can't trust any of them," she whispered. A few minutes ago, they would have thought she was being paranoid. Not now! Tyler patted her left hand and reassured her.

"There's a guard on your door, and in future, nobody will be allowed in without proper identification. They will be accompanied at all times by a WPC, which I have just arranged."

"The Houghbury witness is a retired Major Stubbs. He saw a TV programme about Malaya." She paused for a deep breath, which made her wince with pain because of her cracked ribs.

"What's that got to do with Masood?" Bennett began to show the stress he had been under since Thwaite's arrest.

"The major was stopped at the roadworks alongside Masood's car, which is a newer version of his own. He looked at the driver and his passenger and thought they were too young and too black to own such a car."

"Why should he think that?" Tyler asked gently.

"He's a racist. He didn't like talking to my half-brother previously, because he is from Hong Kong. Stubbs thinks the couple looked like Malayans, were about twenty years old, and could've been twins, a boy and a girl. Nobody except my half-brother and his boss knows about this." Her words became fainter and her eyes began to close as her painkillers took effect.

Tyler looked at Bennett, and when the latter nodded his assent, he leant close to Birdie and whispered, "We will find these Malayans before anyone else knows about them. That should help solve the Houghbury affair and give us a lead on Masood. You just relax and get fit again." Birdie grunted her approval and opened her eyes slightly. Bennett stroked her left hand and reassured her.

"As Inspector Tyler said, there'll be a twenty-four-hour guard on you, Sergeant, so don't worry. You've more than done your duty. Leave the rest to us."

They left her, and Bennett reinforced the instructions Tyler had given the policeman on guard, adding that constant guard meant never leaving there until a replacement had arrived. They also told hospital management to ensure their staff carried ID at all times.

Later that evening, the next constable on guard duty was impatiently waiting for his overdue replacement and was desperate to answer the call of nature. A doctor was passing, so he asked him to watch the room for a couple of minutes so he could go to the toilet. As he went round the corner, he remembered the warning about attackers disguised as medical staff. He looked back round the corner and saw the alleged doctor was not there and the door to Birdie's room was ajar. Horrified at his lack of judgement, he dashed back and leapt into the room with his truncheon drawn. He smashed it against the assailant's arm, causing him to drop the hypodermic needle he was about to inject Birdie with. The crook wheeled around in time to receive a blow to the side of his head. Was he dead or just unconscious? The officer did not care. He handcuffed the attacker, dragged him from the room and called for backup.

Birdie never stirred, and when a real medical team arrived to check her, the officer followed his instructions and stayed with them. His replacement, having been delayed by a puncture, arrived before the backup did. Finally, the beleaguered officer was relieved in every way. A drowsy Bennett arrived with the backup and after checking on Birdie took charge of the arrest of the attacker.

Another one of Masood's men, who will undoubtedly deny all knowledge of him, thought the chief inspector. *Knowledge of Masood! Of course! Doug Evans! Nobody had more knowledge of the crook than Doug. Is that why Thwaite arranged for him to be posted to Norwich? To keep him off the case! I'll arrange for his return immediately.*

Phil Tyler only learnt of the attempt on Birdie's life later the next day. With Inspector Langley's agreement, he had taken all the files on Masood to his own house. There, in his private office, he would be undisturbed and away from prying eyes. He had a link on his home computer to the police system as he hoped to find a connection between the Malayans and Masood.

CHAPTER 18

Pru Gravillons, a small dark-haired woman with a typical Gallic nose, returned to her cold apartment to find her plants dead and a great pile of mail on the floor. She bustled about and made hot drinks for her children, Monique and Gaston. When they were settled, she went to her neighbour and knocked loudly on the door. She muttered to herself in French, "*Vous ne pouvez pas faire confiance à personne de nos jours!*" When there was no reply, she tried more doors until someone did answer.

"Please, can you tell me vere I can find Meester Jenkins in apartment 10?" she asked quickly, before the person could shut the door.

"Jenkins! You mean you don't know?" The query was decidedly hostile.

"Sorry. I've been away for a few months. Where is 'e?" She was puzzled by the reaction to his name.

"In prison where he deserves to be. Filthy pervert. Tried to snatch some poor kid!" The door was slammed shut before Pru could ask for more details.

Her mind was in turmoil: *this is not possible. Maurice 'as always been the best of neighbours and a friend. 'e looked after my children whenever my 'usband and I were absent. We are all very fond of 'im. 'e was supposed to have looked after our apartment while my family and I returned to France to settle affairs zere.* The kids were her first priority, so, having put the heating on and hung up the bedding to air, she took them shopping for essential supplies.

As the police station was near to where they alighted from the bus into Houghbury, she enquired about Maurice. The desk sergeant noted her children and questioned her very politely, as he smiled at the two kids.

"Have you come to register a complaint against him, ma'am?"

"No, no! 'e's a neighbour of mine and I've just been told 'e's in prison. I just want to get more details of why, please." Bob Pollock remembered details of the case and something clicked in his mind, so he asked his question before deciding how to answer hers.

"Did Jenkins read books and comics to your children, ma'am?"

"Yes, all the time. Why?" She was confused.

"If you've no grounds for complaint against him, do you want to help him?"

"Of course I want to help 'im. But why is 'e in prison?" she persisted.

"He was found guilty of attempting to kidnap a small boy. He claimed he was saving him from being run over by a car, but there were no witnesses to that effect. I suggest you see his lawyer, Terry Schott, who is trying to mount an appeal on Jenkins's behalf."

Given Terry's address, she went directly there. Like Sergeant Pollock, Terry's secretary initially thought Pru had come to make a complaint against Maurice. Derek overheard part of the conversation and realised who she was. He insisted on taking her and her kids straight in to see Terry. The interruption angered Terry as it broke into his concentration on a difficult case.

"What have you come to complain about?" he demanded in a frosty manner, before the alarmed Derek could explain. He was still trying to get a word in when Pru took over. Despite her small size and her smart but gloomy apparel, she dominated the room as if under a spotlight.

"**Complain**! Vy does everyone tink I should complain? Well, yes, I do 'ave a complaint! Why wasn't I told Maurice is in prison?" She was very tired and so were her children, who just wanted to get home. Terry's attitude was the last straw, and she fought fire with fire!

"Maurice? Do you mean Maurice Jenkins?" Terry was intrigued by her outburst and calmed down.

"*Mais oui, sacré bleu!* Oo else?" She turned as if to leave.

"I'm sorry. Do you know Maurice Jenkins well?" He indicated for her to be seated and got Derek to give the kids seats as well. Derek returned with two light chairs and some paper and pencils. He sat the kids at the table at the other end of the room and suggested they draw him a picture of their favourite animal.

"But of course! 'e's been my neighbour for years. 'e would always look after Monique and Gaston for us, when necessary. 'e was supposed to be looking after our apartment for us while we were away." She gave a Gallic shrug and spread her hands.

"You must be Madame Gravillons. We tried to contact you. In the turmoil of his arrest, Maurice lost your address and phone number in France. We had hoped to call you as a character witness." Terry jumped in quickly, hoping to placate her and prevent another outburst.

Terry explained the case to Pru. She was astounded and kept muttering, "*N'est pas possible.*"

When he had finished, he paused and added, "I take it you don't believe he could commit such a crime?" She looked at him, open-mouthed, then turned to her kids.

"Monique, Gaston. You remember *Monsieur* Maurice?" They both smiled and nodded.

"Do you tink Maurice would 'urt a child?"

"*Mamma*! You are being silly. Maurice is a good man and we love him, don't we, Gaston?"

"Yes, he's a very nice man. He helped me to read English. Look! I've done a picture of him!" Turning back to Terry, Pru gave another Gallic shrug.

"Vat can I add to that, Mr Schott, except to say I vill always trust 'im with our children. 'e is a shy man, but not with children. Someday, hopefully, some lucky children will 'ave 'im as their father. My 'usband was jealous of the children's affection for Maurice until 'e got to know 'im better. Now 'e knows 'im as the good friend 'e is." Terry was elated by her tirade. He had believed Maurice's story from the start. Now there could be no doubt of his character, either.

Pru explained her own circumstances as she could see Terry was curious. Her husband was a representative for a French cheese company, serving as the link with a major English cheese firm in the Houghbury area. They had returned to France for three months to sort out problems with contracts, and some family inheritance matters. Her husband had dropped her at their apartment while he went to visit the English cheese firm. With all these delays and the absence of Maurice, she would have to rush to get her shopping and prepare the apartment.

Terry decided he had better not delay her further and would take her statement the next day. Meanwhile, he got Derek to drive her to a hypermarket and then home. *The change in duties should take Derek's mind off his sister, Birdie.*

The next day, before taking Monique and Gaston to their schools, Pru attended Schott's office. It was in a historic building and suffered from narrow windows and uneven floors. Terry had furnished his suite of offices in very traditional style. This added to the gloom, and the lights had to be permanently on. Pru thanked him for Derek's assistance and hoped they would soon have good news about Derek's sister, whom she had been told about. Terry had prepared a list of questions and recorded her replies.

"There were some items produced in evidence against Maurice. He said he used them to read to your children. Could you look at them, please, and tell me if you recognise them." He showed her copies of the books and comics found in Maurice's apartment.

"*Mais oui*! Zese are typical of ze tings 'e used to help zem with zeir English."

Making sure that the children were fully occupied, he opened a file and felt embarrassed as he placed the photos in front of her.

"They also found these photos of children in suggestive poses, which were really damning." She looked at the photos and then turned away in disgust. She shook her head in disbelief and muttered some French expletive under her breath. Terry reached into his file and produced a copy of one of the soft porn magazines found at Maurice's.

"Some magazines like this were also there. What do you think of him now?" He played devil's advocate. She picked up the magazine, thumbed through it quickly, and smiled.

"Zis is a different matter. I know my own 'usband looks at zese magazines. It only proves Maurice is a normal man with a normal man's desires. I expect you look at zem too, Mr Schott." Terry coughed in embarrassment. Pru laughed and continued, "But those terrible photos! I cannot believe

Maurice would 'ave such tings. Never! Zey belong to a pervert, not our Maurice!" she declared positively.

"If only we could have contacted you earlier, Maurice would not be in jail now. I shall certainly have strong words with the police authority about the disgusting photos. Your opinion backs the statement by Maurice that he had never seen the photos before and they must've been planted," Terry declared, as he overcame his earlier awkwardness. He put the items back in his file.

"What is 'planted'?" Pru asked.

"If the photos didn't belong to Maurice then it means somebody put them in his apartment in order to provide damning evidence against him," he explained.

"You mean zey could've been put zere by one of ze policemen searching 'is place?"

"Yes. Don't worry, I'll sort it out and hopefully the police will find the culprit. Thank you for coming. You have helped Maurice a great deal."

Taking her to the outer office at the finish, he was surprised to find Judith Donnelly there with his paintings. The contrast in the two women could not have been greater. One short with hair cut in the latest Parisian style, and fashionably dressed in drab colours; the other tall, with masses of uneven blonde hair and very casually dressed in pale blue jeans and a bright yellow jacket.

"Ah, Judith." He looked over Pru's shoulder at the artist, winked and held a finger to his lips.

"I'd like you to meet Madame Gravillons. Judith's done some paintings for my office." The ladies shook hands tentatively.

"Madame Gravillons's just given me a character statement for Maurice Jenkins. You may remember the case?" He winked at Judith again.

"**Oh yes!**" she replied, now totally confused. Perhaps it was the way she spoke that started Pru off.

"'E vould not be in prison now, if I 'ad been 'ere at ze time. 'E's a lovely man, and so good with my children. I trust 'im completely. People must 'ave been mad to tink 'e could do such a ting!"

It was not just her French intonation that rose; so did her temper. Terry hastily opened the outer door and ushered her and her kids out, saying he would keep in touch with her. Returning, he showed Judith into his own office, ignoring the suppressed laughter from Derek and Eileen. Judith unwrapped the two paintings and propped them on a table for him to view.

"Mr Schott, kindly explain what **that** was all about."

"I'm sorry, Mrs Donnelly. I hope you'll forgive me for using your first name, but Madame Gravillons might've realised who you are if I'd used your surname. As you probably noticed, she can be a trifle volatile."

"I did notice. But why would she be more angry if she knew my name?" Judith was still puzzled.

"Madame Gravillons is Jenkins's neighbour. He used to look after her two children, aged seven and five, whenever she needed him to. He taught them to read English. Also, he was supposed to look after her apartment while she went back to France with her family for three months. She's just given me a statement about how she and her husband trust Jenkins completely. She explained how Jenkins is very shy *except* with kids." He offered her a seat while he examined the paintings from all angles. She was considering carefully what he had said and finally looked up at him.

"I see, or at least I think I do. Did you know of her at the time of the trial? That she could be a character witness?"

"I wish I had. Then I would've done my utmost to contact her." He shook his head with regret.

"Why didn't Jenkins tell you about her?"

"I'm not sure. It could've been nerves. More likely, it's down to his psyche. He's a dreamer, and about the most self-effacing person I've met. He has latent potential yet is embarrassed by praise of any kind. This is why he was in a rut with a mundane job. The day he saved your little boy was the day he made his pact with Arnold Phillips."

"The day he snatched my boy, you mean!" she angrily corrected.

"No, I mean saved, which is what I truly believe."

"I'm sorry, but I'm still not convinced! As a loner and dreamer, making a pact with a total stranger could've seriously altered his persona. People do alter and not always for the better. It'll take a lot more to convince me you're right about him!" The sight of Charlie struggling in Jenkins's arms was deeply etched in her memory. Terry shrugged his shoulders.

"One day, I hope to convince you. Meanwhile, I love these paintings. They're exactly what I want. Could you have them framed to match this, please?" He went to the light switches and pressed one. A display light came on at the end of his office, revealing a painting of similar size.

"What desperate faces, and so dark. Who are they?" Judith enquired.

"It's a painting I had done of Ruggero Raimondi and Angela Gheorghiu, from a photo of them in *Tosca*. I had it at home until recently, when I placed it there to go between your paintings."

"How on earth do paintings of deadly fungus relate to opera?" Knowing *Tosca* was an opera was the extent of her knowledge. She and her husband were fans of folk and jazz music.

"The man played the part of *Scarpia*, the most evil man in any opera. He tries to poison the mind of Tosca against her true love, so he can have his wicked way with her. I won't spoil it for you in case you ever do get to see it, in the theatre or on TV. Suffice to say, the music by Puccini is glorious and moving, though it is a tragedy." He could see her interest was superficial, so he changed subject and took one of her paintings to hold alongside the opera one.

"They will look all right here, won't they?" She stood up and moved about the room.

"Yes. I'm most surprised, but they go well together. Just one thing, though." She paused and sighed aloud.

"What's that?" Terry asked.

"They make the room very depressing. What will your clients think?"

"I'd thought of that. That's why I've had the lighting rearranged so nobody will notice them. I will just put the display lights on when I am alone."

"Won't that make you depressed?" She began to think she was dealing with a mentally disturbed person, who should seek help.

"It most circumstances, you could be right. However, in my case, it's a sort of reverse psychology. You see, during my formative years in the legal profession, I noticed that many of my peers became isolated from the real world through their status and their work. I decided that I would be more able to empathise with my clients if I were to keep both feet on the ground, so to speak. These paintings may be viewed as depressing by an uninformed observer, but they remind me firstly of my passion for opera and secondly of my fallibility as a human."

"I can see the counterbalance there." She frowned and

continued. "Why fallibility? How or when have you failed? Or is that too personal?" Terry looked at her and chuckled.

"Cross-examining the defence lawyer? You should be in my profession. Yes, I've failed. I failed to prove Jenkins's innocence. You won't want to hear more of that. I failed to take Arnold Phillips the whole way home for the sake of saving time and money. I saved an hour of my time at the cost to him of his whole life." His whole being reflected the sombreness of his words, and Judith became alarmed. She did not need a degree in Psychology to recognise that Terry could be on a slippery slope. Her customer and erstwhile adversary needed help.

"Why is the opera painting off-centre?" she asked, breaking his self-imposed gloom.

"Eh! Oh yes. There were pipes or something in these ancient walls, which prevented the electrician from putting a display light there." He stared at the wall as if to return to his former state and thoughts.

"The wall will only look balanced if you have four paintings on it. I could provide you with the perfect one to make up the four as it would also balance the subjects and mean you wouldn't have to hide them from public view. After all, if you do want to keep your feet on the ground, you should be sharing with others, not hiding things!" She was on her feet, lecturing him, and he enjoyed it.

"Are you trying to help me or just trying to sell more paintings?" he asked warmly.

"Both, I hope. I've a photo, which I've always cherished, of a young girl running through blossom falling like snow from a tree. It's a true picture of spring and it'd not only brighten up your gallery, but you as well. It'd remind you of new beginnings and new hope." Terry frowned as he peered at the end wall and imagined what she had suggested.

"I've lost on two counts. I still can't convince you about Jenkins and you've convinced me about my paintings. Send me your spring photo, and if I like it, the commission is yours, Mrs Donnelly."

"Please, call me Judith. You've already done so, and broken the formalities anyway," she interjected pleasantly.

"All right, and you should call me Terry then, short for Terrence," he added.

"No! Surely not!" She feigned a look of horrible surprise. "I thought it was short for Terrible." He grinned as he handed her the two paintings at arm's length and assessed their meeting.

"Curses! You found me out. I'm not used to being psychoanalysed in my own office. Now, before you uncover any more of my flaws, you'll have to excuse me. I've got to work extra hard to catch up with all this lost time and to earn the money for all these works of… Judith!" They shook hands as they both laughed, and she left to inquisitive stares from the pair in the outer office.

Back in his own office, Terry reflected on the meeting with Judith. *Why do the intelligent and attractive women I meet always turn out to be married? That Judith could sell me anything! I was like putty in her hands. It's wrong, I know, but I can hardly wait until our next encounter. To convince her about Maurice, of course*, he added to himself.

"Your post, Mr Schott." Eileen interrupted his thoughts.

"Oh, thanks, Eileen." He tried to turn his dreamy look into one suitable for a lawyer considering a serious case.

I must be more careful – make sure my expression does not mirror my thoughts. Our Eileen sees everything, and like the romantic she is, she's always trying to get me attached. I think she hates to see a man still single at my age. To her, it's the ultimate challenge. Perhaps I can find an excuse for my next meeting with the sexy Mrs Donnelly to be on neutral ground, away from prying eyes. What am I thinking? There lies the slippery slope! I must get her out of my mind. Face the facts, Schott! You're a lawyer in a country town and mustn't get involved with clients – or married women. Still, she is certainly a highly *desirable woman. Stop!* **Stop!** *Aha! The Nettles case.* He reached for the file connected with an envelope he had opened, and studied it.

CHAPTER 19

"Do you think your Major Stubbs could produce a photofit of the Malayans?" Tyler asked Derek urgently, as they stood beside Birdie's bed. The tight security surrounding her had enabled the inspector to know her brother was visiting her.

"He's hardly **my** Major Stubbs, particularly after the way he almost threw me out. No, it was my boss, Terry Schott, who got him to talk. To answer your question, **no**. You'll have to produce actual photos to stand any chance of Stubbs identifying them."

"Okay. We'll see what we can do. If he does come up with any new information, please make certain it comes to me. The fact these Malayans exist is being kept secret, even from other police personnel. You can see what Masood's associates did to Birdie. That's why she's under constant guard and nobody else knows the full facts." Tyler gave him his mobile number. "I'll leave you with Birdie now she's waking." He shook Derek's hand and left.

Lying in a hospital bed and being pampered made Birdie feel guilty despite the pain. She'd had an operation to re-pin her shoulder and reset her forearm; the ribs were left to reset themselves. Her bruises were slowly disappearing, and her eyes were almost back to normal. She had only been there for five days, yet it seemed an eternity. The cheering news that Ivor had pulled through was offset by the depressing statement that he may never regain full use of his legs. Although she knew Tyler and Bennett would be more than capable of carrying on with the Houghbury-Masood link, she still wanted to be involved.

They were advised by Birdie's doctor and the consultant not to get her excited in her current condition. Thus, they did tell her enough to quench her thirst for information, but nothing to rouse her mentally or physically. The news that Doug Evans was back on the Masood case, after being kept away by Thwaite, helped her relax a little. *If he is anywhere near as good as Ivor has told me, then the case is in the best of hands*, she thought, though her curiosity was aroused. *Just what sort of person is this paragon?*

It was Derek, who, in telling her about his talk with Tyler, did get her excited.

"I told them what the major said. Obviously, I didn't tell them the full consequences," she whispered.

"What consequences?" Derek regretted telling her as soon as he saw her wince with pain.

"I checked one Asian, an Arun Ramas, who may've been the Malayan driver, only to find he'd been hanged in his prison cell. If the major was shown his photo, he might provide a positive identification."

"Okay, I'll tell Tyler. When are you getting out of here?" Derek looked at her anxiously.

"Ah! Therein lies the rub," she replied grandly.

"Forsooth, what could'st thou mean?" Derek fired back at her.

"I could be out in a couple of days. However, my limited movement, plus the fact I live alone, plus the security requirements, means I'll be here for at least another week or more." Her vexation was umistakable.

"That's easy to cover. I'll take you back to stay with us until you're better." He grasped her left hand and she smiled back at him.

"But what about security? I don't want to put you and yours at risk." Her smile faded as she reviewed the possible consequences. He squeezed her hand.

"Don't worry about that. I've got a couple of days to sort something out. If I can't, then you're stuck, my little sister!" he stated very seriously, but she laughed aloud and then grimaced as it hurt her ribs. "Why do you laugh?"

"I shouldn't have. It's just that my wounded colleague in the next room is a good friend and calls me little sister!"

"I didn't realise you had a boyfriend." He grinned at her suggestively.

"Friend, yes, Derek. Not my lover! We've become very close during this investigation, but it's purely platonic."

"Oh good! Terry will be pleased to hear that," Derek blurted out.

"Terry?" Birdie was mystified.

"Yes, Mr Schott, my employer. You met him when you visited us."

Yes, I remember him, quite a pleasant man – for a lawyer," she qualified. "Why'll he be pleased exactly?"

"He's not said anything, but I think he found you good company!"

"Oh dear! Perhaps I'd better not stay with you after all. Apart from anything else, he's certainly not my type."

"That's no reason not to stay with me, is it?" Derek protested.

"Well, I'd probably meet him if I did stay with you, and if he made advances, which of course I'd reject, he may hold it against you."

"Never! He's not interested in you in that way, and he's not that sort!"

"He's not what sort? Do you mean he won't actually attack me?" she said, cross-examining him.

"Don't try your police tactics on me, Birdie. You know full well what I meant. He's not the sort to hold a grudge against me because you're rude or indifferent towards him. He's a very fair man." He admonished her as he would have when they were kids.

"That's strange. We must be talking about different people. The lawyer I met was definitely not fair." She paused for effect. "He looked more like a dark Spaniard than a blond Saxon." As she grinned at her brother, he shook his fist at her in mock rage.

"Very funny! I'd put you over my knee if you weren't incapacitated," he threatened.

"If I weren't incapacitated, you wouldn't be able to – any longer," she added, as she remembered their childhood fights. "Or do you think you're better than that Sid Cracken?" Derek ignored her threats and humour, and returned to the matter at hand.

"Anyway, I could be totally wrong. Terry's not one to show his emotions, even laughing inwardly at people's idiosyncrasies. Of course, I can inform him that you have a boyfriend. That would be easier for all our sakes. Anyway, our secretary, Eileen, thinks he fancies the mother of the little boy at the heart of our case. I can't believe it as she's married, and Terry is always very proper in his behaviour. But then, Eileen *is* a dreadful romantic."

It was agreed with the doctor she could leave in two days. Agreeing it with the police was much more difficult because of the security requirements. Though they thought

Masood's mob might no longer see her and Ivor as having damaging evidence, they knew the gang's honour demanded early vengeance. Vengeance for uncovering their inside man, Thwaite. To keep her potential move secret, Tyler contacted Chief Inspector Watson of the Houghbury CID. Watson agreed to handle the matter himself. He would check on any safeguards required for Birdie as, even in the West Country, he had heard of Masood's reputation.

Driving around his patch, he carefully observed the Lee household and its environs. He checked all approaches for the possibility of an attacker getting in unseen. Then he looked in the local telephone directories. He reported his findings directly to Tyler. Derek's house was too open to intruders and it was listed in the directories. With recent austerity measures, Houghbury Police would be unable to provide adequate cover. Tyler contacted Derek and explained the move was not possible, and was told about Arun Ramas. Later that day, Terry noted Derek's faraway, gloomy look.

"Is there a problem, Derek?" he enquired softly.

"Yes, but it's a private one, so I couldn't bother you with it." He tried unsuccessfully to smile.

"Come on, Derek. We've worked together long enough. I might be able to help you. After all, a problem shared... as they say." He pulled up a chair and sat beside his assistant.

"It's Birdie. You know she and her boyfriend are in hospital after their set-to with crooks?" He looked carefully at Terry.

"Yes. Though I didn't know it was her boyfriend." Despite his courtroom training, he failed to disguise completely an element of surprise and perhaps disappointment.

"Well, she can leave hospital tomorrow if she has somewhere to go. I wanted her to come to me, but the police said no, because where I live is considered a security risk. I've been trying to think of somewhere nearby that would be safe and let me visit her." He sighed worriedly.

"No problem!" Terry announced grandly. "She can stay in my spare room. My apartment building has a first-class security system, including CCTV and an alarm system linked to the police. She'd have her own space and we can both keep an eye on her. To satisfy the police, I can change the entrance code to my apartment so only you and I and your sister would know it. I can even arrange for my cleaner to only come when I'm there. Mind you, I'll expect you to play your part. I keep very little food in, so you can do the shopping for whatever you think she'll fancy." Derek looked at his boss with amazement and pondered on the offer.

"You'll have to let us pay a proportion of the overheads. What about any medical visitors?" He tried to think of all possible problems.

"Fair shares! You provide the food and drink, if she's allowed any, and the rest is down to me. As to visitors, I'll leave that to you. If you need to absent yourself from the office to accompany a doctor or nurse, I'll understand. What about her boyfriend?"

"We needn't worry about him. He'll be in hospital for some time yet, and when he does get out, I doubt if he'll be in any condition to visit her."

Derek phoned Tyler immediately. As the latter was unavailable, he was careful not to leave an explanatory message, only that Sergeant Lee's brother wanted to speak to him.

Eventually, her move was agreed after consultation with Chief Inspector Watson, who knew the building she would be staying in. To cover her destination as far as possible, Tyler collected her from hospital and drove to the police station. There, he swapped cars and used an indirect route out of London, to be sure he was not being followed. Then he transferred her to Derek's car in a previously agreed quiet spot. Then Derek transferred her to Watson's car outside Houghbury, and so she eventually arrived at Terry's place.

"I'm sorry to hear how bad your boyfriend is," Terry said, as he explained the layout of his abode. Fortunately, Derek had explained Ivor's new status on the way from London, so she was prepared.

"Thank you, Terry. Is it all right if I call you Terry?"

"Certainly, and I'd like to call you Birdie, as we'll be... er... living together." He sounded a trifle embarrassed to mention it, though it did fit her pre-formed opinion of him. Watson deposited her two heavy suitcases in the middle of the lounge and shook her hand tentatively.

"Let me know if you need any help, Sergeant Lee. I have to get back to the station before questions are asked. It's an honour to shake the hand that floored Cracken – and live to tell the tale," he added with a laugh.

"Thank you so much, sir. At the moment, a child could floor me." She forced a smile and watched him leave. The simple efforts involved in her transfer were more painful than she had imagined. She turned slowly to Terry.

"And thank you for letting me stay here. It's very kind of you. I hope I won't upset your routine too much." Her breathing was still difficult if she exercised or talked too vigorously.

Then in a sudden devil-may-care attitude, Terry bowed low with a sweep of his arms. "Honoured to be of service, fair maiden!" he announced with a laugh.

This did not fit her picture of him. Pleased as she was to be out of hospital, she had some misgivings about staying with Terry. She had imagined how dreary it could be and how awkward it could be trying to make polite conversation with this wooden lawyer. *Perhaps I should brush up on interesting court cases so we do have something to discuss; or perhaps I should keep to my room until Derek appears. Is* this *a part of his real character, or is he putting on a special show just for my sake?*

Her police training made her scrutinise each room she was shown, looking for clues. Clues to what? His personality, she guessed. The rooms were bigger than she expected and the décor reflected the male occupant. There were some paintings, which impressed her, and he had a good selection of non-legal books. There was one large cabinet in the lounge that caught her attention, as it seemed out of place. She made a mental note to check it when he was not there.

Her room had a small double bed, a good-sized wardrobe, a small TV and a bedside radio. There was a small table and a chair facing the window, which had a clear view across some of the town's historic rooftops, though, at that time, dusk was creeping over them. Terry hoisted her cases on top of the bed with surprising ease, and left to make some tea. Instinctively scrutinising the room, she decided it was rarely used for any visitors. Such furniture as there was looked suspiciously new. The plain off-white walls must have been the original décor, and desperately needed some pictures to soften them. Even the bed and its covers were unadorned, softened only by the large bunches of flowers he had gone to the trouble of placing on either side of the bed.

Gently removing her coat, she rejoined him in the lounge for tea and a biscuit. He nervously explained in excessive detail where things could be found and how to operate the various gadgets. She was unable to disguise her tiredness, and he excused himself and left for his office. Taking her routine painkillers, she lay beside her cases, fully clothed, and slept.

It was completely dark when she awoke to find the cases had been removed from the bed and she was covered by the bedspread. There was a trace of light coming under her door and sounds of movement from the other side. Her mouth was parched, so she used the bathroom and cleaned her teeth. Not wishing to appear ungrateful, she thought she should speak to Terry before retiring for the night. He was busy preparing the dining table for two persons.

"It's very kind of you, Terry, but I don't think I could manage dinner tonight." He was startled by her sudden arrival and looked at her questioningly. Then a look of realisation produced a deep laugh.

"This isn't for dinner! It's for breakfast! You've been asleep for over twelve hours. Your door was ajar when I returned last night, and I noticed the curtains were open. With all this worry about your security, I went to close them. That's when I removed your cases and covered you up. I hope you don't mind." Again, he seemed embarrassed, and she began to feel sorry for imposing on this confirmed bachelor.

"I couldn't ask for better care. I know I was tired last night, but I must've taken a sleeping pill with my painkillers by accident. If you'll excuse me, I'll put on fresh clothes and have a shower. Then, if it's not too much trouble, I'd love to join you for breakfast." Her mind was clearing now.

"Might I be so bold as to suggest you put on fresh clothes **after** taking a shower!" He laughed again, and it was so infectious she almost forgot her wounds and joined in.

The atmosphere was fraught during their light meal together. The considerable discomfort she endured during her ablutions and in dressing made her angry. When she was in that state of mind, she became Sergeant – 'Ice Maiden' – Lee once more. Forgotten were his kindness, consideration and humour. Instead, she viewed him as a typical lawyer, a representative of the profession she had often crossed swords with in court. A profession she despised as being detached from reality, unlike her own employment. She would tolerate this man for her brother's sake and for her own convenience.

A woman in my sanctuary! I'd not given it a second thought when I made my offer to Derek. Now it's actually happening! Perhaps my appreciation of his sister's abilities and my sense of duty to Derek have breached the defences I've built around my emotions over years. The sound of someone in my shower has definitely added spice to my imagination. No! It is a sick woman entrusted to me by her brother – my assistant. Yet, now I'm about to have breakfast with a woman – a fairly desirable woman! – at my own table? I can just imagine the possible implications. Not least how it'd be presented in court, and in the press. I can see the headlines now: 'LOCAL LAWYER FOUND IN CLANDESTINE LOVE NEST!' Good job this is being kept secret for security or it—

"You shouldn't have waited for me. I'm sure you've plenty of work to be getting on with."

Her interruption broke his darkening thoughts, putting him mentally off-balance. Looking at her, all fresh and sparkling from her ablutions, he was overpowered by lust. *Forget toast, there's a woman in my home and I could eat **her** for breakfast!* He shook his head vigorously, trying to rid himself of animal thoughts.

"Are you okay? Sorry if I startled you." *This is one strange man,* she thought. *I don't know how Derek can work for him.*

"No. No. It's me that's sorry. I was deep in thought about one of my cases, when I should've been making the tea. Or would you prefer coffee?" *Lying and clutching at straws! I'd never get away with it in court. I'm not in court! I'm in my own home, about to have the first meal of the day with one sensual female, and I'm not dreaming.* He steeled himself and raised his protective barriers.

"Coffee, please." Her social skills deserted her. *I'm in the home of a man who doesn't seem to be completely with me. Is he thinking about work? My police skills inform me he's lying. Then there was that disturbing look on his face when I first spoke to him.* Her official persona returned and she became frostier than her nickname.

The quick meal lasted an eternity for each of them. Conversation was limited to the necessities. Neither could wait for him to leave. He was thinking how he could have misjudged this cold person. She was thinking her judgement of lawyers was correct. *They are all overformal and underemotional!*

"Make yourself at home," he said, without sincerity. "There are CDs and DVDs in that cabinet. I doubt if they're to **your** taste. Let me know if there's anything I can get for you. Derek will be round later." He regretted saying it so sarcastically and hoped she hadn't noticed. *Like it or not, I've offered her my hospitality and that's what I must give her.*

I object to the manner in which he spoke to me, but I will tolerate it to keep the peace in his home, thought Birdie.

After he departed, she turned her thoughts to Ivor and his condition. Inevitably, comparison with Terry occurred. *I wish I was with him instead of a man with whom I've nothing in common. There'd been those few moments at our first meeting when I believed him to be a fellow art lover, yet there's no evidence of it here. I'll get depressed if I don't do something to take my mind out of this place, I know. I could watch TV. At least he's got a good-sized one in the lounge, and with surround sound! He doesn't need that for game shows, surely? Now I'm being rude! Let me see what corny rubbish he* has *to offer in the way of DVDs.*

She perused the room and decided they must be stored in the large corner cupboard. She unlocked it with trepidation. Would it be legal codswallop, documentaries, or… she hesitated… or erotica? Throwing the doors open, she stepped back with a gasp of disbelief! There were a few documentaries and comedies. The rest were all **opera**! Could she have misjudged him? She consoled herself by considering the operas must have been a job lot he bought by mistake. **Or** he could have got them for show, as some people do with books on their shelves. Books that never get read!

Which one do I watch first? La Traviata? No, it'd make me think of poor Ivor. Ah, one of my favourites, **Tosca**! *The film made at the actual sites in Rome, with Gheorghiu, Alagna and Raimondi.* She was going to make coffee and changed to tea when she noticed he had Darjeeling. With a mug of tea, a biscuit and a box of tissues, she settled down to watch *Tosca*.

CHAPTER 20

Poor Spencer died and went to heaven. An angel met him at the pearly gates and led him down a long corridor. They passed a room from which came merry boisterous singing. "Who's in there?" asked Spencer.

"That's New-age Christians," the angel replied. The next room emitted lovely choral singing.

"Well, who are they?" enquired Spencer.

"That's the Welsh Baptists," answered the angel.

At every room they passed, the angel explained whom the occupants were, according to the different sounds being made. Then, as they were about to pass one particular room, the angel motioned for Spencer to be quiet. Further on, he asked the angel why they had to be quiet passing that room. The angel looked at him, smiled and replied very quietly, "That's the Roman Catholics. They think they're the only ones up here!"

The email made Sean laugh. He had never received a joke before, and he appreciated Miguel's attempt to cheer him up. He had spotted the one from his Spanish friend immediately when he started clearing his email in-tray. *It must have been sent soon after we parted. How am I to reply? I've not reached any decisions, and I consider it too soon to tell him about Maria. I must email her immediately, even if it's only to let her know I'm home, well, and thinking of her.* When he had finished and pressed the send button, he noticed with a degree of panic that he had signed it – *Love, Sean.*

Has my holiday really caused my heart to rule my head? he worried. *I'd expected my return home would also return me to my pre-holiday ways of life and thinking. Perhaps it'll take longer than I thought. Now for Miguel. The best reply I can give him presently would be a joke to show I appreciated his. Where do I get a joke? The ones in my sermons would be out of place in an email.* He decided he would reciprocate with a religious anecdote, as follows:

> *A Catholic priest and a rabbi met on a liner. They spent many hours debating which was the true religion. The ship hit an iceberg and began sinking. As they were getting into the lifeboats, the priest saw the rabbi cross himself.*
>
> *"My son!" said the priest. "You have crossed yourself and are saved as a good Catholic!"*
>
> *"Nonsense!" replied the rabbi. "I was not crossing myself. I was just checking that I had everything of importance." He demonstrated by touching his face, his crotch, his left and right breasts while saying – "Spectacles, testicles, watch and wallet."*

Emails cleared or replied to as necessary, Sean met his replacement priest and gave him a few pointers about various members of the congregation. He still had his old room in the priest's house, and he retired there for an early night. *I'll put off seeing the bishop until tomorrow.* Reflecting on his experiences in Malaga, he fell asleep. The bishop enquired about his health and holiday, leaving it to Sean to raise more serious topics.

"My vacation was invaluable in helping me to review my beliefs. However, I've not reached an answer as to where my long-term future lies. I realise I can't possibly resume my duties here. If you agree, I'd like to spend the next few weeks as holiday relief in new areas, where my faux pas is not known," Sean requested.

"Actually, that'd be very suitable, as your replacement in Houghbury was due to cover for Father O'Reilly at Bellborough. The town is outside the TV region covering Houghbury, so you'll be a stranger there. It's for five weeks – Father O'Reilly is making a pilgrimage to the **Holy Land**."

Sean understood the implication of the last remark. *O'Reilly is a devout priest doing the proper thing, whereas I have spent a month lazing in Spain.*

In the few days before he left for Bellborough, he inevitably met several of his former congregation. The reception he received in most cases was decidedly cool. A few adopted a more 'Christian' attitude and enquired how he was. Although he was sad to be leaving Houghbury, he welcomed the challenge of his new assignment, however temporary it was. *One pressing engagement I have to fulfil before leaving is to visit Maurice Jenkins.*

He cleared the visit with Terry Schott first. The latter was delighted with the suggestion and explained all that had happened. He told Sean how such a meeting, handled properly, could help Maurice's depression. Maurice was astounded to be told he had a visitor who was a priest.

"I know I'm in poor condition after my fight with Sid, but I don't think I'm ready for the last rites!" he joked, as he trudged to the appointment. He laughed again when he realised the priest had come to receive absolution from him. Sean apologised profusely for his outburst on that fateful day. He explained how the incident had changed his life.

"Bless you, Father, for you've sinned. You must say five unjail Jenkins," he joked, seeing the funny side of the situation.

"I believe I will as I'll explain in a minute. Is it all right if I call you Maurice?" He smiled nervously at his unusual mentor.

"I've no phone, so you can't call me." He grinned at Sean to show he was being funny and continued. "To my face, you may address me as Maurice, and to other parts of my body, but not Tuesday!" His light-hearted approach was infectious, and Sean knew there was a catch.

"Why not Tuesday?" he asked, dreading the answer.

"Well, my name is Maurice, so don't call me Tuesday!" He paused to laugh and enquired, "As I'm not religious and you're not my father, what can I call you?" He raised his eyebrows quizzically and waited.

"True. Don't call me farther or nearer. My name is Sean," he retaliated, and this little repartee dissolved any awkwardness in their relationship.

"So you've suffered as I have," Maurice suggested.

"Not entirely, Maurice. I'm still considering where my future path lies. Not only have I had second thoughts about my true calling, I've had them about your alleged crime."

Sean went on to explain how nobody really sees anything until something unusual draws his or her attention to it. He mentioned the incident of the woman's hat in front of Miguel's car. Their relationship evolved rapidly, and Sean unburdened his quandary about Maria, as if to a real confessor. They did find parallels in their respective positions and agreed to another meeting when Sean returned from Bellborough.

The benefit of the Church's bureaucracy and uniformity was that Sean soon fitted in with his new duties. The people were different yet conformed to a mould he had come to expect. His stimuli were his sermons and his daily emails to Spain. *Strange that one moment of foolishness altered my cosy existence, forced me to move and produced two valuable friends. Friends I've had more contact with than anyone since college. My relationship with each of them's not advanced since I left Spain. I find it difficult to express my true feelings or have deep debates through the impersonality of emails. Sometimes, I sense each of them is waiting for a positive decision from me.*

That'll have to bide its time until I find answers. From where? Divine inspiration? My mind through analysis? Or from my heart? As a priest, I'd controlled my emotions until that fateful event in Houghbury. Since then, there've been those moments of weakness in Malaga. Weaknesses? There was Christ's passion and that of legions of great minds throughout history. Were my Malaga moments weaknesses or building blocks helping to make me a better person? Am I being overcautious about making a decision because of the Jenkins incident?

Noticing he had been subconsciously doodling flowers on his paper, he crumpled it and threw it into the waste bin. Taking a new sheet, he started to write his sermon again. *Where to start? Of course... with my earlier contemplations.* So he based it on the topic of passion.

Bellborough Church was quite modern; made of brick with some striking, coloured glass windows. The altar was a single slab of slate mounted on granite pillars. The contrast to Sean's old church could not have been greater, so it was a surprise to find the majority of the congregation seemed older and more conformist than at Houghbury. *Conformist! Conforming to what? My ideas of wooden worshippers? Or is it what the hierarchy expects? Perhaps the bishop could see the devil in me, because I have decided to make my sermon controversial. It should awaken many from their too-comfortable religious duties. Hopefully, it will inspire them to renew their faith.*

Access to this church was very limited due to excessive vandalism in recent months. Although Sean had a key, he knew the verger was obsessed with security and had to double-check all doors and windows after each service. Fortunately, the rather bare interior meant miscreants could not easily hide. Due to the pleasant weather, and perhaps people's interest in this new young priest, there was a refreshingly large congregation on Sunday. His sermon appeared to be received with good attention, as evidenced by the number who questioned him about it afterwards.

"Do **you** think we should give in to our basic emotions?" a rather grand lady demanded, with nods of agreement from the others.

"As a civilised society, we've evolved a culture over hundreds of years, which teaches us to restrain many of our basic emotions." He could see many were trying to get a word in, so he continued quickly and slightly louder to ensure they all heard. "**By basic emotions**, I mean certain animal instincts, which we have to control to be able to live together. These instincts are mostly outlawed, such as murder, rape, assault and theft. Then there are some emotions that can be accepted, largely because they do not harm anyone; in fact, they could be beneficial." Pausing for a deep breath, the self-elected spokeswoman leapt to the attack.

"Exactly **which** emotions are you eluding to?" she enquired with much pomp.

"I'm sure *you* could name many." Sean looked straight into the woman's eyes and smiled. "Let me help you by naming a few. Firstly, there's the most powerful emotion – love. It's definitely the one where the heart rules the head. Then—"

He was interrupted by someone at the back of the group muttering, "How would he know?"

"As a Catholic priest, I am trained to have my head rule my heart in most matters. Though I must **confess**," he paused as he emphasised the word 'confess', "it is often very hard for me. I'm only human. I could give you examples, but I'm not here to act as your role model. Instead, I'd like each of you to consider moments in your own lives when heart and head've been in conflict. Think of the emotions that can make us better people by helping others, such as sympathy, sadness, or straightforward kindness. Think also of the emotions to avoid or suppress, such as anger and hatred. I'm sure you can each make a list."

He was moving to leave when one wag said, "Are you giving us homework?"

"No, but I hope you do carry thoughts of your beliefs into your everyday lives." Sean enjoyed discussions with his two Spanish friends, not with this group of 'Sunday Christians'.

"Father O'Reilly doesn't give sermons causing after-service debates," the spokeswoman announced frostily.

"I am sorry. As devout Christians, I thought you'd welcome hearing another view of our faith." Sean had not slept well the night before, and this woman's overbearing attitude was wearing his patience thin. *I'm just repeating my sermon*, he thought. "If you'll excuse me, I must disrobe before the church is locked up." The group left grudgingly, with the spokeswoman still pontificating.

Later, as he was walking to the rectory, a young couple stopped him. "Father Anderson. We'd just like to tell you how much we enjoyed your sermon," the woman enthused, and the man added, "It was a breath of fresh air, and it will certainly get the old biddies talking. That's certain," he added for good measure.

Sean shook their hands and thanked them. His tread was much lighter for the rest of his short walk. *I'm not isolated,* he thought. *There are people who can understand the message I'm trying to convey. Perhaps if I stir them up a bit more, I can get my supporters to balance the complainers, by telling the bishop.*

In his room, he tried listing his thoughts about his future. *It's hard to quantify and results in deadlock always. Do I ask God or my friends for help, or do I wait for some external factor to alter the balance? I love my work as a priest and can see no other role for me. I've faith in God, yet I can understand the views of non-believers. I've no homosexual desires, but I did enjoy the company of Miguel. Lastly, but not least, I've strong desires and other emotions for a woman I only knew for ten days.* As he pictured Maria, he finally went to sleep.

The next morning, he checked his emails. Another joke and a conundrum from Miguel. A daily update from Maria, which informed him that she was going on a refresher course in Madrid. She was going by coach, as it would give her a chance to relax and enjoy the scenery. She would contact him when she got back in a week. Sean sent an immediate reply wishing her a good time. Feeling more comfortable after a good sleep had relieved his Sunday stress, he added, *Not too good a time or I will be very jealous. Love, Sean.*

After he pressed the send key, he reread his email. *Oh dear,* he thought. *Have I let my guard down so much I have committed myself to her? Is that a bad thing? Has the sanctuary of the Church, as witnessed yesterday, become too much for me? My faith's as strong as ever. What do I really want?*

The debate raged in his head for the next week. It was only disturbed by what felt like minor duties and drafting the next sermon. The latter was much easier as he did the time-honoured method of elaborating on text from the Bible. Even so he inserted, in his own terms, what he intended to be a couple of rabble-rousers. These caused the split in the congregation he had anticipated, and he rode the ensuing storm without too much difficulty.

Monday came and there was no email from Maria. Sitting down to breakfast, he perused the newspaper absent-mindedly. One small item caught his eye – 'Tragic coach crash near Malaga'. His heart seemed to stop and breathing was difficult. He read on – 'Most of the passengers and the driver were killed outright when a coach from Madrid careered off a mountain road'.

There were no more details, as there were no British involved. Desperately, he used the internet to get a Spanish newscast for the Malaga region. Heart pounding, he read the list of deceased, hoping… hoping – *No! There it was: M Caballeros.*

"THERE IS NO GOD!" he screamed. It brought the housemaid dashing into the room. With misting eyes and unable to speak for the lump in his throat, he waved her away.

In moments of maximum stress, you should keep as busy as possible, or so the experts say. Sean did just that. He kept exceptionally busy by constantly exceeding his terms of reference. He visited all the old and sick in the area. On one unfortunate occasion, he was visiting someone in a care home and found the residents listening to music. It was *Ave Maria*! It made time stand still for him and, try as he might, he could not prevent a tear welling up in his eyes. One of the staff noticed and assured him that the woman he was visiting was healthy apart from her arthritis. The comment freed him from his time warp.

He undertook menial tasks around the church, much to the surprise of the regular churchgoers. At the end of each highly active day, he would finish as he had started, with a brisk walk around the town and parts of the nearby countryside. He kept up his email correspondence with Miguel and still omitted any reference to Maria; not from diplomacy, as before, but because it was too painful. He was trying to hide her existence and his feelings for her from everyone, including himself.

Should I contact her family? That would be the priestly thing to do; I can't. Why? Because the pain of her loss is being replaced with remorse and bitterness. Remorse that I've not been brave enough to seize life with all my abilities and commit totally to a woman I now know I loved absolutely. I'm tempted to join Miguel in Spain. However, he was rational enough to know that a partnership or even close friendship formed in the aftermath of such a loss needed the passage of more time for its certainty.

As his final week at Bellborough drew to a close, he researched the internet for openings more suitable for his current mood. Something that would keep him fully occupied and would use his people skills. Something that would get him away from the church and his familiar surroundings. Destiny called! A multi-faith organisation wanted volunteers for a six-month tour of duty in central Africa. The exact location would depend on current requirements in the various countries. He applied immediately.

It might be dangerous and I might be rash to apply, but it is just the penance I feel I deserve. Some people could think me brave to undertake such a task. I know it is cowardice. I am using it to escape from the anguish of my current life.

He was accepted subject to references and an interview, and he notified the bishop immediately. His Grace was relieved to find one of his staffing problems had been resolved. He agreed to give proper references and a suitable early release date for Sean to leave church and country. Sean finished his duties, shutting out all memories of his vacation in Spain. He blocked them so completely he forgot to send a final email to Miguel.

Honouring his promise, he visited Maurice again. He explained how fate had determined his future.

"So you'll understand why I won't be visiting you in prison again. I'm sure you'll be a free man when I return. Is there anything I can do for you in the few days I have left here?"

"There is one thing you could do, which would best be done by a priest. You know I want to help the Phillips family. Well, I wonder if you'd visit them and smooth the way for me to help them?" It was a shot in the dark. Sean readily agreed as it would keep his mind off his own troubles.

There was an emptiness in Helen Phillips, which her children and daily chores covered enough to ease the pain of her loss. Not a day went by without her thinking of Arnold, but she could never dwell on sad thoughts with the demands of life pressing on her. Outwardly and inwardly, she was a very changed person. To strangers, she was still a very attractive young woman; to friends and acquaintances, she was no longer the radiant Helen they had all admired. Her eyes were altered from bright and welcoming to narrow and cold. Her whole visage was older and less friendly, reflecting normal years of trials and tribulations condensed into a moment of loss. A loss that would last her a lifetime. Comfort food was starting to disguise her figure, while carelessness showed in her apparel, her hair, her makeup and her demeanour.

Sean Anderson felt compelled to visit her after the

reconciliation with Maurice. He comprehended Maurice's sense of obligation towards Arnold's family, and his difficulty in helping when she had proclaimed her hatred for him. He discovered from Terry Schott when she was most likely to be at home, and caught a bus accordingly. Though there were few other passengers at that time of day, he was conscious of their glances in his direction. He had worn his priest's garb to facilitate the meeting.

What a difference a collar makes! Mine protects – a jewelled one beautifies – a metal one manacles – and a rope one kills. This trip truly is a penance! Travelling by bus to meet... what? Probably some dull, dumpy peasant woman whose only topic is the weather. What is happening to me? Am I really becoming that contemptible? Never prejudge! Still, it could be hard to fill the hour until the next bus back.

When Helen opened her door, she was as surprised to find a priest as he was an attractive woman, however unkempt. After introductions, Sean explained his regrettable part in Maurice's incarceration, and how he now realised he was almost certainly innocent. He had been made to suffer unduly for an act of heroism and was also suffering pangs of guilt over Arnold's death. Sean pointed out that this was totally wrong. Far from causing Arnold's death, he had befriended him in an unwritten contract of mutual advancement.

The fact both men had suffered indirectly as a result of their agreement was neither man's fault. Who could have foreseen that a child falling off his scooter would have such dire consequences? He explained how Maurice was overcoming his bitterness for being imprisoned, and was anxious to prepare for release when the true details were produced at his appeal. Maurice had tried to help her husband and was very keen to help her and her children in any way he could.

"You say you're going to Africa. Are you a missionary?" Helen enquired disinterestedly.

"Not exactly. I've resigned from my post in the Catholic Church, and am leaving the country for central Africa to help with aid work," he admitted.

"Leaving sounds a bit final! So does resigning from the Church. What happened to your calling and your faith?" This unusual man intrigued her, and curiosity about him broke her lethargy.

"My outburst when Maurice Jenkins was arrested was seen on TV and resulted in me taking a month's leave in Spain. I made some friends there; one taught me to question my beliefs; the other made me question my celibacy." He hoped his summary would close the painful subject.

"Your celibacy! Were your friends male or female?" Her interruption forced him to amplify.

"The first is an atheist hairdresser – a man. The second was a nurse – a young woman." He stopped as he tried to hide his emotion at the thought of Maria.

"Was a nurse?" Her curiosity was relentless. Sean swallowed and took a deep breath.

"She died." Sean pretended to cough as he fought back an impending flood. *I wish I had never come. For a rustic with limited education, she is far too incisive.* He got that right! She may have been preoccupied with daily living, but she was a keen observer of nature and people. Arnold had once called her a regular Sherlock Holmes. She studied her quarry's face carefully before offering her opinion.

"I think the hairdresser is probably effeminate, and being an atheist in a strongly religious country, he could be gay. Both facts would've taken you out of your comfort zone. The mere mention that the nurse died, without any further details, makes me think the subject is too painful for you. I think you're in love with her and her death's the trigger for your current move."

As she finished, instead of feeling triumphant at her analysis, she felt despicable. *How Arnold would have despised me for being so cruel to a man who had come to help me. Have I become so bitter that I'm ready to bite any hand offered me?*

"I'm sorry. I shouldn't have said any of that. I'd no right to ask your details, let alone analyse them. Please forgive me." She was at a loss as to what else to say when she noticed his eyes watering. Without thinking further, her maternal instinct took over and she went to him. She knelt beside his chair and put an arm around him. He sobbed on her shoulder; all his reserve and the resentment for his fate were washed away. He clung to her as if to life itself. Finally, she pulled away and, without a word, went to the kitchen to make the English cure-all: some tea.

"Thank you for the tea and for being there for me. I've been avoiding the truth and seem to have lost the ability to resolve problems through faith. You're so right! Miguel is a homosexual, and I loved and still love Maria. We never consummated our love as I had to weigh my feelings for her with my position as a priest. I came to the conclusion that she was all that mattered. Then she was killed in a coach crash. I resigned from the Church and sought work where I'd help others and lose myself."

He was calmer as he supped his miracle beverage. She remained silent and expressionless. "I've not had time to visit you earlier. If you'll pardon the expression, you are one of the loose ends I had to tie up before leaving the country," he explained, trying to lighten the atmosphere. Finally, Helen's expression changed.

"Good heavens! I've never thought of myself as a loose end, particularly as for me, everything, from time to money, is so tight," she laughed, and Sean no longer considered himself an unwanted embarrassment.

"Can you forgive Maurice?" he entreated hopefully, returning to his mission. Her smile faded and she looked from him to a photo of Arnold on her mantelpiece. She gazed at it in silence for a few moments and bit her bottom lip.

"You're right. I've no real reason to dislike... er... Maurice, and Arnold wouldn't want me to. Perhaps you'd let him know before you leave for Africa?" she asked softly.

"Of course I will. He'll be very grateful, I know. He wondered if he could help you financially at all?"

"No, it's okay. The insurance paid off the mortgage, and apart from a small allowance from Arnold's work, I've a small income of my own. We get by."

"I'd like to help you myself, but I've only got three days left. If you **can** think of anything, here's my phone number." He gave her his card, knowing it was a futile gesture.

Am I dreaming? Are my emotions rebounding from the loss of Maria? Whatever it is, he reflected, as she showed him out, *I've bonded more closely with this lovely woman than any other, except Maria. I visited her at Maurice's request, to explain his position and desire to help. I finish up revealing my own problems. It's a good thing I'm leaving the country, or I might find myself bounding into love with this highly desirable widow.*

As he was leaving to catch the bus, her kids returned from school. They were intrigued to see a priest coming out of their home, and, full of trepidation, they dashed inside. They were relieved to find Helen was all right and pestered her about her visitor. She explained as much as she considered their young minds would grasp while she prepared their dinner. One thing they did latch onto was that their father had a friend who was in prison, and they pestered her to tell them more about him. Reluctantly, she gave them more details, omitting her earlier dislike of Maurice. The bitterness, which had started as hatred for Maurice, had eased a bit since the unexpected meeting with Sean.

"If he's innocent, Mummy, why's he still in prison?" Nicola reasoned.

"Because he has to wait for the outcome of an appeal, which is going to produce witnesses that were not available at the time he was convicted." It seemed strange to be speaking on behalf of the very person she detested, though perhaps she shouldn't.

"Why weren't they available, Mummy?" Roger joined in.

"Well, one didn't know what had happened until Mr Jenkins's case and guilty verdict appeared in the local newspaper. Another one, whose children Mr Jenkins had often looked after, was in France when it happened. And the third and most important witness doesn't live in this area, and has only just been found." She gave them the facts as well as she could remember them.

"Poor man!" Nicola exclaimed. "It's almost as if he's been punished for doing a good deed."

"Bet he's angry! He'll want revenge when he gets out!" Roger proclaimed loudly.

"No, he won't! He's not like one of your cartoon characters, Roger. In fact, he says he wants to help us, out of respect for your father." She only mentioned this to quell Roger's violent imaginings. Instead, it met with Nicola's enthusiasm.

"Gosh, Mummy! Wouldn't it be exciting to have a convict working for us!"

"**No**!" She paused and looked at each of them. "We really **don't** know what sort of person he is, and – he's not yet been found innocent of kidnapping. The only thing he ever did for us was get your father and me interested in doing further education." The change in emphasis was successful and made both kids think how proud they had been when their parents were going to go to college.

"Why aren't you going to college now, Mummy?" Roger queried.

"Don't be silly, Roger! She can't go 'cos Dad's not here to help look after us," Nicola said, pushing him.

"She could do it all at home if she wanted to." Roger pushed her back.

"Stop it, you two! You're both right. I couldn't go to college for lessons, because your father isn't here to help, although I suppose I could do an Open University course from home." It finished the conversation and they carried on with their usual routines.

The seed had been sown in Helen's mind and the very next day she set about applying for an OU course. *Which course? It has to be something that would allow me to work from home if possible, and is helpful to the kids. And something I am capable of. Accountancy? No. I would be able to work from home, but it would not inspire the kids – or me—*

"Why can't I have a computer like the other kids do, Mummy?" Roger interrupted her thoughts. It was one of those 'eureka' moments! She did not know if she could afford it, but she would try.

"Yes, dear. We'll get a computer," she announced enthusiastically.

"Can we afford it, Mummy?" Nicola asked like a cold shower.

"Course we can!" Roger would not be deterred.

"No! She's right to ask. I'll have to check carefully."

When they had gone to bed, she sat at the kitchen table and researched her finances. She had heard one could get a government loan to cover the cost of the university fees, which would be repayable over the years one had sufficient income. That left the cost of a computer and other materials. She found some adverts for computers in an old magazine, and realised the prices must have gone up since it was published. With servicing due on her old car, she knew she could not afford one at present. *Perhaps I could get hold of a used one. Who can I ask? I could try one of the families I work for. That priest was very kind. He may know where I can get a cheap one.* She knew he was leaving for Africa very soon, so she contacted him the next day. She had barely finished her enquiry when he interrupted.

"You're in luck! You can have mine. I'll have no further use for it, and my replacement has his own. I'll bring it all to you first thing tomorrow."

I'm delighted to think I can help the poor woman, yet I'm worried that I'm putting my emotions at risk. He posted a letter to Maurice, explaining the outcome of his visit to Helen and what he had been able to do for her.

Nicola and Roger had gone to school when Sean arrived, so there were no awkward questions. He handed over all his computer gear and gave her a rudimentary lesson in how it worked. This was very hard to do as her closeness distracted him to such an extent he almost put his arm around her. He explained how she would have to pay for a broadband connection, if it was available, in order to get the best out of the internet. As she was due at her first work appointment, he had to leave; sad to separate from her but glad to have temptation removed.

Still, the apparent joy he had brought to this attractive woman temporarily relieved his anguish over Maria. *What is wrong with me?* he thought. *I shouldn't be thinking about the fairer sex like this! I was married to the Church, but now I'm like any male animal, just seeking a mate.*

After clearing all outstanding matters, Sean left for Africa. He had no photo of Maria, which would have been unnecessary as her whole being was imprinted in his memory. Helen was excited by her gift, and knew the children would be as well. There was something more! She was stimulated by Sean!

Much as I miss my Arnold, I felt myself drawn to this attractive young man who has been so kind and considerate to me. There was that wonderful moment of tenderness when I comforted him. Then there was his closeness while he demonstrated the operation of the computer. I did tense as he brushed against me, but I think I relaxed as I concentrated on his instructions. I was very conscious of his proximity, his warmth and the smell of the soap he used, when he reached across me to press a key. In those moments of contact, I temporarily forgot my pain over the loss of Arnold.

Mentally, she shook herself and said out loud, "He's a priest! Widowhood is giving me hallucinations! He's just being kind. And yet? No! I'm going to work, and that's that!" She hid the computer stuff and left.

Though she was itching to show them their new equipment, Helen put it off until both of the kids had finished their homework. Then it was like Christmas! She insisted they watch while she went through the basics that Sean had shown her. They were totally underwhelmed by her demonstration and just stood nodding their heads until she had finished.

"Very good, Mother! Now let Roger show you a few more things. He's better than me." Both kids laughed loudly, and Roger took Helen's seat. She looked embarrassed and they both gave her a loving cuddle. They explained how they had both been to lessons on computers after school, on the days she had to work late.

"That explains why you'd only just finished your meal when I got home. Why did you let me go through what little I've learnt, when it's all old hat to you?" she asked sadly.

"Because we love you, Mummy!" they chorused.

They all slept peacefully that night, until dawn, when Helen woke up in a sweat; she had been having a romantic dream about a certain priest!

CHAPTER 21

"How do *I know* if she's attractive? I've never met her before, I tell you. And, yes, I know she's probably young enough to be my daughter. Just listen, will you?" Inspector Phil Tyler was desperately trying to explain for the third time why he had to collect Suzy Ramas from Gatwick Airport. "For the *last* time, the reasons it has to be me that collects this young person are: one, she is a vital witness; two, the case involves criminals who kill witnesses against them; three, only a very few people know about her, and four, it was decided that she should be met by a more mature officer to reassure her."

"More mature! You mean older, don't you?" his wife taunted him, to cover her initial jealousy.

"I'll ring Ron Bennett and you can ask him about the need for absolute secrecy." He picked up the phone and started entering the number.

"Don't think you can fool me with this old buddy act. You're in it together. You've arranged what he's to say to me! If it comes to that, how come he knows if it's so secret?"

Phil was annoyed at her lack of understanding and wished he had actually told lies about his trip to Sussex. On the other hand, he did feel rather flattered that, after all their years of marriage, his wife could get jealous still. To an observer, it would seem most unlikely. Phil had never been nature's gift to women, and Brenda had definitely accepted him for his inner self. Outwardly, he had deteriorated over their twenty-five years of homemaking. Now he was very unfit; rotund is putting it politely. His beard was scraggy, and he had less hair on the top of his head. He was slow physically and quick mentally. In desperation, he put a hand on each of her shoulders and made her sit. The sudden, almost violent, action was totally out of keeping for Phil. It made Brenda gasp and stare at him in amazement.

"Shut up and listen to me! This girl is a vital witness and is in danger. Her brother has already been killed. You will tell anyone who asks that I've gone to collect the daughter of an old friend. If the criminals learn the truth, it will be my life on the line as well as the girl's. The only other person on active duty who knows about this girl is Ron Bennett. You do not say anything apart from the old friend bit. Is that understood?" He shook her shoulders, dreading a negative reaction.

"**Ooh, Phil**. You can be so manly when you try!" She gazed at him in admiration. Phil let go of her and stepped back in amazement.

"What do you mean? Do you think I'm womanly the rest of the time?"

"Well – no, but you're so masculine when you're aggressive." She continued to look at him as if he were some god. Phil drew himself up to his full height and folded his arms meaningfully across his chest. Then he adopted a deep voice and frowned at her.

"So, woman! You like a bit of rough stuff, do you? Just you wait until I get home tonight and I'll show you who the king of the jungle is!"

"It's a double secret then, is it?" She glanced coyly out of her lowered eyes.

"What do you mean – double secret?" His voice returned to normal.

"There's your secret mission this morning. Then there will be our secret role-playing tonight." She fluttered her eyelids, trying to appear as seductive as possible. Phil gasped and collected his briefcase and coat.

"We've not role-played since before I got promoted!" He pulled on his coat with renewed vigour and turned to kiss her with much more passion than usual. "I definitely won't be late for dinner, darling."

The flight from Switzerland was fifteen minutes late. It suited Phil because it gave him time to compose himself for meeting Suzy. He knew she was twenty-four years old, dark-skinned, not very tall and a fully qualified nurse. He had no idea where she rated in the beauty stakes, and guessed she would be like the last couple of Asian nurses he had seen, who were about as attractive as himself. He prepared the chief immigration officer by explaining she was a witness he had to take in for questioning. Then he prepared himself for the impending interview, in which he would have to tell her the bad news of her brother's death.

Though it was past 8am, the planeload of packaged skiers were paying the price of economic deals with brutally early starts, and were mostly bleary-eyed and longing for sleep. The border control officer who inspected Suzy's passport advised his boss, and he promptly conducted her to the private interview room where Phil was waiting.

"I'm Inspector Tyler from the Metropolitan Police." He showed her his identity card. "Please be seated." They both sat down, and the immigration officer left them alone. *My god!* Phil thought, as he could not help staring at her. *She's beautiful! Brenda really would be jealous if she could see me now; alone in a secluded room with such a gorgeous young female. Whoever described her as dark-skinned must be from another era! She has the colouring that modern white women spend hours striving to achieve.*

"What do you want with me?" Her worried query broke into his flight of adulation. He coughed. "Do you have a brother named Arun Ramos?" He sounded colder than his original intention in an attempt to cover his momentary lapse in formality.

"Yes. Why? What's he done now?" There was panic in her voice and she continued before Phil had a chance to reply. "I told him those friends of his are dodgy. I warned him time and again to give them up and try to get back into college." Phil seized upon her words to follow up.

"How do you mean his friends are dodgy?"

"There you are! You're the police and you think they're dodgy!" She sounded desperate.

"I'm sorry, but I don't know who these friends are that you're talking about. Perhaps you could explain more?" He pressed her softly to continue.

"He's never told me exactly what they do; which is suspicious in itself. Whatever it is, they seem to have plenty of money but no obvious source of income. Then there's the fear!"

"**Fear**?"

"Yes! Arun's attitude towards the head of the group was definitely more fear than respect; almost as if he's some sort of godfather figure." Her analysis came from long-term consideration.

"Godfather figure?" Phil queried.

"You know. As in the Mafia. Anyway, what do you want to see me about?" Phil began to wish he had brought a female colleague with him, as he could not hedge his news any longer.

"Your brother is dead!" he stated bluntly. There was a dreadful pause as the information was digested, then she cried loudly. A passing immigration officer flung the door open.

"Is everything okay here? Can I help at all?" he demanded.

"I've just given the young lady some bad news. Could someone bring her a cup of tea, or even water, please?" The officer nodded and left them alone again.

"Your brother hung himself in prison," Phil explained, predicting her next question.

"He'd never kill himself." She sobbed and took Phil's proffered handkerchief to wipe her face. "However desperate or depressed he was, he would not commit suicide! It's against our entire upbringing and beliefs. Why was he in prison?" Her training in the face of death, even though very personal, took control.

"He was accused of dealing in drugs." Phil went on to explain the circumstances more fully as she just sat hunched and sobbing into his handkerchief.

"**Why** have you come to tell me this at the airport? Couldn't it have waited until I got home?" Her grief was turning to anger and she slapped the table between them.

"We don't think it was suicide, either. We think he was killed because he could've been a valuable witness against your godfather figure. The murderers do not know, at present, that you may also be a useful witness. When they do, your life will be in danger. This is why I've had to meet you secretly and arrange for you to be housed in safety."

When she had finished her tea, they left via staff areas to his car in an official car park. After taking a tortuous route to ensure they were not followed, he left her in a temporary safe house in Brighton.

The town was selected as a stopgap because with the large

number of Malayans at university there, she would not seem out of place. At the flat in Tooting, which she had shared with her brother, Chief Inspector Bennett's gamble hit the jackpot. He had decided that Masood's gang would probably know Arun Ramas had a sister and may have worked out that she accompanied him on the fateful trip via Houghbury. Furthermore, it was very likely she knew what Arun did for them, and might be tempted to inform the police in revenge for his death.

Consequently, Bennett had the Ramas flat and its approaches watched with clandestinely placed CCTV.

The day Suzy was due back, a car parked within sight of the flat's entrance and nobody got out. When it left four hours later, it was replaced by another car with a hidden occupant. Although neither the car's owners nor occupants could be identified, Bennett felt fully justified in his decision. It had to be Masood's gang watching for Suzy. If they had gone to the trouble of murdering Arun in prison, they would have no qualms about eliminating Suzy, lest she did know anything.

Bennett and Tyler were very worried. They had to move Suzy immediately as Thwaite or some other spy might know details of the safe house in Brighton and tell Masood. They drove down to Brighton that evening, hoping they would be in time to move her. En route, they discussed where to take her that would be safe and unknown to the crooks or their informant, Thwaite. First, they thought of all the places they knew. Then they considered people who might be able to help. Or people who knew people who might help, and so on, in ever-confusing tangents. As they got stuck behind a slow-moving army convoy, Bennett snapped his fingers.

"Can't see the wood for the trees? Of course! My brother!" he exclaimed.

"Why your brother?" Tyler queried, as he accelerated past the last of the army vehicles.

"He's a wing commander in the RAF! He'd know somewhere." He sighed with satisfaction. They collected a confused Suzy, and while she repacked, they each phoned their wives to advise them of the change in their routines. Brenda was particularly upset, as she had prepared for their special evening, with a stimulating meal and her most seductive apparel.

She only calmed down when Bennett spoke to her on Tyler's phone. Bennett rang his brother, who was not pleased at being woken as he had early operations the next day.

"Is this one of your practical jokes, Ron?" Peter Bennett demanded.

"No. This young woman is a crucial witness and is in danger from a vicious gang, which has police contacts. We have to house her somewhere completely secure for at least a few days. **Why** do you think it's a joke, Peter?" It had been a very long day, and all were getting a bit distraught.

"Simply that your witness is Malay, and my wife, Nur, is from Singapore. You said the case will be held in Houghbury?"

"Yes. Why?" Ron Bennett replied.

"Well, that's another bit of luck for you, as I'm stationed only 35 miles from there. She can stay in our spare room. She'll be good company for Nur, who is currently housebound after falling off her horse. I'd better warn the guardhouse you're coming. They are very touchy, what with all these terrorist attacks around the world. What car are you coming in, so I can tell them?

"We'll be in my silver Ford Focus," Ron explained, giving him the registration number.

Suzy was ready and the two policemen had refreshed themselves with some strong coffee, so they left for Peter's. As they moved away from the safe house, Ron watched in his mirror as a silver-coloured Vauxhall pulled into the kerb some distance behind them. When they got to the first corner, he glanced back and noted the Vauxhall appeared to be following them. By taking a tortuous route out of Brighton, he confirmed they were being followed and told Phil quietly so he did not alarm Suzy.

"We daren't head west immediately, so I'll take the road to London, and after the ring road we can take the M4 west. That way, they won't know if our ultimate destination is west, south-west, north-west or north," Ron whispered. They had a stop to have a break and change driver, stopping in a highly public area. The Vauxhall parked well away from them, its occupants unaware they had been spotted. Phil and Ron decided they could not risk calling for backup. They would just have to lose their followers before they revealed their destination. They did not wish to let the followers know they had been observed, or they might call in some others.

After several miles on the M4 motorway, Phil noticed a minibus pulled onto the hard shoulder, and drove in behind it. Then he got out and approached its driver to offer assistance, which thankfully was rejected as the RAC was coming. Meanwhile, the silver Vauxhall slowed but had to keep going to avoid suspicion, and Phil and Ron pretended not to notice.

Travelling along the motorway again, they had only done about 10 miles when they approached an accident. Recognising the silver Vauxhall, Phil slowed and asked one of the police what had happened.

"Hit and run, sir! Three men dead and the fourth in a critical condition. Move along, please." Phil showed his ID and beckoned the policeman closer.

"Don't show that we're police, but we must know what happened."

"Yes, sir. We believe it's premeditated murder. A witness saw the lorry parked facing the wrong way down that slip road and it drove straight into this car, backed up and sped off."

"Do me a favour, Constable. Let Inspector Langley of the Met CID know about this. Tell him that I said the accident was planned for me. Also, I'd like you to keep the names of the victims under wraps for at least twenty-four hours." The policeman agreed and played his part by angrily waving them on.

They arrived at the airbase nearly five hours after leaving Brighton. Peter came to the security gate to collect them and took them straight to his house. There, Suzy, who had slept for most of the journey, was introduced to Nur and they chatted away in Malay, to the consternation of the others. Ron Bennett and Phil Tyler asked to speak to Suzy alone.

"We need to take a brief statement now, though you will be questioned more fully in a few days. Can you remember where you were on the seventeenth of October last year?" Ron asked, while Phil made notes.

"Not really. Should I?" she enquired drowsily.

"Were you near the town of Houghbury?"

"Houghbury? Oh yes. How could I forget? Arun…" she paused to control her grief "…took me for a trip in a car he had use of. He'd some parcels of stationery to deliver urgently in Dorset."

"Did you visit Houghbury on that trip?" Bennett asked meticulously.

"Yes. Well, not really."

"Could you be more precise, please?"

"It was off our route, but I asked Arun to go there, because I wanted to see the old town. We would've stopped, but the place was crowded and there was a terrible traffic jam due to some roadworks."

"Do you remember anything else about the town?"

"Yes, I definitely do! First, there was the old man in a car beside us in the queue, and Arun kept gloating at him. You could tell he was getting mad, so I told Arun not to be so childish."

"First? Did something else happen?" Ron was beginning to think they should have left the interview until she was fully awake.

"My god, yes! Could I ever forget? We'd cleared the traffic lights and Arun put his foot down to catch up some time. That's when it happened." She paused and shook her head in disbelief at the memory. "A small child fell directly in front of our car. Arun wouldn't have been able to stop in time! A man on the pavement snatched the child out of our way just in time. It's a wonder we didn't hit the man. He was a **real** hero. I wanted to stop, but Arun said he daren't as we weren't supposed to be there and he'd get into trouble." She looked from Bennett to Tyler and back. "Is that what all this is about? Is that why they murdered my brother?" she demanded.

"Yes, that's what it's about, but we don't know if or why he was murdered." Ron turned to Phil, who was busy writing.

"I've made a précis of your statements, which I'd like you to read and sign, please." Tyler handed her a sheet of paper. She perused the page and duly signed it.

As she handed it back, she said casually, "I guess that man must've been honoured for his bravery."

"**No**! He was sent to prison for attempted kidnapping of the boy. Nobody else in the vicinity saw him, save the boy, and just assumed he was trying to snatch him." Suzy stared at each of them in disbelief, and realised they were serious.

"Is there no justice anymore?" she queried, shaking her beautiful head.

"That's what we aim to achieve by keeping you hidden," Ron assured her.

Ron and Phil left her and were able to have a couple of hours' sleep before returning to London. Phil ate a light breakfast with the firm intention of going to bed for the remainder of the morning. It **was** firm until Brenda started her inquisition, and he had to explain what he had been doing for the past twenty-four hours in detail, except for the exact location Suzy was left at.

"Well! Was she?" Brenda demanded an answer. Even in his torpid state, he knew what she meant but decided to string her along for a while.

"Was who well, dear?" He blinked to illustrate his condition.

"Not who was well!" she retorted angrily.

"Sorry, what was well, then," he interposed, before she could continue her tirade.

"**Not what or who, nothing well!**" She accentuated each word.

"Nothing well? Sounds a bit sick to me, love," he leapt in quickly.

"There's nothing sick about it. What—"

"That's all right then." He interrupted, yawned loudly and prepared to rise from the table.

"*SIT*!" she commanded, in the style used to teach young dogs.

"Ooh! You're gorgeous when you're so imperious." He sat back and raised his arms in surrender.

"What do you mean, impish?"

"Not impish. Imperious – you know, dominating," he explained with a laugh, which only fuelled her ire.

"Stop changing the subject!"

"I didn't change it, you did."

"Don't split hairs with me! Just listen!" She was becoming exceedingly angry, and he knew he would have to stop twisting her words.

"Tell me what you want to know then." He tried to sound like the voice of reason, which was difficult in his current state. She paused, sighed and sat down opposite him.

"All I want to know is – was the girl attractive?" A question as potentially loaded as the time-honoured one, "Do you think I'm getting fat?" – where the negative answer has to be timed so carefully. Say it too quickly and you're not paying attention. Say it too slowly and you're showing that there could be a degree of doubt. Phil decided to humour her.

"Nearly as attractive as you were at her age." Immediately he finished, he knew he was in trouble.

"So I'm not attractive at my age then!"

"You'll always be attractive to me at any age. And," he paused to add fuel to her flames of vanity, "she won't be nearly as attractive as you when she reaches maturity. Forgive me, dear, but I really must go to bed now. Wake me for dinner this evening." He rose to his feet and turned as he was leaving the room, to add in a deep, suggestive voice, "**Then** you'll find out just how attractive you really are."

At the police station, Bennett, having had some sleep on the journey home, covered for Tyler and carried on with his normal routine as far as possible. He decided to leave after lunch, when the rigours of the previous night began to catch up with him. Clearing his desk, he thought about earlier events and phoned Brighton Police for a check on the safe house. He was alarmed to learn the house had been broken into a few hours earlier. *The Masood case is becoming ever more mysterious. Firstly, why are the crooks anxious to find Suzy? After all, she's only Arun's sister, and they couldn't know she was in Masood's car in Houghbury. Secondly, how do they know about the place in Brighton?*

He did a quick check and found another potential safe house had been entered illegally. *Not only do the gang know the places exist, they've worked out the most likely ones to be used for Suzy. We assume Thwaite's the one protecting Masood, and that it's only a matter of time before we catch him. Now it looks as if there could be other forces at work for the master criminal… is he paranoid or just plain ruthless? Why have people been eliminated to cover up what, on the surface, looks like an innocent journey?*

Suzy Ramas mentioned her brother's fear of Masood; a fear obviously shared by the two who beat up Sergeant Lee and nearly murdered Ivor. That's another problem! Ivor will have to leave hospital soon, but he'll need constant care – and he'll need to be secure. We need to find a place like we found for Suzy Ramas. That's it! If we could get him installed on a military base, he'd be safe and there'd be medical attention available.

"Hang on, Ron." He started talking aloud to himself. "Following this line of reasoning to a logical conclusion, I wonder if Peter could help again. If he can arrange to get Ivor housed there, perhaps Suzy could help with the nursing requirements."

The door to his office opened and a colleague entered.

"You all right, Ron?"

"Yes. I was just thinking aloud that I must ring the hospital and check on Ivor."

The news of Ivor was not all bad. The doctor told Ron that the bullet had struck his spine at thoracic level 12, so he was classified as an incomplete paraplegic. He then amplified the diagnosis for the layman, by explaining that Ivor was now able to control his breathing and other body functions but could not move the lower part of his body. He was having physiotherapy and would need someone to help with the various exercises for many months.

There was a chance that he would be able to walk with help, such as crutches, in a year or so. Given Ivor's reputation, and knowing how damage to a person's ego can hamper recovery, Ron could not resist asking the million-dollar question.

"He's always been a great ladies' man, Doctor. How will this affect his sex life?"

"I don't think I should discuss that with you. You're not family, are you?"

"No, I'm not. I'm his boss and a concerned friend, and as he has no family in this country, I feel I should be in a position to tell him what he may be too scared to ask you directly. I can promise you that I'll tell nobody except Ivor Kowalski."

"Okay. You're probably right; he will want to know. In lay terms, he should eventually be able to enjoy sex again one day, though he might only get an erection from physical, not mental, stimulation. Is anyone making arrangements for his care when he leaves here soon?"

"Yes. I'm looking into that now, and will let you know by tomorrow, hopefully." He nearly told the doctor his ideas for Ivor but remembered his phone could be bugged. He would try making arrangements well away from the office. For extra security, he borrowed his son's phone, drove to the top of the nearest hill, and made the call to his brother. He explained his requirements for Ivor. Peter understood immediately and offered the use of a vacant house next to his own.

"You've fallen on your feet this time, Ron. I'll arrange its use with the group captain; I'm sure it'll be all right. You have to contact Suzy's hospital to explain her absence, as **you** abducted her and won't allow her to use the phone." He sounded very cheerful.

"Why have I fallen on my feet?"

"Well, not only have I got suitable accommodation for your wounded policeman, but I've a fully trained nurse on hand with nothing else to do at present." Ron could almost sense his brother gloating for thinking of Suzy caring for Ivor before he had a chance to mention it.

He replied with false reluctance. "True, and I think she'll be safe from Ivor's notorious charms, at least while he's immobilised."

"There's one thing you forgot in your scheming, Ron." Peter's voice was deadly serious.

"What's that?"

"My reputation! What on earth do you imagine the rest of the air base thinks about an officer living with two women? I've had the necessary security checks done, very confidentially, on Susan. With her agreement, and in view of all that's happened, she's agreed to having her name changed by deed poll," he explained, with considerable satisfaction.

"What, from Suzy to Susan?" Ron had noted the change.

"Yes! From Suzy Ramas to Susan Kumar." He dropped his news like a bomb.

"I don't get it. How is changing her name to Kumar going to save your reputation?"

"It's my wife's maiden name. We are letting everyone know Susan is her sister."

"Actually, that's a brilliant idea! Tongues can wag in your area without endangering Suzy... I mean... Susan. I can let slip that Suzy has been moved to somewhere up north, and that'll take the heat off. I'll have to arrange a similar subterfuge for Ivor. Thanks once more, Peter. I owe you."

With things going right at last, Ron was able to sleep soundly that night.

CHAPTER 22

"There is no evidence that Mr Masood is, or has been, involved in any unlawful activities. Therefore, he has to be viewed simply as an informant. Former Police Superintendent Bernard Thwaite may have benefitted in his career from Mr Masood's information, but there is no evidence that Mr Masood benefitted from information he may have received from Thwaite."

Each time Ron Bennett and Phil Tyler heard the term Mr applied to Masood, they cringed. Internal Affairs had completed their investigation into Bernard Thwaite and had presented their evidence to the Crown Prosecution Service. Because of the potential harm a public case could do to the already damaged reputation of the police, it was decided to have this private meeting with a judge.

Judge Reynolds continued. "Thwaite is being dismissed from the police with loss of pension rights. Given these circumstances, I agree with the Crown Prosecution Service that further punishment is unlikely and a public case would be detrimental to the police force."

Undoubtedly influenced by their vivid memories of Birdie and Ivor in hospital, Ron and Phil were horrified by the outcome. They were not empowered to speak or protest, only to observe. This they did intently.

During their discussion afterwards, they carefully analysed each person involved in the hearing. If Masood had influence over Thwaite, he could have some over other people in important positions. The CPS spokesman had presented the case almost as a lost cause from the outset. He rarely looked at the judge, but often at a colleague seated beside him. Could one or the other have been 'got at' by Masood? Judge Reynolds was well known for his honest and straight talking, though in this case, Ron and Phil were surprised by him calling Masood – Mr. As it was a hearing in camera, they would have expected him to be more plain about Masood's reputation.

"If we had the staff, we could run an in-depth check on these officials," Ron lamented, biting his lip and frowning in concentration.

"Would you include Reynolds in that?" queried Phil.

"I suppose so, despite his impeccable reputation, but it's all hypothetical."

"Good reputation or not, I find it very hard to trust anyone who speaks so respectfully of Masood. And the deep bags under his eyes could be due to burning the midnight oil – or a physical *or* mental disability!" Phil continued with a degree of malice.

"I can understand your disapproval of the man, but we mustn't let it colour our judgement. We could investigate them all thoroughly if we had the manpower."

"Or womanpower!" Phil declared triumphantly. *Gosh! My mind's on fire after this morning's events.*

Deep in thought, Ron nodded and repeated like a zombie, "Or womanpower." Phil laughed and gripped Ron's shoulders.

"Don't you see, Ron? We do have the womanpower! Sergeant Lee! Even on sick leave, I bet she'd welcome the opportunity to do some checking." Ron's eyes lit up and then narrowed.

"A good idea, but there are certain difficulties that may be insurmountable. How do we get hold of the right materials to check, without arousing suspicion, and – how would we get it to Birdie?" Phil's face reflected his disappointment. There was a long silence while each of them considered the options.

Phil spoke first. Looking around to ensure nobody else could hear, he whispered in Ron's ear, "I've a friend who helped set up the CPS computer system. He could help us access their personnel records and case archives."

"That's illegal!" Ron burst out, and pulled away. Phil indicated for him to quieten down.

"Not if it stays within the service. We'd simply be exceeding our terms of reference!"

"**And** the end justifies the means," Ron added, after thinking carefully.

"The big problem will be finding and getting a computer to Birdie without arousing suspicion. Then she'd have to connect to the internet." Phil listed their hurdles.

"The computer's no problem. I'm buying one for my son's birthday in three months' time. I'll get it now and let her use it. She's staying with a lawyer, poor kid, so he's bound to be connected to broadband. You could get it to her via her brother." It was agreed and carried out accordingly, avoiding any possible leaks.

Meanwhile, at Houghbury, Terry had returned to his apartment with Derek, to make sure Birdie had settled in satisfactorily. Imagine his surprise and delight when he discovered her playing his *Tosca* DVD.

"You never told me your sister liked opera!" he protested, turning to Derek. Their arrival interrupted her enraptured viewing of the final moments of the film, and she heard what Terry said.

"Yes, Derek! The same goes for me!" She managed a slight laugh despite the sad scene she was witnessing.

Attacked on both sides, Derek retaliated. "Why should I tell either of you anything? Let alone tell Birdie she likes opera, which she already knows!" Amused by his reaction, she looked at Terry and smiled warmly.

"You must be a genuine opera fan to have a collection like yours." She pointed at the still-open cupboard.

"Genuine?" Terry queried. "Is there any other sort?"

"Yes, there's my friend Ivor who pretended to be one so he could…" she swallowed "…get to know me. You can't be all bad then," she blurted out, embarrassed by what she had nearly said about Ivor.

"All bad? What's Derek been telling you?" He feigned horrified surprise.

"**Me**? You know me better than that, Terry!" Derek protested. Birdie grimaced at the confusion she'd caused, and stood up slowly and painfully.

"It's a police thing. We get a trifle irritated by the treatment we get in court from lawyers, so we don't see them in a very favourable light." She was trying to explain when she noticed Terry pushing his tongue against his cheek and grinning. A glance at Derek revealed him smothering a laugh. "You rotters!" she exclaimed. "You're winding me up! If I wasn't *hors de combat*, I'd teach you both a lesson!"

"**Wow**! That could be exciting. Derek. You told me she's in the police, not a whore!"

Terry ham-acted astonishment, as he savoured his moment of levity with a woman he had finally decided he should get to know better. Derek released his pent-up mirth in an outburst of loud laughter.

"That's it!" Birdie erupted, as she struggled towards them. She tried to swing at Terry, who gently held her arms to her sides. Face to face, there was a tangible moment of shared emotion followed by an awkward silence. Derek, embarrassed by the fraught atmosphere, felt obliged to cut through it with an attempted joke.

"Perhaps you two'd like to be left alone?" He turned as if to leave.

They flushed and pulled apart, uttering in unison, "Don't be silly!" All three laughed and the erstwhile moment of magic was broken. Having made a list of her requirements from the shops, the two men left.

Later, she got a call from Tyler about the proposed task they had for her. Once she knew the judge's decision, she readily agreed, acknowledging the dangers involved. The exact details of the job were concealed from Derek, who collected the materials, and Terry, who agreed to the use of his broadband.

Two days later, Sergeant Lee was back in harness, as well as bandages. She was pleased to have the work as it kept her occupied and took her mind off the mental and physical pain. Mental, because that moment with Terry had unaccountably disturbed her. *He's a stiff, word-watching lawyer; he's not my type; yet he's a kindred spirit with opera, and – there is something about him.*

Terry had the opposite dilemma. His regard for her was growing into something stronger, and he hoped the moment would lead to a closer friendship.

As the days passed, she became totally absorbed in her work and treated him as casually as before. *It must be this boyfriend of hers,* he reasoned. *She has to control any warmth towards me for the sake of her love and loyalty for him.* Birdie did her work when she was alone to save any embarrassing explanations. A quick check of the documents and computer records revealed nothing untoward, so she looked more closely at the cases the suspects had been involved in. The CPS pair had not handled any cases with unusual characteristics on the surface. Judge Reynolds seemed as straight as his reputation. None of them lived beyond their means, and they had all achieved their current positions through their own endeavours.

If I was Masood and I wanted to bring pressure to bear on an official, how could I do it? There's bribery or blackmail or fear; the last can be brought to bear either by direct threat on the person or indirectly on relatives or friends. Bribery should be reflected in the recipient's affluence, and I've not noticed it with these three. Blackmail would be for some dark secret, and, as such, I'm unlikely to find it with my limited resources, particularly if it involves payment by actions and not money. Fear? I could check their associates for any strange incidents, but it'll require more records, though records won't show a case of pressure through fear.

After four days of blind alleys, she was getting frustrated. Terry came home early on the fifth day, and she automatically closed the laptop and pushed her papers together.

"Top secrets, eh?" he joked, and pretended to snaffle the papers. She snatched them back, pushing him away. She was in no mood for his humour. One heading caught his eye, and he expressed his surprise.

"Judge Reynolds? Is that Clarence Reynolds?"

"Yes. **Why**? Do you know him?" She was angry at his prying.

"Not personally, but I remember my tutor at university mentioning him." He frowned in concentration.

"What did he say about Reynolds?" Any information must improve her present knowledge of the man.

"Only that he was an example of how some people can break the mould. Apparently, he was very poor at university, and yet he obviously blossomed later."

"Was your tutor surprised that Reynolds became a judge?" Birdie pressed him further.

"Very surprised." Terry looked at her with increasing interest. Birdie thought long and hard.

"It's been difficult for me to hide my investigation from you, so I'll just have to trust you. What I tell you mustn't be told to anyone else." She peered deeply into his eyes.

"I promise. After all, client confidentiality is part of my profession," he stated in earnest. Birdie recounted the Masood case, from where it was refreshed by the Jenkins incident to her own kidnap. She explained the suspicions of her colleagues as a result of the Thwaite case heard in camera. She asked for his thoughts, and they closely paralleled her own. Uncluttered by emotional or official ties to the case, Terry suddenly, through lateral thinking, asked a question that surprised her.

"Is Masood his real name?" Giving him a quizzical look, Birdie opened her laptop and used her password to log on to her station's criminal records.

"Masood's name first appeared twenty years ago, and there's no suggestion of any other," she told Terry, who explained his line of thought had been generated by some cases he had studied at university. In one of them, it transpired that the accused had changed his name shortly after arrival in the UK, to avoid racial prejudice!

"It's often done. Remember, even our royal family changed their name from a German one to Windsor to avoid any problems during the First World War," Terry suddenly recollected. He then explained the necessary procedure and helped her trace Ali Masood on the National Register. He had entered the UK officially as Ali Masood!

"Thanks for your help, but I'm afraid it's another dead end." She looked warmly at him, sitting beside her.

"There's one other way you can check to see if he's ever used another name here." His persistence she considered obsessive, but did not wish to appear rude to her host.

"How's that then?" she asked bluntly.

"From his records, you have his place and time of birth?"

"Yes. **So**?" *Is this legal expert trying to teach me my job?* she wondered.

"And, do you have access to all records of all court cases over the past, say, thirty years?" he continued.

"Yes. But it'd take ages, even with a computer, if you want a birthplace and date check." Birdie understood where he was going with his line of thought.

"Not if you set it up with tight parameters. Here, let me show you." He moved the laptop in front of him and started his analysis.

An hour passed with them both so engrossed in the figures they were leaning against each other. Then it came; the result she believed impossible. A man with the same birth details as Masood had been accused of running a brothel. His name was Ali Parouk, and, against all odds, he had been found not guilty. The prosecuting lawyer was Clarence Reynolds!

"Yes! Yes! Yes!" Birdie gasped, giving Terry a hug and a kiss on his cheek.

"Yes! Yes! Yes!" he repeated, turning towards her, spreading his arms for an embrace and pursing his lips.

"No, no, no, sir! Pray, unhand me!" she mocked, holding her hands in front of her face and turning it away from him.

"Woe is me for I've been sweetened by the lips of Venus and am lost forever!" Terry orated, standing erect and clutching his hands to his chest. Birdie hung her head and covered her eyes in mock terror. In truth, it was to hide the transition of powerful emotions within her. In those few seconds, which seemed an eternity but were to last a lifetime, she journeyed from elation of mind to ecstasy of heart.

It's all wrong. This can't be happening. It mustn't happen! He – is – not – my – type! She continued to cover her eyes long after the mock action required, as her mind was in panic.

"Are you all right?" He was concerned and lightly placed a hand on her good shoulder. That slightest of touches sent lightning charges through her body and threw her mind into total chaos. Her ice-wall had melted, and the total control she always had over her feelings disappeared. Turning her face away from him as she rose to her feet, she mumbled, "Excuse me," and retreated to the bathroom.

Left alone with diverging thoughts, Terry was tempted to resort to a whisky. Then he decided on a pot of tea, as alcohol could create more problems than it could solve at this time.

When Birdie emerged, suitably refreshed, her defences were almost back to normal and her mind was fixed on her task.

"If Ali Parouk is Ali Masood, and Reynolds was responsible for the verdict, what hold did Masood have over him?" she queried, as Terry handed her a cup of tea. He sipped his own tea and stared into the cup, as if searching for an answer there.

Answer the police sergeant, he told himself, in an attempt to calm his emotions. Strange how small things discovered at college are recollected in later life!

"Now I think back, my tutor's point in using Reynolds as an example was twofold. One was the possibility for anyone to turn failure into success. The other was to concentrate on one's studies, unlike Reynolds, who was an obsessive womaniser. This, of course, was told to me in strictest confidence during a one-to-one session." He was trusting her not to 'drop him in it'! Again, he had come to her rescue, and she was tempted to hug her white knight.

"Of course! I think you've cracked it. He was probably a customer of the brothel and Masood was blackmailing him. Then when Masood returned with his new identity, he could've used Reynolds just as he used Thwaite. In doing so, it benefitted him to further their respective careers." She clapped her hands in delight to restrict other tempting movements.

"Sounds credible to me, but you'll need hard evidence," Terry reminded her. Then a phone call from the police station took him away to see a new client, and he left Birdie to make herself a light dinner. She sent an email to Bennett privately:

Congratulations! You have won a prize in the Grand Draw. Contact now for details. The Bear Facts Company.

The name had been agreed earlier, and he knew he had to ring her outside via non-listed mobiles. She explained what she had discovered and what she thought she needed to prove it. He agreed, and told her about Ivor's impending move.

Discussing it with Tyler, they recognised their limitations in finding the evidence required and decided they would have to involve John Langley, the CID inspector, more.

They had known and trusted him for many years, and

would have to do so again. They had a meeting with Langley, away from the office, and explained the work they had done on the Masood case, and why it had been kept so secret. Ever-cautious, Bennett and Tyler never mentioned the locations of Ivor and Birdie, explaining that the knowledge itself could put him in added danger as they had become prime targets. Also, they never mentioned the existence of Suzy Ramas. Langley was delighted with the news of the criminal's probable earlier life.

"I have the perfect man for the job! I'll give you one guess."

Bennett and Tyler looked from him to each other and then spoke in unison. "Doug Evans!"

"Yes! Now he doesn't have Thwaite to chain him up, we can release '**The Hound of Masood**' once more!" Langley almost gloated.

"Why does he have such a personal vendetta against Masood?" Tyler asked.

"Keep this under wraps as he doesn't really like anyone knowing. His younger sister was the apple of his eye, to put it mildly. She went to college, got in some bad company, was drugged and gang raped by suspected associates of Masood, and committed suicide. Nobody was punished. Exactly why has never been established, but a cover-up by officials now seems increasingly likely." Langley relayed the information with obvious distaste.

"That could explain not only his obsession with Masood but also his apparent lack of social female companions," Bennett surmised.

"Don't let's get into that now. Doug will investigate personally to verify Parouk was Masood, and to establish the link with Judge Reynolds. I've heard of the treatment of Thwaite and it's made me uneasy."

Doug found that the National Records had no trace

of an Ali Parouk and discussed it with Langley, who was able to use his personal contact at Interpol. The Met's facts about Masood's suspected organisation linked in with other suspect cases Interpol had in Spain and France, which had been missed previously. Interpol knew the organisation had branches in several countries, including North Africa, but hadn't identified the mastermind behind them all.

Now they would add Masood's name to the list of possibles, particularly because of his connections in the field of law enforcement. It seemed they had several on the list. Some they knew by name; others were shadows identified by a place, not the person. Three times they thought they were close, only to have the suspect die in mysterious circumstances each time! Once, they really thought they had the right man, only to finish up with a bunch of tourists in southern Spain. Reliable sources would be used to check Masood's history back to childhood. The news of their progress was passed to Tyler and Bennett. Hearing that top suspects had mysteriously died when Interpol was getting close confirmed to them the wisdom of keeping their witnesses secure.

Meanwhile, Birdie felt the association with Terry was taking a turn she did not welcome, so she asked if she could be moved. News of her request filtered back via Derek to Terry, who confronted her.

"Why do you want to move? Have I done something to upset you? I thought we were getting along very well, **aren't we?**" he demanded. She had been staying with him for only a short while and he had grown accustomed to her presence, as well as growing in love with her. The mere thought of her leaving sickened him. Here he was, a mature professional, acting like a lovesick teenager. Then there was concern for her safety, and jealousy because of whom she might be going to.

"It's just that I feel our relationship is not helping your work or mine. You've done nothing to upset me; quite the contrary, in fact," she admitted reluctantly. Her words were nectar to him.

"Our relationship?" he repeated hopefully. She felt she was the guilty party being cross-examined in the witness box, and he was putting her on the spot. *How can I wriggle out of this?* she was thinking.

"I hate to admit it, but I feel there's been a bond growing between us, which has been disrupting my concentration." She looked directly at him and smiled weakly.

"I agree. There is a growing bond, and I welcome it with all my heart. You must know how I feel about you now. I hoped you'd feel the same about me." *Revealing my love for her might encourage her to reciprocate.*

"That's the whole problem! I guessed you were fond of me, and admit I like you very much. However, I don't know the true depth of my feelings as I've no real experience of love outside my own family. Thrust together like this could be a recipe for disaster until I'm absolutely certain how I feel. That's why I thought it'd be better if we were separated until this matter is resolved," she announced, hoping that cold logic would overcome emotion.

"Reluctantly, I can see your point. You **are** a temptation to me that's hard to resist. I'm worried for your safety and admit to considerable jealousy over this boyfriend of yours. However, I don't want to tie you down until you're ready, so I think I've the solution. I know of an empty apartment on the edge of town, which is just as secure as this. I'm sure I can get the owner's permission to use it, and you'd be doing him a favour by looking after it. Only he, Derek and the neighbour, who I trust, would know you were there. Derek and I would check on you daily to see what you needed, and I'll arrange a broadband connection in my name." He explained his flash of inspiration with triumph.

"Sounds too good to be true! Who exactly is the owner?"

"It's Maurice Jenkins, the man whose case brought you here in the first place."

"Extraordinary! That poor man's still in prison, yet his action has led to major developments in a case against international crime organisations. Wait a minute! I can't go there! He's going to be out soon."

"Not unless you know something I don't. I'm his lawyer, remember. The appeal's not due yet." Terry revealed his frustration at the lack of progress.

"No, I forgot. You've not been told yet because of all these security arrangements. The driver of the car he saved the boy from had a passenger. She's being kept safe, and her evidence corroborates Jenkins's version of events. Because of the danger to her, we'll get her sworn statement and pass it to you," she confessed. "I'm sure you'll be able to get an early release in the circumstances."

She relaxed more, now she had been able to give him the good news. His delight was evident, until he remembered why the subject had arisen. Considering alternative accommodation for her, he put another suggestion to her.

"There's an empty flat on the floor above this. If you don't mind staying in the same building, I can arrange to rent it for a few months." He paused and looked closely at her. "Or would it be **too** close to me?" he added.

"Don't be silly!" She prodded him affectionately in the chest. "I'd have my own space. That's all that matters at the moment."

So it was agreed, and two days later she moved to her new home.

CHAPTER 23

Ron Bennett and Phil Tyler drove down to formally interview Suzy, alias Susan. The policemen took a circuitous route, starting due west on the M4 motorway and then zigzagging cross-country, to ensure they were not followed. At the gate to the airbase, they were delayed by security checks, which had increased due to a terrorist alert. There were three vehicles in front of them when they arrived, and soon there was a large black car behind them. With all their precautions, they were not unduly concerned but still kept a wary eye on all that was happening. Constantly checking their rear mirrors, they were alarmed to notice the occupants of the black car seemed to be discussing them, and never took their eyes off them.

When it came to the inspector's turn to be checked, they were asked to leave the car. As they did so, one man got out of the following car and approached them with his hand in his jacket pocket. Instinctively, Ron and Phil moved further away, putting the RAF police between them and their pursuer. The latter had a word with one policeman and they were preparing to produce their IDs, reaching into their pockets, when all hell broke loose. The man checking the underside of Ron's car shouted a warning. Guns raised, the RAF police seized Ron and Phil and dragged them towards the guardhouse. The pursuer dashed after them and his mates leapt out of their car and hastily followed. In the guardhouse, they were handcuffed and given a quick check for weapons. Then the man with his hand in his pocket entered.

"Look out! He's got a gu—" Ron's words died as the RAF personnel stood to attention, and one addressed him.

"Sir. We found their bomb before they got a chance to explode it!"

"Good. We thought they were acting suspiciously. They started reaching for something in their pockets. Could be remote detonators. Better have a look," the officer commanded.

"We thought **you** were acting suspiciously. We were going to warn your men and produce our IDs. I'm Wing Commander Bennett's brother," Ron hastily explained.

Once their IDs had been inspected and Peter Bennett advised, they were released. Their supposed pursuer turned out to be the group captain in charge of the base, and he had a good laugh with his men at the idea that he looked suspicious. Ron explained why they had to be so cautious and that he thought someone might want them dead. The group captain instructed his staff to ensure the specialists they called for gave the full picture to Ron.

"They're a bit like us, I suppose. We all have a job to do for the safety of Joe Public, but all we get for doing it is complaints!" Phil said with resignation.

"I don't know about Joe Public, Phil. It was certainly lucky for us we got checked. Why would anyone want to kill us? We don't have any vital information, yet. And getting rid of us would just bring somebody else to do the interview," Ron reasoned.

"I wonder why the bomb's not gone off already?" Phil questioned, fearful over what might have happened. Luckily, they had taken their briefcases from the car, so they had their recorder, notes and other papers required for the interview. After a much-needed break and some tea, they were able to meet Suzy. Even in a pair of worn jeans and a loose sweater, with her hair pinned back severely, she was sublimely attractive. She pulled nervously at the sweater as she sat down, enhancing her wonderful figure. Formal identifications completed, in her real name, they proceeded to take her statement, which she gave lucidly with minimum prompting.

"I'll always remember the seventeenth of October last year for several reasons. My brother, Arun, invited me to join him on a trip to Dorset. He had to deliver some stationery in a car and wanted company. He knew it was my day off. As I'd nothing planned, I thought it'd be fun. The first surprise was the car we went in. It was a beaten-up old Ford Escort GT, and in a horrible green colour!" She smiled and shook her head, as if remembering her disbelief when she first saw it.

"How'd you know what the car was?" Phil asked.

"Several years ago, an older cousin once took me for a ride in a used one he'd bought. He was so proud of it and how fast it'd go. I remember it smelled strongly of the polish the dealer had used." She smiled again, and Phil wished he was single and younger as her beauty captivated him. Ron nudged him back to the task at hand.

"How long ago was that?" Phil demanded, as sternly as possible.

"It must be at least twelve years ago."

"So this one you went to Dorset in was about fourteen years or more old?"

"Yes. That's about it."

"What happened to the Ford? You were in an Audi in Houghbury."

"It turned out that was the whole reason for the journey. Arun had to deliver the Ford to Lyme Regis and return in the Audi." She became serious, as if something was troubling her.

"Was there anything unusual about the Ford?"

"Er... no."

"Do you have any idea why your brother had to deliver an old car to Lyme Regis?"

"No. Though I had my suspicions."

"Tell us about them." Phil pressed her.

"The strangest thing was that the boot had some sort of seal on it, and Arun had strict instructions not to open it. Originally, I was told we were just delivering some stationery, but then I wondered if there was pornography or even drugs or other illegal items secured in there."

"What happened in Lyme Regis?" Phil indicated for her to keep talking in the direction of the recorder.

"I don't know. Arun dropped me at a café on the edge of town, because I wasn't supposed to be there. Imagine my surprise and delight when he returned about half an hour later with a new Audi. While we had a snack at the café, he said nothing about the business, except that the swap had gone okay."

"Tell me about your experience in Houghbury." Phil continued his interrogation as Ron made notes, sometimes pointing at them for Phil's benefit.

"It was a diversion so we could see the place. Had we known about the dreadful roadworks, we wouldn't have bothered."

Did anything happen while you were stuck in the traffic jam?" Phil prompted her.

"Yes. There was this old codger queuing alongside us. He kept glaring at us, and Arun made faces at him until I made him stop. When we did get away from the lights, Arun put his foot down and raced away. That's when it happened." She looked at the two policemen.

"When what happened, miss?" Phil was anxious to get the pertinent facts from her.

"When this little kid fell off his scooter right in front of us. A man on the pavement acted like lightning and snatched the kid from certain death. Arun would never have been able to stop in time. It all happened so fast, it was a wonder we didn't hit the man. I told Arun to stop, but he was too frightened that his boss'd find out he'd not stuck to the proper route."

"Could you identify the man who saved the child, or the child itself?" Phil questioned hopefully.

"I only had a fleeting glimpse of them, but they were fully illuminated in our headlights. The scene is imprinted in my memory, so I suppose I may be able to." Due to the needs of her safety and the security of their evidence, Ron had managed to get photos of Maurice and Charlie, and a selection of similar-looking men and boys for comparison. First, he spread out the men selection on the table in front of Suzy, in random order, explaining what he had done for the benefit of the recorder.

"Look at each photo in turn, don't rush, and decide which, if any, of these is the man you saw save the child," Ron instructed her precisely. Suzy looked slowly at each one then went back over them. The two policemen looked at each other and grimaced in despair. They had thought they were onto a winner, but their hopes were sinking fast. Unable to be patient any longer, Phil spoke first.

"**Well?**" She looked up at them and smirked wickedly before answering.

"I think I know that one." She pointed at a photo and watched the disappointment show on their faces. Then she laughed aloud and had difficulty in continuing with her statement for a moment. "I think he's one of your policemen!" She laughed again at their frustration.

"However," she paused provocatively, enjoying this teasing of such serious officials, "the one who saved the boy on the evening of the seventeenth of October last was that one." She turned to the recorder before either of the delighted men could speak. "For the record, I'm pointing at the third photo from the right." Then she sat back in her chair and laughed again. Phil and Ron were so euphoric they slapped each other's hands very noisily.

"For the record again, I must add that the sound you just heard was that of Inspector Tyler and Chief Inspector Bennett giving a high five." The men looked at her with new admiration. Not only was she beautiful, but she was clever enough to play them at their own business.

"Why did you take so long over the identification if you were able to select the correct man so quickly?" Ron asked out of curiosity.

"These last few days have been very stressful for me, and humour is a way of relieving it. Also, I do tend to see the funny side of any situation, particularly this one. You should've seen your faces when I procrastinated. I wish I'd had a camera. What's wrong, Inspector Tyler?" She gasped as Phil clutched his chest and struggled to breathe. As his head dropped forward onto the table, he winked at Ron, who grabbed him and looked at Suzy in alarm.

"It's his bad heart. I think you pushed him too far. Can you do anything for him?" he begged the shocked woman. She dashed round the table and pulled Phil upright. As she leant forward to check him, he burst out laughing.

"I was hoping for the kiss of life, but then I realised my wife'd be bound to find out." He chuckled some more. "Two can play jokes, miss. Ron and I are old hands at it."

She looked from one to the other, smiled and said, "Touché!"

"If you two have quite done, I would like to finish before it's too late! Fortunately, I switched the recorder off when you explained your sense of humour, in case anyone took it the wrong way. Interview continues after a natural break. If you'd continue, please, Inspector Tyler," he added, as he switched the machine on.

"You're absolutely certain that's the man you saw on the seventeenth of October last save a child from in front of the car you were in? You'd be able to pick him out in an identity parade?"

"Yes. That's definitely him. I've no doubts at all."

"For the record, Miss Ramas has identified Maurice Jenkins," Phil announced to the recorder as Ron spread eight more photos on the table in front of her.

"Can you identify the child he saved, please, from these eight pictures?" Phil requested.

She studied them carefully and admitted, "This is a lot more difficult. Not having much to do with small children, I think they all look much the same."

"Perhaps you'd select a couple, just in case it'll be required. Don't worry, we'll not tell you if the actual child is the one you choose, so we won't be accused of influencing you," Phil urged.

She looked at each photo in turn, held close to and at arm's length. Finally, she closed her eyes as if trying to recall the images of that eventful day. Ron and Phil grimaced at each other.

"Yes, I think I've got him fixed in my mind now. It's a bit like hospital duty where I have to identify patients in my care very quickly. I'm almost certain it's this little boy. The runner-up would be him." She pointed at two photos in turn. She had picked Charlie Donnelly correctly. They were very pleased and realised they had to mention it for the record.

"For the record, please note that the witness has identified Charles Donnelly." Phil spoke very precisely into the machine. The interview was concluded with a few minor points being duplicated to prevent any misunderstanding.

They discussed her new identity and explained how they hoped she would care for their disabled colleague, who should be arriving soon. She was delighted to assist them. She explained how she had grown very fond of her new 'sister', but needed more to do.

They confirmed her hospital had been advised of her absence on the grounds that she had family problems in Lancashire. To alleviate their consciences and prevent future problems, they warned her that Ivor was a notorious ladies' man but assured her that he was genuinely incapacitated. Ron could have said more but remembered his promise to Ivor's doctor. They had a meal with Peter, Nur and Susan before they left. It was decided to explain Ivor's presence as a wounded soldier requiring Susan's specialist attention.

Meanwhile, their car had been checked thoroughly. The booby trap was designed to explode when someone sat in it again after an hour away. Thinking it through, Ron and Phil calculated that together with the homing device experts found earlier, it was intended to kill them after they had revealed the whereabouts of Suzy. It was a belt-and-braces job; if the homing device failed, the report in the media, of the explosion, would betray the locality of their crucial witness. At their request, the bomb specialists reset the bomb to start again. The homing device had been taken for a quick flight in a fighter aircraft and then switched off. Once Ron and Phil got onto the M4, they switched it on again. It was hoped that the erratic course would make the owner of the device believe it had temporarily gone wrong.

The group captain rang them to wish them '*bon voyage*'. He explained how the bomb incident had been suppressed by making it part of an exercise to test the camp's defences. His remaining problem, for which he blamed Ron, was that the staff at the base were now calling him the 'godfather'. This was for appearing to be a gangster to a stranger, but he undermined the true reason by becoming a godfather at the christening of an officer's child.

With some trepidation, they drove north via Oxford, never stopping for more than a few minutes, until they reached the outskirts of Manchester. They reckoned their very devious route would look like an attempt to lose any pursuers. There, they met other members of the bomb squad in a disused quarry, known for its bad satellite reception. A weight equivalent to a person was hung on the driver's seat, and after an hour it was released. The ensuing explosion totally destroyed the car and could have killed anyone within 20 or 30 metres of it.

Meanwhile, Ron and Phil were on a train back to London. They alighted at Milton Keynes and were met by John Langley. The crucial question was how to continue. They would be presumed dead by Masood's organisation, so they should use this to their benefit. However, as they could not disappear for long, it was decided to hide them in a safe house for a week. During that time, they could type up Suzy's statement and perform 'paper' checks they now knew they required, with a computer and some extra records.

After much consideration of their wives' and families' health, they decided only Langley would know they were alive. Phil even joked that his temporary death might make his wife appreciate him more. Listening to their copy of the recording from their interview with Susan, they simultaneously stiffened.

"Why take an old car all the way to Dorset?" Phil spoke first.

"Yes, Masood is not short of cars," Ron replied.

"The answer must lie in the sealed boot!" Phil announced emphatically.

"Agreed, but if the contents were simply illegal, they could've been quickly removed without the need to involve another car," Ron cautioned Phil.

"What if the car **was** part of the ultimate plan? We can't approach the local police for news of an old green Escort." Phil shrugged his shoulders. They both sat quietly thinking, and Ron doodled.

"The media!" Ron declared loudly. "We can check on the computers all the local media around the seventeenth of October for any news concerning the car."

Two hours later, their frustration was showing and they ate their microwave meals.

"There's absolutely nothing on TV or radio about the car," Ron declared soulfully.

"The only item in the papers, other than car test reports, was some man committed suicide by driving off a cliff," Phil said, as he cleared the table. Ron sat quietly, deep in thought.

"Did they say what make it was?" he asked, making polite conversation.

"No. All it said was that it was believed to be suicide, although it could've been a simple case of brake failure due to the age." His eyes widened and he nearly dropped the plates he was carrying. "**Due to the age!**" he almost shouted. Ron got to his feet and punched the air.

"That's it! If it was the Escort, the chances are the driver was already dead or drugged before the car went over the cliff. It looks like Masood's way of getting rid of someone." He slapped Phil on the back, and continued. "The victim must've been sealed in the boot. After young Ramas delivered the car, Masood's local associate would've rigged the accident. And who would ever associate an incident in Dorset with gangsters in London?" There were no details of the car or its driver, as it exploded on hitting the rocks and was totally burnt beyond recognition.

"We'll have to get John and Doug to check with the local police for more details. They could also check the list of Masood's known enemies – and associates – to see if any disappeared around that time." Phil made notes as he spoke.

CHAPTER 24

Terry Schott had started the appeal procedure against Maurice Jenkins's conviction on the basis of Diana Gumbrill's evidence. This had been stalled by the allegation of Inspector Banbury that there was an unlawful conspiracy between her and her husband, who had worked with Maurice. Subsequent information from the police in London and Houghbury had substantiated Diana's evidence. Then the appearance of Pru Gravillons as a character witness had enabled Terry to have a date set for the appeal. This was another reason the two London police inspectors hastened to get a full statement from Suzy Ramas.

A copy duly certified, and with an explanation of her inability to attend, was sent to the appeal court. The outcome was a foregone conclusion, and Maurice was freed, with a handsome compensation payment. After settling the debts that had accrued while he was in prison, he insisted the residue should go to Arnold's widow, Helen. It was returned to the court and forwarded to Maurice. He was determined she should have it, but he would have to find some other method to ensure she did profit from it.

He was able to thank in person or by letter all those who'd had faith in him or had helped in his release. The three items on his list for immediate attention included meeting with Helen Phillips, but Terry advised him to wait until her unwarranted dislike for him had moderated further. The next item was to meet with Judith and Charlie Donnelly. As soon as she had heard the full facts quashing his conviction, she insisted on meeting him to apologise for her original misconception and to thank him for saving Charlie. The last item was Sid Cracken. Having discovered another side to the lout and taking him under his wing, he felt a responsibility towards him. He knew he would have to visit him whenever possible but wished there was more he could do for him.

He was dreading the meeting with Judith, which Terry had arranged to be held in his office. He was worried that seeing the child again, after all that their last encounter had caused, might arouse some deep sense of injustice. It should not happen, he reasoned.

If Nelson Mandela could overcome any resentment he felt after years of incarceration, then I should be able to after a few months. I just hope it does not affect the boy. He did not know how he should respond to the mother's apology. As a loner, he had always shunned anyone's attempts at praise or gratitude. *This meeting is a duty I have to perform for the sake of the others involved. Duty to my fellow mankind was instilled in me by Father.* With no current employment to distract him, he arrived early at Terry Scott's office and was warmly greeted by Derek. Over coffee, they chatted until Terry was able to see them. It helped Maurice to relax.

"Your incident certainly put the cat among the pigeons!" Derek exclaimed with a laugh. "Who'd ever have thought the simple, brave act of saving a toddler's life would have international repercussions?" he continued rhetorically.

"I knew the police were using the facts in some ongoing case, and I'm sorry your sister suffered so. I **didn't** know it was international in its effect." Maurice was genuinely curious. "How is your sister now?"

"She's recovering slowly, thanks. She's being kept in... er... what-do-you-call-it – a safe house until the current problem with these criminals is resolved. The gang she was after is now known to be part of an international organisation. Your action has exposed their informer in the police. **He** was a senior officer! It's jump-started a case that had been stalled for years. Ah! There's Terry now." Maurice stood up quickly and shook Terry's hand vigorously.

"I hope you're not going to do this every time we meet, Maurice. You've already thanked me enough when I brought the news to you in prison." His client's overwhelming gratitude embarrassed Terry. Maurice released his hand and took a step back.

"Sorry! It's just that what you did for me must have exceeded the normal duties of a man's lawyer. Your faith and confidence in me helped me survive at a time when I was at life's lowest ebb!"

"True. I've always believed in you, but I have to admit that your case has been of great benefit to my business. So you see, I've had my reward commercially."

He led Maurice and Derek into his office and seated them at the table at the opposite end of the room to his desk. Maurice lost his balance slightly and bumped the table. Terry noticed and gave a polite laugh.

"From the outside, it looks rather grand to have offices in a medieval building, but, as you've discovered, the downside is the uneven floors!" Derek joined in the laughter, clapping his hands.

"Very droll, Terry. You're on good form today, then."

"I don't know what you mean, Derek."

"I do!" interjected Maurice. "It was the **downside** of your floor, which I found to my cost."

"Oh yes," Terry acknowledged blandly, lost in thought.

"What's wrong, boss?" It was a term he had never used and he knew it would rouse Terry. The lawyer waited until they were seated comfortably, then he placed both of his hands on the table and looked directly at Derek. He delayed, as if seeking the right words.

"Nothing's wrong, or at least I hope it isn't. My problem, or rather worry, is how you'll take some news I've to give you. I've left it until Maurice is with us so he can explain the matter more fully." Derek looked from Terry to Maurice and back.

"What news? For god's sake, spit it out, Terry! I've never known you procrastinate before."

"I'll tell you." Maurice spoke up, as he had been forewarned that Terry would raise the subject. "The thing is, Derek, I've befriended Sid Cracken." It was the briefest of statements and its effect was like a bomb to Derek.

"**You what?**" he spluttered.

"Sidney Cracken is now my friend," Maurice said quietly, dreading another outburst. Derek stared at him in disbelief, then at Terry, and then slapped his hands against his cheeks.

"How can you possibly be friends with the... the shite who tried to rape my sister and who gave you a beating?" He started to enunciate each word carefully, and finished up spluttering in fury. Maurice explained in great detail the events leading to his bizarre friendship; from his attack on Sid to Sid's reformed character, with hope for a better future as a good citizen.

"The prison psychiatrist was extremely interested in Sid's case. He'd ignored him as just another lout, until someone mentioned the change in him when he moved in with me.

I can't remember all the mumbo-jumbo he told me about. You know, things like psychosis and dopaminergic, et cetera. The principal diagnosis is that Sid suffers from autism. This explains his anti-social and violent behaviour, and why he's become more normal now he's found he does have real skill at something." Derek's wide-eyed stare at him was unsettling, and Maurice looked around the room. It was then that he noticed the paintings. He turned in his chair to observe them more thoroughly. Derek was still digesting the information about Sid.

"Those fungi are very good. Are they by a well-known artist?" he asked, and Terry was glad for the change in topic to ease the tension.

"Not well known yet. But you're about to meet her. Judith Donnelly did them for me. In case you don't recognise them, it's amanita phalloides. It's the fungus that killed Arnold Phillips."

"Why do you want paintings of such a deadly plant?"

"It's to remind me of the incident and how temporary life is, and to keep my feet on the ground." He nodded his head as he too looked at the paintings.

"Autistic! Well, well. I'd never have believed that such a lowlife **could** be capable of redemption, let alone have a skill. What's he good at, apart from violence?" Derek's sudden return from silent thoughts caught them by surprise, and they turned to look at him.

"**Art**! He has an amazingly good ability at art. He's a natural when it comes to drawing and he has an eye for colours. What he desperately needs is proper tuition, which he doesn't get in prison," Maurice explained to a calmer Derek.

"He still tried to rape Birdie! But for her agility and skill at unarmed combat, he would've!" Derek protested. Maurice held up one hand to prevent him saying more.

"In reality, no! He might've slapped her about and pretended to try and have sex with her, but he couldn't actually have sex as he is one of those rare examples of Homo sapiens who's asexual! The psychiatrist believes it could be part of his problem." Stopping for breath, he was interrupted by Derek.

"How? Sounds like the sky-pilot is searching for excuses for someone who's just plain bad!"

"I thought that too, at first. Then I took his theories on board and compared them to the person I shared a cell with for my last few weeks. He has a large body with muscles to match. He has the mental ability of a seven-year-old. At school and in later life he was the subject of much ridicule, and from constant repetition he accepted that he is, to put it mildly, stupid. From all the sexual banter he heard, he understood that he's somehow different. The whole world was against him, so he reacted with violence. Violence, which juveniles of limited intelligence found exciting. This became, literally, a vicious spiral. The rougher he became, the more the young louts liked him and the rest of society detested him." Maurice broke off for a moment's reflection.

"Unwittingly, when I took the blame for the beating he gave me, partly from honesty and partly from fear of him, I broke the mould. Being confined in prison with such little thought as he's capable of, my simple action stimulated him. Suddenly he could see a glimmer of hope at the end of his erstwhile black tunnel of life against society. That same spark of light..." Maurice's voice trailed away as he recalled his depressed thoughts on that fateful day in October. *How I decided my life needed a spark. Never in my wildest dreams could I imagine it coming from a retarded criminal.*

"Are you okay?" It was Terry who broke the silence.

"Sorry. Where was I?"

"Talking about a spark of light," Derek muttered impatiently.

"Oh yes. In olden days, they would've talked about some form of divine intervention. What happened was more like a reaction between two chemicals. Sid benefitted from my supposed honesty, and I did from the realisation that he's not the ogre I'd feared. He's an overgrown, unruly child in need of help. I used him for the physical pain I believed would ease my mental anguish. Now I'm left with a feeling of responsibility towards him. I sought something apart from beating up people that he might be good at, more in the hope of alleviating my conscience than actually helping him." He nodded as he remembered.

"His ability to draw, and in such delicate fashion, was more than a revelation; it was a eureka moment. With the help of the psychiatrist, we managed to get him some art materials. He was an object of derision, called such names as Simple or Silly Sid. Now he's become known as Pencil Cracken or the graphite king of Kindleford Prison." Maurice looked at his audience to emphasise it.

"Prisoners and guards queue up to have Sid draw their portraits. Even the governor's had one done. He could make a small living from it when he gets out. I'm no expert, but I think he's capable of much more. Have we locked away a potential genius? With current economic restrictions, the prison service is unable to give him the help I think he needs. Despite the best efforts of the psychiatrist, Sid'll not be allowed to attend outside courses because of his record. There are no courses inside and it's unlikely that anyone would be brave enough to teach him individually." Maurice's heartfelt oration ended with a note of despair.

His listeners sat in silence, thinking differently about what they had just been told. Terry wondered if there might be a *'cause célèbre'* for him to take on. Derek weighed the facts and tried to reconcile his memory of the monster he had met with the picture Maurice was painting. The door, which had been left ajar, was opened by the clerk.

"Mr Schott. Mrs Donnelly and her son are here. I didn't like to interrupt while Mr Jenkins was talking." She addressed everyone formally, though she knew all their first names. The three men stood up and turned to face Judith and Charlie. Terry stepped forward briskly and shook both of them by the hand, closely followed by Derek. Maurice's mind, which had been racing as he expounded his lonely campaign to help Sid, came to an abrupt and embarrassing halt. He stood awkwardly, shifting from one foot to the other, like some disobedient child reporting to the head teacher.

"You know Derek, of course, and this is—" Terry started to make the introduction to ease Maurice's obvious tension, but he was overtaken by Judith. She stepped forward smartly, with her little boy clinging to the hem of her short summer dress.

"No need to tell me! It's Maurice Jenkins. I hope it's all right if I call you Maurice?" She grasped his hand, which had been dangling at his side. Completely disarmed by her warm approach, he replied as he had with Sean.

"Much better than Fred or Brian, or even calling me next week." The frozen face he initially presented to her broke into a smile as he tried to ease the situation. Terry and Derek looked quizzically at each other.

"You're right. Maurice is better. Calling you 'next week' would sound dreadfully feeble." Judith burst out laughing. Once she realised how wrong she had been about the incident and how much she owed him, she knew she would have to meet him and apologise in person. That it was her duty made it no easier. She had been very nervous about the meeting and had practised on the phone with Tom what she intended saying. Delayed in Terry's outer office, she had overheard Maurice's articulate plea on Sid's behalf, and was intrigued enough to forget her nerves. She was still clasping his hand in both of hers as she continued brightly.

"I apologise from the bottom of my heart for all the trouble I've caused you." Maurice flushed and tried to withdraw his hand, but she clasped it even tighter. "You bravely saved my son's life at the cost of many months of your own." Maurice managed to get his hand free only for Judith to place a hand on each of his arms as she gazed into his eyes. "I've no idea of the dreadful life you must've had in prison, and all through the fault of a stupid, hysterical woman. Our family owes you a debt of gratitude we can never hope to fully repay." Maurice gave a sickly smile and almost wished he was back in prison, where he was safe from such plaudits. Judith pulled Charlie between them.

"This is the wonderful man who saved your life, Charlie. You're still too young to understand the full implications, but I'll **never** let you forget it." She was close to tears with her heartfelt emotion. Terry had some tea brought in and they all sat around the table. As there wasn't a suitable seat for the boy, Maurice sat him on his knee and helped him draw on some paper Derek provided. No longer face to face with the over-beholden female, Maurice felt able to reply.

"I'm no paragon, but the experience has taught me to be thankful for those blessings I **do** have. On the day it happened, I was depressed and lonely. I met Arnold Phillips and we agreed to make fresh starts with our lives. Arnold is dead, perhaps due to our agreement. Anyway, I owe it to him, and society at large, to better myself. Prison had its drawbacks and its benefits. I look back on it as a salutary lesson and know I've gained from the experience. Look, this is a smiling face and this is a sad face. Now, you copy them."

He paused to draw and instruct Charlie. Judith grinned at a scene she would never have thought possible only a short while ago. Never before had Terry not been in full command of events in his own office.

"Just what have you learnt inside, Maurice?" Terry stirred from his lethargy.

"About people less fortunate than me, society's cast-offs. How to record everyday events with a view to using them in a book or play. Then there's the degree course I've started. Then, of course, there's Sid, a veritable monster I touched with my magic wand, or something, and restored to a human being. For that last, at least, I shall always remember my incarceration with some amount of satisfaction. That's very good, Charlie." His gaze returned to the scribbling of the little boy on his lap. Judith reached out and patted Maurice's arm.

"Tom and I'd like to help you any way we can. He's sorry he can't be here himself. You say you're doing a degree course. Well, if you ever need any help in understanding or presenting your work, do let us know." She took a deep breath and continued with determination. "One way we can repay you in some small measure would be for me to help your Sid with his art." Derek, sitting patiently listening to the others, had to intrude.

"**You can't possibly do that**! He's little better than a savage beast. You don't know what he might do. He tried to rape my sister! And then there's all the other convicts. It's not a safe place for a woman." He could not believe what Maurice had just told them, and still envisaged Sid as the person he had met in the car park.

"I can't blame you for thinking that way, Derek. I love Judith's suggestion and can guarantee she'll be quite safe. First, I'd like Derek to come to Kindleford Prison with me to arrange it. He can meet the new Sid and see the change for himself," he reassured him.

"The governor could make one of the education rooms available for the lessons. I'll take Judith and introduce you to Sid, but I must warn you—"

"Here it comes!" Derek interrupted. Maurice smiled at him and continued.

"I must warn you about dressing as you are today. A beautiful woman like you in a provocative dress could cause a riot. You'd have to wear old jeans and stuff." He gave a mock bow.

"When you put it like that, Sir Galahad, how can a simple woman refuse? You never warned me that Maurice is such a smooth talker, Terry." Her face glowed with the compliments. So it was agreed, reluctantly by Derek, and a date set.

Maurice contacted the Kindleford governor and made the arrangements for three of them to visit Sid, and in a classroom used for crafts. Derek opted out. He had no wish to meet the person responsible for many nightmares, even though Terry assured him it would be for his own good; facing up to his fears would help to dispel them. At the last minute, Terry had to go to court and could not possibly attend the prison.

"I don't like to do this to you, Derek, but I'm afraid you'll **have** to go to the prison in my place," he ordered him, with the best air of reluctance he could muster.

"Why can't Maurice and Judith go on their own?" Derek begged.

"Their psychiatrist says it'd be quite safe. However, the governor is ultra cautious and is only too well aware of the field day the press would have if anything went wrong. 'Governor allows ex-con to bring woman to cellmate', or words to that effect," Terry explained seriously.

"Well, all right then! But don't expect me to be nice to him or even talk to the lout," Derek answered grudgingly, shuffling papers loudly to show his displeasure. "I'll go as a duty, never as a pleasure. What on earth will Birdie think when I tell her?" he added, bending over his work.

"No need to worry on that score. I've told her all about Cracken's alleged change of attitude, which she too finds hard to believe. She firmly agrees that your meeting him can have only positive results, hopefully for both of you," Terry assured him.

"So you've been seeing my kid sister, have you? I thought she moved to another apartment to get away from you," Derek retaliated, with satisfaction at changing the subject.

"She just came to my place a couple of times for a meal and to watch one of my operas. I'm amazed how emotional she gets over them. Not the picture I formed of the tough cop nicknamed the Ice Maiden. Anyway, I think Birdie is old enough to make her own mind up, and more than capable of keeping me in order." He laughed at the thought of it.

Derek joined in and added, "Tell her I insist *she* visit Cracken as soon as she is able to."

As suggested, Judith had changed her appearance for the visit. She was wearing paint-covered jeans and a sloppy sweatshirt; her hair was tousled and she had on a pair of horn-rimmed spectacles. Maurice and Derek stared at her in disbelief. The attractive, cultured lady had become a rag-a-muffin art student. Her musical giggle and eye fluttering as she lowered her head in mock modesty only added to their amazement.

"Good job you're happily married," Maurice exclaimed. "I've had naughty dreams concerning kinky art students."

"Only dreams?" queried Derek, raising his eyebrows.

"Yes, unfortunately. I did meet one I really fancied, and I'm sure the attraction was mutual."

"What happened?" Judith asked, as he got a distant look in his eyes.

"**Nothing**! By the time I'd plucked up enough nerve to consider talking to her, she'd gone from my life **forever**." He emphasised the last word.

"Only death is forever," Derek growled, illustrating to the others that he was determined not to enjoy the day's experience.

Safely housed in the supplied classroom, with only a handful of prisoners paying any attention to Judith en route, they each prepared for the forthcoming meeting in their own way. Maurice had differing memories about the place as they went to the room, though he was anxious to meet his former cellmate and protégé to see if he was continuing to make good progress in his conversion. Judith's emotions were split between welcoming the challenge – or was it a crusade? – and trepidation at having to teach a man convicted for his brutality. Derek definitely did not want to be there at all, and was unsure how he would react when meeting the thug who had tried to molest his sister.

A few minutes later, a guard brought Sid into the room and started to handcuff him to one side of the table.

"There's no need for that, George! Sid'll be quite all right with us, won't you, Sid?" Maurice put his hand on the guard's arm.

"Okay, Mr Jenkins. It's **your** responsibility." He removed the handcuffs and left the room. Maurice moved to Sid and shook his hand warmly as he rested his other hand on the big convict's shoulder.

"How are you, Sydney? Have you got a new roommate yet?" The ruffian's face showed a sense of pleasure that nobody would have thought possible only a couple of months ago.

"I'm fine. Got the cell to myself, 'cos I'm so busy doing pencil portraits of everyone. I've done one of the governor. Still want to do painting. tho'. Who are these folks?" He let go of Maurice's hand and turned to look at the others. Derek remained frozen to the spot and looked with astonishment at the man before him. He did not look at all threatening, as he had the last time they met.

It hardly looks like the beast I remember. How's he different? Derek thought, staring open-mouthed. *He is smart in his prison uniform and his hair is neat, but there's something else. He's no tattoos on his face – and he's smiling!*

While he completed his analysis, Judith advanced. "Hi! I'm Judith. It's my little boy that Maurice saved, and I'd like to repay him in some small part by helping you to paint. **Will** you let me try and teach you how to paint, please?" She took his hand and gave it a gentle squeeze. Sid's mouth dropped open and he just stared at her and then began to blush. He looked desperately at Maurice as if seeking advice, and got a large nod of approval.

Turning to Judith, he started to stammer, paused, made a loud gulp and spoke. "Gee! I'd love that, miss. How'd I pay you for your time and stuff?" he mumbled.

"My time and stuff – is free. It's the very least I can do to repay Maurice for saving my boy and mistakenly ending up in prison. Maurice insists on paying for the materials because he considers himself to be in your debt," Judith explained to him slowly.

"What you mean, debt?" Sid blurted out.

"I was feeling very bad in my mind, Sid, and you helped me to get better. You've made a new person of me, and I'll always be grateful to you. In other words, I owe you for giving me a better life." He patted Sid on the back.

"Blimey! You lot 'aving me on? Nobody's never owed me nuffink before. And – nobody's ever offered to 'elp me for free. Must be summink I can do in return," he prattled.

"There is one thing you can do for me right now, Sydney." Maurice adopted a more serious tone. "This other gentleman is Mr Lee. It was your attack on him and his sister that brought you here. I'd like you to apologise to him for your **dreadful** behaviour." Sid studied Derek closely as if trying to remember the event, then advanced slowly towards him. Derek began to ease away, but Maurice quickly stood beside him. Sid held out his great rough hand towards Derek.

"I'm sorry, sir," he said, like a naughty schoolchild carrying out instructions. Reluctantly, Derek held out his hand for it to be crushed by Sid's. As they stood there, hands clasped but not shaking, a look of recognition came over Sid.

"Your sister was the one that flattened me!" Derek tried to withdraw his hand but it was gripped too tightly. Then Sid began shaking it vigorously. "I was very wrong to attack you and your sister, and I'm very, very, **very** sorry. Your sister's done me a great favour. She gave me a lesson when she dumped me on the ground. And this prison sentence stopped me getting into more trouble, and, above all, it brought me Maurice. 'E's the first person to take the blame for me; 'e's the first person to treat me like a 'uman, and 'e's the first to be a real friend to me." Sid stopped because he thought the others would be laughing at him for the length of his oratory.

They were all too mesmerised by what he was saying in such a heartfelt fashion to laugh.

Derek was no longer trying to pull his hand away, and was patting Sid's with his other. His fear of the erstwhile thug had gone; and been replaced by an embarrassed need to comfort the huge man in front of him who showed all the signs of starting to cry. There followed an awkward silence, which Judith broke.

"I think you've some drawings to show me, Sid?" Sid released Derek's hand and opened a large black file. He pulled out half a dozen sketches and spread them on the table.

"Why, that one's of Maurice!" she exclaimed. "They're **brilliant**! You mean you're entirely self-taught? I can't believe it. Such natural talent deserves to be recognised. It will be an honour for me to show you how to handle paints. I've brought some watercolours for you to try out and a small potted plant as your first subject." She reached into her voluminous bag and laid the items on the table. "If it's all right with you, Sid, I'd like to borrow these drawings to display in my art club's latest exhibition. Can I sell them for you, if there are any offers?"

"Yer. I suppose you could ask for a quid, or even two, for each one. Except the one of Maurice. I want to get that framed and give it to him as a mem—"

"Memento," Maurice corrected, adding, "I'll be proud to accept the drawing, Sid."

Derek had been quietly observing.

"If I gave you some photos of my family, Sid, would you draw them for me? I'll pay you well." *Did the words come from my mouth?* Derek wondered. *This is unbelievable! How'll I ever explain to Birdie my change of heart?*

"No payment needed. I'll be glad to do them after all the trouble I caused." Judith gave him instructions on the basic use of the watercolours and asked him to do a painting of the plant ready for her next visit. The guard collected Sid and the visitors left.

"You've convinced me, Maurice. I wouldn't have believed such a transformation possible. There's just one thing bothering me, though. What happened to all his nasty facial tattoos?" Derek enquired of Maurice as they got into his car.

"They weren't real. He only painted them on to give him the aura his dreadful friends expected of him. He was too scared to have real ones done," Maurice said with a laugh.

*A binman and a child's scooter and a protégé in prison! Even with my numerous thoughts for a story, I could not have dreamt of such a scenario. Well, I may not have a job at present, and I still have to find some way to help Arnold's family, but I am **free**! Yes, free and with new friends. **Free** to seek out a new life and more... real sparks!*

End of Part I

This book is printed on paper from sustainable sources managed under the Forest Stewardship Council (FSC) scheme.

It has been printed in the UK to reduce transportation miles and their impact upon the environment.

For every new title that Troubador publishes, we plant a tree to offset CO_2, partnering with the More Trees scheme.

For more about how Troubador offsets its environmental impact, see www.troubador.co.uk/sustainability-and-community